THE
HANG OUT GROUP
AND THE BROKEN BALANCE

TAYLOR J. GASE

INK START MEDIA
5710 W Gate City Blvd Ste K #284
Greensboro, NC 27407

The Life and Death of the Devil

There was a time when God was alone. There was nothing yet created, just God and his thoughts. God's power was something called Loomation, and with that, he made his home, Heaven—a very large, bright, and peaceful place. God wanted to fill his home with others, so he was ready to make life. God knew that making life was a powerful act, and he felt that there should be some restraint with this power. Just because he could didn't mean he should So, God made something more powerful than himself—free will. God proclaimed that all life he created would have this power.

God then made the devil, a very different being compared to himself. God wanted to make everyone he made different, and the devil was far from God's personality. God was loving and patient while the devil seemed more cruel, sadistic, and cold. Despite the devil not showing any positive affection toward God, God still loved his creation and planned to make more.

Over time, God made the archangels, and they showed extreme love and loyalty to their father. The archangels, on the other hand, never gave the devil the time of day. So God made the horsemen, and they were more comfortable being around the devil than the others. The devil tolerated the horsemen, but he didn't really care for them. The devil didn't like that God kept making life after him; everyone made after the devil was less powerful than his first creation. The devil was used to a high powerful presence in Heaven during that time when it was just the devil and God. The devil didn't fully hate the others; they did carry Loomation powers like he and God, but not on the same scale as the two. The devil would learn just how much he could grow to despise life when God wanted to show everyone his latest creation.

God was away from Heaven for a while working on his projects, so the archangels would say. When he returned after a long absence, he gathered everyone up to take them out of Heaven to show them something. God showed them earth; he was able to elevate the viewers high off the ground to see the humans who were living on it. The powerful beings were watching the humans as if they were high up in a private box seat. There were only two humans at the time, but God had plans to populate the whole land with them. The archangels, the horsemen, and even the devil had never seen God so happy. They all could tell that humans were God's favorite by far. The archangels said a few positives things about the humans while the horsemen kept silent.

Seeing that they carried no Loomation inside them, the devil was disgusted by the humans. Without that, they were weak and powerless. The devil expressed the negative thoughts he had about the humans to God, but none of it changed God's view on them.

"Do they even have free will?" asked the devil in a harsh tone.

"Of course they do," God delightfully replied.

The archangels were stunned by the devil's attitude toward their father. No one ever talked to God the way the devil did. The archangels were too respectful to ever question God, while the horsemen were too intimidated by his presence to ever raise their voices to him.

"How can you tell?" the devil questioned.

Once again, the archangels were growing furious with the amount of disrespect the devil gave God, which was the main reason they never liked the guy. The horsemen couldn't help but grin at the strong angry glances the archangels were giving the devil at that time. God never grew irritated by the attitude the devil gave him. He still had great love for his first creation, even if the humans were now his favorite.

"I planted a special tree within the Garden. I have personally asked the humans to never eat the fruit from its roots," God said while pointing toward the tree. Not too long after that, everyone retuned to Heaven. All except God, of course; he wished to continue his watch over the humans.

Back in Heaven in the devil's corner of the area, the devil was chatting with the horsemen. The horsemen now felt more comfortable expressing their dislike for the humans. They were impressed that the devil was able to express his hatred while being in front of God himself. One of the horsemen discussed the other creatures living on the planet, claiming that the animals were stronger than the humans and that some of the wildlife within the Garden carried Loomation inside them. "Heck, the humans are so weak that they could catch a deadly disease carried by the smallest of insects!"

One of the horsemen declared that without the measurement of one's Loomation to reveal the strongest, the humans would struggle to find leaders among themselves, which would drive them to debates, fights, and even war.

"With how weak they are, they are going to need so many things to survive. The desperate need to stay alive will cause them to demand more from others, more than what they need, and some will even grow to steal to survive," one of the other horsemen stated.

"Their time on earth will be short. They all will die, then continue their existence in Heaven. They can die very easily, even by killing each other," the horseman Death mentioned.

"None of them will ever do anything disheartening," claimed the devil. "If God asked these lesser beings to follow him, all he has to do is simply request it. They will, in turn, remain the peaceful and loyal humans God wished them to be."

The horsemen were all looking at the devil as if they thought he was coming up with a plan. The devil wanted to prove to God that the humans did not deserve such high praise. The devil said he was going to drop down to earth to have a talk with God's favorites. The devil then left Heaven and landed on earth within the Garden of Eden.

It wasn't long for the devil to find the two humans, Adam and Eve, living there. The two were alarmed by the visitor at first, but they felt that nothing inside the Garden could hurt them, so they weren't scared for very long. The humans asked kindly who the stranger was. The devil didn't wish to give away his name, so he told them that he was from God's home. Seeing someone from God's home fascinated the humans and caused them to let down their guard and trust the man instantly.

The devil talked to the humans with a kind voice, doing his best to deliver his lies in such a believable way. He told them only the ones who carried Loomation could enter Heaven. The humans didn't understand what Loomation was. The devil said it was power, the same type of power God possessed. He told them that there was a way for them to receive this power and become just as powerful as God. This information made the two humans swell up with joy. Thinking about the idea of becoming stronger and being able to enter God's home made them excited.

"What do we have to do?" wondered Adam.

The devil pointed at the forbidden tree and said, "The fruit from that tree will grant you the power of Loomation."

"But we were told not to eat from that tree," Eve timidly replied.

"That's because God wants to keep you weak. He doesn't wish for you to have any powers. Once I ate from the tree, I was granted such tremendous power and was able to enter Heaven and experience the wonders of the place. Trust me, one bite will give you more than what God could ever give you!"

That was the convincing line for the two humans to succumb and eat the fruit. Both Adam and Eve walked up to the tree. Once they reached the tree, they started to have second thoughts, but the devil's words were still sitting heavily on their minds, and so they both reached up and plucked fruit from its roots. They both took a bite simultaneously and felt nothing but the taste of the fruit. Immediately after taking a bite, they knew that they were in the wrong, that they were tricked, and that they were in trouble.

God came down to the Garden within a flash of bright light. Once God was on the ground in front of the humans, Adam and Eve both knelt, begging for forgiveness. Adam said that they didn't mean to eat it, while Eve told God that they were tricked by the stranger. The devil pointed out to God how humans would lie and blame others when things looked bad for them. God ordered the devil to stay silent and said that he would talk to him after he finished speaking to Adam and Eve.

God ordered the humans to leave the Garden at once. The humans didn't wish to make God any angrier, so they did as he wished without any fuss. Once they stepped out of the blessed land, a barrier grew up around the border of the entire Garden. All Adam and Eve saw when they looked back was a mountain that would forever conceal the Garden.

Inside the Garden, with the newly built high stone walls now surrounding the place, God and the devil had an argument. "Why did you trick them into breaking the rule?" God asked the devil.

"I wanted to show you how weak they were. I knew that they weren't strong enough to break the rule on their own, so I had to put the thought into their heads somehow."

"They could have done it on their own. They do have free will!"

"Yes, but your presence is so overwhelming to the humans that they will blindly obey your orders without ever having an idea of disobeying!"

God then turned his back on the devil, struggling to keep a straight face. God was holding back tears because he knew that if the devil was around, he would continue to lead humans down the wrong path. God's thoughts went to a dark place for he thought that his first creation must die for humanity to live in peace. God made a sword grow from the grip of his hand, a sword that would reveal the evil ones by a glowing gold light with a blade strong enough to kill the devil.

"They can't exercise free will when you're the only direction in their head! They're too weak to know that. That's why I did what I did, to prove a point to you!" the devil shouted.

Then God got an idea and discovered a missing piece to the human's free will. God now found new purpose in the devil and thrust the sword away so fast that the devil didn't even see it. The sword pierced the wall of the barrier and was lodged into the rock. God turned toward the devil and told him that he was right. "Free will isn't anything without an option of good and bad decisions."

God said that the humans would have an even set of choices, one leading them to being a good person, and the other leading them to be a bad person. A balance of good and evil, he called it, saying that without the balance, free will was pointless. God told the devil that he wanted him to be in charge of the evil side, to be the voice inside the humans' heads trying to get them to do negative things. God would be the voice to set them on the right path. The devil agreed to the job and to the terms of neither side ever overstepping the other.

"But you did trick the humans, and I can't let that go unpunished," God sadly stated. "If you would have brought this up to me before your actions toward the humans, things would have gone differently."

"What punishment?" asked the devil, showing concern.

"I won't let you leave this place," God said as he looked around the land.

"What are you talking about?"

"I'm saying that I'm the only one with the power to teleport out of here. As long as this barrier remains intact, there is no spiritual realm. Not even you can teleport without that."

"How am I supposed to do my job if I'm trapped in here?" asked the devil with a frustrated attitude.

"You still have the power to communicate with the horsemen on the outside. You can give them instructions to carry out in order for the evil side of the balance to be where it needs to be. But you should warn them that if they participate in the orders you send, they will be banned from Heaven. I won't have spirits who bring harm to humans live in my sacred home."

"You really think that the horsemen won't go over the balance?" the devil asked, dumbfounded.

"If the evil side of the balance ever tips higher than the good side, I'll temporarily release you from your prison to correct the situation. But if you ever let the evil side purposely go over, I'll strip your Loomation powers from you! Without them, you'll be nothing more than just a human. The thing you hate the most."

The devil was outraged by all this. The only consolation was that he was able to make the humans' lives a little bit more miserable. "If you love these powerless humans so much, then I won't let any of them live if they ever become more than what you intended!" These were the last words of the conversation. After that, God left, leaving the devil locked away in the Garden.

Things in Heaven changed after that. God banished all evil spirits from his home and even put up a gate around the area. The horsemen were getting their orders from the devil, and they happily carried them out. God had some cleaning up to do on earth now that humans were living out of the Garden; there were tons of threats out there from God's past projects. The archangels created angels in order to execute God's plans to protect the humans due to them not wanting to be bothered with it.

Over time, the good side of the balance was now being run by the souls of the passed-away Saints on earth. The Saints were making good spirits to help the good side of the balance. The horsemen designed more negative spirits, and they branched off to make more as the population of humans grew. All evil spirits were getting their orders from the devil, while the angels and positive spirits were getting their orders from the Saints.

There was only one time when the balance was tipped. A spirit was causing too much evil in the 1600s. The Saints were able to let the devil out only to eliminate the threat to the balance. After the devil killed the spirit, he was returned to the Garden. Once the awesome power of the devil was demonstrated, no other spirit ever dared to tip the balance again.

The devil had been working on his way out of the Garden ever since he was trapped inside it. He used an exhausting amount of power to pull a meteor from space to strike the outside of the barrier, causing it to pierce a hole in the wall. After the action was done, the devil fell into a deep sleep to regain his strength. When he woke up, he found a rope hanging from the hole on the side of the barrier. He figured someone must have entered the Garden while he was asleep. But he didn't care; he climbed up the rope and gleefully walked out the tunnel unnoticed and reentered the outside world. Once outside, the devil traveled the world in secret. Once free, he performed some of the actions needed to cause the evil side of the balance to be where it needed to be.

Then the devil saw a newspaper clip about seven men who turned in a giant-size diamond. The devil knew where that diamond came from, and he tracked one of the seven men down and discovered that the man had the power of Loomation inside him. The devil killed the man and then tracked down the others to kill them next. Due to the balance of good and evil, the devil couldn't personally kill more than once a month. But when he was down to two, he tricked one into killing the other and offered the last one a chance to give himself up. The last man, possessing an active Loomation, was able to teleport away and was able to elude his deadly grip.

The devil was able to use his power to track down the final man, always finding him during the final days of the month. The man was good at escaping, but the devil was in no hurry to kill the final man, so he just let the game of cat-and-mouse go on for years. Until one day, the devil discovered the last man hanging out with others who also carried Loomation. The devil managed to kill off one of them and then ran off before a fight broke out.

Not even a full day later, the devil got permission from the rest of the Loomation carriers he discovered to come and kill them. The devil heard their prayer from inside the Garden and went there to murder them all. The devil managed to kill one of the humans inside the Garden before he faced his final fight and ended up being killed by the same sword that was made to kill him. He was killed by seven boys who referred to themselves as the Hang Out Group.

The Broken Balance

Sunday, August 1, 2010

There are a few buildings at the gates of Heaven. The largest one was where the Saints worked. As there was no work allowed in Heaven, the Saints must remain outside of Heaven in order to do the job God himself asked them to do. The Saints found new purpose in their afterlife, a chance to watch over God's creations and to help the living. One of the jobs the Saints had to do was to keep the good side of the balance where it was meant to be. They would retrieve prayers from the humans, mainly the ones asking for help with an obstacle or a wish for care after a tragedy. The personal prayers would go to God himself. The Saints would craft hypotheses to find out who needed the help most. Then they would send out orders to the positive spirits and angels to spread the good into the world.

In a large office, a saint named Peter was working on a ship in a bottle. The Saints did need to give their minds rest from all that stressful work from time to time. Most slept while others were able to ease their minds by working on hobbies. As Peter was deeply focused on his project, a coworker barged through his door.

"Peter, you need to see something. It's urgent!" the saint said, short of breath.

In a pace that was a little too calm, Peter carefully placed his tools down and rose out of his seat. Peter was led by his coworker into the council room for the urgent news. The room was large with a long oval-shaped desk big enough to seat five. The five in the room were the head council of the Saints. Across the desk was a large hologram against the wall displaying a bar graph. At the bottom of the bar graph were two words with a red line between them. *Good* was written on the left side, *Evil* written on the right side.

Peter's eyes grew very wide when he saw the bar graph in the room. He saw that the green bar over the Good side was right where it should be, at the red horizontal line in the middle. But the green bar over the Evil side was nonexistent. Peter now fully understood the urgency of this problem for the balance of good and evil was now broken.

"Why didn't the evil spirits carry out their orders last month?" Peter shouted to the other Saints in the room.

The Saints in the room were all dumbfounded by the situation. Guesses were shouted out left and right.

"Perhaps they're on strike?"

"Maybe they wish to change their ways?"

"Could it be possible that they didn't receive any orders?"

It was easy to rule out the first two suggestions; the evil spirits had a deep passion for their job, and they would never pass up the opportunity to carry out orders. They were designed to hate humans, so changing their ways was an absurd statement. The Saints now had to address the last option. They couldn't think of any reason why the devil wouldn't send out his orders for the month of July. The devil fully knew the consequences of not fulfilling the actions of his job. The Saints hated it, but they knew they were going to have to talk to the devil. Even if it wasn't his fault the balance was broken, the evil side was his responsibility, so he must be the one to fix it.

The five Saints in the room all scurried to their chairs to open a communication channel with the devil. They spoke as if they were on a phone call with the speaker on. They had only talked to the devil once before. It was a very daunting task, and they wished to never open this channel again. Peter, sitting in the middle of the desk, spoke first.

"Devil, the evil side of the balance is broken. It seems that no evil was cast upon the earth this past July. Do you know why?"

There was nothing but silence on the other side of the channel. One of the Saints pointed out to Peter that the devil was ignoring them. Peter, looking past the dumb comment, repeated his statement in a much higher, angrier voice. Silence was still the response.

Peter, now even more frustrated, called out to the wall in front of them. "Wall, show me the devil!"

The image in front of the wall changed from showing the balance of good and evil to the Garden of Eden.

"Let's see if he continues to ignore us when we have eyes on him!"

When the hologram finished rendering the image of the devil within the Garden, the Saints all received a mighty shock; some even covered their mouths with their hand as they stared at the horrific sight. What the Saints saw was the devil lying dead in front of them.

An uncomfortable hush filled the room for a few moments. They couldn't believe what they were looking at; some even thought that the hologram was pulling a prank on them. Peter was the only one who thought, *This would explain why the balance is broken.*

Francis, the saint on the far right of Peter, got to his feet to take a closer look at the image. The devil had a sword lodged though his heart, pinning him to the ground. He asked the others if any of them had seen this sword before. A saint named Patrick, who sat on Peter's far left side, said that he had studied every weapon in human history, as well as the weapons the angels designed over at the armory next door, and he had never seen that weapon before.

"You think he made it…and used it on himself?" questioned Anthony, the saint to Peter's right.

"No. Just a closer look at the body, you can tell that this was murder," Francis replied. It was disturbing to look at the devil's dead body; what most of the others could only notice was the sword. "There is a diagonal slash across his forehead, along with a bullet wound at the center of it. There is also a large cut on his throat, and not to mention, his entire right forearm was chopped off!"

"Who could have done this?" shouted a saint named Paul, sitting on Peter's left. "How could anyone have done this? The devil was trapped inside the Garden. Who could have broken in?"

"The barrier is impenetrable on the inside. But I did learn that the outside was not as strong. A mighty force could breach the place. But that would require hitting the wall extremely hard from the outside, which should be impossible from anyone trapped inside," Patrick explained.

"Are you saying that someone broke into the Garden of Eden and murdered the devil?" Anthony asked, finding the whole thing hard to believe.

The Saints struggled to process this mystery. The devil knew how to keep his life censored; he was able to use his Loomation powers to keep his actions from being recorded by Heaven so that the Saints couldn't look up his past activities, including the events of his murder. Unless the Saints were using the power of Heaven to view him now, there was no way of viewing any of his actions.

Peter, keeping a level head, spoke to the wall once again, asking it to show the past events within the Garden. But the devil's censored power blocked the entire Garden's past events as well. So Peter asked it to show them something in the Garden that wasn't put there by God. The hologram's point of view flew away from the devil and blurred through the land at a fast speed. When the view came to a stop, the Saints saw two grave sites. Two crosses made of sticks were buried into the ground next to each other.

This startled the Saints for there was now proof that the Garden was indeed infiltrated. Francis, still standing up next to the hologram, read off the names written on the grave markers. "The one on the left says Logan Charles Renshaw. The one on the right says Cain Parker Renshaw."

"Siblings perhaps?" wondered Paul.

"Maybe. All I do know is that the devil didn't bury them. So if we find the grave digger, then we find the assassin," Peter stated.

Patrick asked the desk to bring up the file of Logan Charles Renshaw. The file arrived within seconds and was placed right in front of him. After that, Francis returned to his seat and called upon the file of Cain Parker Renshaw. The two viewed the files and learned that the relationship between the two was father and son. Both died on the same day, Monday, June 28, 2010. Then Patrick found something interesting within the file, and that was the age of Logan at the time of his death, which was 110. When he brought that fact up to the rest of the group, Francis mentioned that Cain died at the age of 80.

This felt like the mystery of this whole situation was only growing rather than being solved. Then Patrick mentioned something within the file. Logan had an active Loomation inside him. The Saints were surprised by this information. The Saints knew that there were some humans in the past who possessed Loomation, but most of them were prophets, and they hadn't had one of them in forever.

Peter asked the readers to jump to the end of the files to see who buried them. The location for both the Renshaws' burials was censored due to the devil keeping the events inside the Garden blocked from Heaven's records. But the file did reveal the names of the ones who buried them. The names were Will Bishop, Tyler Bluth, Hayden Pierce, Blake Lucius, Eric Derole, Beauregard Aday, and Miles Hall.

Once the Saints had the names, they were able to study the boys. They learned that they all contained Loomation inside them. One of the seven had an active Loomation, one of them had the power of flight, and one had immunity to fire.

"So the devil was killed by seven kids with a low-enough amount of Loomation inside them that they still register as humans," Peter said, frustrated while being dumbfound.

"The devil was the most feared living thing in all creation. Even the archangels feared him!" Paul mentioned. "We have lost our biggest enforcer for the balance, heck, our only enforcer! When the other spirits find out about this—"

"They're never going to find out about this!" Peter shouted.

The room got quiet for a moment.

"Not every evil spirit gets a job every month. Heck, most of them don't. And since they don't talk to each other much, we were very lucky that none of them figured out that no one had received any orders last month."

"We can't be that lucky forever! Sooner or later, they'll find out," Francis stated.

"We'll handle the evil side of the balance from now on. We'll send out the orders to the negative spirits under false pretense. We'll make them think that they are getting them from the devil and not us. That way they still think the devil is alive, and that will keep them in line."

"I don't know if I have it in me to send out orders to cause harm to people," Anthony struggled to say.

"We cause harm to millions of people by not responding to their prayers for help because the balance won't let us help everyone," Peter stated.

"Denying a person's prayers is different from causing the actions that make people call out for help in the first place," Patrick explained.

"Look, I know this isn't going to be easy, but there are a lot of Saints in this building who can help us bear the weight. This is the only way to keep the spirits in line."

"But what if one of them does fall out of line, Peter?" questioned Francis.

"That hasn't happened in centuries."

"But what if it does? Or worse, what if they find out that we're the ones sending the orders because the devil is dead? They'll tip the balance, and our angels won't be strong enough to stop them," Francis added.

The tension was running high in the room. The realization of the massive consequence of their secret being discovered leveled a heavy burden on the Saints. But also, the reasonability of maintaining order to the world and keeping the people safe from the evil spirits who wish to rob them from all hope and peace was, and would always have to be, their prime motivation. So they would do whatever it took to keep the secret from ever leaking from the gates of Heaven. As far as the possibility of one of the spirits going rogue, Peter suggested they take another look at the Memphis project.

The Memphis Project

The Memphis project was a designed plan for the Saints to craft a spirit. The Saints had made spirits in the past for the positive side of the balance. But spirit Memphis was to be an enforcer for both sides. The reason for this heavily powered creation was to no longer have to deal with the devil. Back when the balance was broken the first time, the Saints hated their interaction with the devil and wanted to produce a way to avoid any future conversations with the dreaded monster.

Spirits are made with Loomation power, and the designer can control what kind of power they will be especially skilled at. The plan for Memphis wouldn't have any special supernatural powers in him, just pure brute force. With only that in him, he'd fall under as a neutral spirit. The plan was to have Memphis take care of any rogue spirit. The Saints liked the way of having their own enforcer that they were in charge of so they wouldn't have to deal with the devil anymore.

The Memphis design ran into a few problems; his being a neutral spirit made it unpredictable as to where his loyalties would lie. A solution was suggested to keep his brain activity to a minimum. A lack of intelligence would make the spirit unable to think of any original decisions. The name for these types of creatures were called hatched eggs.

Hatched eggs were the lowest forms of spirits there were. They are just spirits hatched from their eggs who obey their designer as if they have no free will at all.

The proposal to make Memphis no more than a highly powerful hatched egg was denied. The Saints were afraid of a spirit being able to outsmart or outwit Memphis, which, sadly, wouldn't be very hard to do. With the level of intelligence needed for Memphis to be victorious, he would have the ability to fully explore his free will, and the Saints couldn't risk someone as powerful as him not joining their side.

The Memphis project was reactivated after the Saints discovered the death of the devil. The design for the being was already underway in the basement of the council chamber. The Saints believed that they had come up with a solution to solve Memphis's alliance. When the archangels made the angels, they imported tons of loyalty aspect into their personalities. This was why the angels served Heaven so proudly.

Monday June 1, 2015

In the basement of the council building, saints Francis and Patrick were checking all the reports on project Memphis. The two were feeling nervous because they were the last Saints needed to sign off on the awakening of the egg that would bring Memphis fully to life. As Patrick was checking the strength levels the man would have, he asked Francis, "With the amount of dry Loomation we pumped into him, is he going to be able to access any of the active Loomation we put in him?"

"Yeah, he'll be able to use it," Francis simply replied as he kept his eyes on some of the documents. "He'll be able to enter the spiritual realm, teleport, and open up communication channels with all spirits." Once Francis said *all spirits*, it made him want to double-check that fact. He knew that Memphis would have access to talk to the evil spirits, but he wanted to see if Memphis could open channels with the positive and neutral spirits as well. Over the past five years, the debates on what Memphis could and couldn't do went back and forth so much that Francis didn't have it all straight.

"Would he be able to track anyone down?" asked Patrick.

"No, he won't be powerful enough to perform that action. The devil had a lot of power, and it still took him more than a few weeks to track down a human," Francis said as he searched for the report on Memphis's communication abilities. When Francis had his hand on the document he was searching for, he read the information. What he said to Patrick about Memphis being able to talk to all spirits was true. It also said that he would be able to talk to any type of angel and that he would have a full index of all types of angels and all kinds of spirits, even the Hogs.

"He'll know about the Hogs? Why?" Francis questioned. "They're only human."

Inside the buildings at the gates of Heaven, the Saints had turned the members of the Hang Out Group into celebrities. With just a little bit of Loomation inside them, they were barely more than regular humans, and yet they were the ones to kill the devil. This was so hard for the Saints to believe. They studied past prophets to find some sort of explanation for this, but they all came back negative. No prophet existed claiming the devil would meet his demise, nor any prophet saying humans would slay the mighty beast.

The Saints studying the Hogs' history revealed that they never received any special orders from God or mission from an archangel. They grew up as average kids with no famous ancestor or some Godlike interferences in family history. The Saints knew everything about the Hogs. They knew the reason they spelled the title of their group with a space between the words *hang* and *out*, which is where they get the Hog reference for the members of the group. They knew who had the nicknames, which one was fireproof, and which one had the active Loomation. They were shocked that one of them could fly, which did fall under a past prophet claiming that the great ones fly. But that one prophecy didn't help ease the reality of the Hogs beating the devil. The Saints still didn't know exactly how the Hogs did what they did due to the devil's ability to sensor all his actions.

"Memphis just knows their names and that they are the ones who killed the devil. He knows nothing about the damage done to the devil, nor does he know anything about the sword used on the devil. He doesn't even know anything about the Hogs' history, just the names and the simple description that they killed the devil," Patrick stated.

"Yeah, but why? Memphis was only made to attack those who harm the balance," Francis said. "They don't carry nearly enough Loomation to be able to affect the system, so they are no threat."

Patrick further explained that the Hogs didn't kill the devil by accident, implying that they could one day be a threat to the balance once again.

Due to the double amount of work the Saints had over the past five years, it was hard to get all the head Saints together to discuss the Memphis project. Many of the of Saints were working overtime to keep up with both good and evil orders for the balance; working on the evil side of the balance had caused loads of stress on the workers, which had caused them to take more rest and recreation. As of right now, fourteen Saints were threatening to resign if the head Saints failed to take the evil order off their work schedule.

Peter was able to convince the other Saints to hold off on their desire to resign, telling them that it would take a while to readjust to the new work. Peter was able to strike a deal for five years of working with the evil orders before fully making their decision. But now that five years were up, Peter had to make a change to keep his staff intact.

The solution to get rid of the negative dispersion from the saint's workload was to have Memphis be the one to issue the evil orders. This meant that he had to be given more intellect to know how to place the spirits and to spread out the necessary malevolence to enforce the balance. Giving the spirit more intelligence such as this caused the Saints to delay the waking of Memphis again. The Saints wanted to pump more reliable and loyal attitude into him so that his alliance would fall to them.

After Francis and Patrick fully looked over everything, they signed the papers to allow Memphis to be awakened. They, just like the others who signed off on the final actions on the project, were still nervous. They felt a little rushed into signing this off due to the large number of Saints threating to quit. Peter was frustrated that it took them as long as it did to sign off. Peter just wanted Memphis to be awakened so that the evil workload would be lifted from the Saints and that the complaints would stop.

Outside the buildings of the gates of Heaven, the Saints stood on what looked to be pure white clouds. To their right were the golden gates that stretched out horizontally as far as they could see. In front of the Saints was the egg that encased the mighty Memphis waiting to be hatched. Due to many of the Saints wishing to view the birth, they moved the egg to the outside. The five head Saints were standing out front with Peter in the middle.

Once all the signatures were signed, the egg started to crack. It took a few minutes for the beast within to emerge from its shell. The Saints shook briefly in fear hearing the crumbling of the egg. When Memphis was fully hatched, he rose to his feet with his back toward the Saints. Memphis's eyes were gaining its first view ever. He had the view from the gates of Heaven's location in front of him and the most magnificent place ever created just to his right. Still, none of this impressed him.

The Saints looking at the monster made them freeze up at first. They were all waiting for Peter to talk to it. Peter couldn't show any signs of fear in front of his subordinates, so he took a step up to the spirit. Peter thought by now Memphis would have turned around to face his creators, but he just kept staring out in the distance.

"Memphis," Peter said in a firm tone.

"Yes," Memphis simply replied, still refusing to turn around to face his creators.

Peter looked back at the Saints for a moment, possibly feeling embarrassed. When he turned back to the spirit, he had to remind himself what he normally said to the new spirits when they were hatched. "We have a job for you," Peter said, still finding it odd that he was only talking to the spirit's back and not to him directly.

"I know what you've built me for," Memphis stated.

"To carry out the orders of the evil side of the balance, yes. We were hoping you could start right away."

"That's not all of it." Memphis's words were starting to make some of the Saints uneasy. "You want me to deliver the orders to the evil spirits while making them believe that they are getting them from the devil. And you want me to eliminate any evil spirit who falls out of line."

Peter didn't know whether to be impressed or disturbed by how much Memphis already knew just seconds after being hatched. "Yes, keeping the lie of the devil still being alive will keep the evil spirits in line."

"And what do the spirits get in return for being so obedient?"

"They get their reward by carrying out their orders. They thrill in spreading their evil. And them staying in line keeps them from getting killed," Peter said, now getting frustrated that Memphis still hadn't faced him yet.

"They wish for more, you know. Some go a long time before they get the call to act, and that angers them," Memphis said as he lifted his head up. "I can feel their thoughts, their desires." Memphis then looked over to the gates of Heaven. "They wish to go to Heaven, you know. A lot of them are miserable, and when they get to do what they love, it only lasts a few moments, and who knows when they get to act again. They know that if they were in Heaven, they would find peace."

"Heaven won't allow anyone who thrives on hurting the innocent or who purposely disrupts the peace for their own personal selfish goals."

"The spirits have stayed in line for so long due to the fear of being murdered. They desire more, and since Heaven will never be an option for them, I think they should make their own Heaven on earth." Memphis then finally faced Peter and all the Saints behind him. "I think they should know the truth." Memphis then closed his eyes and opened a communication channel to all spirits.

"Memphis, I order you to stand down!" Peter shouted as he waved a finger at the monster.

"You made me for the evil spirits, and I want them to be liberated from all said orders so they can be free to do all that they wish!"

Peter then turned around. He ran past the other spirits trying to get to the main building of the gates. Peter pushed open the doors with a heavy force and reached for the button on the side of the wall. Peter slammed his palm onto the button, and an alarm went off. This was a panic button; many of these were located throughout the buildings. When the Saints set up offices at the gates of Heaven, they were given protection from an archangel personally requested by God. An archangel would teleport to the gates if this button was ever pushed and would wipe out any threat present. Peter knew that the power of an archangel would be their only hope to save them now.

But it was too late. The message was already sent, and Memphis had teleported away. The message was sent out to all spirits saying, "The devil is dead…has been for five years. The Saints didn't want you to know so that they could maintain the fear they have over you to keep you all in line. But now that the beast is dead, you all have the chance to live! Go out to the world and do what you love, and if any angel tries to stop you, they'll have to get through me."

The War of the Balance

A house of cards can take much time to build, and one false move will cause the entire structure to come crashing down. There is a feeling of the stomach dropping when accidentally nudging the stabilizing card, followed by the shaken reaction of watching it all drop in front of you. This tragic feeling seemed to be Peter's reaction as he watched the evil side of the balance rise up in front of him. The Saints in the building were all in a panic, running to get to their desks to obtain the overwhelming flow of prayers appearing as letters. Peter had Saints knocking at his door, saying that an archangel was standing outside, furious that the button to summon him had been pushed without any threat found at the gates.

After Memphis sent out his message, it was as if all the evil spirits were throwing themselves a parade on earth. It seemed that they wanted to fully test the no-limits promise. That evil side of the balance was going up so fast, it was unprecedented. Peter then heard Francis knock and asked to be let in. Peter let Francis in. Francis eyed the balance and was a little stunned to see how fast things were moving on earth.

"Patrick, Paul, and Anthony are talking to the archangel trying to calm him down," Francis stated.

"You think that an archangel would be up for an assassin's job?" wondered Peter.

"Only if you can get Memphis back up here to threaten us," Francis sadly replied. archangels never listened to the Saints. Only one of them was given the job to protect the gates of Heaven and the Saints who stayed there. Since God gave him that job and not the Saints, he complied. Back when the balance was broken the first time, the Saints did ask the archangels to terminate the spirit breaking it, but they all refused, saying that the balance was not their problem and that God had already put others in charge of it so that they would never have to.

"Killing Memphis won't fix this, Peter," Francis added.

"I know," Peter admitted. Peter then plopped down in his chair and leaned back, covering his face with his hands. "How do we fix this?"

"Right now they're just testing us." Francis was talking about the spirits. "Once they wreak havoc long enough, they'll eventually fully believe that there is no devil coming for them. After that, things will never be the way they were ever again."

"So it's hell on earth from now on, is it?"

"When the excitement finally comes to an end, they'll settle down to get some rest. The archangels may not want to fight for us, but we have an army of angels who will be ready to get their hands dirty, ready to fight for the good of the world!"

"We knew the odds of beating the spirits weren't on our side before Memphis claimed protection over them. With him on their side now, we don't stand a chance!"

"We still have to have hope, Peter."

⤙◈◈◈⤚

Francis was right. After twenty-four hours of one of earth's worst days in centuries, things finally started to calm down. The spirits had their fun, but Memphis felt that there should be a ringleader among them. In order to build an evil spirit paradise on earth, they would need some type of direction. Memphis had his followers; they believed that he set them free for telling them the news of the devil's death. Memphis even earned the trust of the horsemen; with them by his side, Memphis had almost complete order and respect from the evil spirits.

Memphis's first action was delivering territories to his closest followers. Then the war broke out. The Saints were sending the angels down to earth to defend the balance. Memphis, along with his followers, was able to repel the angels with ease. Memphis's power was too much for the angels, and Memphis grew the nickname the Angel Slayer. Memphis didn't stop at the angels. He had his followers help him find any active positive spirit on earth. Memphis slaughtered them as well and would even seek them out when they were in the middle of working.

The Saints had assigned angels for protection duty over all remaining positive spirits. The good spirits and most angels were all too scared to return to earth as long as Memphis was still alive. The war of the balance lasted five years, and it was a one-sided battle. The Saints theorized that if they could take out Memphis, things could turn toward their side.

Thursday, October 1, 2020

Out in the Atlantic Ocean, a small fishing ship fought through the heavy waves, an unmerciful downpour, and unending stormy weather. On the boat, an angel teleported to the bow of the vessel. Once he was there, he transitioned from the spiritual realm to the physical realm. Being in the physical realm caused him to feel the shakes of the ship more aggressively, and when a large wave pushed the boat, he took a few steps around him to manage his balance.

"James, quit your dancing and get over here!" shouted another angel from the stern of the ship. This vessel had sailed away from its owners a few days ago. The rope used to tie it to the dock had been eaten by a goat. The angels found the ship within the ocean and commandeered it for their mission.

When James walked over to the stern of the boat, he saw five other angels there. Once he was standing beside them, he asked, "Is this it?" James had to shout over the loud winds and heavy raindrops pounding on the boat.

"Six angels counting, you are all who were assigned for this mission," the angel running this mission stated. "Did you get the goods?"

James nodded as he set a briefcase onto the table that was glowing within the boat's light. He was directed to come up to the gates of Heaven to receive a new explosion device, one with the chance to take out Memphis. James opened the case to show off the weapons. They looked like bracelets they would strap to their wrists; to activate them, the angels would have to blast it with their Loomation powers. A small blast of Loomation would set it off after five seconds while a large blast would set it off immediately.

"Angels, take one," Commander Boris instructed. There were six angels for this mission and only six bracelets. Strapping something so powerful to themselves was slightly uncomfortable, but they showed no fear. "I don't know many of you well, and I know that most of you are fighting together for the first time tonight. But the Saints put together this task force to take out Memphis, and we won't let them down!"

The soldiers all cheered with a slight lift of their guns toward the air. Over the years of this war, many task forces were assembled, and these six on the boat were the few survivors from most of the fallen past teams. James and Commander Boris had been together since the beginning of the war. James had seen his commander do his best in many battles, but in the end, they had lost many fights. They went from many survivors from their team to very few survivors, and they were the last two standing from the last battle they fought in. James was nervous, thinking that he had used up all his luck and fearing that this time, he would be one of the fallen.

"I know that many of you haven't fought in the physical realm before, but as long as Memphis has the symbol that turns off the spiritual realm, we have no choice. The symbol's range can be as far as a half mile, but if it's built large enough, it can reach up to two miles. Just know that there won't be any teleporting as long as the symbol remains intact. The humans will be able to see you, so try to stay out of their way. And don't forget that your surroundings can hurt you while in this form!"

In the early days of the war, the angels were able to teleport straight to Memphis's location; it was the only advantage the good side had for a while. But after Memphis learned about the symbol, the angels had to find new way to approach their foe.

"Memphis is currently giving protection for an evil spirit named Sinker. This dirty scoundrel has sunk boats since humans learned how to float objects! The Saints have located the two on a large cargo ship. This is the largest ship Sinker has ever attempted to take down, so it should take a while for the ship to completely sink. Thanks to the Saints looking into this ship, we fully know where it is, and we are making our way toward it now. The plan is take out Memphis at all costs!"

"And save the ship, right?" James aggressively said.

The commander glanced at James with a mean face. "The ship isn't our priority, James," he said with no guilt.

James felt that the Saints' and angels' primary goal of protecting the humans had now faded, and none of them seemed to care. James knew how important it was to eliminate Memphis, but he didn't want to lose his goal of protecting the humans along the way as so many others had.

"What's the worst a spirit named Stinker can do to a ship? What, is he going to pull his finger and make the whole place smell like skunk? How's that going to sink it?" said the only angle within the group who had a set of wings on his back. Not all angels were given wings; winged angles were a rare breed within the angel population.

"It's Sinker, not Stinker, you idiot!" said one of the other angels.

"You really want to insult me while I'm wearing this!" the winged angel replied, shoving his bracelet into the face of the one who insulted him.

"I doubt that you'll fire that thing so close to your target. You luggage department angels never attack your opponent at close range!" said a different angel.

"You know that we don't like that term!" the winged angel said, feeling insulted.

"Given the fact that your kind called it quits first, maybe we should call you winged angels…chickens!" another angel chimed in.

"Knock it off, all of you!" the commander shouted as he stomped his foot. "We all have a job to do, and we won't succeed if we are too busy fighting each other!"

"Commander!" shouted James as he pointed out toward the ocean.

Everyone faced the direction James was pointing toward, and they saw the ship. The massive cargo ship had already started to take in water from a few holes spaced out from the bottom of the vessel. The whole crew had already abandoned the ship, scurrying on lifeboats, for it was only a matter of minutes before the entire ship went under. The angels felt that they were too late and that the mission was already a failure. James was upset that they didn't even have time to attempt to save the boat.

Commander Boris saw that the cargo ship was indeed sinking, but it was clearly a controlled sinking. The boat was lowering itself into the water as if it was on an elevator going down. Normally the water would fill up on one side of the vessel, and that would cause it to tip. It was clear that the evil spirit that was causing this unnatural sinking was still on the boat, and so was Memphis. Commander Boris told his men to jump onto the deck of the sinking ship while they still had time to find their target.

Once the angels' boat was close enough to the shipping container ship, they took a mighty jump to reach to main deck. The one with wings flew safely across the sky to get to the deck. They saw nothing but the containers and heard nothing but the rain slamming onto the metal that was all around them. They didn't have much time to search out the ship. They could feel the vessel lowering itself deeper and deeper by the second. The task force all started to slowly split up in teams of two. Not too long after that, one of the shipping containers swung wide open close to some of the angels, and out came Memphis, charging at the two angels closest to him.

"*Memphis!*" the winged angel shouted at the top of his lungs. The winged angel flapped his wings quickly in order to retreat; one of his wings even smacked the angel next to him in the back of the head. The remaining angel still in Memphis's path pointed his explosive bracelet device at his enemy, but he failed to perform his attack having to steady his head and replace his footing due to his head getting wacked from the wing. Memphis managed to grab the angel's wrist, and then he pulled him in close with just one hand. With Memphis's other hand, he held a dagger and, with no hesitation, shoved it right into the angel's heart, killing him.

There was something odd that happened when the dagger entered the angel's body. When the blade cut into him deep, the body seemed to spurt out sparks of silver light. Memphis then raised his head to set his eyes on the winged angel. The winged angel was shocked with fear as he aimed his bracelet at the monster. Memphis gave a quick whistle, and from the container that was stacked on top of the one that he had just emerged from came a half dozen hatched eggs. Since the winged angel was hovering right at that height, the hatched eggs all jumped onto the body of the angel. Three of the hatched eggs managed to hang on to the angel and started pulling on the wings.

"No!" shouted the angel in much pain. "Not the wings!" He screamed as his right wing was torn clean off. The angel went into a crash dive right into the ocean, and then his bracelet went off under the water, killing him and the hatched eggs still on him in a blast that splashed water onto the deck.

Two of the other angels ran toward the commotion and used their guns to shoot down the oncoming threat of the hatched eggs. One told the other that he'd hold off the eggs as the other fired off the bracelet. But before the angel could make a move to his bracelet, an attack came from the left of the two angels. A large mighty red fur horse came galloping at the two with a powerful stomping attack. The two were trampled unmercifully with its hooves pounding them over and over. Both of the angels reached their arms over to their bracelets to activate them, and before the horse could give the killing stomp to end their lives, the two angels managed to fire off their bracelets at the stallion. Combined with the two bracelets' exploding force, all three of them went out in a large fiery blast.

Commander Boris saw that Memphis was now defenseless. The commander told James that he'd swoop over in front of Memphis while James snuck in from behind. James nodded, and the two took off to proceed with their plan. The commander ran over to charge at Memphis head-on. The commander was able to use his powerful gun to exterminate the remaining hatched eggs with ease. He then unloaded the rest of his gun's ammo at Memphis. Memphis, being built to withstand strong attacks, arrogantly welcomed the bullets exploding onto his chest as his body was built to take a pounding much worse than this.

Boris knew that the few remaining bullets within his gun wouldn't be strong enough to finish off Memphis, but he wasn't using the gun to kill him, just get his attention. James was running around the containers trying to find a path that led right behind Memphis so that he could fire off his bracelet. James ran fast, being able to stay out of sight thanks to the line of containers on his left side. James found a gap between the storage units and turned into it and found himself behind Memphis. James hurried to aim his bracelet.

Memphis, having no idea that James was behind him, chucked his dagger right at the commander. The dagger drove deeply into Boris's shoulder and flung him back off his feet. Sliver sparks were flying out of the wound, and Boris started to feel weaker and weaker. A new feeling came to the commander, and that feeling was water. The deck of the ship had now gotten closer to the surface of the ocean. The commander lifted his head and saw Memphis was hit with an explosion from James's bracelet.

Memphis's body was pounded face first into the water that was engulfing the ship. The commander looked down and saw James standing in the path behind Memphis. James hurried over to his leader, running past the burning body of Memphis. James knelt to help his commander up. The water was rising fast as it was now up to his knees.

With the heavy rain and the water surrounding the entire dock, the fire on Memphis went out in a hurry. There was a large bruise steaming off Memphis's back as he returned to his feet. James and Boris were at a loss seeing Memphis standing strong. They couldn't believe that the blast didn't kill him or hurt him. They were also, at the same time, slightly impressed, and the last emotion that they were feeling was the fear that Memphis couldn't be killed. The spirit was truly built to take a hit.

The commander then activated his bracelet, feeling like he barely had enough Loomation inside him to do it, and then he fired it at the beast. But a floating storage container got in the way of the attack, and the explosion caused a massive but harmless wave within the water. James grabbed hold of his injured leader and dove deep into the ocean, swimming away from the ship fast.

Back on the ship, Memphis looked over and saw the evil spirit Sinker. Sinker was the one who floated the container in the way of the attack. Now that things were safe for the spirits, Memphis looked over and saw his fallen follower, the red horseman, War. He couldn't believe that the angels were able to kill him. Memphis lost his best general, but he knew that this would be the last attack from the angels. He knew by now all angels were either dead or too terrified to continue the fight. The Saints were defeated, and so he really didn't need his top general anymore.

Out at sea, James was struggling to keep Boris above the water. The injured angel could barely move, and the waves were making the swim difficult. James was very relieved to see the boat he came on within a short swim. James swam over to the boat, pulling his commander on board. James rested the man against the side of the boat and removed the dagger from Boris's shoulder. Blood started to flow out of the wound much faster after the blade was removed. James was able to give a healing spell onto the angel to bring him back to health.

"We better get back to the Saints. I can feel the spiritual realm back up, so we can teleport again. We might not have killed Memphis, but we took out the horseman War. That should make the Saints a little happy," James said as he stood up tall and offered his hand to Boris to help him back to his feet.

"I won't be making it back to the gates, James," the commander struggled to say as he opted to stay sitting down on the deck.

"What are you talking about?" asked James in a confused tone. "I healed you."

"That dagger you took from my shoulder was something that the Saints wanted me to keep top secret."

James took a closer look at the dagger in his hand but didn't see anything unique about it. Boris explained that the dagger was one of Memphis's special weapons. This dagger was one of the reasons why so many angels were afraid to go back out in the field.

"Angels get their powers by their connection to Heaven. That dagger cuts off that connection. Once we are cut off from Heaven's power, we're nothing more than a human body," Boris spoke as if all his pride and might had faded away. The angels became afraid of the dagger when they learned about it, which was why most of them had resigned.

James placed the dagger in the briefcase that was still sitting on the table. "I can teleport you back to the gates, and we can find someone who can fix you."

"There is no fixing this, James. I'm human now, and I won't return to Heaven a beaten angel! I won't go back as a useless, powerless failure!"

"I'm not just going to leave you here!"

"You still have orders, soldier. Someone must return to the Saints to give the mission report! Now, you will do what you must and leave me here!"

James stood up, respecting his commander's final orders even if he didn't agree with them. James picked up the briefcase and looked back at Boris, telling him that he would return for him after his meeting with the Saints. James then teleported back to the gates, leaving his commander on the boat.

The Hog Mission

When James arrived at the gates of Heaven, he appeared in front of the main building. His wet hair, skin, and clothes had all dried up due to the Heavenly presence of the area. You would always be clean and smelling good while in this location. James looked down at the briefcase in his right hand, wondering if it was smart to carry the frightening dagger inside the building. He figured that if he kept it inside the case, it would be fine. James wanted to present it to a friend after seeing the Saints; maybe he could study it to find a way to undo its effects or something.

James entered the front door of the main building. Inside he saw a plethora of Saints working at their desks, reading over prayers in letter form, and stressing out that there was nothing they could do. One of the workers noticed James and stood up to impatiently ask, "Did you kill him?"

James painfully shook his head no. The saint asked if James was the only survivor, feeling like he already knew that answer. James said that he was the only one able to make it back, and he then continued on his way to the head Saints' room to make his report. It was odd being the only soldier walking though these halls for the first time. Up until now, James was always with Boris, and he didn't feel right leaving him back on the boat in his condition. James saw that the door to the main Saints' room was already open. The Saints, with a sense of doom, asked him to close it when he walked in.

James took the chair that was opposite of the large oval-shaped desk of the head Saints. The Saints always presented themselves as clean-shaven, nicely-combed-hair gentlemen. They always don themselves in long religious dress robes that came in multiple color choices. The angels and spirits got into the habit of referring to the workers of Heaven's gates as the Robes due to the saints wearing clothing that covered almost their entire bodies. The saints felt the need to present themselves as perfectly as they could; perhaps it was an attempt to hide their flaws. James walked through the entire battle from his point of view the best he could. The Saints didn't care that the angels were unable to save the ship, and they had no reaction when James mentioned the death of his comrades. They just wanted to know if any of them managed to hit Memphis with the new weapon. James, speaking as if he was now annoyed by these guys, stated that he managed to strike Memphis with his bracelet, but it didn't come close to killing him.

"Just one of them hit the spirit. We were hoping all six would," Peter replied in an angry tone.

James reminded the Saints that they fell into a trap and that they were attacked by hatched eggs and even the horseman War. James said that two of them combined managed to kill the horseman, thinking that they'd be happy to hear that the new weapon did kill off a powerful spirit. The Saints again didn't show any reaction by hearing that War was now dead; they only cared about killing Memphis.

James knew why the saint had such a huge obsession to kill Memphis. They knew that they made a mistake by designing him, and they felt like having him killed would undo their mistake. God hadn't reached out to the Saints at all during this whole time. The Saints felt like they were being punished for their actions. The archangels refused to assist the Saints; they were angry at them for building such a powerful spirit. The archangels had been keeping an eye on the Saints' projects ever since Memphis was brought to life. After the frustration that the archangels experienced with Memphis, they passed an act that the Saints were no longer allowed to build anything so powerful. That is why their arsenal wasn't strong enough to take out Memphis.

"I would like to return to earth. I left Boris on the boat, and he's going to need help out there on the ocean." James had already told the Saints about Commander Boris's falling victim to Memphis's dagger.

"There is no need to return to earth on Commander Boris's behalf," Saint Anthony stated as he handed over a stack of files to Peter.

"We shouldn't just abandon him since he's now human." James raised his voice to the Saints and stood up from his chair. "Commander Boris has fought for you guys in every mission you gave him, even when he knew that he was risking his own angel life by doing so!"

"Commander Boris is dead," Peter said as he was looking at the files he received.

"No, he's not dead, he just lost his angel powers," James replied.

"James," Francis said, expressing remorse for the news he was about to give. "After you left him on the boat, Commander Boris tied himself to the boat's anchor and then dropped it in the ocean. He's gone."

James fell back into his chair feeling distraught. James couldn't believe it; he was just with Boris a few minutes ago. James argued with the Saints, telling them that they should have sent him back to him before he did what he did. Francis said that there was nothing James could have done to change his mind. James disagreed with that, claiming that he knew he could have done something to help him.

"James, every time an angel lost their powers and became human, they've all done the same thing," Francis stated with a heavy heart. "Once an angel loses his or her powers, they lose all sense of purpose in life. They were made to serve Heaven, and no longer being able to do that causes them to no longer wish to continue in life. Their entire life changed, and they all see it all as a downgrade. Angels can rest and live in Heaven, but living humans can't. Many of them don't know how to survive with a human life, and they don't want to try it. It's horrible, I know, but trust me, Commander Boris's mind was made up as soon as he was fully human. Nothing you could have said or done would have changed his mind."

James was now truly heartbroken; he lost his commander and was officially the only survivor from the latest attack on Memphis. Along with James's sad feelings, he was also disgusted at how most of the Saints in the room handled this news. The reaction to the tragic report of the loss of his commander was handled with the same lack of emotion. It was like their reaction to any common mission report they had received over the last five years.

"When is the next task force being assembled? I would like to be in for a promotion as a commander," James stated, leaving his grief behind and getting back to business.

"We will be postponing all future task force assignments until further notice," Peter replied, keeping his eyes on the files in front of him.

When James asked for the reason for this, they explained that James's latest attack on Memphis was the Saints' final attempt to take out the spirit. Due to the many losses of their assets over the course of the war, they could no longer risk the extinction of Heaven's forces. That and most of the remaining angels refused to go out in the field as long as Memphis was alive. The plan was to call for a cease-fire on their side until the order to the archangels to make more angels was successfully granted.

James couldn't believe that the Saints were throwing in the towel like this. They knew that the archangels would never make more angels for them. The Saints were officially giving up on ever managing the balance of good and evil again. When James tried to express his thoughts on this idea, they sternly ordered him to be silent.

"Well, if you are so eager to get back in the field, James, we do have a small mission you can take," Peter said, looking away from the files and up to the angel.

James hated the idea of sitting around and doing nothing, so he eagerly took the job offer, whatever it might be.

"Since we are at the moment discontinuing the fight in the war of the balance, it's time to bring in the people responsible for all of this to be judged," Peter explained as he offered the files he was looking at to James.

James leaned forward to grab the files. As James looked at the files, he saw that they all contained the members of the Hang Out Group.

"The Hogs, they have nothing to do with this," James replied in a confused tone. Ever since Memphis released the news of the devil's murder, all angels and spirits were asking how and by whom. The how was never publicly known, but the names of the Hogs were the ones responsible for the murder.

"They have everything to do with all of this! They went into the Garden and committed murder and, in doing, so broke the balance of good and evil!" Peter shouted, displeased with James's insolence.

"Unknowingly broke the balance," corrected James.

"We are doing this very professionally, James," said Francis, keeping a level head. "The Hogs will have their chance to defend themselves in court."

"Yes, and we won't bring them up here to serve the trial until they are aware of the charges they received," Paul explained.

"Which means you'll have to tell them the secret origins of the balance of good and evil, James," Patrick added.

James was quickly growing very nervous; to speak of something such as the origins of the balance to humans gave a consequence of being taken to hell. The Saints had given James permission to speak of the secret only once, so they strongly suggested him to reveal it when they were all together. Once the Hogs knew their charges, they would be sent up to the gates of Heaven where the trial would be held.

The files in James's hand had all the highlights of each member of the Hang Out Group, including their current whereabouts. The Saints knew that this wouldn't be an easy mission for James, especially since Memphis had his followers out on earth looking for any angels or positive spirits. They wanted to give him all the time he needed to fulfill this mission, but according to the latest hypothesis on the Hogs' future, one of the members was projected to die within a few days. This was only a hypothesis, so there was no guarantee of him dying or if his death would fall on the estimated day. But this information did put James under a literal deadline to complete his mission.

James thanked the Saints for the mission and then left the room, placing the files into the briefcase. He then exited the building, walking onto the white cloudlike ground surrounding the gates of Heaven. James then headed over to the armory building, which was a small walk from the building he just exited. He walked with the briefcase in his hand and entered the building to see his friend.

Inside, James met up with his spirit friend Boston, the weapons expert and top designer for the armory. Boston was a spirit built by the Saints many, many years ago to design and keep track of the angel arsenal. Boston was happy to see James alive after his latest battle, but he could tell by James's mood that the mission was unsuccessful. James gave a quick rundown of the attack as he placed the briefcase onto Boston's worktable.

"So the new explosive bracelets failed to do the trick?" Boston asked, although he already knew the answer.

"Well, the combined force of two bracelets did take out a horseman. But it'll take all six of them to kill Memphis," James said as he opened up the case.

"Sorry, James. Saints' orders dictate I can't make anything too powerful. If it wasn't for the archangels' making that a law, I could really make something that could do some heavy damage."

"Well, I want you to take a look at a weapon made by our enemy," James said as he handed over the dagger to Boston.

Boston picked up the dagger and brought it close to his eyes. James warned him that the blade was strong enough to slice off the connection angels have to Heaven. Boston was fascinated by this detail, and he then put the object under one of his microscopes.

"Any idea how Memphis could come up with something like this?" asked James.

"Well, Memphis was made with the strength and knowledge to not only kill spirits, but angels too," Boston said while looking at the carvings on the blade. "Best way to take out an angel is to make us human, and that's done by taking away our Loomation. Since you get your Loomation powers from your connection to Heaven, finding a way to cut that connection would lead to you being human. And it seems that Memphis has found a way to turn that knowledge into a weapon."

"Yeah, it's why so many angels are too afraid to face him. I'm hoping that me now having his dagger would bring the courage back into them."

"How did you manage to get this?" wondered Boston.

"I pulled it out of my commander's shoulder after he and I escaped Memphis."

"Well, I doubt that Memphis carelessly chucked away his only dagger. After taking a closer look at this dagger, I can see that it's made of iridium, and the carvings in it has the symbols of an old archangel language. Spells that were used to make angels but written in reverse."

"Any way to reverse the effects?"

"It'll take an archangel or higher being to restore the connection, that or an amputation transfer from a living angel who still has their connection. Like if you wanted to give your arm to your commander, that might reverse the effects."

James's hope for an easy fix for the dagger's negative results wasn't high, but it was something he had to check on. James then took a seat at the chair around the worktable to take a deeper look into the Hogs' files. Boston asked James if he was being assigned to another task force. James carelessly informed Boston that the Saints were no longer building task forces. Boston wasn't really shocked by this information. With all the fallen angels and most of the rest reluctant to volunteer, it was only a matter of time until the Saints quit.

"So you get reassigned to protecting the remaining positive spirits?" questioned Boston, seeing that it was the only job left for the angels now.

"The Saints want me to gather up the Hogs and bring them up here so that they can stand trial for the murder of the devil," James said as he thought this was a pointless assignment.

"What do the Hogs have to do with any of this?" asked Boston.

"The Saints just want to put the blame of the broken balance on them. They're trying to make it look like the whole Memphis project was the Hogs' fault. I'm sure that if they can make it look like it was their fault, then maybe the archangels will be a little more helpful with the Saints instead of being angry with them."

"It's too bad the Hogs weren't fighters for the order of the balance. That group managed to kill the devil. Now there's a task force that could take on Memphis."

James looked at Boston as if he just said something brilliant. James thought about it and agreed with Boston. The Hogs did kill the devil, who was the strongest being God had ever created. James had no idea how they did it; no one did. But he was about to go down to earth to talk to them. One of them could enlighten him on that information. James felt that if he could get the Hogs on the Saints' side to be fighters for the order of the balance, then James could be a commander of his own task force team.

The problem was that the Saints were dead set on them facing trial as soon as they discovered the information of the balance. James would have to fulfill his mission before having the Hogs do anything. After that, he'd have to convince them to help him fix the world.

James looked at the seven Hogs' files thinking that they were earth's last hope.

James had to plan out his mission; he knew it wasn't going to be easy to get them all in one place, so he would have to channel both good cop and bad cop to get results from them. The hardest part would be avoiding the evil spirits. Evil spirits were granted territory within the borders of each member's residence. Memphis wanted to keep his eyes on the Hogs, so he tagged seven of his followers to follow each member.

The seven Hogs were all split up, some far away. James found a place out of all the evil spirits' territories where they all could meet up, a safe house he called it. James saw that the evil spirit paired up with Will was the horseman War. Since War was now dead, any heavy negative emotions pressed onto Will would now be in the process of fading due to War being killed off. James planned to see Will first due to his having no evil spirit in his area. Will was close to both Timber and Eric, and their evil spirits were still in close range to them, so James planned to have Will pick them up on his way to the safe house.

The next Hog James would go visit would be Juice. His evil spirit wasn't dead but was occupying another one of her territories now, which was the only case for the remaining Hogs. So if James hurried, he could talk to Juice and get out before she came back. James would have Juice pick up Hayden and Miles on his way to the safe house. Once the six were there, James would test out the Hogs' mission skills on having them rescue Gard. Since Gard was the one who it was hypothesized would die, James wanted to keep an eye on him as much as he could. He'd have to be up at the gates of Heaven to do that, so James would be very come and go for the Hogs for a while.

James was very excited about this plan. For the first time in a long time, he had high hopes. James looked over the Hogs' files, this time more than just their whereabouts. He was shocked that most of the Hogs had not seen each other in the last five years. Not only that, but none of them even considered them to be friends anymore. They all moved on from their group years ago, and they all had faced devastating events due to the evil spirit haunting them for the last five years. The Hogs were not who they once were back when they killed the devil. James knew that if the Hogs were going to be able to fight for the order of the balance, they would have to get themselves back to their old selves again. James felt that he had his work cut out for him. But if he could pull this group together, the balance could be fixed.

Come Together

The night was getting late, and there was a storm on its way. Juice was walking home from the movie theater in a bit of a rush due to the chance of getting caught in the rain. As he made his way to his apartment, he had to make a small detour due to an active police investigation blocking off the street. Someone was recently murdered on that street, and the *Do Not Cross* police tape was set up.

Once Juice was on the street of his apartment, he was about to walk past an alley. In the alley, two thugs were getting ready to jump him. But one of them caught a glimpse of the man they were about to mug and called it off. This man had tried to mug Juice once before, and he learned the hard way that Juice was much stronger than he looked. When Juice walked by the alley, he just gave a slight nod to the two potential muggers. The two men, one with a puzzled look on his face, started to walk the opposite way.

Juice made it to the door of his apartment building, and before he opened the door, he saw that all the cars parked on the street next to the building had been broken into. Juice was happy that he parked in the parking garage and not the side of the street as he normally did. He walked into the apartment building and made his way to the fourth floor.

Down the hall of the fourth floor, he spotted his neighbors who lived across the hall. His neighbors were two women, one in her midforties and her daughter in her midtwenties. The mother was hugging her daughter goodbye with tears sliding down her cheeks. The mother worked the day shift while the daughter worked the night shift. So they only had a few minutes to see each other between her getting home from work and the daughter taking off to work. The mother was concerned for her daughter when she took off for her job at the gas station. The place had been robbed at gunpoint twice since she'd been working there, and she'd been working there for only two months.

Juice placed his key into the keyhole and unlocked the door. Juice walked in and quickly locked it behind him. He didn't turn on the lights; he just chucked his keys on the kitchen counter as he walked up to the fridge. Inside the fridge were leftover takeout food and a half-empty pint of chocolate milk. Juice was frustrated that he was out of beer. He could have sworn that he had at least one left. He was even angrier at himself for not buying any on his way home. The coming storm made him concentrate on getting home more than anything.

Juice walked over to his small couch and plopped straight down on it. He looked out the window and saw the rain start to hit the glass followed by a lightning strike. He turned his head away from the view as the lightning was spooking him. After all these years, he still couldn't enjoy the viewing of a lightning storm like he did when he was a teen. The flashing lights in the clouds brought back some disturbing memories.

As Juice turned his head away from the window, he spotted a beer bottle on the couch's end table. He reached for it, hoping that there was still a swallow or two in it. When he picked up the bottle, he felt it completely empty. Slightly frustrated, he slammed the bottle back on the end table. He put too much force in this action and ended up smashing it into pieces. He looked at the table to see the shattered glass. He picked up the largest broken glass piece with his right hand and brought it over in front of him. He stared at the sharp pointed glass for a moment, then looked over to his left wrist.

Before he had another thought, he heard a knock at the door. He faced the door not knowing if the knock was real or just in his head.

Then three more knocks followed in rapid succession. He looked back at the glass shrapnel in his hand and then chucked it against the wall, shattering it into many pieces. He then rose to his feet and made his way to the door. More knocks came to the door, and Juice yelled that he was on his way while muttering to himself that if the visitor would have come a few minutes later, then he might not have been able to come to the door.

Juice opened the door and saw a stranger on the other side. This stranger was James, and he was eager to start his chat. James's original plan was to visit Will first, but James didn't know how long Juice's evil spirit would be out of his territory, so he chose to visit him first and get out of there fast.

"Hi, I'm James," James said as he reached out for a handshake.

Juice ignored the handshake and walked over to the kitchen, leaving the door open for James to let himself in. "What can I do you for, James?" Juice said in an exhausted voice as he grabbed a glass out of the cupboard.

James let himself in and walked over to the kitchen. Juice filled his glass up with the water from the tap. Just before Juice touched the glass with his lips, he offered it to James, as if he just remembered to be nice and offer his visitor a drink. James passed on the drink. Juice told James that passing on the drink was probably a good idea; he mentioned that the water has tasted a little off for the past couple of weeks. Juice took a large drink out of the glass and propped himself up on the counter to sit down.

At this moment, James realized that he had not prepared a speech for Juice at all. James was speechless at first, and Juice simply kept drinking his water. When he finished his glass, he refilled it from the sink again. There was a slight awkward staring competition between the two for a moment. James felt that he had until Juice finished his second glass of water to speak; otherwise, he would kick him out of his home.

"I was sent here to inform you that your presence is requested," James stated.

Juice waited to finish his glass of water before speaking again. After he was done drinking, he dropped the glass into the sink and replied in a slightly annoyed way, "Who wants me where?"

"My orders come from the top…like the highest order out there," James said, feeling lost for words.

"Alright, Jones, I'm not interested in any type of cruise or time share offers." Juice said, already forgetting James's name.

James, no longer wanting to find the easiest way to tell this information, decided to take a direct approach with his words. "Alright, Juice, I have to be straight with you. The world is in misery. I know that you had to face your own misery over the last five years, and I'm sorry for that. But you are not alone. Everyone out there is suffering, and it may be all because of you and your Hang Out Group friends. I can explain why all that is, but I need you to do a few things for me first."

"I don't have to do anything for you. Trust me, the world isn't in misery because of me and my old high school friends. We rid the world of the big bad devil years ago, so you're welcome!" Juice said as he angrily jumped off the counter.

"Killing the devil wasn't a good thing!" James shouted.

At that moment, Juice knew that there was something different about this person. Juice found it odd at first that this man knew his old nickname and the name that he and his old friends used to call themselves back in high school. That could have been researched through social media, but the knowledge of them killing the devil was something impossible for anyone to know. Juice was now stunned and even speechless.

James aggressively set down a few documents onto the counter. "If you can gather up Hayden and Miles and meet me at the safe house location, I will tell you guys everything. Why what has happened to all of you has happened, why the world is in hell, and why killing the devil was a bad thing."

Juice glanced at the papers for a moment. When he looked back at James, he saw that James was already heading to the door. Juice followed and asked how much time he had to do this. James yelled back from the hall that he only had a day to get to the safe house with Hayden and Miles. Juice then looked back at his watch on his wrist and saw that midnight was about to strike. When Juice noted the time on his watch, he heard an unusual gush of wind in the hallway swoosh by. Juice was familiar with that sound and checked the hallway, but it was empty. It was as if James had just disappeared into thin air.

Juice was confused, lost, and full of questions. Why did he have to get Hayden and Miles? How did this guy know where they were? Why was killing the devil a bad thing, and did this strange visitor have the power to teleport?

Juice closed the door of his apartment and started to pack a backpack. He packed the rest of his snacks and grabbed his keys to his jeep. The files were the last thing he picked up on his way out. Once inside the car, he looked at the locations of Hayden and Miles. Seeing that Hayden was the farthest away, he opted to get him first.

As Juice drove out of the town, he suddenly felt a new purpose in his life. If there was some unnatural reason behind his dark past, he had to find out what it was. He was nervous to see his old members of the Hang Out Group again as he hadn't seen them in years or even tried to contact them. How was he going to convince them to come with him? What if he couldn't? All Juice knew was that he had to keep his head focused on the road. There were a lot of bad drivers out there, and he didn't need to end up in the next car accident while traveling to Hayden's place.

Friday, October 2, 2020

James arrived at Will's home while the sun was rising. James knew that Will wasn't in, so he didn't bother knocking at the door. He sat on one of the rocking chairs on the porch and, looking at the neighborhood, saw that it was more pleasant than where Juice was. Will was living in a rental condo on a street full of condos. He was currently unemployed. His time with the military had ended, and he hadn't reenlisted. He had some money saved up to fund him for a while, so he was taking some time for himself to see what his next move would be.

James was still getting used to being in physical form for this longer period of time while on earth. He started to get used to it and started to like it more. He loved the wind on his face and the warm heat from the sun. Being in the spiritual realm, you missed out on so much on what earth had to offer. In the spiritual realm, the smells were weaker, the view was blurrier, and no one outside the realm could see or hear you. It got lonely in there, and James never fully noticed that until he started to personally interact with humans.

Down the street, James spotted Will coming in from his morning run. Will walked up the porch and offered a handshake to the stranger. James, happy to have his first handshake with a human, grinned and stated his name. Just before James could offer his hand, Will quickly pulled away his hand to dry off the sweat on the side of his pants.

"Sorry about that," Will said with a chuckle as he offered his hand again.

"Not a problem," James replied, giving a small laugh.

"What can I do you for, James?" Will asked.

James was a little shocked that Will asked that question. Juice asked the same question last night, but when Juice delivered it, it came off as if he was annoyed and sarcastic. Will's attitude to the question was more positive and uplifting. James quickly thought of a few possibilities on why this was the case. First off, the evil spirit attached to Will was killed just the other night. With the horseman War dead, all the negative thoughts that were heavily forced on Will's mind were now eased off to a more reasonable state. That could lead to Will getting much better sleep. Another theory was that War had to leave Will's area many times through the five years due to his being Memphis's top general and strong fighter for the evil side of the war. With War gone from Will a lot, there wasn't much he could do to him to make his life miserable. James's last theory was that Will had a strong sense of fortitude, that he was able to push back the bad thoughts and keep the sour images out of his memories. Whatever it was, James was happy to see a smiling face.

Will took the rocking chair next to the one James was using. James saw that Will was all ears and was ready to listen to whatever he had to say. James had more time to prepare for his talk with Will, so he started off things slowly.

"So I understand that you were in the military for quite some time. You were the top of your class with all the physical challenges," James stated.

Will didn't deny any of this, but he did feel uneasy talking to this man once he was talking about his training history. It wasn't uncommon for a private security team to try to draft ex-military men, and this man sounded like he did his research. Will wasn't interested in joining any private security company right now, as most of those guys were protecting possible powerful criminals at the time.

"I read that you were a hero for many of your missions during your tours overseas," James added.

"Just because I was the last man standing doesn't make me a hero," Will replied, losing the charm in his voice.

"I fought in many battles in my life, some very recently. The recent ones were the hardest. We lost every battle and lost every soldier who fought by my side along the way too."

"I'm sorry to hear about your loss, sir." Will now changed the tone in his voice again. It shifted to a caring sound. Will now believed that this was a man who was reaching out for a fellow soldier to talk to.

"It's not your fault," James replied, not knowing if he fully believed that. James looked at the rising sun out in the distance. "Why didn't you reenlist?" wondered James.

Will cleared his throat before speaking. "Because I didn't understand the goal anymore." Will leaned forward and used his hands to wipe off the sweat from his face. "It feels like so many new wars have branched out all over recently. And it felt like we were just fighting for the sake of fighting. We fight to end wars, and I didn't feel like that was the goal anymore. I wanted to take some time off to concentrate on the goal. To walk around the place we're protecting, to remind myself why I enlisted in the first place."

"What if I told you that you can fight for something much bigger than you could ever imagine?" James said.

Will looked over to James, no longer feeling like this was a man offering a sketchy job of protecting some playboy millionaire.

"The world is running on a broken system. My bosses believed that you and your fellow Hogs are the ones responsible for this situation. And I believe that you can help fix it all. To fight in a war that seeks to bring hope back to the world."

Will believed what this man was saying and nodded, saying, "That would be something I would like to fight for."

"It's not just you who I want fighting for this goal." James then passed over some files containing the locations of Timber, Eric, and the safe house. "We need to get the group back together."

Will glanced at the files and stated that if James wanted the whole group back together, they would need Juice, Hayden, and Miles. James said that he was already working on getting those guys to the safe house and that Will needed to be the one who gathered both Timber and Eric.

"We won't be complete. Gard had been declared dead not too long ago," Will stated, bowing his head in a moment of sorrow.

"Gard isn't dead. I know where he is. We'll get him last."

Will couldn't believe the news about Gard. Last Will heard about Gard was that he went missing, then the world declared him legally dead. James said something bad happened to Gard, just like something bad had happened to all the others. James said that together, they could help the others, but first they all needed to be gathered up.

"You better get moving to Eric's location. He's the closest to you. After that, you just need Timber, and we'll meet up at the safe house. The others would be there by the time you reach the place."

"How much time do I have?"

"Tonight. Hurry or we may miss our one opportunity to save Gard," James stated.

Will stood up from his chair and requested more information from James. James said that he must be going and that Will should start getting a move on. James left the porch and took off down the street. Will ran back into his house to grab a few things before taking off.

Nice to See You Again

Hayden was sitting in the kitchen inside his small cabin in the deep woods cleaning his guns. He had a few rifles and handguns on the table. Hayden always cleaned his guns the exact same way every time. He set the firearms on the table from largest to smallest, from top of the table to bottom. He cleaned them in that same order. He'd done this so many times, he knew that he could perform this chore with his eyes closed. He didn't have his eyes closed, but he was close. The way he stared straight at the wall with an emotionless face as he did this job made it look like he was sleep walking.

When Hayden picked up the handgun, the final gun to clean, he felt that it seemed a touch heavier than what he was used to. Hayden turned away from the plain boring spot on the wall to eye the handgun. He fired off this gun for target practice so many times that he could recognize an empty gun when he felt one. Hayden believed that he could feel the extra weight of one round left in the chamber of the weapon.

Hayden lifted the gun around, slowly moving it with his arm, wondering if his theory of there still being a bullet inside was true. He held the gun in front of his face, with the barrel facing the left side of the room. Hayden could just check the gun to see if there was a bullet inside.

Another way of finding out would be pulling the trigger. He thought about where to aim the barrel if he chose to pull the trigger. If he aimed where he thought, he wouldn't hear the gunshot after pulling the trigger.

Hayden then heard something on his laptop resting by the sink. Hayden looked over at the screen and saw that one of his motion sensors was tripped. He stood up out of the chair and got closer to the laptop. Hayden had tons of motion sensors placed all around the woods, all to alert him of unwelcomed intruders. The woods he was living in were private, so there was no hunting from outsiders allowed. Hayden liked his privacy and hated people in his woods. He saw which sensor was alerted and knew the intruder was close. Hayden turned away from the computer, placed the handgun on the table, and picked up his rifle, snatching a box of ammo on the way out.

Outside, Juice was now deep into the woods, struggling to find his way. He was following the directions written on the files James left for him. Juice had to park his car on the side of the road and started marching east to find Hayden. Juice had walked for a while now, and he had already passed two No Trespassing signs. Juice was hungry and tired, and he was beginning to hate this hike in the woods.

"Of course Hayden would be living out in the middle of the woods. I'm not in the least bit surprised!" Juice angrily ranted to himself. "I bet that there isn't even anyone out here at all. That guy James must be having a big laugh knowing that he sent me on some wild-goose chase!"

Just then, Juice heard a sound of a gunshot from a short distance. Scared, Juice jumped slightly as he quickly turned his head toward the sound.

"Alright, at least I'm not alone out here," Juice calmly replied to himself. He then fearlessly took a few more steps toward the source of the gunfire sound. Then a second gunshot went off. This time, Juice heard the bullet strike a nearby tree. He saw the struck tree and realized that Hayden was aiming at him.

"Hayden, stop shooting!" Juice hollered while lifting his arms up in frustration. "It's me, Juice! I just want to talk!" Juice, with his arms still up, waited for a response. There was nothing but silence for a moment.

Then Juice heard Hayden's voice say, "Shuffle a few inches to your left, and you'll see a small trench leading up to my cabin."

Juice did as he was instructed, found the small trench, and followed it forward. When Juice found Hayden's cabin, he saw that the cabin was located in the center of a round dirt-and-grass patch of land. Juice saw a solar light panel on the roof, which would explain why Hayden had to cut down the trees surrounding the cabin so they did not block the sunlight. The ground was covered with tons of bullet shells with target sheets hanging in the distance. Along with the shells on the ground were heaps of empty bottles of booze strewn about the ground. Juice was shocked to not see a fire ring, a fire pit, or even firewood. Juice got a good look at Hayden. Hayden was holding his rifle down at ease as he looked right at Juice.

"You look…exactly the same," Juice stated hesitantly.

"Well, of course I do. With this Loomation in us slowing down our aging, you look exactly the same too."

"Yeah, but I just didn't expect you to be so…well groomed," Juice said, trying to find the right words. Juice was expecting Hayden to look dirty, with long hair and a beard. But despite Hayden living in the woods, he still showered daily and knew how to cut his own hair. Hayden did have an on-call job in the small town close by. He was a mechanic. Sometimes when the garage would get overwhelmed with customers, he would get called in, which seemed to happen a lot lately. Hayden did do his best to stay in his woods. It took him most of his inheritance to buy this isolated space, and he didn't like leaving it. Hayden grew his own food, hunted his own meat, and fashioned his own bullets.

"How did you find me?" Hayden said as he turned away from Juice and entered his cabin.

Juice followed, taking that as an invitation to come on in. "That's kind of a complicated story," Juice said as he entered the house.

Hayden entered the kitchen of the cabin, took out some cold premade sandwiches, and sat down at the table. Hayden was planning on eating after his job of cleaning the guns, and he was starving. Juice was hungry also, but he didn't bother to ask him for any food.

Juice stood in the kitchen eyeing the whole place, including the room across the hall. That was when Juice realized that Hayden only had one chair within the entire cabin. Hayden never had company over, so he never needed more than one chair. "Last night, a man came to my apartment and told me that the world is a mess right now."

"You don't say," Hayden said with food in his mouth.

"Yeah, but he added that it was all our fault. Well, not just you and I—the whole Hang Out Group is responsible as well."

"What makes him think that?" questioned Hayden.

"He said that killing the devil was a bad thing."

An awkward pause came after Juice mentioned that fact. Hayden asked Juice how the man knew that information. Juice assured Hayden that he had never told anyone about the devil, the Loomation powers, or anything that happened back in 2010. Hayden then wondered if any of the others told.

Juice asked, "If they did, who would have believed them?"

"Maybe he was hired by Kate or something. She's probably still mad at us," Hayden hypothesized.

"Yeah, but I'm pretty sure we never used the word *devil* in our letters about the incident. We just called it the monster or the great evil."

"She did speak to her father before he died. Maybe he mentioned it."

"Maybe…but I don't think it's as simple as that. This guy, he fully believed everything he was saying. It was weird. He said that he could explain why the world is the way it is. And he said that he can tell us why all the bad things that happened to us happened during the recent years."

"Do you believe this man?"

"I do. That's why I'm here. He's the one who gave me the exact directions to locate you. If that's not a sign that he's legit, then I don't know what is."

Hayden just sat eating his sandwich. Once he was finished eating, he asked Juice where they needed to go. Hayden had a troubling time during the recent years, so hearing that there was a man who could explain why that was, he'd be willing to go see him. Juice said that they needed to pick up one more person before getting to James. Hayden got out of his chair to grab a few things before heading out. Before Hayden took a step away from the table, he picked up the handgun and fired it at the floor. Juice didn't even flinch at this sudden action; he just figured it was something Hayden did on a regular basis. Hayden tossed the gun back on the table, saying to himself, "I knew it wasn't empty."

Out in a big city, Will was on his way to see Eric. As Will walked down the sidewalk, he couldn't help but notice all the homeless on the side of the street begging for cash. Some were kind, asking for some spare change, while a few were very aggressive and mean to the ones who walked by them. One of the homeless signs said "The end is near…I hope." Will checked his pockets and pulled out a few folded-up dollar bills. He gave the bills to the man with the sign, telling him not to give up hope.

Will felt bad that there wasn't more he could do. Then Will remembered what James said. He had a chance to fight for a better world. Will was nervous about his mission, hoping that he could be convincing enough to recruit Eric.

A few steps later, Will found the office building he was looking for. It was the tallest building on the street. He looked up high, knowing that Eric was on one of those floors. Will checked his information that James gave him to find out how to get hold of Eric.

Inside the building, Eric was sitting in an office meeting. A large shipment of the business's supplies was recently sunk at sea the other night. The report said that the cargo ship was caught in a small hurricane and went under with everything on it. There were divers out in the area trying to find anything worth salvaging from the wreckage. The divers were thieves trying to get their hands on anything they might find useful.

Eric worked for a pharmaceutical company; they made and sold drugs to pharmacies, stores, and doctors' offices. Eric's boss was happy that they would receive a massive paycheck from the insurance company for the lost supplies. One of the workers at the meeting asked how long it would be until they could transport more products. The boss said that it would take time to make more batches to send out. But they would deny any overseas outgoing until they received their insurance check from the lost products. The man tried to explain to the boss that something like that could take weeks. The boss didn't care. He knew that rushing another shipment so fast would cost extra, and shipping overseas was always very pricey right after a recent sinking.

"The people aren't going to die if they don't have their pills for a couple of weeks," the boss said, annoyed by the questions.

The cruel greedy nature of the boss made everyone in the room feel disgusted. But the boss raised his voice, and the subordinates knew to remain silent if they wanted to keep their jobs. In this moment of silence, Eric checked his phone, which he kept out on his side under the table. He got a text from the custodian saying, "Down by the fire exit."

"Sir, is that all for this meeting?" Eric asked. The boss let everyone out of the room and ordered them all to start working on calling their stores overseas to tell them that were doing everything they could to get their product to them as soon as possible.

"And what's our motto around here?" the boss yelled out.

"Sell it," the group all simultaneously said with no pep or delightful energy. The people in the room all slowly gathered up their notes and moved to the exit. Eric was the last one to exit the room, but the boss, who still sat at the head of the table, called out to him.

"How many divers do you think are out there in the ocean trying to find our pills, Eric?"

"Hard to guess," Eric replied.

"I would like to say that it's hard to believe how *deep* people will go just to get some free pills. But it's not hard to accept it as being true. People have been drowning themselves over things they think they need since the beginning."

Eric didn't say anything nor let out any positive expression. In fact, he found this whole chat annoying and uncomfortable. Eric saw that the boss had nothing more to say, so he quickly left the room. He headed to the fire exit on the floor and saw the custodian's cleaning cart next to the office room located by the fire exit. Eric stopped by the cleaning cart and looked for the custodian Gary.

"Gary?" Eric whispered.

Gary was in the office room and popped his head out to see Eric.

"Your cleaning supplies are in the box next to the window cleaner," Gary said as he wiped his hands with sanitizer.

Eric reached down on the cart to pick up the box. The box seemed heavier than it should be, so Eric peeked inside the box and then quickly closed it. Eric was angry at Gary, saying that he delivered way too much. He always asked for a small shipment of supplies. Gary said that the other people who he normally delivered to didn't need their supplies today, so he was giving Eric a special large delivery. Eric didn't want to continue his conversation with Gary, so he aggressively took the box and marched off.

Eric made it to his office and closed the door, giving him his privacy. He took one step away from the door toward his desk when the box slipped out of his hand, slammed on the floor, and tipped over. Lots of pills fell out of the box and scattered across the floor. Eric dropped to his knees, praying that no one heard that as he shoved the pills back into the box. When he managed to get them all back in, the stress of all this urgency triggered his desire to take a couple right then and there.

Eric swallowed a handful and then reached for his pill bottle in his pocket to fill it up with the pills from the box. Once the bottle was full, the box still looked almost overstuffed with the pills. Eric stared blankly at them. He knew that there were enough pills here to kill a horse. Eric thought, *Why just stop at one hand full? Why not down the whole box?*

Then a knock at the door came from behind him. This terrified Eric as he turned to face the door to make sure it was indeed fully closed. Another knock came at the door. This time it was followed by his secretary saying that there was a visitor there to see him. Eric shouted out to give him a minute. He closed the lid on the box and shoved his bottle back into his pocket, then hustled over to the file cabinet behind his desk, opened the drawer, placed the box inside, and quickly closed it.

"Alright, the visitor may come in!" Eric shouted.

The door opened, and in came Will. Eric was shocked to see Will for a moment. He wasn't, however, happy to see his old friend; in fact, he was slightly annoyed. Will walked in, impressed by the nice-looking office. He was happy to see his old friend again; he went in and offered his hand for a handshake. Eric looked at the hand for a moment, regained some of his composure, and then shook it. Will then eased back in the chair.

"Want a drink?" asked Eric as he wheeled the chair over to the liquor cabinet. Will said no thanks to the drink. Eric stood up, picked up his bottle, and poured it into a fancy glass. "Well, I hope you're not here for money because I don't give out charity."

"I'm actually setting up a hangout and wanted to get the old group back together."

"We haven't seen each other in years. I thought that we grew out of that," Eric said as he took his first sip of his glass.

"Well, I'm not really the person setting it up. I was just asked to round up the Hogs again."

"Who's setting it up?"

"A guy named James. I think he has a job for us."

Eric took another sip of his drink before speaking. "Sorry, Will, I got a lot on my plate right now. So I'm sorry that I can't join the reunion," Eric said, not feeling sorry at all. "Besides, with Gard dead, James's already going to be lacking one member from the hangout."

"James says Gard's alive," Will replied.

Hearing this gave Eric a real shock, and he then finished his drink in one gulp. "Look, Will, I got to make tons of calls to countries where I don't even speak the languages. I have to sell them lies that we're sorry for the inconvenience. And given all the different time zones, I'll be working all night. Then I have to be on top of tons of insurance agents, which will get me talking to the company's lawyers, and on top of all of that, I need to make orders to produce and ship tons of new product. So I really don't have time for this hangout nonsense at all this weekend—or ever for that matter. So you should just leave now," Eric ranted, trying to keep himself calm.

Will was trying to continue his pitch to Eric to join him, but Eric threatened to call security. Will left peacefully, asking Eric to keep an open mind. After Will left the room, Eric popped another pill from his bottle.

⪻⪼

Meanwhile, a car pulled into the parking lot of St. Anthony Hospital. The facility was isolated, being far away from any town with acres of woods surrounding the place. Both Juice and Hayden exited the car and eyed the building. Hayden yelled out that he hoped visiting hours were still going on. Juice stated that the information that he had said that he would find Miles here. Juice had the idea that Miles was a staff member or something. Juice looked across the street and saw the many trees in the field.

"Reminds you of home, doesn't it?" Juice said to Hayden.

Hayden was not amused. The behavior between the two was nothing like it once was. They seemed to despise each other's company, only traveling together to see what this mysterious James had to tell them. No smiles or laughs were cracked between each other, just rude nods and annoyed faces.

As the two walked up the steps leading to the front doors, they saw that this was a mental hospital. This did slightly shock the two, wondering why Miles would be here.

"Maybe I should have ended up here," Hayden whispered to himself.

The two walked in the dimly lit building and saw that almost half of the lights were burned out. Juice swatted at a moth moments after entering while Hayden found his chance to squish a spider by the door. The two made their way to the front desk. There was a lady at the desk who gave a grumpy look at the two.

"Visiting or dropping off?" she almost mumbled to the strangers.

"We're here to see Miles Hall. Do you know if he's here?" Juice asked.

"He's in the common room with the others," she replied in a louder voice, pointing to the back.

Juice, not wishing to carry this talk any further, took off in that direction.

"Hold it!" she yelled. "You'll need some visiting badges!" She was annoyed at this interaction. She dropped two badges onto the desk.

Both Juice and Hayden took a badge and rushed out of her sight. As the two walked down the hall toward the common room, they both picked up a nasty odor, as if someone recently sprayed some bug killer in this hall. They found a few dead bugs in the hall, so that may have been the case.

In the common room, Hayden tapped Juice on the shoulder and pointed to Miles by the window. This was when the two realized that Miles was a full-on patient in this hospital. He was just sitting at a small table staring at the window with an emotionless face.

"How long do you think he's been like this?" wondered Hayden.

"The file James gave me didn't say, just that he was here," Juice replied.

"You think it's because of his active Loomation?"

"Hard to tell. Logan was the only one we knew who had an active Loomation, and all he suffered from was Alzheimer's disease."

"You think that the heal spell would fix him or something."

"The heal spell only repairs your physical body. It doesn't do anything for your mind."

"What about that time Logan healed you from the dual personality?" asked Hayden.

"He said that was more of an infection. Something was physically on my brain causing that side effect. I always thought he wiped it from my brain, but I think Logan just shut down its side effects," Juice replied. Juice hadn't brought up his dual personality in a very long time. This was the first time he spoke out loud about his thoughts on the infection still being in his head. Juice believed that its side effects had activated once or twice in the past five years.

The two took a few open chairs at the table to talk to Miles, who turned away from the window to look at Juice and Hayden. He wasn't surprised to see them. He didn't say anything to them. He ignored them and looked back at the window.

Juice was the first to speak, saying, "Hey."

Now, Miles was shocked; he didn't think that Juice and Hayden were real. Miles thought his mind was playing tricks on him again. But now, getting a better look at them and hearing them talk made him believe that they were real.

"You're real," Miles said, panic in his voice.

"Of course we're real," Hayden responded, thinking that was a dumb comment.

"Miles, what type of meds do they have you on here?" Juice asked in a rude way.

"I don't know, they give me my pills and water, then they go down the hatch," Miles said, soaring his finger through the air, landing it next to his stomach.

"Well, you need to come with us. Some fresh air will do you some good!" Juice stated.

"Yeah, breathing in all these bug fumes isn't good for your health," Hayden added.

"Well, I was told that I can leave at any time," Miles uttered.

"You're staying here on your own? Well then let's go!" Juice shouted as he got out of his chair.

Miles looked around the room. He didn't realize it until now, but he couldn't remember any of the other patients' names. He spent so much time there and never reached out to anyone. He felt like he was in a turtle shell his whole time there. He only talked to his doctor during his therapy sessions. The doctor always encouraged him to take a few days out of the hospital, but oddly enough, that made Miles wish to stay even more.

Something started to stir inside him. Miles didn't know if it was safe to go with Juice and Hayden. They weren't straight with him, but they seemed to want him to come with them. Miles said that he had no plans for tomorrow or for the rest of the week. So he said that he'd grab his belongings from his room and meet them out in the parking lot.

Miles marched up to his room and grabbed his wallet and a book bag of extra clothes. After he put on his shoes, he felt that there was something he should do before he left his room.

Miles pulled a blanket out from under the bed. The blanket was tied into a noose. Miles untied the knot and placed the blanket on the bed. Miles closed the door on his way out and proudly walked out of the hospital. After he walked past the front desk, the lady there said something rude to him.

"You won't last a day," she said with a sneer.

Miles paused for a moment upon hearing that. He couldn't believe how close he was to the front door. A door he only used once. Miles was asking himself if the lady was right, wondering if going out was the best thing for him. He had never felt a desire to leave this place, and now he was all packed up and ready to walk out the exit. Miles didn't want to keep his ride waiting, so he took a deep breath and pushed the door open.

Outside, Miles could see the sun start to set behind the trees. A running car sat waiting in front of the building with the headlights already on. Hayden, sitting in the passenger seat, waved at Miles to hurry. Miles opened the back door of the car and hopped in. The car took off fast from the building with Juice behind the wheel. He was in a hurry to arrive to the meeting place.

Will was now back in his hometown of Maze. His parents moved away from this town years ago, so going back for a visit was rare. Will knew that there was one member of the Hang Out Group who moved back to the hometown back in 2015, and that was Timber.

Timber was offered a partnership job at the funeral home. Timber took the job, and ever since, business was thriving. Will was worried about Timber; over the years, having that much work could be disturbing. Timber had no wife or even a friend to spend time with, so Will thought that Timber was just hanging out with dead people all day. Will felt like he was running out of time, so he didn't have a chance to drive down memory lane and see the park where he and his friends used to play ball. He couldn't see his old house to see how it had changed. He really wanted to see his old school, but that wasn't on his way.

Will knew that Timber lived in an apartment above the funeral home. When there was no answer at the door, Will checked the funeral home. The door was unlocked, so Will walked in. Inside was a wide room with a closed coffin in the back of the room. Will was then spooked by a maid who just finished cleaning the bathroom. He asked her if she knew how to get hold of Timber. She said that he wasn't in and that he could possibly be out picking up a body. She stated that he received calls like that all the time.

Will informed her that it was very important for him to get hold of Timber right now. She then told him that since it was urgent, he could call his work cell phone number using the home's office phone. She picked up the office phone and pushed speed dial number 2. When the phone started to ring, she handed the phone over to Will.

Timber wasn't on a work-related trip; he was in a dark place at that moment. He was watching the sun set for what he thought was the last time. When the sun was down, Timber looked down below him. He was standing on top of a bridge crossing over a river. There was a drought in this area, so the river was barely knee high. Before Timber could make any move, he heard his phone go off. Timber saw that it was his job calling, probably about another body to go retrieve.

Timber stared at his phone as its ringing was distracting for him. He wasn't in the mood to talk at the moment, so he let it go to voice mail. Timber didn't know why, but he chose to play the voice mail. He couldn't believe that it was Will's voice he heard. He hadn't seen Will in such a long time, and there he was, leaving a voice mail on his phone. This brought Timber to take a step off the ledge.

The voice mail said, "Timber, it's Will. Look, I know it's been a long time, but there is a man who wants to see us. He says we can do some good. I don't want to go without you, but I can't wait all night. I'm leaving you the location of where I'll be going just in case you don't get back in time. Hope to see you soon.

Timber put the phone back in his pocket and returned to his car. He gripped the steering wheel tightly. He didn't know what to make out of all that. Will was vague in his message. He was far from the home, so even if he went full speed all the way, he doubted that Will would still be there by the time he got back. So he took his time on getting back. He didn't mind if he missed Will, nor did he have any intentions on going with Will.

It was late when Timber got to his apartment. There were no strange cars in the parking area, so Timber knew that Will was gone. He parked his car, and when he got to his front door, he saw a letter taped to it. Timber picked up the envelope and walked into his home. He tossed the envelope on his dining table as he grabbed a beer from the fridge. He wasn't sure if he was even going to open it. Then his doorbell rang.

The sound of that spooked Timber as he was in midsip of his beer. Timber sensed that it was Will wanting to talk to him. Timber knew that he couldn't pretend that he wasn't home as the lights of his place were already on, revealing his presence. He then started to hear hard knocks at the door. He knew that he couldn't postpone this interaction any further, so he placed his beer down and went to the door. Timber was surprised at the person at the door for it was not Will. It was Eric. This day just got a lot weirder for Timber. He opened the door and asked what he wanted.

"Timber, you handled the funeral for Gard when he died, right?" Eric asked, getting straight to the point.

"It was just a memorial service. He was only declared dead due to the body being lost at sea," Timber replied.

"So there was never a body," replied Eric.

"We only showed an empty coffin," Timber stated.

"So he's still out there then," Eric said to himself more than Timber.

"I guess it's possible. Say, what's all this about?" wondered Timber.

"Did Will come to see you by any chance?"

"Yeah, but I wasn't here at the time. He left me a note where to meet up with him."

"Where…where is the hangout taking place?" Eric asked, now talking at a fast pace.

"The location is in an envelope, which I haven't opened yet," Timber answered.

Eric requested Timber to retrieve the letter. Timber went to his dining room to pick up the envelope as Eric followed. Timber picked up the envelope, and then Eric snatched it out of his hands. Eric quickly opened it and perused the paper. He skimmed over everything until he found the location of where the hangout was happening. Eric, now knowing where he was going to go, handed the letter back over to Timber. Eric said that he was heading to the hangout.

Timber was so overwhelmed by all this. First, Will called him out of the blue. Then Eric came to his front door asking about Gard. Timber looked at the letter and saw what Will wrote on it. It said, 'The Hang Out Group isn't dead! Please come see and be a part of it again."

Timber then yelled out to Eric to wait; he wanted to go to the hangout too.

The Hangout

Juice was out driving on the highway, making his way to the hangout location. Hayden was resting his eyes in the passenger seat. Juice was feeling very tired himself, but they were so close that he knew he could stay awake long enough to make it to the house. Miles, sitting in the middle in the back seat, mumbled something. Juice ignored everything Miles was uttering and stayed focused on passing the slow car in front of them. He saw that the left lane was crowded, so he eased over to the right lane. As soon as he did, he saw that the lane was about to end, so Juice had to quickly jerk the car back to where it was. The shaking of the car caused Hayden to open his eyes.

"I'm barely awake, and even I heard Miles say that the right lane ends soon," Hayden rudely stated.

"That guy has been mumbling nonsense ever since he got in the car. The one time he says something useful, I completely ignore it!" Juice said, frustrated. "I have been driving since last night. I'm a little tired, so sorry."

Hayden looked at the map and reported that the turn was coming soon. Within the next half hour, the three made it to the house. It was a small two-story house in the middle of the country road. Juice drove down the stony driveway and parked next to the house. The three got out of the car in a hurry to make time for a much-needed stretch.

"Alright, so where's this James?" asked Hayden.

"He's probably inside. *He better be inside,*" Juice said to Hayden while whispering that second part to himself.

The three walked up the porch with Juice leading the way. Juice saw a note taped to the front door. He read the note, which said, "If I'm not here by the time you arrive, please go inside and make yourself at home. I'll be there soon. James."

"What's it say?" asked Hayden impatiently.

Juice relayed the message to the two as he opened the unlocked door. The place was fully furnished, even had a working TV. Hayden saw a minibar and checked to see if it was full. He was pleased to find some bottles and sipping glasses within the bar. Hayden helped himself by pouring a glass. Juice asked Hayden to make a drink for him as well. Hayden complied and handed him a glass. The two took a deep sip while Miles just sat aimlessly in a recliner.

"You want one?" asked Juice.

Miles hesitated before simply saying no.

Both Juice and Hayden returned their glasses to their lips, thinking that Miles was acting strangely. But giving where they picked him up at, it didn't seem that odd.

Hayden finished his glass and started to refill it. "So how long are we supposed to wait here? Until the bottle is empty? Because that won't be too long," Hayden stated before taking a sip of his refilled glass.

Juice finished off his drink and said that he didn't know, but he didn't plan to wait too much longer. He did what he was asked to do and found it rude that James didn't hold up his part of the deal. But he was tired of driving and wanted some time to relax before he did anything else. So he asked Hayden to fill him up with another drink.

About an hour passed, and the three boys were just sitting in the living room watching TV. As they were watching an old sitcom, they heard a car pull up in the driveway. Will got out of the car, praying that he wasn't too late. He was already showing up without Timber and Eric, so he was hoping this James guy was understanding and appreciated the attempt.

Will walked up the front porch steps and spotted the note at the door. After Will read the note, he let himself in.

Will walked into the living room and saw Juice, Hayden, and Miles. Both Juice and Hayden stared at him as if they were disappointed, as they were expecting James to be at the door. They didn't say hello or even give a wave; they just turned their heads back to the TV. Will, on the other hand, was thrilled to see his old friends again.

"You guys made it! It's great to see all of you!" Will said with welcoming arms. But Juice and Hayden didn't have the same reaction while Miles just stared at Will with a confused gaze.

"You're real, right?" Miles asked as he looked up at Will from his chair.

"Yes," Will replied with a confused look.

"Don't mind him, he's been acting weird since we picked him up from the mental hospital," Juice said as he rose from the couch to grab another drink from the bar.

"A mental hospital? Is he okay?" Will asked, the first one who expressed any concern.

"Probably not," Hayden replied.

Will was disturbed to see his old friends so emotionless. They were so careless and lifeless in the living room. Will looked back at Miles and could tell there was something off with him. Miles's mind was so far gone, he didn't even know there was something wrong with him.

"You didn't tell me he would be here," Hayden told Juice.

Juice, now leaning against the bar taking his first sip of his fresh glass, claimed that he wasn't told that Will would be there either. Hayden then turned to Will, asking if he knew why the world was such a mess. This question didn't make sense to Will. When James talked to Will, he shared different information than what he told Juice. Will sadly informed them that he didn't know why the world was a mess.

"Well, according to this James guy, it's our entire fault!" Juice said before finishing off his drink.

"It's all our fault?" Miles asked, now getting his voice into the conversation.

"That's why we're here. To see how killing the devil was a bad thing," Hayden added.

"We really killed the devil, right?" Miles asked in a panicked tone, making sure it was true.

"Yes. Ten years ago. We went into the Garden, and people died, the devil included!" Juice shouted.

Just then, James appeared in the room in front of the TV. This alarmed the four Hogs in the room. Hayden knelt in front of his chair's ottoman, pulled out his gun from his shoulder holster, and aimed it right at James. Juice smashed the bottle of booze he was going to use to refill his glass and held the shattered bottle up as a weapon. Will assumed a fighting pose while Miles was screaming as he ran behind the chair he was using.

"Woo! Calm down, everyone!" James shouted as he put his hands up.

"James?" shouted Will in disbelief.

"You didn't tell me that he had an active Loomation," Hayden replied while keeping his gun aimed at James.

"I might have theorized but didn't want to assume!" Juice yelled.

James pleaded with the boys to let their guards down and assured them that he didn't wish to harm them. Will was the first one to put himself at ease. Will then passed a look over to Juice to follow suit. Juice slowly put his shattered bottle back down on the bar while Hayden put the gun back into his holster. Miles stayed hidden behind the chair, peeking his eyes over at James.

James searched the room and failed to see Timber and Eric. James asked Will where they were. Will was embarrassed to tell him that he was unable to get them to come along. James's body language revealed a frustrated attitude.

"I told you that they needed to be here, Will," James said, holding back his rage.

"I tried. Eric wanted nothing to do with me, and Timber fully avoided me," Will said, trying to defend himself.

"Look, I don't care what you told him to do," Juice said, chiming in. "I did what I was asked to do. I got all my people. Now you tell me what you promised!" Juice ordered with a powerful point.

"I need to wait until you're all here before I do!" James shouted.

Will apologized, feeling sad that he didn't try harder to complete his mission.

"I need to go and find them and to check on Gard. I'll be back!" James then vanished out of the room.

This made Miles turn his head away and cover his head with his hands. "It's all real…I know what's real," Miles whispered to himself.

Will didn't know how to comfort his frightened friend, and he felt guilty for not knowing about his condition earlier. Juice looked over and saw Will was concerned about Miles's shaking.

"He's fine," Juice stated in an uncaring way.

"You just told me that you picked him up from a mental hospital!" Will replied as he stepped closer to Juice.

"Yeah, so he's not at 100 percent, but it's not like any of us are. Mr. Fireproof over here didn't have a fireplace in his yard, nor did he ever take out a lighter to play with the entire car ride over here. And I have my own problems going on," Juice said as he returned to his seat on the couch. "We all came here to find out why that is…to get an answer on how we managed to break the entire world."

Will looked at both Juice and Hayden. He could tell that they were not the same friends he used to spend so much time with in his past. For Hayden to not have a fire ring at his place was very unusual for him. And Will had a strong guess on what Juice meant when he said he had his own problems.

"We're the cause of the world's problems. It's all our fault!" Miles said while hiding behind the bar with a newly opened bottle in his hand. Miles then started chugging the drink.

Hayden stood up quickly to snatch the bottle out of his hand. "We don't need the one with the active Loomation to get drunk. Your mind is already not at a solid state. Making it worse could cause you to turn us into frogs or something!" Hayden said before he started to drink straight from the bottle. Hayden returned to his seat while Miles sat on a barstool.

Will was hoping that this reunion would be more of a heartwarming moment. But the hearts of the people in that room had been cold for far too long.

Then they heard two cars pull down the driveway. Will hurried to the front door window to see who was arriving. Hayden asked if it was a pizza delivery person. Will was happy to announce that it was Timber and Eric coming to the door.

"Great, now they show up!" Juice uttered.

Will opened the door for the two, hoping that they would be bearing a positive attitude. When he said hello, Eric walked past Will into the house and asked, "Where's Gard?"

Will was sad to inform Eric that Gard hadn't arrived yet. Then Timber made it to the door. Will was happy to see that Timber got the note he left at his house. Timber wasn't fully sure why he was there, and part of him wished that he didn't come along. Will opened the door wide and stepped back for Timber to have plenty of room to enter. Timber walked in and saw the rest of the Hogs in the room.

"Who knows where Gard is?" Eric asked.

"Isn't he dead?" Hayden said.

"James says he's not dead," Will replied.

"Who is this James?" shouted Eric.

"Apparently, he knows that we killed the devil, and he's going to tell us why that was a bad thing," Juice said, raising the volume of his voice.

"What are you talking about?" wondered Eric.

"Oh, and he has an active Loomation," Hayden added.

"Another guy with an active Loomation wants to talk to us. What does this one want from us, to kill Hades?" Eric yelled.

"We killed the devil. That was real," Miles muttered to himself.

Eric faced Miles and could tell that he was speaking nonsense and had clearly been on some type of medication. Will, on the other hand, couldn't believe everyone's attitude. He was amazed seeing so many Hang Out Group members in the same room, something that hadn't happened in years. And none of them seemed to care. Eric didn't even say hello to any of them. These guys weren't here to hang out or to reminisce with each other. They were just here to relay information and be on their way.

Then James appeared in the room in front of the TV again. This caused everyone to jump in fright, but not as much when James arrived the first time he showed up. James was thrilled to see that Timber and Eric made their way to the house. James said that there wasn't much time and that they had to act fast.

"Look, we have some questions for you," Eric said, demanding his needs be addressed before he did anything for him.

"If we don't hurry, Gard will be dead." James did his best to deliver that urgent news with a calm voice.

Eric settled down and was now ready to comply.

"Gard is, right now, in another country. I can't give away the how and why on how he got there, but I will tell you that he's trapped within a cave mine. He's passed out, so he's helpless. If he doesn't suffocate from the lack of oxygen, the bomb set to explode on a timer will finish him off," James explained.

"How could you possibly know all that?" shouted Juice.

"I know…because I know. Now who's with me?" James said as he reached out his hand.

Everyone in the room was unsure if they should believe James or not. Eric couldn't take the chance of James being wrong, so he took James's hand as if he were giving a handshake. Will walked across the room to place his hand onto the handshake.

James looked at the rest and said, "There isn't much time."

When Hayden heard the possibility of there being an explosion, he passed on going. He didn't want to be around fire. Miles was nowhere near being ready to teleport at the time. He didn't think his mind could handle that kind of action right now. Timber was still unsure about believing James; he was still trying to figure out why he was even there in the first place. Juice then made a move toward James. He thought, *Why not?* Worst thing that could happen was that he died.

James teleported Will, Juice, and Eric to the outside of the cave where Gard was trapped. The landscape was tropical, the humidity was strong, and there was no wind. When the Hogs arrived at the cave, they saw a man in front of them lying dead. Will went up to the dead man and saw that he died from a bullet to the heart. Will looked back at James and asked if they were too late. James regretfully said there was nothing he could have done for that man. James couldn't elaborate on why that was. If James had showed up earlier to save him, he would have gotten into a battle with the evil spirit that was hunting Gard. The evil spirit had just left a few moments ago after the man was killed. But James couldn't tell them any of that just yet, so he changed the focus on them saving Gard.

James said that Gard was still in the cave. Eric, without hesitation, dashed into the cave with Will, Juice, and James following. There was a row of lights that had fallen off the side of the tunnel; luckily, not all of them were shattered. The Hogs reached a pile of rocks blocking their way.

"Gard!" shouted Eric.

"Can you hear us?" Will yelled out.

Many calls for help were yelled out by a group of people on the other side of the wall. Will asked James who all these people were. James, with hands on the rock wall, quickly stated that they needed their help. Will, Eric, and James all started to use their advanced strength to lift and chuck the rocks out of their way, tearing down the wall. Juice, staying back, happened to notice something blinking within a metal cart that looked out of place within the tunnel. The blinking light in the metal cart was some sort of bomb, and the timer was counting down fast.

"Hey, guys, there's a bomb on a countdown in this cart. Should we be worried about that?" Juice asked calmly.

"Can you stop it?" shouted Eric.

"Oh yeah, let me check my smartphone on how to deactivate a bomb!" Juice yelled back.

"Roll it out of here then!" Will shouted as loudly as he could.

"I'm not risking the bomb going off from the heavy shaking of the cart!" Juice argued.

"He's right if that thing is too sensitive. Wheeling it out of here could set it off early and kill us all," James added.

"How much time do we have left?" wondered Eric.

"Looks like less than four minutes," Juice said as he eyed the timer.

"Less than four minutes? Are you kidding me?!" Eric shouted.

"Get your butt over here and help us!" ordered Will in a demanding voice.

Juice rushed in to help with the stone wall. The combining might of the four caused the rock wall to crumble. Once the stone wall was down, the people came out, running for freedom. Will told everyone to head to the exit as he waved his arm like a windmill. Eric stopped one of the men on his way out to ask him where Gard was. The man pointed to another wall, saying that Gard was deeper inside the cave, and the rocks blocking his way collapsed first. Eric immediately charged at the second rock wall and started pushing off rocks. Once everyone was clear out of the cave,

Will started to help Eric. Juice was closer to the outside, making sure no one bumped the metal cart containing the bomb. Once everyone was outside, James led them to safety away from the blast zone. James was able to speak in a language that most of them could understand. He told them the good news was that they were all free from their captivity and then pointed them in the right direction to find civilization. After that, James dashed back to the cave.

Eric moved a rock that allowed him to see to the other side of the wall. There were a few busted-up lights on that side giving enough light to spot Gard in the room. The Hogs all called out to him, but he wasn't awake.

When James entered the cave, he checked the bomb and saw that they were now under a minute and a half. James charged down the tunnel and saw the three Hogs removing the final rocks from their path to the other side. Eric ran up next to Gard and, for a moment, thought he was dead.

Will leaned in and checked if he was still breathing. "He's still alive," Will stated.

"Well, we're not going to be if we don't get out of here fast!" Juice yelled.

James then rushed over and told everyone to grab on to him. Will picked up Gard and placed his hand on James's arm. Juice and Eric placed their hands on James's shoulders. James then teleported everyone out of the tunnel just in the nick of time. The bomb went off, sending flames in all directions and soon engulfing the tunnel all around the cave, causing a strong cave-in.

James teleported everyone back to the safe house. Will placed Gard down on the couch. Hayden, still behind the bar, asked them how it went. Juice said that they were all still alive, then asked for a drink. Eric asked James if he knew if Gard would be all right. James said that Gard would be fine; he was just doused under the influence of a heavy amount of chloroform. James suggested that he sleep it off.

"So I'm guessing that you're not going to tell us what you know?" Juice asked, feeling like he already knew the question.

James painfully stated no, that he'd tell them all in the morning after they all had a good night's rest. James said that there were a few beds upstairs that they could use. James said he had to take off to see his bosses and that he'd be back in the morning.

"You better be," Juice added.

After that, James was gone, leaving the seven Hogs alone. Timber asked the guys if they were all right. Will said everyone was fine. Eric said that he was going to go up and find a bed. He had had enough excitement for the day. Will looked around and asked if everyone was staying the night. Juice headed upstairs saying that he might as well wait until morning; otherwise, the whole trip wouldn't have been worth it. Hayden sat in the recliner saying that he'd be staying. Miles just headed upstairs, implying that he was staying. Will looked at Timber, wondering where he stood. Timber still wasn't sure if coming was a good idea. But he didn't want to turn back home now, so he headed upstairs to find a bed.

Will looked at his friends still in the living room. Hayden was happy sleeping on the chair while Gard was already passed out on the couch. Will knew that the group may not have been their usual selves, but he loved that they were all back together. Will took the second recliner in the room to sleep on for the night. He and Hayden stayed up watching old sitcoms until they fell asleep.

The Secret Information

Saturday, October 3, 2020

Gard was having a nightmare. He saw a fiery explosion coming right at him, filling up the mines he'd been working on for almost two years. He could hear the terrified screams from the other prisoners being engulfed in front of him. Then just before the flames reached him, he heard a sound from outside of his dream, and this sound woke him up.

Gard leaned up from the couch in a frightening motion. The sound he heard was the front door opening. The person at the door had already walked away from the entrance, leaving the door wide open.

Gard looked around and found himself lying on a couch alone in a living room. Gard was stressing out for he had never seen this place before. Gard was trying to review his memories, and the last thing he remembered was being in the far back of the cave with Mitch. Gard couldn't remember anything beyond that moment. Then Gard saw a familiar person walk to the open door. It was Hayden. It was he who made the sound that woke up Gard. Hayden left the house while Gard was still asleep, but when he returned to the house, he opened the door too loudly. He left the door open because he still had stuff in the car to bring in after dropping the stuff he brought in already. Hayden stopped walking when he saw that Gard was awake.

"Back from the dead?" Hayden asked.

"Still trying to figure that out," Gard replied as he moved his body from lying down to a sitting position.

Hayden then went out the door, heading back to the car. Gard twisted around to see out the window. He saw that the cars out in the driveway had American license plates, so Gard was able to confirm that he was back in the States. Gard knew that there was no way he slept the whole way through where he was back to the States. Now that he saw Hayden was here, he figured Miles must be here as well and had teleported him here last night.

Gard got up and followed Hayden outside. "How did you guys find me?" Gard asked as he walked up to Hayden.

"James knew where you were," Hayden replied as he took out a cup tray containing four cups of coffee.

"Who's James?"

"Isn't that the million-dollar question." Hayden then handed the tray of cups over to Gard before grabbing the second tray. Gard was confused by what Hayden said, but Gard knew that Hayden was always very vague with information. When Gard saw the second tray of coffee containing four more cups, Gard counted eight cups of coffee altogether.

"Who's all here?" wondered Gard.

"All of us," Hayden said, knowing that he knew Gard would understand what that meant. Hayden walked past Gard to bring the tray of cups to the kitchen.

Gard took a moment to soak in all this information. He couldn't believe that they were all here in this little house, and he wasn't really up for a reunion right now.

Hayden placed the tray of coffee cups next to the box of donuts he brought in earlier. Gard walked in and placed the tray he carried on the counter next to the other. Gard picked up a coffee and walked around the long dining table to sit at the foot of it, making himself as far away from Hayden, who was standing by the counter.

"I didn't need you guys to rescue me," Gard stated before taking his first sip of the coffee.

"First off," Hayden said before taking a bite of a donut, "I didn't help rescue you." He then swallowed. "And from what I was told, you were trapped in a cave unconscious with a bomb about to go off." Hayden then took his second bite.

Gard wasn't aware of all that information. He thought that would explain why he had no memory of being teleported to this house.

Then the front door opened. It was Will coming back from his morning run. When Will spotted Gard awake sitting in the kitchen, he rushed up to him. Will gave his old friend a pat on the back as he took the seat next to him. Will gave Gard the details on what happened while Gard was asleep. Will was sad to tell him that there was a man already dead from a shot to the heart when they arrived at the cave. But he was happy to inform him that they managed to save the others trapped inside.

"What were you doing there anyway?" Will hesitantly asked. Will saw all the scratches, cuts, and bruises all over Gard, as well as his dirty clothes. He was afraid that Gard would be in some kind of shock from being at that place and not wish to talk about it.

"I was on vacation," Gard quickly replied. Then without hesitation, Gard shouted out to Hayden for him to toss him a donut. After that, Juice exhaustedly walked into the kitchen, not knowing the last time he was up this early. Juice picked up a donut and a cup of coffee. Juice looked at Hayden and asked him if he got these supplies.

"Yes," Hayden answered.

"You travel to the place on foot?" Juice asked before bringing the cup to his lips.

"You left your keys in the car," Hayden replied, not feeling guilty for taking the car without permission.

Juice took his breakfast and sat to Gard's left. Will told him good morning. Juice just gave a hum for he had coffee in his mouth at the time. Juice put the coffee on the table and said, "I hate coffee."

"Then I'm taking yours," Gard said as he snatched Juice's cup. Gard was still very tired and had already finished his cup before stealing Juice's.

Upstairs, Eric was in the bathroom looking in the mirror. Eric swallowed a few pills from his bottle that he kept in his pocket. He took a few extra before going to bed last night. The stress of all the events yesterday took an extra toll on him, and that was before he was trying to break through the caved-in walls to save Gard before the bomb went off.

With all the extra pills Eric consumed within the short amount of time, he checked himself in the mirror. He remembered how quickly he could tell that Miles was on medication last night. Eric had to make sure that his facial features didn't show his drug use. Eric believed his face looked fine, so he focused on cleaning the dirt off his hands. Moving all those rocks from the cave-in left his hands a mess that he was too lazy to wash off before going to bed.

Eric was the last to join the group in the kitchen and sat at the end of the table opposite of Gard. Will thought that since Eric was so concerned for Gard's safety yesterday, they would at least exchange hellos to each other. But the tension between the two seemed to be an unpleasant one. Gard couldn't help but to give Eric a nasty glance while Eric seemed to feel guilty about something.

Will found it odd that no one was talking, so he said in a cheery voice, "Can any of you guys remember the last time we were all at the same place at the same—"

"How long is this going to take?" Eric asked, interrupting Will. "I got to get back to work soon."

"They keeping you busy at work still?" Gard rudely asked.

"No one leaves until James tells us what he knows!" Juice yelled.

"Who is this James?" shouted Gard.

Then James appeared in the room by teleport. This made the Hogs gasp heavily; Miles even let out a small scream. Gard jumped out of his chair; this being his first time seeing James teleport, he was the most surprised by this action.

"That's James," Juice said with food in his mouth while pointing with the donut still in his hand.

"This place has a front door!" Hayden shouted to James while he spit out some of the food he was chewing.

The mystery of this man was a heavy wonder to the Hogs. Besides a small interaction with Kate, the Hogs had never told anyone about their fight with the devil all those years ago. So how did James know about their actions, and why confront them now? Juice did receive an angry letter from Kate about five years ago where she discussed her hatred toward the

Hang Out Group. Back then, Juice was still slightly in communication with a few members, and they never believed that she would do anything to threaten them. Juice, along with the others, had no thoughts on James working for Kate in anyway. They didn't think Kate would go that far to bring them all here just to hurt them. Not to mention James was in the rescue mission to save Gard last night. If this man didn't wish to harm them and would do a lot to make sure that they were all together alive and well, what exactly did he want from them?

James took a long glance at the seven men in the room. They were not much to look at given the fame that was attached to them. They looked like your usual run-of-the-mill grown adults getting close to their midtwenties. Hayden was the tallest, slightly taller than Miles and Gard. Gard had the longest, shaggiest hair with a scruffy beard along his jawline. Timber had the expensive haircut look, always feeling the need to look presentable. The physical evidence of their advance strength was not presented in their muscles. Juice looked to have the weakest-looking physique of the group, while Will looked to be the strongest one despite being the shortest. Eric's years of working at a desk showed, but keeping himself in fancy suits made his look to be more impressive rather than being slightly out of shape. Miles, on the other hand, looked like he really needed a sandwich; the guy was all skin and bones as his fitting clothes looked baggy on him.

The time of hesitating had passed. Everyone in the room was eager to hear what James had to say. James was well aware of this, having all eyes in the room on him as they patiently waited, chewed on their breakfast, and sipped their drinks. James's speech to deliver the forbidden information was something that made even him shiver slightly. In the high mood to get his speech underway, he introduced himself.

"My name is James, and I am an angel from Heaven." James paused for a moment to let the Hogs allow that information sink in.

Before James could deliver any more information, Juice spoke up. "You don't look like an angel."

"Well, in the Bible, it says that God made man in his own image. That was a very universal image. Every type of angel, spirit, devil, or human all seemed to be built in a similar structure." James was about to move forward in his speech, but Hayden shouted out something.

"Where are your wings? Don't angels have wings?"

Judging by how the questions were being delivered, it seemed like the people in the room didn't believe James.

"There are some angels who do have wings. I'm not one of them. But to be honest, those winged angels are a little stuck up and pretty rude to the nonwinged angels."

"Guys, this isn't too out of our reach of belief here. We fought the devil within the Garden of Eden, remember?" Will brought up to help support the idea that James was who he said he was.

"In Logan's research of Loomation, he did theorize that angels were built to carry this special power. This guy can teleport, which means his Loomation is active. And after seeing him move those heavy rocks from the cave-in last night, he showed off the kind of strength that a dry Loomation provides. We've never seen a person who has both," Eric said, thinking out loud to the group.

"Alright, I'll admit that I did believe that God and his angels once existed. But my theory was that they all died a long time ago, leaving the devil to be the last of his kind. And we killed him, so I thought that they were all now extinct," Gard said with hand gestures.

"Well, you're wrong. The only one of the devil's kind who is no longer around is the devil himself. He was someone who carried a very important job."

"That's it, isn't it? That's why it was bad for us to kill the devil because he carried a very important job." Juice was pointing at James, practically jeering at him.

James nodded, and then the floor was his to speak again. James told them the story of the beginning of life and their free will and how free will was bestowed upon the humans. He told them about the argument between God and the devil about the humans. This argument led to the balance of good and evil being built, which was settled by having the devil being in charge of the negative spirits causing the evil part of the balance. James told the Hogs about the Saints and that they were in control of the good side of the balance. James explained to them that after the devil was killed, there were no orders being delivered to the evil spirits to cause the evil side of the balance. This, in turn, led to Memphis being built, and Memphis's actions fully tipped the balance over to the evil side, causing the war and the constant mayhem they all had been experiencing. James explained the war of the balance and that the Saints have officially called it quits on restoring the proper balance of the world.

After James explained the reason for all the pain and suffering the world had faced over the last five years, some of the Hogs still had a few questions. They understood the importance of the devil's job and could see how things could go horribly wrong with him being dead, but they still had questions about the balance of good and evil.

"So the good spirits go out and help the good people, while the negative ones go out and make things bad for the bad people?" asked Gard.

"No, that's not how it works," James said, now feeling like he needed to go in a little deeper in explaining that part of the story. "A bad person who sells illegal drugs his whole life may never get arrested, while a good person who gives to charity on a regular basis may never win the lottery."

"So how do you win the lottery?" asked Juice.

"When it comes to risk where the odds are way against you, or if you challenge yourself to an activity where the flawed consequences are on par to the success, you won't receive any positive or negative effect from any spirit. So that the challenge is fair and the victory is well earned."

"So the world still has that sense of fairness in it?" Will asked, looking for confirmation.

James said that when the balance was in perfect order, the answer was yes. But after the balance broke, there became fewer true chances and little to no fairness in the world.

"Say a farmer couldn't get his crops to grow, he prays for rain…what do the people upstairs do about that?" questioned Hayden.

"We've had a ton of farmland cases over the course of human kind. There was a time when an evil spirit caused a massive drought over a farmer's land. The farmer prayed for rain, but since the good side of the balance doesn't undo the evil side's actions, the guy just had to wait out the drought. The orders for the negative spirit's action stopped at the end of the month. After that, the natural rain came in for the farmer."

"I bet that farmer was praising God when that rain came in, even though God nor the Saints did nothing to provide it," Gard stated.

"Yes, the farmer did praise God when the rain came, but he still participated in God's plan. Everyone in this room knows that God's plan for us isn't all good weather and happy days." What James said made the group grow silent. "Now that the farmer had experience on getting through hard times, he was more obligated to help others who were facing a hard time themselves. Reaching out and helping others is a common thing that people do after they experiences a bad time in their life. Not all of them do it, but that's how free will works. Some change for the better while some grow crueler."

"So what is it that you actually do then?" asked Eric.

"We sometimes point a search party in the right direction. Make sure a scout gets to the game where he'll spot a young player who would launch him into a strong career. We can make sure that the printer actually works when you really need it to sometimes."

James then started to explain how spirits could affect one's mind to nudge them to make decisions. He said that they might find it odd that a lot of evil spirits don't press negative thoughts onto bad people. The evil spirits know that there is a nine-out-of-ten chance that a bad person would do the bad thing, whether or not the spirit was pushing for it. The negative spirits would push for the nice guy to do the bad thing; if the nice guy could block all the nasty ideas, then that's a sign of a strong will. But until the balance was broken, the negative spirit had a limit on how much they could push. Now, they had no boundaries. They pour a heavy amount of negative influence on the people. Even the strongest-willed people have had trouble, sometimes succumbing to temptation.

James said that when Heaven receives prayers from people who are wishing for help from a family or a group of people who suffered a tragedy, most of the time the Saints don't have to do anything about it. "Sometimes terrible things happen to people, and there is no evil spirit to blame. That's called human interaction. That can go both ways. Now the Saints could send a positive spirit down to earth to help the people in need. But that would take away people's chance to do something good. After the events of a house fire or someone being robbed by a criminal, people chime in to help out. The Saints won't take away the chance to have people do the right thing. When people donate or help rebuild out of their own free will, that's called human interaction. But when all the good is taken out of the world, it's very easy for people to not provide anything positive for others. When people live in a world that is nothing but hate, greed, and pain, the people tend to stop helping others."

The Hogs felt that they had failed to provide any help to anyone over the last five years. James was right; seeing a world on fire when you're already engulfed in the flames really makes you no longer to care about others. Makes you no longer care about your best friends. Makes you no longer care about yourself. The Hogs were once together, but they all branched off into their own lives and simply lost touch with one another. Beside Will, none of them were happy to see each other after all this time. They all had lost their passion of maintaining a strong friendship.

"So now that you know the situation and the history behind it all, I now have to read you your charges," James regretfully stated.

"Charges?" Eric repeated with an off-put tone.

This made the group tense up.

"The Saints are charging you with the murder of the devil. And they demand your presence up at the gates of Heaven to stand trial to see if you are fully responsible for the broken balance or not."

"That is absolutely ridiculous!" Gard shouted as he stood up out of his chair.

"I want my lawyer!" Eric yelled out.

"Those guys in robes can't put the whole blame on us. That's outrageous!" Juice said as he slammed his hands on the table.

"We weren't the only ones trying to kill the devil that day. We were just the last ones standing!" Hayden added.

"What would happen to us if they find us guilty?" wondered Will.

"They haven't told me that yet," replied James.

"Well, we are definitely not guilty! It was all self-defenses actions. We were in a kill-or-be-killed situation!" Eric said as he stood up to retrieve his cell phone to get in touch with his lawyer. "Why don't I have any signal? I had it this morning!" shouted Eric, looking at his phone.

"It's because they're bringing us up," James replied as he looked around the house.

At that moment, the Hogs all eyed the windows and saw a white light start to glow in from the outside. Not only did the white light start to cover the whole outside, but the house felt as if it was being lifted, a similar feeling of being on an elevator.

"They're beaming us up now, Jimmy? I didn't agree on going to the gates of Heaven!" Juice said, getting out of his chair and trying to open the back door of the house.

"They told me that they'll send you up after you were informed of your charges. I'll get there to inform the Saints of your arrival," James said as he disappeared from the room.

"No, wait!" shouted Eric to James.

But James was already gone.

"Push harder, Juice," Gard said as he reached the back door to help Juice push open the door. Both Juice and Gard were slamming their shoulders into the door, trying to force it open. But the whole house seemed to be impenetrable; not even the combined forces of both Juice and Gard were able to leave even a dent on the door.

Eric picked up a chair and smashed it against the window. The chair shattered, but the window was scratch-free.

"I'm not facing any trial. I can't go back to jail!" Hayden shouted as he ran to the front door to try his luck on getting out there. Hayden tried the knob, but it wouldn't turn. Hayden then removed his gun from his shoulder holster and fired off five shots at the window of the door. The bullets harmlessly dropped to the floor after colliding with the window. Hayden then tried to kick open the door many times after that.

The elevation of the house started to speed up much faster now, and the white glow from outside had now completely filled the windows. The sound in the house was similar to the sound of a plane taking off, and it was getting louder by the second. Miles was under the table feeling like he was about to have a panic attack.

Eric got down on the floor next to Miles. "Miles, you're our only hope getting out of this!" he shouted to him. "You teleport us out of here, and I'll give you all the pills you could possibly want!"

Miles just covered his head with his arms, trying to calm himself during this overwhelming time.

Will pulled Eric away from Miles for he was scaring him. Eric then turned the blame on Will, saying it was Will's fault why he was there.

Gard shouted that they should have left him in that cave. Will reminded Gard that he would have died if they didn't come after him.

"Yeah, but now we may be facing something worse!" Timber shouted.

This made the Hogs experiences a new type of fear. None of the Hogs wanted to imagine the type of punishment they would face if the Saints found them guilty. There was an awkward moment of silence within the group as they all pictured the worst.

"I shouldn't have come," Timber moaned.

"At least you had a choice! I was dragged here!" Gard shouted.

"Gard, if you complain about getting pulled out of that cave one more time, I'm going to throw you back in it!" Juice yelled out in frustration.

Most of the Hogs were angry, and all of them were scared and nervous to face what's to come next. Hayden walked back into the kitchen, returning his gun back in its holster. Once they were all in the same room, they all grew quiet, as if they knew it was pointless to put the blame on anyone. They figured this would have happened one way or another. There was no hope in trying to escape, so they just stood and waited for this ride to be over.

The wind noise grew louder, and the white glow started to fill up the whole inside of the house. Then they felt the shaking of the entire house, as if the house had finally come to a landing. Most of the Hogs headed to the window by the back door. They saw the white cloudlike ground. And out in short distance, they saw the glowing gold gates of Heaven.

The Trial of the Hogs

With most eyes looking out the window, Will turned back and offered Miles a hand up off the floor. Miles turned toward Will and took his assistance in getting up. Will asked him if he was alright, and Miles gave a convincing positive response.

"I feel fine." Miles was finding himself a little surprised on how well he felt. Miles no longer seemed easily spooked, and when he talked, it no longer sounded like random nonsense.

"You back at 100 percent?" wondered Will, seeing how much better Miles was acting.

"Not quite there yet, but a lot closer than where I was."

"You think you'll be able to teleport us out of here?" asked Hayden.

"I don't think I'm at that level of concentration yet, but I'm past whispering to myself," Miles replied.

The Hogs didn't fully realize that they were now in a much calmer mood. Their anger, fear, and frustration all seemed to calm down. Miles's state of mind was the most noticeable, perhaps because his mind was the most clouded. Miles then stepped to the back window to see the gates and asked what do they do now.

Gard placed his hand on the back doorknob and remained motionless before turning it. Gard let out a small breath and turned the knob, feeling relieved that they could now exit the house.

The seven men exited the home and stood on the ground. The ones wearing the dirty clothes from being inside the cave last night were now donning the same clothes, but somehow they seemed to be clean and feeling soft. All the Hogs all seemed to have perfectly clean bodies and nice-smelling hair. The side effects of being that close to Heaven seemed to clean not only their bodies but also the minds.

"It's hard to believe that God's home is just beyond those gates," Will said in a whimsical moment. The gates were about two football fields away from where the house landed.

"You think a place so perfect and full of peace wouldn't have gates," Gard uttered. Hayden noticed a few large buildings to their right close to the gates. It was hard to believe that they didn't see those buildings before. They seemed quite obvious now that they spotted them. Besides the massive golden gates that reached from left to right as far as they could see, the buildings were the only other things around. Hayden started marching over to the buildings, but Timber thought it would be best to stay at the house until James came back.

Before anyone could vote on that, the house started to lower itself down under the ground to return to earth. The Hogs were quite spooked by seeing their only familiarity disappear into the ground. They arrived in the house, and now it was gone. The questions were, how do they get back, and will they be able to go back?

"Looks like we're heading to the buildings," Gard said as he took the lead to the edifices.

The visual height of the three magnificent structures seemed to be growing as they grew closer to them. The three buildings all had title signs that hung above the archway doors. The far left had the words The Armory. The building on the far right said Hall of Records. And the building in the middle said Main Office.

"Pretty big step up from the Garden of Eden, am I right?" Juice mumbled over to Hayden.

"Yeah, literally," Hayden replied.

In the center building, James opened the doors from the inside and signaled the boys to come over to him. James led them toward the entrance. Inside were high ceilings with tall granite arches supporting them. Large dark brown office desks were scattered on top of the gray marble flooring. The windows were made up of brightly colored stained glass material while the walls were covered in magnificent art paintings of famous Saints. Aside from the Hogs and James, the room was empty.

James led them to a table so that he could give the Hogs a rundown on what was about to happen. "Alright, now all the Saints are waiting in the courtroom down the hall over there," James said while gesturing toward the hall. "You'll be seated across from the Head Council. They'll read off your charges, and you'll enter your plea. If you plead not guilty, then they'll ask you questions and allow you to make your argument."

Eric was frustrated to learn that the trial would start right away. Eric complained about him not wearing his court suit and was embarrassed by what the others were wearing. Eric then lashed out his complaints about not having his lawyer present. James said that originally, the Saints weren't going to allow the Hogs to have anyone to help defend them. But James argued that the humans barely had any information on the balance of good and evil and were also almost completely unaware of what the Saints were in charge of. The Hogs wouldn't be able to defend themselves without someone on their side who knew how things were meant to be handled by the Saints.

"In America, if you don't have an attorney, one may be provided for you without the need to convince the government for one. This place sucks," Hayden stated.

"Did you just say that the gates of Heaven suck?" Juice asked, thinking how odd and ironic that statement was.

"It's not America up here, Hayden. The justice system at the gates works differently than what you may expect. The Saints will ask you questions. They will, in turn, allow you to elaborate and let you give out statements. So try your best to keep a level head," James informed the befuddled group. James told the Hogs that he will be handling the defense side, meaning that he was going to be the Hogs' lawyer, but also assured them that they can represent themselves as well.

Eric wanted to know if James had a defense tactic. Eric was pushing for their plea to be not guilty, claiming that their actions on the devil were all in self-defense. James asked the rest of the group if they all agreed with that plea. The rest of the boys simply nodded, thinking that it was the right choice.

Before any more information was relayed, a saint walked out from the hall that led to the courtroom. The man called out to James, saying that it was time for the trial to start.

A fearful chill suddenly ran down each of the Hogs' spines when they heard this news. Things were really happening fast for them. Just a few minutes ago, they were on earth eating donuts, not having a clue on why they were gathered up. Now they were about to face the Head Council and had to convince them that they killed the devil in an act of self-defense.

Down the hall under the dark archway was the location of the courtroom. The Hogs could hear the chanting of the Saints as they walked in the dimly lit tunnel. All talking had come to a complete stop when the Hogs reached the light of the room. All eyes of the Saints were bearing down strong glances upon the Hogs when they walked into the room. The place was built like an arena, with thirty-some Saints filling up the bleachers that covered half the room. In the center were the two tables, one for the Hogs and one for the Council.

The Hogs felt very intimidated as they walked up to the front of the room. They kept their hands to their sides and tried to keep their eyes straight. The awkward silence was disturbing, and the long walk down the floor just didn't seem to end soon enough.

"James, are all these people dead?" Will softly asked James.

"Yes, all the Saints have all died a long time ago. Here they are just souls. They are fortunate souls who were able to manufacture themselves a body. They don't have blood, organs, or sweat. But here at the gates of Heaven, the spiritual realm allows them to be visible to the living. The gates of Heaven is the only place where the ones in the spiritual realm can be seen by people who are in the physical form," James explained.

When the group came to the table, they all took a seat. From left to right sat Miles, Hayden, Juice, Gard, Eric, Will, and Timber on the right end. James stood up standing between the two tables. Then the Head

Council arrived from behind the room, taking their seats at the table across from the Hogs. Peter sat in the middle with Anthony and Francis on his right, while Paul and Patrick was on his left.

James started things off by addressing the council. "Saints, I have informed the Hang Out Group members, or Hogs as they like to be called, the origins of the balance and the importance of the job the devil once had. So they are now ready to face their trial."

After a small acknowledging nod, Peter proceeded to read out loud the document in front of him. "This case number is classified and is being viewed by the entire staff of the Saints here at the gates of Heaven. We are also broadcasting this trial live over the spiritual realm communication channels for the archangels to listen in, which leads us to suspect that other spirits, whether they are good or bad, could also be listening. Since *how* the devil was murdered is highly classified, we will not be discussing any fighting style, weaponry, or any other resources used to assist on killing the devil. We are not here to find out the *how*, just the *who* is responsible. The humans brought here today are Will, Tyler, Hayden, Blake, Eric, Beauregard, and Miles. The charges they face are the murder of the devil and the actions of disrupting the order of the balance. James, you may deliver their plea."

All eyes were on James when he announced that the Hogs were pleading not guilty. After that statement, the audience started to chat with one another. A lot of Saints were wagering on what the Hogs' plea would be. The majority of the bets were on them pleading not guilty. Peter waved his hands like a band conductor for a quick motion. After Peter's motion was made, seven Bibles appeared on the Hogs' table sitting right in front of them. Patrick instructed them that to continue forward, they all must be sworn in under oath. The Hogs did comply and were wondering what was going to happen next. They weren't sure how Heaven court would go. Would there be opening statements, witnesses, evidence presented, or even a jury? James told them before entering the courtroom that if they plead not guilty, then they will have to convince the Head Council that they were right. So it seemed that the five Saints sitting across from the Hogs was the jury. Everything was relying on James within the Hogs' minds; they were just hoping that he knew what he was doing.

"The angel named James will be defending the Hogs, but each member of the Hang Out Group is entitled to add any comments they wish to bring to our attention due to this being a rushed trial. James, you have the floor," Peter said.

James didn't feel too nervous about being the defendants' lawyer. He had a heavy thought on how this was all going to end. If things went the way he's wishing, then the hard convincing part would take place after the trial.

"We're all here because the devil is dead. Murdered, says the Saints. Now, we know that the devil had no expiration date in a way. That dying of a natural cause was not an option for the beast. So yes, someone is responsible for the death of the devil."

"Where is he going with this?" Eric whispered over to Will, thinking that this opening statement wasn't helping their case at all.

"Just give him a chance to see where he's going with this," Will replied, having more confidence in James than the others.

"The devil was killed on the last Monday of June 2010. Since the devil had the power to sensor all his actions from any records being documented for the Saints, there is no true proof that the Hogs killed the devil. The only evidence the Saints have on the Hogs is that they can place the Hogs being in the Garden the same day the devil was killed. They have nothing more than that to prove my clients' guilt."

Eric was impressed by this statement by James. Without any sound evidence of the Hogs killing the devil, the Saints couldn't prove their claim. Most of the Hogs thought that this was a closed case.

Peter, on the other hand, didn't care about the lack of proof the Saints had on the Hogs. He surmised that them being inside the Garden the same day that the devil was murdered was enough evidence to bring the Hogs to court.

"Miles," Peter said, making heavy eye contact with the defendant, "are you and your friends responsible for the devil's death?"

"Objection, you just can't straight up address the defendant a question like that!" Eric said as he stood up from his chair in a rage. "He's not even in the witness stand!"

"You've all taken the oath, and with our system that places you all as our witnesses, we can ask you any question we want," Peter replied, not liking Eric's bold outburst.

James looked over to Eric and gave a face expression to sit his butt back into his chair.

"Miles, please answer your question," Francis said before repeating the question. "Are you and your friends responsible for the death of the devil?"

Miles let out a heavy sigh and responded with a regretful yes.

"Objection!" Hayden shouted, practically out of control. "We picked this guy up at a mental hospital yesterday! Who knows what kind of state his mind is in? Can his comments even be taken as a reliable source?"

"Okay then, Hayden. Same question to you. Are you and your friends responsible for the death of the devil?" Francis inquired.

"Well, that's a misleading question." Hayden looked over to eye the people sitting at the table with him. "Most of us haven't seen each other in years. So I wouldn't exactly call us friends." Hayden bowed his head and answered the question. "But yes, we are responsible for the death of the devil."

James then made the claim that the Hogs were acting within self-defenses. Eric stood back up from his chair to state that he and the others at his table were in a kill-or-be-killed situation. The devil wanted them dead, and the Hogs were just defending themselves.

"Due to maintaining the balance of good and evil, the devil is allowed to kill a life of a human once a month. With that order given, the good side of the balance can miraculously save a life in the same period of time. Such as a person who is able to walk away from a deadly car crash without even a scratch. It's a miracle that is only allowed once a month, but to keep the balance, a human's life on earth must be cut short with any means the devil wishes," Anthony explained to the Hogs.

"But with the devil being locked up in the Garden, he never personally carries out the assignment. He always assigns this hideous task to the horseman Death or the Grim Reaper spirit," Paul added.

"So even if you somehow knew that the devil was going to have one of you killed for that month, you were still merely being a part of the system of the balance, making your plea of acting in self-defenses invalid," Peter stated.

"Now that is not true!" Juice said, standing up in a rage. "We've seen the devil personally kill a man right in front of us, and we weren't even in the Garden when it happened!" Juice was referring to the murder of Ray. Juice, along with the others, was still haunted by the gruesome screams Ray emitted when the devil burned his body alive. The guilt of standing by and hiding in fear still rested heavily on the Hogs.

The mention of the devil not being in the Garden at some point caused a stir in the gallery. The crowd was loud, and even the Head Council was passing confused chats among one another.

James leaned in closer to the Hogs, asking them if the devil ever being outside of the Garden was indeed true.

"Yes, it is true. The devil escaped from the Garden years ago and chased a man named Logan Renshaw for decades," Will answered.

"James, was there any responsibility that the Saints had for making sure the devil was locked away inside the Garden?" wondered Eric.

"Absolutely there was," James said with a slight thrill. James believed that this could help the Hogs' case. James informed the Saints that the devil was free from the Garden for decades, and the Saints were totally unaware of his disappearance. James said that if the Saints were doing their job by making sure that the devil was always in captivity, then the Hogs wouldn't have had to defend themselves from the devil's deadly threats. James knew that the Saints had blundered big time on not being able to track the devil's longtime flight of freedom. With information like this, the archangels or even God may demand the Head Council to step down from their position due to a lack of diligence in maintaining contact with the devil's presence.

"I know that there is another prison out there containing powerful spirits, and I bet you never forget to check that one to make sure it's still being occupied. So what kept you from ever checking the Garden to see if the devil was still there?" James asked, feeling the momentum turning toward the Hogs. The Hogs felt that they could get out of this trial with their freedom due to the Saints' mistake of simple guard duty.

Unfortunately, the Saints used the devil's power of censoring his actions to justify the lack of evidence of the devil actually being out of the Garden at all. All they could prove was where the devil's dead body was, and since that was in the Garden, there was no proof of him ever escaping.

Eric once again stood up from his chair outraged, saying that he and everyone at his table were eyewitnesses to the murder of Ray by the devil, which took place outside the Garden.

"This trial isn't on whether or not the devil was out of the Garden. If he was, it doesn't take away the fact that the devil was still working within the guidelines of the balance of good and evil. He is entitled to execute one human a month, and he never broke that rule," Peter replied.

"The devil personally targeted us for execution!" Gard shouted. "So his work on the balance wasn't random at all. He wanted us all dead, and he tried to kill us all at once!"

"The balance doesn't hinge on whether or not the victims are chosen at random," Patrick commented. "But him trying to kill all of you at once does cross the line of his given responsibility and limits."

"So if the devil tried to kill all of my clients at once, then their self-defense plea is valid," James said, sensing a newfound hope in his case.

"Tell me something, Hogs. If the devil was out of the Garden, how did he end up back inside, and why was he trying to kill you all at once?" Peter asked.

"Excuse me, I informed my clients that they would be receiving their questions individually, so you can't address them all at once with a question," James commented with growing confidence brewing from within.

Peter then addressed the question to Will. Will painfully glanced over to the others at the table because he knew answering this question would ruin their chances of winning their case. "We entered the Garden. And once there, we cried out to the devil saying that we gave him permission to kill us. He heard our intentions and came to answer the call."

Eric gave a heavy pound on the table for he had completely forgotten that part. It had been ten years, and it was still the most disturbing, most terrifying event of their lives. It was easy to forget certain events of that day due to the Hogs trying their best to wipe clean the memories of that horrible time. Now that the Saints had the knowledge of the Hogs giving the devil an open invitation for him to come and kill them to allow for the opportunity to set a trap, this completely ruined their self-defenses claim.

Even James had no positive turn on this situation. All James said was that the Hogs had no idea of the existence of the balance, so they didn't understand how and why the devil could have gotten away with his deadly actions. "All that my clients knew was that the devil wanted them dead, and their will to live pushed them to fight back to a point where they will never have to worry about the devil's threats ever again."

"Humans are made to die, James. The devil wasn't," Peter harshly stated. "The Head Council finds the defenses guilty of the murdering of the devil."

With that said, the bewildered Hogs felt their stomachs drop, and hearing the words out loud caused them to grow silent. They were too stunned to feel any anger or rage. They fully felt guilty and even started to wonder if they should feel regret for what they had done.

"For the charge of them being responsible for the balance being broken, I would like to state that my clients should be innocent on that. The rules of the balance say that humans can't affect the levels of either side of good or evil." James added.

"With the Hogs now found guilty for killing the devil, we hereby establish the Hog Declaration," Paul stated.

"The Hog Declaration? What's that?" questioned James.

Francis explained that the Hog Declaration comes into effect when a human finds a way to interfere with the balance of good and evil, which, up to this point, was thought to be impossible. The Hog Declaration is the action of a human or humans killing the one responsible for sending out the orders for either side of the balance. The other way a human can affect the balance is killing off a spirit who is holding territory. This action takes away all future progress the spirit was causing to the balance. In summary, the Declaration is when a human disrupts the balance by ether killing the messenger or the provider of the negative or positive influence."

"So then what happens to us now that we're found guilty?" Gard asked, raising his voice.

The Head Council's next action was to head back to their office to discuss the punishment for the Hogs' crimes. After they left the room, all the Saints in the audience headed toward the exit. The Hogs and James were the only ones left in the room. The place being empty really displayed just how wide and hollow the room felt.

James looked over at the group; they all had their heads down and were feeling pretty down at the moment. The group had to pull back memories from their tragic past, and now they had to face the consequences of their actions. The guilt of knowing that they were responsible for the depressed and tortured world suddenly fell on their shoulders. Now all they could do was wait for the Saints to return and deliver their sentence.

James told them that he was going to check in with the Saints. He wanted to see if there was anything he could do to soften their punishment. James didn't like the idea of leaving the group in such a depressed time, but he had an idea that he wanted to pitch to the Saints.

James entered the Saints' room. The Saints at first told him to leave, but James refused. James said that after completing his mission of bringing in the Hogs for their trial, he felt that he earned a few minutes of their time. He was interested in the Hogs' punishment.

Peter was pretty straightforward. He reminded James that the Saints didn't have the power to condemn any soul to either hell or Heaven. God did the judging for that, but not until the human dies. The Saints were planning on speeding up the wait for their judgment from God by ending their life right away.

"You're going to kill them?" James asked in high disbelief and shock.

"They ruined a system that was set up during the times of the first humans. They murdered the first creation. We consider this mercy," Peter stated.

"The Hogs were only responsible for the balance being broken once. It's your creation Memphis who's the reason why it's not yet fixed!" James argued.

"We believe that once we punish the ones responsible for the beginning of all this madness, then the archangels would be more cooperative on helping us out on fixing it again," Paul added.

"And when they still refuse, what would be your plan then? I doubt you have any backup plan if this one fails because this one is such a desperate act for help, it's pathetic!" James yelled.

"Then what do you expect us to do then, James?" shouted Peter.

"Give me another task force, and we'll take out Memphis once and for all!" James replied with a sense of confidence that it could actually be done.

"No angel will fight by your side! They've all called it quits. We have no more operatives!" Peter stood up from his chair. Peter's mood slightly changed after shouting this out, as if he just now realized that James was right. Peter never admitted defeat, but he just reminded himself that Heaven was out of soldiers. Peter knew that this long shot of getting the archangels to help after punishing the ones responsible was a hopeless act. Peter didn't have any plans when this one inevitably failed, and that truly scared him. He was asked by God to take care of the humans, and he felt that he failed. And now he wanted to kill a group of humans who were just defending themselves from a monster—a monster that instilled fear in Heaven's strongest creations. Peter fell back to his chair feeling lost.

"We don't need angels to help us restore order to the balance. After everything that just happened out there in that courtroom, we learned that humans can affect the balance! Right now Heaven doesn't need the angels. It needs the humans, it needs the Hogs!"

"The Hogs aren't fighters for Heaven," Patrick uttered.

"If you grant them full access to being fighters of the order of the balance, then maybe they will fight for earth. Thanks to the Hog Declaration, we fully know that if humans kill spirits who occupy territory, then they can affect the balance. These guys have killed the mother of all evil. A few evil spirits should be a piece of cake for these guys. Once Memphis's army is weakened, he'll fall, just like the devil."

"You are offering to lead the Hogs with this task? We can't force them to fight. You'll have to convince them too."

"I'm ready to lead my own team."

"James, what makes you think they have a chance?" wondered Francis.

"The balance has been responsible for many great and awful things during the course of human kind. But some of the greatest achievements have been caused by untampered human interaction. When that happens, it's a great reminder of the belief in humans. I know that the humans right now are crude and insolent. Trust me, the Hogs are no exception to that attitude. But we must have faith in them and believe that human interaction is going to be how the world is fixed. So let me ask you. Do you still believe in humans?"

James's pitch was powerful for the Saints. They agreed to James's plan. The Saints said that the Hogs will be set free. The compromise of bearing the title of the murderer of the devil and breakers of the balance satisfied the council.

After James's meeting with the Saints, they all returned to the Hogs to tell them that there was no punishment for them. But bearing these titles may affect God's judgment on them when they died. The Hogs were so thrilled to hear this news. They didn't care about carrying the titles; they were just happy not to be condemned to hell or have their life cut short.

The Hogs were unaware of what James wanted out of them in return for getting them out of their punishment. James was responsible for taking the Hogs back to earth, and after that, the Saints said James was free to continue the fight for the order of the balance. James was going to wait until they returned to earth to tell them. His hopes for them to join him in the fight for the order of the balance were pressing hard on his mind. James gathered up the Hogs in a circle, and he teleported them back to earth.

Returning Home

When everyone was teleported back to earth, it was now nighttime. The men were standing in a damp grassy area. It must have just finished raining because the Hogs could smell the petrichor odor emerging from the plants in the area. The only light source was natural light from the environment. Many stars were shining bright from above, and lightning bugs were in the distance glowing off their tiny lights. The temperature was very pleasant, no need for a sweater, but wasn't too hot for pants. The Hogs looked around the place and recognized their location after some drawn-out looks at some parts of the area.

"Are we at the swamp?" asked Juice.

"This place was in your records as a home away from home as you called it," James stated.

Hayden knew that their old campsite was nearby, so he took off toward that direction while the others stood still. Eric was upset for not returning to the house where they were last before heading to the gates. Eric said he wanted to get into his car to head home now. James explained that there was more to clarify to them, and he wanted a peaceful place to do that in. James said that he won't teleport them anywhere until morning. It's too late to walk anywhere, so they should stay the night at the campsite.

"You've already told us everything we needed to know for the trial. And the Saints let us go to live out the rest of our lives. So just leave us alone, James," Juice angrily replied as he walked past James and followed Hayden's walking path toward the camp area.

Timber, Eric, Gard and Miles followed Juice. Will stayed behind, telling James to just give them some time, and they would come around.

Hayden reached the long stretch of perfect soft green grass that bordered around the old cabin that was still in pristine shape. After the first step into the grass, the bugs that were hovering around Hayden had scattered away. The transition walking onto the land was still amazing, but Hayden has been on and off this land so much that he didn't even notice. The land still had the clear, clean watering hole within the location with the healthy tree growing next to it. Hayden saw his old pop-up camper out on the far end of the border of the comfort zone. Hayden left it there years ago. The fire ring was still there, but no woodpile. Last thing visible on the land was an old run-down pickup truck. The truck was once Will's, but he couldn't part ways with it, so he parked it at the Garden and left it there.

Hayden reached the cabin with the words "The Diamond in the Rough" engraved on top of the door. Hayden pushed open the door and walked in. Inside was a bunch of stuff—a sleeping cot, a worktable, and a framed newspaper clipping showing a photo of Logan and his old travelers. Along with these items were folded up chairs and a couple of empty water containers and boxes containing more camping gear. Back when the Hogs used this place for long weekend breaks during college, they turned the cabin into a storage unit. This left the majority of the camping supplies inside the cabin and made packing for the next trip much easier.

Hayden searched for the box that contained the lighters and gasoline, the things they used to start the campfires. Hayden snatched up these objects and walked out of the cabin. Hayden walked up to the watering hole and chucked them into the water. As Hayden watched them sink, he was happy to know that there wouldn't be any fires being made here. Hayden then walked back into the cabin and pulled out a lockbox from under the cot. Hayden turned the combination lock on the box to open it. Inside was a key to Hayden's pop-up camper. Once the key was in hand, he locked the box back up and placed it under the cot.

Hayden then marched out of the cabin and headed to the pop-up camper. By this time, the rest of the Hogs reached the camp area. They figured since James wasn't going to teleport them anywhere, they might as well set up camp for the night. Will went to his old pickup truck, opened the car door, and hit the high beams of the truck's headlights. The headlights lit up the campsite from the cabin on the far left to Hayden's pop-up camper on the far right. Will was both shocked and pleased that the truck battery was still capable of doing this. Will then headed to the bed of the tuck to remove the cover. Under the tarp were a few tents along with air mattresses and other sleeping units. Underneath it all was an old futon comforter. Will gave the comforter a press and was happy to know that it still felt in great comfy shape.

Eric was the first at the truck to pick up his tent. Eric had a whole tent to himself along with his own a large air mattresses. Eric took his stuff and walked over to his old set-up spot. Juice grabbed the hammock from the bed of the truck and opened the back door of the vehicle. The back seats of the truck were all stuffed with extra pillows and blankets. Juice grabbed one of each and headed off to two nearby trees to hang up his hammock.

"Are you going to place that up high in the trees like you used to, Juice?" Will yelled out to Juice as he was walking away. Juice had no response. Back in the past summers and long weekend days, Juice used to hang that hammock high up in the tree line. He said that he had to stay clear from the wild land-walking animals, and he also wanted to be the first to know when it rained. But tonight, Juice was only hanging the hammock at the normal height.

Miles took hold of his tent bag. It was just a small thing that could be carried like a duffel bag. Gard came by to open up the back door of the truck. He said that he was planning on sleeping in the cabin, so he was taking a pillow and blanket. Timber then grabbed the last tent in the back. Once the group had what they needed from the truck, they positioned themselves in their usual places within the camp area.

Will took a good look at the old rusted dark blue truck that was about his age. Pleasant, nostalgic feelings returned to him as he placed his hand on the hood of the car. This was the truck he bought during his college days. He just needed it to get him to class on time and to get him home during the holiday breaks. Will was happy to see that the rust didn't grow worse over the years of letting it sit in the campsite. With the diamond pebbles from the Garden of Eden still buried under the cabin, this old place had always remained a perfect land.

James then accompanied Will at the truck.

"Man it feels so good to be back here. It was our home away from home. I wish you could have been here during its heyday. We got these white Christmas light packed away in the front of the truck, and we used to hang them from the tree over by the watering hole, to the cabin, to the pop-up camper at the edge of the border, to the truck, then back to the tree. We had some support beams buried into the ground outside of the comfort zone at some places to help support the lights. It was pretty easy to set them up every time we came here. Juice would fly around with the line of lights, and in the end, we would hook it up to the truck's battery."

"Sounds like the place to be," James replied, smiling.

"The place is still as perfect as we left it, but it's just the people who are different," Will said as he looked around the area, wishing his friends were feeling the old nostalgic feelings as he was. But none of them seemed to be happy being at the swamp again, and Will knew that there was something not right about that.

Hayden unlocked the pop-up camper and walked inside. The place smelled of old mothballs. Hayden hit the light switch, but nothing happened. Hayden just now remembered that he took the batteries out of the camper when he was last there. Hayden switched on his cell phone light to see. In front of Hayden was a couch, and under it was a safe. This safe also had a number combination, and Hayden placed the numbers in the right position and opened the safe door. Inside was Hayden's old hunting rifle. Hayden did have a nostalgic feeling seeing and holding that old weapon again. This was the same gun Hayden used to shoot the devil in the head. The memory of that attack was something he wanted to lock away, but at the same time, he wished to keep it as a souvenir. Then Hayden saw what he really wanted to find inside the safe. It was his old knife, the one with the infused diamond chips on the tip of the blade. This knife was strong enough to cut the skin of the devil, so Hayden knew it was powerful. Hayden had a hunting knife sheath inside the safe. Hayden placed the sheath around his waist and placed the knife in its storage area. Hayden was very upset at himself for never going back for this knife. Just having it strapped to his side had already made him feel a little more protected.

Eric was struggling with putting up his tent. His tent was so large that there was need of a second person to support the weight of lifting the roof off the ground. Eric really wanted to get it up all on his own, but he couldn't be in two places at once. So giving in to his pride and stubbornness, he yelled out, "Could someone give me a hand with this?" Eric spotted someone walking nearby and looked up, thinking someone was responding to his call.

Gard was the person who Eric saw. Gard was carrying some folding chairs that were covering up the cot in the cabin out to the yard when he walked past Eric. The two had a troubling glance, not saying a word to each other. Gard then walked on. Eric turned away and removed his pill bottle from his pocket. He looked at the bottle, craving a few pills. He then remembered his time up at the gates. Things got stressful while up there, but he didn't have any urge to take any pills. He figured that it was being at the Heavenly place, and he wished that feeling didn't go away so fast. After taking two pills, he tucked away the bottle and looked down, thinking about trying to raise the tent on his own again. Before he tried, he heard someone responded to his call for help.

"I'll give you a hand," Miles said.

Eric looked over and saw Miles standing close by the tent. Eric instructed Miles to grab the support bar on the right side of the tent while he grabbed the support bar on the left side. The two tilted back on the bars, and with that simple motion, the tent was standing tall. Eric did a quick check of the tent to see if there if there was any more to do to it.

"Alright, it's up. Thanks," Eric said, turning his head to Miles to thank him. Miles said no problem. Miles's tent was placed next to Eric's, and he returned to it to finish setting it up. Eric hesitated to ask, but he forced himself to ask Miles if he needed help with his tent. Miles said that his tent was so small, it could only hold one, and he couldn't even stand in it. Best part of his tent was how easy it was to set up, and he could do it all on his own in under a minute. Miles's tent was only waist-high and looked like it could barely fit Miles lying down in it. Eric's tent had a front room and a back room with high ceilings and large windows.

Will, Hayden, Gard, and James were around the fire ring putting up the foldout chairs. Will asked if they should start a fire. Hayden shut down the idea of starting a fire, saying that they didn't need one as he placed his chair back to the fire ring. The Hogs felt weird sitting at this place without a fire. Hayden of all people refusing to have one was weird. Some of them wanted to ask, but many of them were hiding things from the others, and they weren't going to share it, so they didn't expect Hayden to share what he was hiding.

After Eric finished airing up his mattresses, he took one of the chairs in the circle. He asked Miles if he wanted to use the air pump, but Miles said that he always slept without a mattress, saying that the grass here was so soft that he didn't need one. Timber wished Eric offered him the electronic pump as he had to blow up his mattress with a hand pump.

Once everyone was sitting around the half circle, James was ready to tell the Hogs the dark truth about their past. James was pacing while gathering his thoughts. He started with how Memphis was programmed to know about the Hang Out Group. He told them that Memphis only knew them as the people who killed the devil, but never knew any of their past aside from that. James said that after Memphis became the leader of the evil spirits, he started granting territories. He planted a spirit on each member of the Hang Out Group over the last five years.

"Why would Memphis target us?" Will asked.

"You guys are famous among the spiritual population. He wanted to keep an eye on you and keep your morale low."

"You're saying that we've had an evil spirit hovering over us for the last five years, making our lives worse?" Juice questioned.

When James said yes, the group grew silent with their heads hanging low. James knew that the Hogs were taking in a lot of shattering news today. They were still feeling depressed about knowing that they were responsible for the broken balance, and now they learned that they were being targeted by the evil spirits who were free to trash their lives as much as they wanted due to the devil being dead.

"You want us to kill Memphis, don't you?" Eric asked, knowing all along that this guy wanted something like this out of them.

"What makes you think we can kill Memphis? The way you make him sound makes him sound unkillable," Timber mentioned.

"You guys killed the devil, a person who no one ever wanted to be threatened by. The spirits should fear you if they don't already," James stated.

"We barely killed the devil! We had one chance to pull off our planned attack, and since he was so off guard when we started, we were able to perform our attack to perfection. It took us a matter of seconds to do what we did. And trust me, if it would have taken longer, we would have lost that fight. And I fully believe that if we had to do it again, we would not be able to pull it off a second time," Gard explained.

"You guys are earth's last hope, so I beg you to sleep on it for a while," James said as he turned his back on the group. James then waved his hands around the air space in front of him. A green light was coming out of his fingers as he waved his hands. The light seemed to be staying in place of where he placed it. James was painting the air with this green light. James looked like a band conductor as he was crafting his hologram-like image. When James was finished, the Hogs saw what he had made.

The glowing image was the balance of good and evil. It denoted a graph. On the bottom were two words: *Good* on the left and *Evil* on the right. There was a glowing green bar above the evil side of the balance and no bar on the Good side. James pointed to a spot in the middle of the green bar, saying that the evil and good side should be right there. James said that the good spirits and angels will return when they hear that Memphis is dead.

"We just need to kill Memphis, and everything will go back to normal?" wondered Will.

"It's not that easy." James looked over the group and knew that they weren't ready to fight Memphis. "See, I've fought Memphis, and he's no joke. He was built to kill and to take massive hits. Last time I fought him, I was with a team who didn't care for each other. A team who, at a moment, was ready to fight each other before fighting the evil spirit. And seeing how you guys are now compared to when you fought the devil, you guys won't last long in such a fight with Memphis."

The Hogs looked at each other and knew what James was talking about. They didn't have that powerful spark that Logan saw in them so many years ago. The way they were acting at this moment in time would highly disappoint Logan, their old friend. They felt that the friendship between Cain and Ray was stronger than how they were right now.

"Lucky for you, I know how to return you all to your old selves. Or at least close to it, I guess."

"What do you mean?" asked Juice.

James said that the heavy negative emotions they were feeling are due to their evil spirits' influence over them. James said that once they find and kill the evil spirit who has been haunting them for the past five years, their mind will be at ease. "The strong nightmares, the heartbreak, hate, regret, greed, and dishonor you all feel is a heavy emotion being pushed down by the evil spirits. It can be eased up. All we need to do is find them and kill them! And trust me, the evil side of the balance will start to drop with every kill we make. The Saints even referred to the actions of a human killing a spirit who carries territory as the Hog Declaration, saying it's one of the ways a human can affect the balance of good and evil. So we can do this. We all work together to save each other, then we take on Memphis. We can bring good back to the world again!"

The idea of finding the ones who caused their most painful moments and killing them felt pretty good to most of the Hogs. But some were not sure. This sounded like a battle that they were doomed to fail. Will was the first to stand, saying that he'll fight by James's side. Will looked at his friends, hoping that another would stand up.

Hayden did stand up from his chair. All eyes were on him to see what he was going to say. Hayden, like the others, was very troubled by his past. The way he didn't want to even look at fire was a sign of his tragedy. He knew if he found the one responsible for what happened, he would risk his life to make that spirit pay for their actions. "I'm in too."

Some of the others weren't sure, so no one else stood up. James begged them to at least think about it for a few days. The remaining Hogs felt that they owed James that. He was the one who helped them out during the trial. Who knows how bad things would have turned out if he didn't step in.

The Hogs went to bed for the night. James left the daunting image of the balance of good and evil up in the swamp. The Hogs could see it glowing from inside their tents or through the windows of the cabin and the pop-up camper.

Juice was in his hammock, Hayden was in his pop-up camper, Eric and Miles were in their respective tents, while Gard was in the cabin. Will was sitting in the bed of his truck, about to sleep on the futon comforter. Before he closed his eyes, he saw someone walking up to the truck.

Will turned and saw Timber. "What's up Timber?"

"You're really in on this whole fixing-the-balance thing?" asked Timber.

"Yes, I am. I think we owe it to the world to fix our mistake. I can't stand seeing you guys the way you are. And if killing some spirits will make you guys better, then that's what I'm going to do."

"You're a good man, Will. So I'm going to fight with you. I don't think we'll win, but you'll be a good friend to fight beside."

After that was said, Timber turned and headed back to the tent. Will was smiling because he now fully believed that things were going to get better from this moment on. Will knew that once the Hogs were back to their normal selves, they could win this fight. He had to keep believing in this and keep believing in his friends.

Help From Above

Sunday, October 4, 2020

Deep into the night, the Hogs were struggling to stay asleep. Failure to get a full night's rest was common for them. Most of them faced nightmares or depressing dreams when they slept. For a moment and not too long before sunrise, all the Hogs were sound asleep. During that moment, the swamp was visited by a mysterious flying man. James, who stood guard on the land, spotted the flyer making his landing within the camp area. James knew who this man was and was very surprised to have him grace them with his presence.

"Gabriel, is that really you?" James asked the man in disbelief.

"The one and only," Gabriel said with arms stretched out.

"I can't believe you're here. Are you going to help us fix the balance?" James couldn't believe he was standing in the presence of an archangel. Their power was ranked up high on the Loomation power scale; they were more powerful than the combined force of ten standard angels. With someone as powerful as Gabriel fighting by their side, James felt that everything was going to turn out okay, and they would surely defeat Memphis.

"I'm only here to help one of these humans."

When Gabriel stated that, James's felt a huge disappointment strike his mood. James thought that for once an archangel was actually going to do something with all their power. James felt a type of pride in that thought, thinking that the Saints couldn't get them to help, but James managed to get their attention. But Gabriel not wanting to help the whole group was very predictable. The archangels were made with so much power, but they never liked using it. They were like children who had the energy to walk the family dog, but just found it easier to let the dog run around the fenced-in backyard.

"Are you one of mine?" wondered Gabriel as he took a good look at James.

"No, I'm one of Michael's." James was stating that he was created by the archangel Michael. The standard angels were all made by the archangels. Over the years, it was proven that the angels made from Michael were the most loyal and most eager to serve Heaven.

"Oh yes, Michael always likes to present himself as very strict with great poise, but deep down he's just a teddy bear. Don't tell anyone this, but he always cries at the end of family films that have a big heartwarming moment." This made the two share a small laugh. "But really, don't tell anyone that. It'll probably be the last thing you ever do."

An odd quiet moment sunk in after that statement. Then James asked Gabriel who he wished to help. Gabriel pointed over to the tree line where Juice was sleeping in the hammock. James felt that he should have guessed it was Juice. Juice and Gabriel had something in common, so it made sense that he wanted to help him.

"You have a flyer on your team who doesn't fly. I will help him get back in the air."

"I was going to get started on helping him today. I'm planning on helping all of them," James replied.

"Look, I read Juice's file. He was usually the one who could change the mood of the group to something positive. He being on your side will be a lot better than him being one who needs help. All he needs to do is to get back into the air, and then he'll be able to take out his evil spirit."

"You're going to help him kill his spirit?"

"I'll coach from afar."

James wasn't sure if he should let Gabriel take Juice. James didn't like Juice taking on his evil spirit without the group. He wanted the whole group fighting side by side when going into battle. Gabriel was a little pushy, saying that Juice will be fine and that he won't let him die. Gabriel just reminded James that he had a lot on his plate, and having one of the Hogs already cleansed from their evil spirit's troubling mood would move things along more smoothly. James felt that he had to go along with Gabriel's plan and trusted him to take Juice. After their chat was over, Gabriel teleported Juice away, and James waited for the rest of the Hogs to wake up.

<hr>

When Juice woke up, he found his face buried in white sand. For a second, Juice thought that he was back at the gates of Heaven. But when he started spitting out sand from his mouth, he knew he was still on earth. Juice rolled over on his back, seeing the empty blue sky, trying to remember how he got to this location. Then he spotted someone drifting off in the sky. Juice turned his head at the flying man and was highly confused at what was going on. In a quick motion, Juice got to his feet to get a better look at the man.

"Good morning, Juice, how did you sleep?" the congenial Gabriel nicely asked.

"Well, this wasn't the worst place that I've woken up from, so yeah, I slept well, I guess." Juice then looked around; he saw nothing but white sand as far as he could see. "Where am I?"

"The White Sands of New Mexico. You been here once before, remember?"

"Yeah, I remember losing my favorite action figure out here," Juice said as he looked back at the flying man. The sun was shining brightly from behind the man flying in the air. "Who are you? One of James's coworkers or something?"

"Let's say that I'm upper management when it comes to James. I'm an archangel, and I'm also flyer."

"Yeah I can see that. Aren't all angels flyers?"

"The ones with wings can. But only a few without wings can." Gabriel landed next to Juice. Gabriel took out a water bottle from his jacket pocket and handed it over to Juice. Juice took the bottle and started to use the water to help get the sand out of his month. As Juice took swigs of water from the bottle, Gabriel asked him to take flight, informing him that no one was around, so it's okay. Juice spit out some of the water after swirling it in his month to help remove the sand and said that he'll pass.

"I haven't been able to do that in years," he added.

"Why not?" wondered Gabriel.

"I just lost the knack for it. I can't do it anymore," Juice said as he started to now chug the water.

"See, a power like that just doesn't go away like the hair from the top of your head. It sticks with you always. My diagnosis is that you're mentally blocking it. That evil spirit who Memphis ordered to target you has really done a number on you. To get a flyer to deny his true power can be done by a number of effects. Self-doubt is extremely common. But you've always felt unworthy to possess such a power, and that has never kept you down before. See, after reading your file, I thought it was your broken heart. But no. That heartbreak is just the negative burden that the spirit has placed on you. So why do you think you believe you can't fly anymore?"

"Look, if I make an attempt to fly, would you drop it?" Juice replied in a frustrated tone. Gabriel asked him to take off and clear the sand dune west of them. Juice let out a deep breath and took off running down the hill. Juice then jumped, diving forward into the air, aiming his body to glide over the hill. But instead, he smashed straight into the hill getting covered in sand. Gabriel ordered him to try it again.

<hr>

Back at the swamp, all the material to set up the eating area was left outside of the cabin by Gard the night before. Will and James set up the canopy and the foldout table under it along with the small foldup chairs around the table, along with the coolers and the beverage dispenser placed within the shade of the canopy.

"So he just took him?" asked Will after getting the rundown of the archangel visit. James assured Will that Juice will be fine, and when he comes back, he'll be back to his old self. Will and James had just finished tying off the anchor ropes of the canopy. Once that was done, the two walked over to the chairs placed around the fire ring. On the chairs were the food supplies that needed to be taken to the coolers. Will said that he was happy that one of the archangels was willing to help as he lifted the four bags of ice. But then he asked why wouldn't the archangel help them fight for the order of the balance?

"The archangels were not put in charge of the balance, so they don't see this as their problem. When it comes to them fixing problems, they don't like to help groups, they'd rather just help individuals," James said as he picked up some grocery bags to carry them over to the table.

"Why Juice then?" questioned Will as he started to pour ice into the coolers.

"There is prophecy out there…written by a few prophets, actually, that says, 'The great ones fly.' Gabriel is the source of where that prophet came from." As James was speaking, he separated the cold food from the dry food on the table.

"Are you saying that Juice is a great one?" asked Will in slight disbelief.

"Anyone who carries Loomation inside them, whether it is dry or active, is a candidate for being a flyer. I don't know why the ones who can fly can. Mine and many others' theories suggest that it has something to do with inspiration. Someone who inspires others to be better."

Will never thought of Juice having a title of being a great one before. But what James said felt that it had some meaning to it. Juice was good at inspiring others to be in a better mood back when the group was still together. Will then remembered his last visit with Juice about two years ago. Will now felt that he understood why Juice didn't fly anymore and prayed that Gabriel could help him return to the air.

Will then spotted Hayden exiting his pop-up camper. Will told James to get the food ready, knowing that these guys were worst when they were hungry. James went shopping while the others were asleep last night. He bought enough food for a week. When Hayden sat down, he said he wanted water and a cereal bar. Will sat down and joined Hayden in eating while James continued to organize the coolers. Not too long after that, they heard Gard exit the cabin.

Gard had a shovel hanging over his shoulder in one hand. The shovel had toilet paper wrapped on the edge of the handle of the shovel. In Gard's other hand, he was carrying the camping toilet. Gard was marching out to the east side of the swamp, out past the campsite where they normally placed the toilet. It was obvious what Gard was doing, and Hayden yelled out that he was going to get to that after eating.

"I'm used to digging in the morning!" Gard hollered back.

The Hogs at the table knew that this must have been a hint at what Gard was doing when they found him in the cave. They looked at James to see if he could shine some light on this, but James said that he refused to give away someone's past.

Out in the White Sands of New Mexico, Juice was tumbling down a sand hill from yet another failed attempt to fly. He slowly got to his feet as Gabriel landed next to him. Gabriel pointed out that he didn't stay in the air that time. Juice brushed off the sand from his clothes in annoyance. Juice asked if they could be done with this now, admitting that he gave an honest attempt several times.

Gabriel knew that using physical force wouldn't be enough to make Juice fly, so Gabriel told Juice to take a seat in the sand. Gabriel sat next to him and offered him the water bottle again. As Juice took in sips, Gabriel asked him about the first time Juice took flight. Juice admitted that it wasn't anything special; he just jumped up high to get the attention of his friends. He added that he didn't come down after his jump, saying that he found himself stuck up there. Juice expected Gabriel to find his story on his first flight to be underwhelming, but Gabriel thought it was pretty interesting.

"Your friends must mean a lot to you," Gabriel stated.

"I guess they did."

"Why did you lose touch with them?"

Juice took a large swig of water before replying. He simply said that things like that happen, adding that friends move away, grow apart, saying it's hard to keep your friends when you get older.

"When would you say that you started to lose touch with your friends?"

"Back in late 2015, I received a letter from a friend, Kate Renshaw. See, before that time, she had a busy life, but we still managed to stay in touch by writing letters once a month. One day I got an angry letter where she admitted that she hated the Hang Out Group. She fully blames us for her family dying. She told me not to get in touch with her anymore."

"And how did that make you feel?" wondered Gabriel.

"I talked it over with a few Hang Out Group members. They were upset about this news but also understood her anger. They felt that it was best to respect her wishes and leave her be. Not too long after that, I moved to a new town, got a new apartment, and then…"

"Then you started seeing someone," Gabriel said as he knew about this story from reading the files.

Regardless, Juice continued on with the story of his tragic past.

"My tragic past started with a girl named Jess. I never really had a serious girlfriend before, so I was head over heels with dating this girl. We seemed perfect. We never seemed to have any disagreement and had the same sense of humor. Dating this girl caused me to stop staying in touch with my friends. I felt that Jess was all I needed in life. I had to let go of past friends such as Kate, so letting go of the rest of my friends came easy. Then after a long time of dating, she suddenly broke off the relationship. This breakup came out of nowhere, and I was deeply crushed by it. I was ready to tell her about my Loomation powers and my days fighting Big Foot and the devil. Finding someone who I felt comfortable sharing that information doesn't come around often, so it was very sad to see her go," Juice said as he picked up sand and chucked it.

"Then after months of blocking myself off from people, I was introduced to a new girl named Grace. Grace and I went on a few dates, and over time, we became a couple. Grace and I found ourselves in arguments a lot and couldn't decide on anything together. One day, Grace came over to my house to end the relationship, saying that she had been cheating on me with another person. I didn't take that too well. I was depressed when Jess broke up with me, but when Grace broke up with me, I found myself angry all the time.

"After that, I didn't care if there was no one in my life. I didn't want any friends or girlfriend, and I was okay with that. But Jess came back into my life and wanted to get back together. I hated the idea of getting back with her. One reason why was that I still didn't know why she called things off the first time, so what will keep her from ending things again? After she spent weeks of asking for forgiveness and pleading with me, I chose to get back together with her. I figured she was the only one who I almost shared my secret with, so I gave her another chance," Juice said, taking another sip of the water bottle.

"And this led to your last flight," Gabriel stated, knowing the ending of the story.

"We had plans on going to a movie, but she said she had to work late. I was just going to stay at my apartment for the night. But then I got a call from an old friend, Will, saying he was in town." Juice explained that this was the first time in three years since he'd seen a member of the Hang Out Group. He kind of wanted to say that he was busy, but he wasn't doing anything that night, so he made plans to meet up with him at the bar.

"I got to the bar a little early to get in a few beers before Will showed up. And as I was sitting in the booth, I looked over, and there's Jess making out with another guy." Juice then finished off the water in the bottle after that. "And boy, did I lose control." Juice admitted that he felt an uncontrollable closed-off dual personality take over his actions. This buried personality was created by one of Ray's inventions. It was an invention that implanted a dual personality on Juice's brain. He thought it was removed by Logan's healing spell, but it turned out that Logan just turned off the acting side effects. Once Juice felt that rage, the side effects came back to him very strong, and he felt his alter ego take control for the next couple of minutes.

"I marched out of my seat and pushed the guy kissing Jess to the ground hard. Jess was freaking out, demanding a chance to explain. But she grew silent when I looked at her, waiting for an explanation. She truly couldn't think of a way out of her situation at the moment. She knew she was caught in the act and was frozen.

"Then the guy rose up and tried to shove me away. Yeah, he just ended up sliding himself away from me. If I would have been upset, then yeah, that guy would have been able to beat me up. But I was ticked off to the max. I begged for him to hit me again, which he did, and he was able to land a few punches. It didn't hurt. In fact, it hurt his fist more than it hurt me.

"And that's when I was about to throw my first punch, one that would surely break his nose and make him cry." Juice paused to regain his breath. "As I was swinging my fist at the man, it was suddenly put to a stop by someone who came to my side. I looked over, and there was Will, asking me what was I doing."

"You think Will stopped you from sending someone to the ICU?" asked Gabriel.

"Oh, for sure." Juice nodded. "At the time, I completely forgot why I was at the bar in the first place. When I saw Will, it all came back to me. Will then pushed me out the back door of the bar. When we got out of the bar, Will was trying to get some answers out of me. I tried to get back in, but Will refused to get out of my way. So then…I rushed at him at full speed and carried him off the ground through the air. I flew out of the alley, slammed him into a building, then rotated my body and flew down the street to slam him into another building. Once Will was up against the building, he pushed off the wall, forcing me to crash into the street." Juice went on to say that was the last time he had flown. He was very lucky that it was in the middle of the night by a broken streetlight, and all the people were inside, so no one saw it happen.

Once they were on the ground, the fight seemed to stop. That dual personality in Juice's head seemed to calm down, but was still in a state of not caring about anything. Will was a little overwhelmed by the situation but felt that Juice just needed to get his rage out, and he would rather it be taken out on him rather than some helpless guy with no advanced strength. Juice explained that Will's visit was to ask him to attend Gard's funeral with him since this was the time Gard was presumed dead. Will thought that the Hang Out Group should attend. Juice was not interested on going to any Hang Out Group–related event, including a funeral. Will could tell that Juice was just angry and asked him to at least think about it. But Juice never went, and Will didn't have the courage to ask anyone else to go. It was a dark night for Juice. He officially decided to keep himself alone after that night.

Gabriel placed his hand on Juice's shoulder, telling him that he was sorry for his sad past. Gabriel then told Juice that a lot of his past was blamed on the evil spirit known as the Siren. "She's a worker for Memphis with the job of keeping an eye on you and to make your life as miserable as she can. The Siren is the spirit of false love. She was made back when the earth was in need of an aggressive expansion in some low-populated areas. The villages needed more life to be born, otherwise, the village wouldn't survive in the late future.

"The Siren was to spread false love to people to stir up unmitigated passion, causing people to give in to their primal instincts, urging them to do activities that sometimes lead to procreation. The couples were never a perfect match, far from it most times. But the Siren was able to have the humans ignore the negative features in each other and continue dating. She made people fall for the wrong person, and sometimes she would remove the thoughts of love, making them no longer want to be with that person. The time of doing it for procreation didn't last long, but she still loved the power of tricking people into saying 'I love you' when she knows they are under her influence.

"But over time, humans were falling for the wrong person without her influence. People were staying in bad relationships all on their own. So she barely got any orders from the devil, and that made her angry. When Memphis released the news of the devil being dead, she spread her false love to so many people, you included. She was asked by Memphis to keep an eye on you, and she did and played all her tricks on you, and in the end, she grounded a flyer. She was granted vast amounts of territory from Memphis after that."

"So she's the spirit who I need to kill to finally get over my lost-love pain?" asked Juice.

"It will be a strong help. And she's doing this to so many others throughout the planet. I'm not saying everyone will be happier when she's gone, but they will be able to see the bad relationship they're in more clearly. And the ones with the heartbreaks, they'll be able to move on easier."

Juice stood up, looked at the sky above the white sand, and wondered if he had what it took to take out the Siren. Juice said that if he can take flight, he would have more confidence on achieving this mission. So Juice tried to take off again, jumping high in the air, hoping to stay up.

Making Progress

Back at the swamp, James had everyone sitting at the eating table as he was now ready to tell them all about their evil spirits who had been following them the past five years. He first explained that the reason Memphis wanted them followed was because they had important information. That information was how they killed the devil. Since the Saints kept the detail on how exactly the devil was killed a secret, it grew to be a huge mystery among the angels and spirits. Lucky, none of the Hogs ever mentioned how they killed the devil, so no spirit has ever found out.

James started talking about Will's evil spirit, saying it was the horseman named War. Will felt the fact that War was following him over the last five years made sense. Will was a marine and was always stationed in places that never had any attacks until he showed up. Peaceful lands all of a sudden were being bombed by terrorists everywhere he went. James was happy to let Will know that War was killed during James's last assassination attempt on Memphis.

The Hogs now knowing that Will's spirit was killed understood why Will seemed to be the most positive of the group. The idea that they could feel that way by simply killing off their spirit felt too good to be true.

"I want to know mine," Hayden said while raising his hand.

James said that Hayden's spirit was named Phobia, the spirit of fear. Phobia lived up to his name, causing people to be afraid of heights, flying, spiders, and crowded spaces. Hayden knew exactly what this spirit made him fear, and he was more than willing to kill him for revenge, and maybe he can see what he once loved again.

"Timber, you had the horseman Death. Eric, you had horseman Famine. Gard, you originally had the evil spirit of greed, but he died during one of the battles with the angels. After he died, the Grim Reaper took over. And Miles, you have the horseman Pestilence."

The Hogs figured that Pestilence being Miles's spirit explained his mental health problem, a problem that seemed to have faded away after his visit to the gates of Heaven. Eric asked James if any of their spirits had been killed off recently. James said that War was the last one killed off. James mentioned that the evil side of the balance was once higher, but after the death of War, the bar dropped a bit. James said that the bar will keep dropping as they move forward to kill off the spirits, and the Hogs will feel so much better afterward. James could see that some of the Hogs were unsure of joining him on this fight.

"When we find theses spirits, how are we supposed to kill them?" asked Gard.

"How did you manage to kill the devil?" The big unknown question was finally asked by James, and he was a little shocked by how casually he asked it. James checked and saw that no evil spirit had territory anywhere near the swamp before making that their home base, so it was safe to discuss this information.

"We had a sword," Timber uttered.

"Hayden shot him in the head with some modified bullets," Miles added.

"I stabbed him in the throat with Hayden's diamond-tipped knife," Gard mentioned.

"That, and we were in a place where humans feel no pain," Eric brought up.

"But overall, it was the sword that did the trick," Hayden stated.

"Yeah, Cain was able to use that thing to slice the devil's arm clean off," said Timber.

"Where did this sword come from? The workers in the armory have failed to craft a blade strong enough to cut deep into Memphis's thick skin, let alone his bone," James replied.

"Logan said that the sword came from the Garden," informed Will.

James couldn't think of any sword that came from the Garden of Eden. But if it was strong enough to kill the devil, he could understand why the Saints wanted to keep the weapon top secret. James told the Hogs if they can get their hands on that sword again, then fixing the balance may be easier than they thought.

Some of the Hogs shied away from the idea of returning to the Garden. A lot of bad, scary, sad memories lay there. The Hogs still remembered the way to get in: two people who carried Loomation needed to touch the rock that covered the entrance. That alone was an annoying task to do. Hayden stood up, saying he was going to retrieve the sword. Gard said he'd go along with Hayden, saying he's in the mood to stretch his legs.

"I would like to go retrieve my car. I left it at that house that took us to the gates of Heaven. And if you guys want me staying here any longer, I'm going to need some supplies besides food. Like a toothbrush and some clean clothes," Eric stated.

"I can teleport the ones who still have cars parked back at the safe house so they can drive home to pick up their stuff," James replied.

"Does this mean that you guys are on board on fixing the balance?" Will asked with hope in his tone.

The answer was still unsure for Eric, Gard, and Miles. Will was happy that they were sticking around to take their time on their decision.

"James, just teleport Juice's car here. My bag is already in there. All of my stuff was able to fit in a duffel bag," Hayden said.

Miles added that all his stuff was also packed into a bag located in Juice's car.

"I haven't been to my place in almost two years. I have no idea where my stuff is," Gard mentioned.

"Well, I bet it's all sold, with you being declared dead and all," Timber said.

Gard was shocked by that information. He had no idea that he was declared dead. His shock went away pretty quickly because it was something he theorized. Just hearing it out loud made him grow silent.

"Hey, if James's teleporting you guys to your cars, how are we supposed to get to the Garden?" Hayden asked to get things back on topic.

"Miles, you can do it, right?" Eric asked, looking at Miles, thinking he was now healthy enough to do it.

Miles felt put on the spot. Just a few days ago, he would have said no way, but with his mind a little clearer, he was willing to give it a try.

"Do any of you even have a phone?" wondered Timber.

"Yes, I do…unfortunately," Hayden mumbled.

"If you guys get in trouble, you call us," Will brought up.

Hayden asked what his number was. Hayden then put the numbers of Will, Timber, and Eric inside his phone. James gathered up Will, Timber, and Eric, getting ready to teleport them to the safe house to retrieve their cars.

After they disappeared, Miles walked over to Hayden and Gard. Miles with nervous hands rested them on the two. And with a deep breath, Miles was able to teleport them to the mountain that contained the Garden of Eden.

<hr>

Back at the white sands of New Mexico, Juice once again failed to stay in the air. Juice was growing frustrated. He dropped his butt onto the sand to rest up as Gabriel stood in front of him to block the sun. He told Gabriel that maybe he couldn't do it anymore because he doesn't like the person who he became. He was thinking that he may no longer carry what it takes to be a flyer. Gabriel assured him that every part of Juice is a flyer. He just needed to remember the feelings that made him have the energy to fly.

"You once cared deeply for your friends. You were the one who wanted to be there for your friends whenever they needed help. You stopped wanting to do that at the worst possible time. But now you have your chance to be that person again," Gabriel said, trying to find that spark to make Juice fly.

"Maybe it wasn't fully me," Juice said, thinking of something inside him. "There is this infection inside me. It once made me a different person, a person who hurt my friends. And I think it was active again. I hurt Will when it became active. Maybe I need to remove that part of me in order to be my true self again."

"Look, I can fully remove that evil side of you out of your mind. But only if you show me that you can fly first."

"I think you're missing the point here. I can't fly until I'm happy with who I am, and I can't do that with this other side of me attached to my brain."

"You were always able to fly with that infection inside your mind. And I think what's keeping you grounded now is your focus on the past. Try to focus on what you want to do next. Forget the past, focus on your future!"

Juice felt that what Gabriel said was a good point, so he rose to his feet. Juice closed his eyes and thought about what he was going to do after he accomplished his goal at hand. He knew that he wanted to be there for the Hogs again. But he knew that there was another friend who he wished to make an amends with first. And the idea of helping others again caused his feet to be lifted off the ground.

Juice opened his eyes and looked down. A whimsical feeling took over his mood, and he felt a burst of energy that he used to skyrocket up high in the air, causing the sand below him to be tossed into the air in every direction. Juice was as high as a cloud, and he cheered out loud in an expression of joy. Juice was taking off all around the air, feeling the joy of the wind on his face once again. He didn't think that he would ever ride the high winds of the sky again, and he was so happy to be wrong.

Juice landed back on the ground and ran over next to Gabriel. "Did you see that? I'm back in the skies again!" Juice yelled in a happy tone.

"Alright, flyer, a deal's a deal," Gabriel said as he placed his right hand on Juice's forehead. "Now stay still, and I'll have that infection permanently removed from you."

Juice stayed still as Gabriel worked his active Loomation powers on him.

All of a sudden, the sand around Juice started to get caught in a swirling windstorm. The wind grew wilder, and there was so much sand drifting in the air, Juice could no longer see anything but Gabriel and the twisting sand. Then Juice felt a heavy pressure slam against his head, and he took a step back as if his whole body was being pushed. Juice felt that he had the wind knocked out of him as he felt that something was pulled out of his entire body. Gabriel even felt winded from this event, being shocked on how much energy this took to accomplish. They were both barely standing as the winds died down, leaving sand piles all around them.

"You okay?" asked Juice.

"Yeah, just thought removing that thing would have been easier, I guess." Gabriel then checked to see how Juice was doing. Juice said besides being a little light-headed, he felt great. He was 100 percent sure that it worked; the dual personality that had haunted him for so long felt completely gone.

"Good, because now you need to kill the Siren. After that, you'll be ready to return to the Hogs being your good old self."

"There is one more thing I want to do first. I was wondering if you can take me to someone first," Juice asked, pleading in a way.

"I know exactly who you're talking about, and I know where she is." After Gabriel said that, he placed his hand on Juice and teleported him away.

Not too long after the two left, a sand pile that was behind Juice started to shake from underneath. Then a hand emerged from the white sand, followed by a head. This person buried in the sand had the same face as Juice. The man was, in fact, Juice, but not really. He was the living embodiment of Juice's dual personality. The power Gabriel used to remove the infection from Juice's brain seemed to activate something that brought him to life.

The man took his first breaths and clambered out of the sand pile as if he was being born into the world from the sand.

An Old Friend

Hayden, Gard, and Miles were standing at the entrance of the Garden of Eden. Hayden, not wanting to waste any time, placed his hand on the rock. Hayden eyed the two others, wondering who wanted to be the key for the door. Gard quietly volunteered and placed his hand on the rock. The rock started to drain the two humans like they were beverages being consumed by a straw. The two Hogs dropped to their knees while their hands were still stuck to the rock. The rock moved out of the way all on its own to reveal the great Garden of Eden.

Once the door was open, both Hayden and Gard dragged themselves to the ramp that was in front of them. Being fully past the rock and onto the ramp, their strength started to come back to them to a point where they could stand up. Miles walked onto the ramp, and the three looked out into the beautiful sight of the Garden and felt and thought nothing of it. This place was ground zero for all their terrifying memories. Over the last five years, they'd all faced new horrors, but this place still topped them all. Fighting the devil to the death would make any place lose its beauty.

"Come on, let's go get the sword," Hayden said, wanting to get a move on.

As Hayden started heading down the ramp, Miles spoke out and said something. "This is where Juice made us take that photo. Remember?"

Hayden stopped his walk to turn back at Miles. "You know, you're right," Hayden replied.

"I can't believe that was ten years ago," Gard uttered.

The picture was still hanging on the outside cabin wall right next to the front door. But none of the Hogs bothered to look at it when they returned to the swamp last night.

"Juice thought that we would never be back here again. How I wish he was right," Miles said.

The three Hogs had a nice memory during their time in the Garden, and if it wasn't for Miles mentioning it, they would have forgotten all about it. The three then marched into the Garden to retrieve their sword. Hayden led the way, but all three remembered the area where they killed the devil.

When they arrived, it was just as they left it. The devil's body was exactly the same way it looked the day he was killed. The sword was still stuck into the ground, with the devil's body between the ground and the handle. It was truly a disturbing image.

Miles squatted down, taking a good look at the sight. "You know, there was a time when I thought that this wasn't real, that we never entered the Garden, and that there was never any devil." Miles then looked over to Hayden and Gard. "I was going through a bad time. I thought my active Loomation powers weren't real. I got to an unhealthy point where I didn't know what was real and what wasn't. I couldn't understand basic feelings such as hunger, tiredness, or even loneliness. I once went three days without eating because I thought my hunger feelings weren't real. I did my best to avoid sleep because I was terrified to dream. That's how I ended up in the mental hospital."

Both Hayden and Gard didn't know how to react to Miles's opening up speech. They felt bad for their friend and was happy to see him doing much better now. It was a needed reminder to prove to him that what happened was real, and he was a fool to ever deny his own mind.

After Miles's speech, Hayden walked up to the corpse and removed the sword from the dead body. The blade was covered in blood, so Hayden used the grass to wipe it all off. Holding the sword gave Hayden a mighty feeling. He forgot that powerful burst of energy that came from holding the handle of the sword. Holding that sword again made Hayden feel braver, and he needed that feeling. The three had what they came for, so they marched their way out of the Garden.

⋘◈◈◈⋙

As the sun was going down, Juice and Gabriel arrived in the town where Kate lived. Gabriel figured that Juice would want to see her, so he checked her whereabouts from the gates of Heaven's hall of records. They teleported to a vacant alley hidden from the bustling city traffic. They peeked out of the alley and spotted Kate entering some bar.

"Same bar every football Sunday this season," Gabriel stated. "She always sits at one of the small tables close to the TVs and always orders a large rack of ribs."

"Got it, I'm going in," Juice replied as he walked past Gabriel onto the sidewalk.

"Just send me a prayer, and I'll be back to pick you up. I got to run up to the gates to pick up something," Gabriel said before teleporting away.

Juice gave a thumbs-up just before Gabriel vanished. Juice made his way to the bar to have a talk with an old friend.

Kate found her usual seat and gave a wave to the bartender, signaling him of her arrival. Kate always preordered her ribs so that they would be ready by the time she got there. She sat down with three different TVs right in her view so she could keep track of her fantasy football teams. Watching football was something she used to do with her dad, so she always made time to watch Sunday football.

As she was watching the screens, Juice popped up in her view, taking the chair across from her.

"Hey, Kate, mind if I sit here?" questioned Juice politely.

"What are you doing here? How did you even find me? Get out of here! You're blocking my view of the TVs!" Kate yelled out in anger.

"I'm going to take that as a yes," Juice said as he moved the chair over to not block Kate's view.

"I told you guys to leave me alone."

"If it helps, I came alone."

Just then, the bartender delivered Kate's plate of ribs. "Here you go, Karen, and here is your whiskey."

As the bartender walked away, Juice asked for a glass of water. "Karen? I thought you were done with the fake names," wondered Juice.

"What do you want, Tyler? Why are you even here?" she said as she grabbed her food.

"I missed my friend." Juice actually found it odd that it took him so long to say that about any of his friends. "You used to come to and see the Hang Out Group when you were free from work and even came to a few of our Thanksgiving dinners. I just wanted to know what changed your view on us."

"You really want to know why?" she said as she turned away from the TV and put down her food.

Juice nodded, knowing that it'd help to get the information out in the open.

"It was back in 2015. I finally decided to legally change my last name back to Renshaw."

"Well, that's fantastic! I know it was something you always talked about doing."

"Yeah, well, it turns out my father's enemies were a lot more than just Ray. And when they found out that there was another Renshaw out there, they learned that I was his daughter. So my father's enemies tried to kill me. And at the time, I was still running Salt Water Chemicals, which made things worse! Did you know that back in the day, if you wanted Cain Renshaw—or Cain the animal, as most people knew him— the common phrase was 'They're always hiring at the SWC.' Well, it turns out that phrase was still remembered by some people because I had my father's enemies come right up to my office trying to be a part of a team fixed on killing me. I bet you can image their surprise when they found out I was in charge of the office!"

Juice had no idea about any of this. He wished that she would have asked the Hogs for help back when her life was threatened. She mentioned that she could protect herself and be able to defend herself from most of the threats. She was a skilled fighter and was able to land a bullet on target when needed.

"The thing that made me shut down the factories and go on the run under a new name was when the Havocs showed up to my office."

"The Havocs? I thought the remaining members were either in jail or dead."

"Well, some of them escaped prison, and some of the members who left the group before you guys got the remaining members arrested came back to the group. The guys were able to rebuild the group, and they've been doing a lot of work ever since."

Kate mentioning the return of the Havocs was just another thing on Juice's fear list making a comeback.

"They wanted me to lead their group and take charge of the mission on tracking down the Hang Out Group."

"Why would they want to find us?"

"They believe you still have the cube. And not to mention you guys are the reason why the group was destroyed back in 2010."

Juice felt that he kind of knew that answer when he asked and felt a little dumb for asking it. Juice asked why none of the Hogs had seen or heard from any Havoc member in all this time. Kate said that since she didn't join them, they knew that they would have to wait until their forces were strong enough to take out seven Loomation carriers.

"The more missions they do, the more money they get, which leads to better guns and more members. They're not going to underestimate you guys like last time," Kate said as she took a sip of her drink. Kate saw that this information was a lot for Juice to take in.

Juice didn't tell Kate this, but he and his friends had a lot to deal with already. Adding the return of the Havocs to that list was very overwhelming.

"I knew that the Havocs would one day come back to me. I feared that they would use me to get to you guys. The guys just knew your hometown. They couldn't remember any of your names or addresses. So I shut down the factories, took my fortune, and moved from place to place under a different name. But not until I first wrote the group a letter expressing my anger for being in this position!"

"Kate, your letter didn't mention anything about your death threats or about the Havocs."

"Yeah, well, I had my dad on my mind as I was writing it out. I was thinking if my father was still alive, he would be able to handle all this for me. But no, he was killed. And the people who were supposed to watch his back failed and got to walk out of the Garden with their lives still intact," Kate said before shoving her drink back into her mouth. "I just got my dad back after a twenty-year coma, such a little time before I lost him forever."

Kate now started to tear up from her loud conversion.

"My father loved me! He was the strongest one out there, and every time he left the mansion, I knew he would always come back alive. He came home in a coma once, but he still wasn't dead."

Kate's loud words started to turn into a softer tone.

"Then he goes into the Garden of Eden with a grandfather who I didn't even know existed with the Hang Out Group, and there I lose my only family I had left."

Kate couldn't stop the tears falling down her face. She absolutely hated showing any signs of weakness. It went against all that her father asked of her. Never show fear was his motto to her, and she just couldn't help but to think that she was letting him down every time she did. Juice was pretty shocked with all this information. He could tell her what she had already been told a dozen times by the Hang Out Group. He could have told her that her father died in an attempt to keep her safe from the great evil from ever attacking her. But she didn't need to hear what she already knew; that wouldn't cheer her up.

"You left your entire life just to protect the Hang Out Group," Juice said, thinking of her as a true friend. "I don't think anyone has ever done something more kind and loyal for us than what you did. And trust me, we just made a friend who got us out of an execution sentence." Juice then gave her a small shake on her shoulder. "Kate, what you did is exactly what a Renshaw would do. Leave their entire life to keep the ones they love safe. Your grandfather abandoned his wife and newborn son for decades in order to keep them safe. Your father went into a fight where he was up against a threat that was stronger than he was because he wanted to make sure his daughter will be safe. You are a Renshaw, and you don't need a legal document to prove it!"

Kate then faced Juice. Juice told her that the Hogs were her friends, and they owed her a thousand favors. Kate smiled, starting to feel the friendship she once had with Juice start to reignite. She did add that it wasn't just protecting the Hogs' identification on why she left. There were still enemies of her father trying to kill her every now and then.

"So just got out of an execution sentence, huh. What have you boys been up to?" Kate asked in a friendly tone.

"It's a real long story. It goes all the way back to the beginning of humans actually."

"Why am I only slightly surprised," Kate said with a small laugh, not thinking it was true. "It's always something with you guys."

"The group is currently going through some issues at the moment. We're in the need of some dangerous, life-threatening therapy. And I'm about to face mine, and I wanted to make sure that we were okay before I go, in case the worst happens to me," Juice said as he picked up Kate's phone from the table.

"Life-threating? What are you talking about?"

"I promised myself that I wouldn't go back to the Hogs until I took care of my problem. This means I need to face this threat by myself." Juice then sent himself a text message from Kate's phone so now he would now have her number. "If you don't hear from me, can you go to the Hogs and tell them I'm sorry? We're staying at your grandfather's old cabin in the swamp." Juice then placed her phone back on the table and headed to the back exit.

Kate ran after him feeling like she needed more information. When she made it to the exit, she found herself standing in a poorly lit parking lot with no Juice in sight.

Juice flew off as soon as he could before Kate could reach him.

Killing the Siren

After Juice's meetup with Kate, he returned to Gabriel on a nearby rooftop. Gabriel asked how his visit with Kate went. Juice was happy to say that he thinks that he was able to rekindle that old friendship. Gabriel was happy to hear that because he had everything ready for Juice to face the Siren. Juice was eager to face the spirit who has tortured his and hundreds of others' love lives.

Gabriel had an angel rifle (also known as an AG weapon) strapped to his back and swung it off to present to Juice. "Here's some gates of Heaven heavy artillery!" Gabriel said as he handed it over to Juice. The weapon was gray, six feet long, with a barrel that could fire off green rounds that were the size of a baseball. "The weapon can only be fired by someone who carries Loomation. This is a newer model, made specifically to be fired by nonspiritual forces. A feature that we only just recently added due to Memphis pilfering AG weapons from fallen angles after battles. It's fully loaded, but you're only going to need one bullet for the Siren. One shot on her will cause her body to instantly decay. Now it would take multiple shots for someone as powerful as a horseman, so try not to use up all the ammo."

"Okay. Now I'm not going to get in trouble by killing this spirit, am I?" asked Juice, remembering the consequence of killing the devil.

"The Saints allow you to live so you could be a fighter for Heaven. So taking out any spirit who's not respecting the rules of the balance is allowed to be killed off due to their defiant crime," Gabriel stated. Gabriel then informed Juice how to fire off the gun so he would know what to do when it was time to fire the weapon. "Since the Siren isn't as powerful as some of the others, the Saints were able to find out where she is." Gabriel paused before revealing the next part. "She's your landlord, Juice."

Juice turned his face away from the rifle to face Gabriel. "Susan? That monster!" Juice said with a shocked look on his face. "I knew she gave me way too good of a deal on that apartment! And now that I think about it, she did introduce me to both of the girls who ended up breaking my heart. So yeah, that does make sense now that I hear it out loud."

"Now a little information you should know. She's strong, so don't let her toss you around. She can release a defense spell, but most spirits hate doing that while in physical form. And whatever you do, don't fall in love with her."

"With how rude she's been to me over the years, I'm surprised I haven't fallen in love with her already," Juice said, making his first joke in years.

"I'm serious, she's the spirit of false love. With one look, you could be head over heels for her and go from trying to kill her to wanting to buy her flowers. To be honest, that's why I think it's best for you to go up against her alone. She loves making people fight for her hand."

"Well, fine, I promise I won't fall in love with her. I'll just make sure I kill her before I do!" Juice said, starting to feel a little overwhelmed by what he was about to do. It's been years since he faced off against something stronger than himself. He was starting to get nervous, and as a result of that, he started yelling.

Gabriel let out a joyful laugh at Juice's response. Gabriel teleported Juice to his apartment and was ready to leave him on his own.

The two stood in the apartment looking around the place. Juice didn't bother turning on the lights in the room as all the light bulbs were burned out. This was why he didn't have any curtains; the outside streetlights were able to keep the place from being pitch-dark. Juice asked one more time if Gabriel was sure that he didn't want to help him. Gabriel said that he helped enough, and he doesn't like to get into a fight if he didn't have to. He did say that if Juice survives the attack, he'll return to teleport him back to the swamp. With those words, the archangel disappeared from the room.

Juice then retrieved his phone from his pocket. He saw that he had a few missed calls and unopened text messages from Kate. But Juice ignored it; he wanted to keep focused on his mission and made a call to his landlord Susan. She picked up, and Juice said, "Hey, Susan, so my water has been tasting funny for a while now. I know it's late, but I was wondering if you could stop by to take a look at it."

Susan said that she was about to head over to the building, so she can stop by the room to check out the sink. She said she'd be there in less than an hour. Juice said okay and ended the call. Juice's heart started to beat fast because an evil monster was on her way to his apartment. He felt that he should clean up the place real quick since guests were coming.

After Juice did all he could do around the apartment to keep himself busy, he started to pace back and forth for the last few minutes. The knock at the door made Juice jump up and let out a small scream. "Alright, Juice, the spirit of false love is right behind that door. Just open it up for her and stick to the plan," Juice whispered to himself as he was frozen with fear. Then more knocks came to the door. "It's open!" Juice shouted, being too scared to get the door himself.

Susan opened the door and walked in carrying a toolbox. "Hey, Tyler, sorry it took so long, but I made it, so let's take a look at that sink," she said with a big smile. She headed to the kitchen, dropped the toolbox on the ground, and crawled underneath the sink to take a look at the pipes.

Juice walked into the kitchen and leaned against the fridge. He then eyed that small gap between the fridge and counter. He saw the large towel stuffed in the spot. Behind that towel was where Juice stashed the angel gun.

"Do you have a problem with the electric also? Why are all the lights off?" she asked with a silly tone as she switched on her small flashlight.

"Oh, all the light bulbs burned out and such. I have been meaning to go out and buy some new bulbs, but I found out that the electric bill is way lower this way."

Susan emitted a friendly laugh at that response. "Well, I may have some extra bulbs down in my office in the basement. I can have that new tenant bring them over to you. She was asking about you when she moved in."

"That new girl who works at the gas station? She asked about me?" For a moment there, Juice almost forgot what he was going to do. The girl was using her powers, and Juice almost didn't notice it. Juice's plan was so simple. Once the spirit was under the sink, he'd dash to the gun and shoot her. But Juice was having second thoughts on this; she didn't look like some evil spirit made to cause humans to feel pain, anger, and hate. She was really sweet and kind. When Juice saw the devil, it was a nightmare image accompanied with a horrible voice. Juice had to be sure that this girl was an evil spirit and not some nice girl with beautiful hair.

"You know after my last relationship, I don't feel ready to start dating again."

"Hey, I know that Jess cheated on you, but that's no reason to keep yourself from getting back out there."

Juice was shocked to hear Susan say that. Juice talked about his breakup with Jess the second time, but he never mentioned the fact that she cheated on him. Juice knew how she was aware of that information—it was because she was the Siren. Juice felt that it was now or never, so he sprung for the gun behind the towel. With the weapon in his hand, he aimed it at the Siren.

"I'm sorry, but I'm now a fighter for the balance, and I have to take out any who breaks that order," Juice said as he pointed the rifle at Susan. Juice couldn't fire the gun right away; he had to add pressure to the handle of the gun. The gun needed a boost of Loomation power from the one holding it in order for it to be fired. Since the dry Loomation in Juice was at a low amount, it took a few seconds to warm up.

"Tyler…you're not going to use that on me, are you?" the Siren asked with the most innocent face she could deliver. She batted her big eyes at him and issued him a coy smile.

Juice lowered the gun, gave off an embarrassing blush, and said no.

"Good," she said as her innocent smile turned into a sinister grin. She flung her feet back and slammed them into Juice's chest.

Juice was flung back and landed on the coffee table in the living room. The Siren took out a large red steel pipe wrench from her toolbox and marched up to Juice.

Juice had the air knocked out of him and started feeling a strong stinging pain in his chest. Juice now knew for sure that his landlord was indeed the evil spirit. Juice faced the spirit and received a swing from the wrench to the face that knocked him to the window. After Juice smashed into the window, he used his flying powers to keep himself from falling out of the room. Juice flew back at the Siren, charging in for an attack. But the Siren was too fast and was able to tackle him down to the ground. She placed the wrench sideways on Juice's throat and pushed down with all her might while Juice did his best to force the wrench off his throat.

You're back to flying now, Tyler. You know Memphis gave me a lot extra territory for being able to ground the flyer," she said as she continued to strangle Juice. "Did those Saints remove your dual personality?" She brought her nose up to Juice's head. She could no longer detect the infection inside Juice, which meant Memphis's experiment may have worked. She took a moment while she was suffocating Juice to send Memphis a telepathic message to let him know that the Cider project may have worked.

After she delivered her message, a knock at the door was heard.

"IT'S OPEN!" Juice shouted with all his might, hoping that a miracle was behind that door.

The door opened, and in the hallway was Kate.

"Kate, there's an angel gun in the kitchen! It can kill her!"

Kate eyed the fancy-looking gun in the kitchen and dashed toward it as fast as she could. The Siren took the wrench off Juice's throat and swung it across Juice's face, hitting his face with a mighty blow. While Juice was feeling the massive pain on his head, Susan ran after Kate to stop her from getting to the gun. Susan pulled back on Kate's shoulder just before she reached the gun. Kate turned her body toward the Siren and delivered a strong right punch to the spirit's face.

Susan had no idea that Kate had advanced strength, so she didn't expect that punch to be so painful. Kate didn't stop at one punch; she started up her boxing training and threw three more punches at Susan before showing off her kicking skills by kicking her hard in the chest, knocking her to the back wall. Kate turned back to the gun and picked it up while Juice shouted out the instructions on how to fire it.

"Press down on the handle until you feel a slight twitch, then pull the trigger!"

Kate heard the gun start to boot up as she held down on the handle of the gun. The Siren got to her feet and ran straight at Kate. Just before the spirit reached Kate, the gun gave off the twitch in her hand, and Kate pulled the trigger. A green spear blasted out of the gun and struck the Siren dead center of her chest. The impact of the green bullet pushed her back, slamming into the wall, causing drywall to fall around her. Just like that, the spirit was gone.

Kate saw no moment from the threat, so she put the gun at ease and ran over to check on Juice. She helped him to his feet and checked his eye. She said that it was really swollen. Juice tried to say thank you, but his throat was hurting too much, he only whispered. It really hurt for him to shout out the things he said to her, but it saved their lives, so he didn't care.

The two looked at the fallen Siren and saw it start to decay. The ammo that killed the spirit was safely melting the body away, leaving no trace of the spirit. Kate had never seen anything like this before. She only heard of the great evil that her dad died from, so now seeing a spirit of evil made her believe the stories of the Hogs' fight in the Garden even more.

Juice thanked Kate for the save and asked how she found him. Kate said that she looked Juice up on social media and saw that he lived only an hour away. After Juice left her at the bar, she jumped into her car to find him. She could tell that he was going to do something dangerous and didn't want him to face it alone. Juice gave his friend a hug, saying that she saved his life.

After that, Gabriel arrived in the room. He congratulated the two on their first evil spirit kill. Gabriel gave Juice a heal spell, and his body was now in perfect condition. Juice could yell without any hint of throat pain. Juice introduced Kate to Gabriel, and they shook hands. Gabriel asked Juice if he was ready to return to the Hogs. Juice said he wanted to grab some stuff first, but he wanted to take Kate somewhere before returning to the swamp.

After Juice packed up everything he thought he would need, he told Gabriel to take them to the entrance of the Garden. Kate smiled because she never knew it, but she had always wanted to visit the Garden. Once there, both Juice and Kate was the key to open the door. Juice showed Kate the beautiful land, and they walked up to the burial sites of her family.

Kate sat in the grass between the two grave markers. Juice said that he'll give his friend some space. She read the names: Logan Charles Renshaw and Cain Parker Renshaw. She teared up as she started to talk to her father. Juice stood far enough away to not be able to hear her. After she waved him back over, Juice walked up to her. She thanked him for bringing her there. She really needed this; she needed to say goodbye and to have closure.

Juice then thought of something. He then dug his hand into the spot between the buried crosses. Juice pulled the cube out from the ground. Juice thought that this cube could come in handy in the fight for the order of the balance. Juice asked Kate if she was ready to go. Kate took out her phone and took a photo of the place so she could always look at it whenever she missed her family. After that, the two left the Garden.

"Are you sure you don't want to help? You kicked that spirit's butt back there," Juice stated.

"I think you boys need to solve this together. Just give me a call when it's all fixed."

"What are you going to do next?"

"Well, you guys are helping the world in the spiritual way. So I'm going to find a more down-to-earth way to help. I'm going to be reopening the factories. I'll be offering the past workers their jobs back and also offering new jobs to people who could use a solid paycheck."

"Well, I know that you can handle yourself when trouble comes your way. If they're smart, they'll stay away."

"And you guys stay safe. Not just the evil spirits, but from the Havocs as well. They'll be coming for you, so make sure you're ready."

"We will."

After that, Juice and Kate had one last hug, and Gabriel teleported Juice back to the swamp. But Kate was fine staying on the side of the mountain. She had money to get back home on her own. She wanted to stay in the place where her grandfather hiked to; she wanted to walk around the place for a chance to feel closer to him.

Back to Life

Monday, October 5, 2020

That morning, Hayden was out on a walk around the swamp area. He stepped back on his old hiking trails that he used to march on when the group would visit the area. He was trying to recapture that nostalgic feeling of the good times staying out there. But still, he didn't like being back at the swamp; it wasn't the same. He could tell that the others were having that same feeling. Will was the only one who was enjoying his stay at the campsite. Hayden would have given anything to have that same feeling, but nothing was working for him. He knew what the swamp was missing—it was the campfires he used to build. But he couldn't bear the sight of fire, so he couldn't bring himself to start or allow any fires.

He started to make his way back to camp. While on the way, he spotted Will on his morning run and gestured to him a wave.

Back at the campsite, Miles saw James holding the sword that was retrieved from the Garden. James was fascinated by the weapon as he held it close to this face.

"How long are you going to be looking at that thing?" wondered Miles.

"The Saints never wanted the spirits or angels to ever know about this," James said as he gave the sword a twirl. "And now I understand why. A blade strong enough to kill the devil could possibly be the most powerful weapon in existence. Power like that shouldn't be in anyone's hands. I now know why the archangels refuse to let the Saints build more powerful weapons. This is the weapon that destroyed the balance, and now it's the only hope on fixing it."

"You know, I think Hayden used to use it to chop up firewood that summer when we had it in our possession," Miles said as he took a bite of his Pop-Tart.

"A weapon like this shouldn't be used for foolish chores!" James snapped at Miles. "It shouldn't be used at all. It should be locked away, buried, never to be spoken of again." James set the sword back on the table and took one of the chairs. He looked back up to Miles, who was still munching away on his cold Pop-Tart.

"I'm sorry I raised my voice. It's the sword…holding it gave me a sudden gust of strong energy that pierced through my body. It was incredible."

"Yeah, that's how the others described it. A powerful blast of confidence hit them like a mighty ocean wave," Miles said, looking at the sword.

"Did you have the same feeling when you touched it?" wondered James.

"No, I never touched it. When it came to carrying weapons, I had my active Loomation to keep me safe and alive."

"How have you been feeling by the way? Your teleporting trip to the Garden and back went well? You think you'll be ready to fire off defense spells again?"

"Look, I'm still not sure if I want to fight for the order of the balance. I'm not the same fighter I once was. I have been doing well *thinking*-wise since the trip to the gates, but I feel like I'm slowly drifting back to the guy Juice and Hayden picked up from the mental hospital," Miles said as he lowered his head. "I'm afraid of freezing up in battle and not having the concentration to use my active Loomation."

"Well, I'm glad that you're still here. I think you spending time with your old friends is helping. And now that we have this sword, we can kill the horseman who has done this to you."

James and Miles had a nice chat. James was happy that Miles has been opening up to the others, sharing his fears and his past. James believed that when push came to shove, Miles will find the old warrior that was inside him.

Not too long after that, Timber and Eric joined the two at the table for breakfast. When Will and Hayden returned, Will asked the nagging question. "When is Juice coming back?"

"He got back late last night. I'm surprised none of you guys noticed," James said as he pointed high up the tree trunks of the nearby trees. That was when the group saw him lying in a hammock high up in the trees with a blanket resting over his head to keep his face safe from flying bugs.

"Juice, you're back up in the tree!" Will shouted with joy.

This call out to Juice woke him up, and he pulled the blanket off his head to emerge into the morning sunlight as he turned toward to his friends. "Good morning, Hang Out Group!" Juice cheered out as he flew out of his bed and landed by the table.

"Oh great, he's back to flying again," Eric said with a sarcastic tone. The reminder of Juice flying nonstop while they were out in the swamp came back to the group, and he remembered that it did get a little annoying after a while.

"It's so good to see you all again!" Juice said as he patted Eric on the shoulder, along with Timber, Miles, and Hayden as he circled around the table. When he reached Will, he delivered a high five.

"We've been together for the last few days now," Hayden mumbled.

"Juice, did you kill your spirit?" Will asked with a bright mood.

"Absolutely not. In fact, she came close to killing me. If it wasn't for Kate showing up, you guys would be down a flyer," Juice said with a humorous tone. "Kate killed the spirit, but how she got there, well, that's a completely different story altogether. She's fine and trying to relaunch her business. But when I got back here, I noticed that the bar of the evil side of the balance dropped a little last night." Juice pointed over to the balance.

The glowing balance James painted into the air worked as a nightlight. In the dark, it was easy to see, but in the bright sunlight, it was very transparent and faded.

"That's great, Juice! So you're in for a fighter for the balance now?" James asked.

"Yes, I am! Thanks to my help, people are able to see the bad relationship that they are in. Couples are losing the heavy urge to cheat on their spouses, and the ones with the broken hearts can move on sooner. And if taking out the other evil spirits would lead to others feeling this peaceful, I want to do all I can to make others feel this great too!"

James was so happy to hear this, and he could see how the others were envious of Juice's newfound joy. James had never seen Juice like this before; it was like he was seeing a completely different person and was so happy to have him on his team.

"Where's Gard? He needs to be out here with us. He needs to know that it feels great to be alive!" Juice yelled as he rushed over to the cabin. When Juice reached the cabin, he opened the door wide, bellowing, "Good morning!" Juice's happy face turned into a frown because the cabin was empty. Juice checked under the sleeping cot just to make sure there was no one in the cabin. Juice popped his head out to inform the group that Gard wasn't inside. This made everyone grow uneasy because no one noticed Gard leaving the cabin. The last anyone saw of him was last night before going to bed. Hayden and Will both got up early, but they both took off on hikes within the swamp.

James didn't even know where Gard was, and the Hogs grew concerned, wondering if he had been taken by an evil spirit. James said that if an evil or positive spirit would have visited the swamp, he would have known. James said that it was possible for Gard to have left the swamp while he wasn't looking. The Hogs wondered why Gard would leave without telling anyone. Where would he go, and would he be alright on his own?

Will didn't know if Gard was safe out there on his own and wanted to start a rescue party in order to find him. Juice said that he'll start circling the swamp from the skies, thinking that maybe Gard didn't get too far.

After Juice took off into the air, Hayden pointed northwest, saying that the closest town was in that direction, thinking that maybe Gard headed that way. Hayden then pointed south, saying that the next closest town was that way, claiming that Gard could have gone in either direction. Will said that they'll spit up into two teams. Will, Eric, and James will head to the northwest town to look for him there while Hayden, Timber, and Miles will head to the southern town to search there.

Miles was a little nervous about having to be the teleporter for his search group, but Hayden reminded him on how well he was able to carry him and Gard to the Garden and back yesterday. Miles almost forgot about that and was worried about how fast he was forgetting things. He feared that his mind was falling back to what it once was. But he had a job to do and felt that he could carry out this mission.

"Maybe he doesn't want to be found?" Eric stated. All eyes were on Eric. "Maybe he didn't want anything to do with the fight for the order of the balance drama and chose to take off. He might not have been in the mood for some pep talk or a strong pitch to reconsider, so he just left in the middle of the night."

"Eric, don't you want to know if he's okay? Heck, you finding out he was still alive was the information that got you to the safe house in the first place," Will said as he walked up to Eric. "Now for all we know, he could be in the same amount of trouble he was in when we found him in that cave. You wanted to make sure he was okay back then, so why not now?"

Eric hesitated and looked down at the dirt away from Will before responding. "Fine, let's go northwest," Eric said, not wanting to press this conversation any further.

Juice returned to the campsite while staying suspended in the air within shouting distance. Juice reported that he couldn't find Gard anywhere within the swamp, so he must be long gone. Will told Juice to stay at the swamp in case Gard returned while the rest of the guys gathered up in their search groups.

"Before you guys go, you should have this just in case," Juice said as he removed the cube from his hammock and tossed it over to Will. This made the group very angry for none of them ever wished to see the cube again. The Hogs yelled at Juice, saying that the cube was safer being inside the Garden and that he shouldn't have removed it. Juice tried to defend himself by saying that the cube was a very valuable object when they faced the devil, so he thought that it could be useful once again. Juice's words were convincing, and since there was no time to continue the argument, they agreed with him.

"What do we get then?" asked Hayden, thinking it was unfair that the first group got something and they didn't.

"How about this?" Juice asked, showing off the AG rifle.

Hayden let out a large uncontrollable smile and gracefully accepted.

"How did you get your hands on that?" questioned James with a high shock.

"Gabe gave it to me!" Juice proudly admitted.

After the two groups received their objects from Juice, James teleported his group to the northwest town, while Miles teleported his group to the south town.

⊰◦◦◦⊱

Gard was in the northwest town sitting in a library, looking up information on one of the public computers. Gard was looking at the report that declared him dead. A cargo plane from North America to South America crashed flying over the ocean, and all passengers drowned. Gard's name was on the manifest. Gard was on that plane, but to say all passengers drowned was false. Not only did Gard survive the crash, but so did a few others. Gard pulled drowning men and woman up from the depths of the ocean and managed to get them onto floating wreckage. They floated for two nights before finding shore. By that time, only half of them were still alive.

Gard was all too aware of what happened after that. The people fought so hard to paddle toward the shore and encountered rescuers they were not hoping to find. They were a paid group of trained enforcers. They used their guns and chains to make all the survivors prisoners. The odd part was that the plane that crashed was originally heading to this place to drop off the people as a prisoners' exchange. When the armed men saw Gard, they already knew him. The people offering the prisoner exchange demanded a lot of money for him. They described him as strong, tough, and relentless. Gard found out that the people who he owed money to captured and sold him to the men in the country to cover his debts. Gard spent the next two years digging in mines and being treated like an abused animal.

There was no information on the criminals responsible for forcing him and so many to do heavy labor work every day. Gard even looked into the history of the land he was digging at to find out what was so important to find. For two years, Gard never knew what they were searching for because they never found a thing.

Gard eased back from the computer to cover his face with his hands. He couldn't believe that he was finally free from that place. He was still used to waking up and knowing that he had to start digging, or the men with guns would start shooting.

Gard then put his fingers back on the keyboard. He logged into his social media account. He caught up with all the people who were once in his life. It wasn't that great. It turned out the rest of the world didn't have much to celebrate in these recent times. He learned that a lot of his relatives had passed while he was missing. Gard typed a status on his media page saying "I am alive."

Before Gard clicked send, he looked at the statement again. Gard found it odd on how simple and uneventful it was expressed. He didn't even end the message with an exclamation point. These plain-written words was all that he could muster to describe himself. And Gard didn't even feel the desire to push send. He felt that he wasn't truly alive; he knew that he was still breathing, but to him, that didn't mean he was living.

Gard never pushed send to his message about being alive. He thought that maybe the world should just go on thinking he was dead.

Gard left the computer and headed outside. He walked for a while and found himself standing in front of a bar. Gard checked his pocket and pulled out a twenty dollar bill. Gard had had this bill in his pocket from the day he was captured and forced onto the plane. It stayed in his pocket when the airplane crashed and while he floated in the water. It was the only scrap of paper he had while he was kept prisoner. Gard wrote out a suicide note on this bill. He knew that one day he would act in a way that would cause the guards to kill him on site, or if he got himself close enough to the men's guns, he would turn it on himself. A small paragraph written in small handwriting was all that was scribbled on it. At the bottom it said, "I wish you would have helped me, Eric."

Gard walked into the bar and used that bill to order some beers.

As Gard was drinking away his misery, he didn't see how fast the day outside came and went. It was early evening now, and Gard had used up most of his cash. He had enough for one more bottle of beer. After receiving his drink, a man sat at the stool next to him.

"Keeping yourself hydrated, Gard?" asked the man.

Gard recognized that voice and couldn't believe his ears. Gard very slowly tilted his head over to the man and saw his face. It was Mitchell, a man who was kept prisoner alongside Gard. Before the Hogs rescued Gard, Mitchell was the last person he saw. Gard couldn't believe that the same man was sitting next to him right then and there. The man mentioning the staying hydrated comment was an inside detail. The armed men would splash water at the prisoners whenever they got too smelly or were in need of water. The men would shout, "Make sure you stay hydrated!" in an ironic way.

"How is it that you're here?" Gard said in disbelief.

"As soon as you disappeared, I started searching for you. I figured that you would access your social media account someday, and once you did, I was able to find the location of the computer you used to log in with. After that, it was easy."

"That was hours ago. There is no way that you could have gotten here that fast."

"That would be true if I were human…but I'm not." Mitchell slowly turned his head to look at Gard.

Gard saw Mitchell's face reveal his true look, the look of a pure white skull. Gard fell out of his barstool, and his butt slammed to the floor. Gard started to crab-walk away from Mitchell.

Mitchell stood up from his chair, and once he did, his clothes transformed into a heavy dark cloak with a hood covering the top of his skull. Due to this frightful sight, Gard's heart started to beat so fast and hard, his chest started to bruise.

Gard did a quick look around to see if anyone else in the bar could see the Grim Reaper inside the building. But the people only had eyes on Gard, for he was acting like he was having a mental breakdown of some kind. What Gard was seeing was all in his head. The Reaper was attacking Gard within the spiritual realm, causing him to see things that weren't really there.

"The mercenaries only had funding for two years of digging," the Grim Reaper stated as he slowly moved closer to Gard. "They were planning on reselling the bombs they didn't end up using. They were afraid that the two they already planted within the mines wouldn't be able to wipe out the loose ends of the failed project. They did figure it would at least trap the prisoners within the cave. But what about Gard? they thought. If the bombs only caused a cave-in, then he could manage to dig himself out. So they made Mitchell a part of the plan." The Reaper reached out for Gard.

Gard rolled away and started to dash toward the door.

"They told Mitchell that they would let him live if he knocked you out before the bombs went off."

Gard now could remember being deep in the back of the cave with Mitchell. Mitchell hit him with chloroform, knocking him out. The Reaper informed Gard that after Mitchell delivered the news of Gard being unconscious to the mercenaries, they killed him on site. Then the mercenaries fired off the implanted bombs. Once that failed to kill off the prisoners, they rolled their last bomb that they were hoping to resell into the cave, set the timer for five minutes, and then took off in their helicopter.

Gard kept trying to push open the door to flee the Reaper but was failing. The Reaper said that he received permission form Memphis to kill him, and he was going to succeed in doing so. Gard saw that the door was a pull, not a push. Gard was overwhelmed with so much fear that he wasn't thinking straight. He managed to exit out of the bar, and as he ran, he kept looking back at the bar to see if the Reaper was following him. Gard ran straight into oncoming traffic, and a truck slammed into him hard. This instilled in Gard's high level of fear, and his heart pounding so hard, he was knocked out from this collision. Due to his dry Loomation working off his emotions, his fear put him in a dire need of an ambulance.

Gard's unconscious body was taken to the hospital. They had him connected to a heart monitor and saw that his heartbeat was racing out of control. The doctors did all they could to help him, but Gard was failing to wake up. From within Gard's mind, he was dying by the hands of the Grim Reaper.

In Gard's mind, he woke up in a hospital bed. Gard didn't know he was experiencing a dream. He at first thought that he woke up for real and was in an actual hospital room. Gard felt no pain from the car accident; it was like it never happen. Gard looked around and saw an empty room, so he got to his feet, headed to the door, and entered the hallway. Gard looked over and saw an exit sign and headed toward that direction. As he walked, he heard the voice of his father in a room down the hall.

Gard ran to the room to look inside. Inside was a truly shocking image. He saw both his parents holding him as a baby for the first time. Gard saw his parents young, and he had no doubts that the baby was him. Gard didn't say anything as he knew that they couldn't see him. They would have spotted him at the door by now.

Am I going crazy? Gard asked himself.

"You're not going crazy," the voice of the Grim Reaper said as if his voice was coming out of an intercom. "You're just fully exploring your mind for the first time."

Gard looked all over, trying to find the source of that voice. Gard left the room, and as he walked closer to the exit, he saw a version of himself at the age of six visiting his pediatrician. Gard ignored that and just stayed focused on the door. When he walked through the doors, the bright white sky blinded him at first. When his eyes adjusted to the light, he saw that he was standing on Main Street of his hometown. Gard knew that there was never a hospital in that location of town before.

"You're dying, Gard." The voice of the Grim Reaper came to him again, this time sounding like it came from the sky.

Gard looked up to see if he could see Grim Reaper, but instead he saw a billboard with the words "full diaper" printed in big letters. These were Gard's first words.

"Enjoy the highlights of your life for they will be the last things you see until you cross over." The voice gave off such a sinister tone, and it made Gard shiver when he heard it. Gard ran down the street and felt that the town was all based around his life. Every building had large glass windows, and inside had a different theme of his life displayed.

The first window Gard glanced inside showed off Gard's sports life. Jerseys alongside the cleats, basketball shoes, and running spikes were all displayed within the window. Jerseys he donned over the years. Preschool soccer, kindergarten tee ball, and the high school football, basketball, and track jerseys were the largest placed in the back.

"What is all this?" Gard shouted to the voice.

"You managed to slip though death's fingers so many times within the last five years. It has really kept you on edge. The fear of your next possible life-ending event had always made you stress out…that and the nightmares."

All of a sudden, a car parked on the street exploded, causing Gard to duck for cover. This was the same car that the mob blew up in order to show off their deadly threats to Gard when he owed them money. This was the first time Gard was almost killed during the last five years.

"Deep down, you were petrified and stressed out. But you've always been successful in bottling that up. Now that I've smashed that bottle, all that fear and overwhelming feelings are hitting you hard and is causing your heart to pound at a dangerously high rate."

Gard dashed into one of the buildings to get away from the street in fear of another car exploding. He found himself in a room that was presented as a bank on one side and a casino on the other. One of the casino employers asked Gard by name if he would like to place another bet. Right after that, one of the bankers informed Gard that his request for a loan was denied. So many memories were pressing onto Gard that it was hard to get the sequences of events straight. Gard ran to the back of the room to get away from the clerks and casino workers.

Gard entered a room where he saw the mob bosses who he wagered his bets to. Gard could see himself sitting at a table with them, making his first major bet. The dealers were shocked by Gard's high bet. They asked why he would make such a high-stake gamble. Gard remembered his words he used to reply to that question and said it simultaneously with his past display memory.

"I'm looking for a thrill in life. I'm looking for something that makes me feel alive!"

Gard remembered winning that bet, which was a shame because he continued to make more bets after that. Whenever he lost, he quickly made another bet to cover his losses. Some of the bets he made to cover his losses wouldn't have results until the end of the week, and sometimes the mob grew very impatient on the payoffs. This is what led to the car explosion.

Gard couldn't stay in that room anymore, so he looked over and saw a flight of stairs and ran up them. There was a door at the top, and on the other side, he was led to his old apartment. Gard looked over and saw someone about to attack him. Gard's memories started to hurt him as he was now reliving a past situation. Gard was attacked by a group of people to shake the money out of him or to give him a beating to send a message that they wanted their money.

Gard fell into the same motions as he did the first time this happened. He got hit with a baseball bat from behind, got punched in the face by a mean right hook by a second man, and the third guy wrapped a piano wire around his neck and started to pull back hard. Gard, again following in the same steps he did when this happened the first time, fought back and badly hurt the three men. The men outnumbered Gard, and in the struggle, one of them manage to shove Gard out the window. This was the fight that made the mob know just how strong Gard really was.

As Gard was falling, he fell through a roof of another building leading into another memory. Gard didn't want to relive this memory. Gard was now lying on the floor of an office, Eric's office. In 2018, Gard was deeply in debt with the mob and found himself so desperate for money that he dragged himself to an old friend.

Gard was once again watching a memory of himself, watching him plead to Eric for enough money to make another bet...a loan that, if won, could fully pay off everyone.

As Gard watched his memory, he saw that Eric seemed to hate this visit from Gard and wasn't going to give him a cent, let alone the amount he was asking for. Eric even ended up calling security to remove him from the building.

Gard couldn't take watching this memory anymore, so he ran to the closest door and found himself back on the road. Gard saw his past self being dragged into a van. The mob was gathering up people to sail to a private archaeological dig, and they charged a lot for Gard due to him being very strong. The mob got their money from Gard that way. Once that memory came and went, Gard looked up and saw the plane he was once forced on in the air. Gard watched the plane crash off in the distance. After that, a huge wave of water came right at him, splashing him off his feet. This was the memory of the plane crashing into the water and the fight to reach the surface.

The water wrapped Gard within a current and carried him all around town. The wave of water slammed him into a building, and the building crumbled with the sound of crushing rocks. The broken parts of the building looked like the rocks and dirt that he spent two years moving. All these tragic memories being piled up on him was causing his heart to pound even harder and harder.

"WHY ARE YOU DOING THIS TO ME!" Gard shouted as loud as he could.

Outside of Gard's mind was Will, Eric, and James standing by an unconscious Gard. When they heard of a man under the description of Gard being hit by a car, they hurried to the hospital. The doctor told the three that they were doing everything they could to lower Gard's heartbeat to a normal pace, but nothing was working. The doctor let the three in the room with Gard for a moment to go check with the nurses.

"James, could you give him a heal spell?" asked Will as he closed the door.

James placed his hand onto Gard's forehead in attempt to heal Gard. "It won't work. He's got the Grim Reaper inside him. The spirit is keeping Gard from being healed," James sadly informed the other two. "His heart will just keep beating faster until it stops completely."

"Is there anything we could do for him?" Will asked, hoping for a positive response.

"Right now, Gard is in a duel with himself and the Reaper. The Reaper will hit Gard with all of his negative, fearful past memories. After that, Gard will be begging for the Reaper to end his life."

"No, I won't accept that. He'll pull thought, he always does!" Will said as he looked at Gard.

Back inside Gard's mind, Gard was running from more buildings crumbling all around him. As the buildings that outlined the city were falling down, the white light started to grow over the empty spaces. Gard saw that he was running out of places to run. He felt that this was the end, and he'd end up falling into the great white light soon. This was all truly terrifying for him, and the waiting for the inevitable was making it unbearable.

The Reaper spoke to him once again. "I can put all of this to an end, Gard, just come to me. I'm at the center of the town. I'll make this all go away, and you can finally move on from this nightmare."

Gard looked around the corner and spotted the Reaper in the middle of the street. Gard saw no way out of this and just chose to give in to the evil spirit. As Gard walked up to the Reaper, he looked over at the buildings on the side of the road. He saw a large banner hanging over a window with the words *The Hang Out Group* written on it. Photos, group T-shirts, and playing cards were all displayed though the window. One of the photos was the one of the group at the Garden of Eden. The TV was showing Gard's first hangout with the other members, all of them having a good time.

The playing cards was a very unique touch. The playing cards was some fantasy-based game that he used to play when he was a kid. At the time, none of Gard's friends played this game, so it was hard to find people to face. Then he found someone who was a fan of the game—this person was Eric. The two bonded over the game and were close friends before the Hang Out Group was even a thing. The group never played the game; it was just an Eric-and-Gard thing.

Gard despised Eric after he rejected his request to borrow money, so much that Gard never thanked Eric for going into that cave to pull him out of it before the bomb went off. Gard now realized that Eric felt bad for not helping when he should have and was trying to make up for what he did. Then Gard realized how much of a jerk he was to Eric. If the tables were turned, Gard wouldn't have let anyone borrow that amount of money. Besides, the bet Gard was going to make with that money would have put him into an even deeper hole. For the first time in a long time, Gard wanted to live. He couldn't let Eric go on thinking that he resented his friend.

As Gard was walking up to the Reaper, he saw that he was holding a scythe. Ever since Gard entered this Grim Reaper's dream, he was looking for any kind of weapon. That scythe was the only one he found, and he believed it would be able to kill the spirit. The only problem was that it was in the spirit's grip. Gard had to think fast. If he could launch a surprise attack at the spirit, he could steal the scythe right out of his hands.

When Gard reached the front of the Grim Reaper, he knelt down in front of him. The Reaper lifted the scythe high with both hands. When the Reaper reached the peak of height, and just before he started to bring it down, Gard made a leap forward right into the spirit's arms, clashing his body into its arms.

The collision made the spirit lose his grip of the weapon, and Gard pried it out of his hands. Once Gard had the scythe, he planted his feet back down and started to wave it like a flag twirler all over the spirit's body. The scythe sliced through the spirit's body like butter. After the third swing, the spirit was now dead.

For a moment there, within his heavy breathing, Gard felt victorious. Then Gard looked around and saw the white light getting closer. More of the buildings were being knocked down. Gard may have killed the spirit, but his death attack was still active.

Outside the dream, Will, Eric, and James saw that the heart monitor had now suddenly went from a fast pace to an almost nonexistent pace. With the spirit now dead, the intense fear Gard was having had gone away. But since Gard's life was at the moment ending, the heart was pumping slower and slower.

James said that he could give Gard a heal spell, but that wouldn't save his mind from the spirit's dream. He knew that Gard was on the verge of going brain dead, and it would take more than a heal spell to bring him out of it.

"The cube!" shouted Eric in a sense of desperation. Will quickly removed the cube from his pocket and handed it over to Eric, for he was the one who could solve it the fastest. Eric, with steadying hands, managed to put the pieces in proper alignment to get the cube to appear as one solid piece. Eric then crunched down on the cube, making the Loomation light up. Eric then brought the cube close to Gard and then released its energy.

A white shock wave blast was released from the cube, hitting Gard and Eric. Will was able to keep Eric from fully falling backward by steadying him from behind. Gard woke up right away from the blast feeling like a new man. He smiled when he saw his friends. James saw the doctors running back to the room, so he teleported them all back to the swamp.

The four were standing in front of the cabin within the campsite. Juice shouted with joy when he saw that his friends returned. Juice staying back at the swamp put himself out of cell range, so he had no communication on what was going on with them finding Gard. Once Juice heard the story of what happened, he pointed over to the hologram displaying the balance, saying that he did noticed the evil side lowered a little. The four turned toward the balance and did see that the evil side was now lower than when they saw it last.

The green hologram was the only light source within the swamp. At nighttime, the light was glowing soft as a large nightlight. Juice then ran over to the parked truck within the campsite. He said he wanted to show them something. Juice then picked up two different cords resting next to each other.

"Get ready for this!" Juice said just before he contacted the two cords. Once the action was done, white Christmas-type lights went off all around the Hogs. The light bordered the campsite and also the entire comfort zone of the swamp. Seeing the lights turned on brought back some good, fond memories for the group.

Gard's face let out a large smile seeing the lights. The old place was starting to look more like home now.

"Awesome job, Juice!" Will shouted.

"Now we don't have to sit in the dark anymore!" James added.

"This was what you were doing all day?" Eric asked, not being moved by the lights.

"Well, not really. Turns out hanging lights is easy when you don't have to be constantly repositioning a ladder," Juice replied with a laugh.

Gard walked up to Juice to give him a high five and told him nice work. Juice could tell that Gard was now free of his evil spirit haunting his state of mind and mood.

Hayden, Timber, and Miles then arrived at the swamp by teleporting. They were impressed by the hanging lights Juice put up. While the three were in the south town, they received a text from Will saying that he found Gard, so the three did some grocery shopping. Gard dug into the bags, and within Hayden's bags was a case of beer. Gard took the beer out and asked the group, "Who's up for a drink?"

The Hogs were sitting around the cold fireplace; some were enjoying a beer while some were just happy with a bottle of water. The last two nights, the Hogs just ate a bit and then spent most of the night within their own sleeping areas. With it being so dark, no one was in the mood to do anything. But sitting around the hung lights got them in the mood to sit out together.

"I never thanked you guys for saving my life. Not just today but back at that cave," Gard said as he started to open up to his friends. Gard told them his story, his gambling problem, his rising debt, the plan crash, and the two years of being prisoner forced into working in the caves.

"Couldn't you escape?" asked Will.

"I tried once, got pretty far away from them too. But they took me down and dragged me back. They told me that if I ever get spotted taking a too-long-glance at an unguarded path, they wouldn't shoot me, they would start shooting the other prisoners. They knew the chances of them catching me again were slim, so the threat of killing the others was what kept me there."

Gard then talked about the day the mercenaries were finished with their digging and were going to kill the prisoners to keep the project secret. That was the day the Hogs were there for him to save his life.

Juice was inspired to share his past with the others after Gard was done talking about his story. Juice stood up because he liked to pace back and forth when bringing up his hard times.

Juice talked about his past girlfriends. He now knew that the Siren caused all the false love feelings from both sides of the relationship. He then said that there was a day when a friend was there for him.

Juice looked over to Will. "Will, that day you showed up to see me, you kept me from making a huge mistake. I in return turned all that vicious attitude on you, and that resulted me in taking my last flight for a while." Juice then took a sip of his water before going on. "But I really needed a friend that day, even if I didn't know it. And even though I acted in my most unfriendliest way that night, you still have treated me as a good friend this whole time. So I thank you for being there, and I'm sorry how I acted at the time."

Juice returned to his seat, and Will gave him a tap on the shoulder saying all is forgiven, and it's all water under the bridge.

Gard glanced over to Eric, seeing the similarities of Juice and Will's situation. Besides Will and Juice, only Eric and Gard were the others who had seen each other during the last five years. Gard wanted to tell Eric that he was sorry for coming to him for money and that he wasn't mad at him for not being granted it, but couldn't find himself to say it just yet.

Eric then stood up, finished off his beer can, chucked it out in the field, and said he was heading to bed. The rest of the Hogs felt that they should be off to bed as well. As everyone was heading off to their areas, Gard called out to James, saying that he's in on fixing the balance. He said that he didn't want to tell the world that he's alive until they finished what the group had started.

Eric took the last of his pills from his bottle. It was a very stressful day for him, and the pills helped him fall asleep easier. Eric was hoping that he could find more pills in his suitcase in the morning. If not, he'd have to return to his office.

Urgent News

Tuesday, October 6, 2020

That morning, Eric was searching his suitcase to see if he packed any extra pills. Him not finding any had ruined his morning routine. After he checked his entire tent, he exited it and made his way to his parked car. Eric didn't bother waving or nodding to the other members of the Hang Out Group; he just stayed focused on getting to his car. Eric didn't know how he was going to function without his pills. After he searched throughout his car, he slammed the door in frustration.

"Looking for something?" asked James from behind the car.

Eric was shocked due to him thinking he was alone by his car. Eric said that there was nothing he was looking for. James responded with a head tilt, as if he knew Eric was lying. Eric took a hard glance at James and realized something.

"You know what I'm look for, don't you. Those Saints gave you files on all of us. So you know all of our dark secrets, don't you." Eric then walked up to James. "So why not tell the others? I'm sure that these guys would love to give me an intervention."

"I'm not here to reveal secrets. They're not mine to share."

"Well, there's nothing to reveal. Millions of people are taking antidepressants all around the world every day. Given the shape the balance has been in the last five years, that's not surprising," Eric said as he walked past James.

"That's true, but you're not one of them," James replied.

Eric ignored James and just kept walking over to the eating table where most of the Hogs were sitting. Eric informed them that he needed to get back to work. He only took a few days off and claimed that he really needs to return to the office.

"Would you be back?" asked Miles.

"Yeah, what about fixing the balance?" Timber added.

"Look, last I checked, fixing the balance was optional. And I just can't continue to abandon my life just to fix something that the forces of Heaven can't fix."

"Yeah, but we're the ones responsible for breaking it," Juice stated.

Eric took a moment to let that information sink in once again. Eric looked around and could tell that he may be the last one to sign on for getting this balance fixed. Juice then told Eric that they needed him. Eric started to sweat; the withdrawal side effects were already starting to kick in. Eric wiped his face and started to think about that large box of pills tucked away in his office desk.

"Look, you guys can handle this project on your own. I have other responsibilities to get to." Eric then went to grab his suitcase from his tent and head off in his car. The Hogs sitting at the table felt that they should have tried harder to convince Eric to stay. James walked up to the table and took a seat.

"You see that Eric left?" Timber said.

"Yeah, but it was his choice to make," James replied.

"You said Eric's evil spirit was the horseman Famine. What did he do to him?" questioned Miles.

"Telling other people's stories isn't how I work."

"What do you mean?" asked Timber.

"I'm so used to being an angel that I still follow the rules, even when the system is corrupt," James said as he looked at the faded hologram of the balance. "In the heat of the moment, I'll teleport you fighters to safety, and if our paths face an evil spirit, I'll be right by your side ready to fight. But an angel's help isn't meant to be seen and not to be displayed so directly. We know information that we can only learn by receiving the news from the gates of Heaven. Information like that being passed around the humans can tip the balance. We angels can help open people's eyes, minds, and hearts to help them learn that information on their own. But the best way to learn about someone is to ask and see if they want to share. Angels can help push someone to open up, but sometimes that doesn't work."

"Isn't that what you've been doing?" Juice inquired. "You know that simply killing our evil spirit isn't enough to fix us right away. It takes a huge burden off our shoulders, but even without that, we still wouldn't have really changed our mood. We have to talk about our problems to someone who wants us to get better, someone who has also suffered our miseries. In the end, people save people. The angels only provide a slight assist."

James gave a simple nod for what Juice said was right. James then checked his watch and said that he made plans on meeting a colleague soon. James asked Timber to use the walkie-talkie to call in the others. James then got up from his chair and started to head west, saying he'll be back with someone soon. The Hogs at the table thought that James was going to elaborate on who exactly he was going to see. But he didn't, so Timber did what he was asked.

Out in the swamp, on the east side of the campsite, Will, Hayden, and Gard were weapon training. Hayden was shooting at some beer cans with his rifle while Will was using a handgun to shoot at some targets nailed to the trees. Gard was working with the sword, swinging it around as if he were in a duel.

"You guys should have seen me fight the Grim Reaper. I was on fire!" Gard said as he swung the sword around like a knight. Gard then turned over to Hayden. "You remember fire, don't you, Hayden?"

Hayden then fired his rifle six times, knocking down the six cans perfectly. Hayden didn't say anything to Gard; he just started to reload.

"Why don't you use the angel gun?" asked Gard.

"It only holds seven rounds, and Juice already fired off one of them when he fought the Siren," Hayden replied.

"Yeah, but I know for a fact that you went into battle with the devil with only two bullets," Gard added.

Hayden grew back to his silence and marched forward to reposition the cans.

Gard walked over to Will and asked "Was I this cut off before I killed my evil spirit?"

"No," Will said. "You were much worse."

This comment made both Will and Gard laugh. Gard couldn't remember the last time he laughed, let alone a small chuckle. Gard put his hand out for Will's gun, implying that he wanted to fire off a few rounds. Will traded his gun for the sword. Gard aimed the gun at the target. Gard fired off a few rounds and hit the target multiple times. Nothing dead center, but he never missed the target.

"You think this hot lead is going to be enough to kill a spirit?" asked Gard.

"According to James, that angel gun isn't powerful enough to kill the more powerful spirits out there. It killed the Siren with no problem, but a full seven rounds on Memphis would only tickle him."

"Well, at least we got the sword. That's our advantage that the angels didn't have."

"We'll have to have Juice show us how to wield it."

"I keep forgetting that Juice took multiple sword training classes back in 2013," Gard said as he fired off a few more rounds at the target. "It's weird thinking back to those times. You know we're all here for the actions we did back in 2010. And we've all had a troubled last five years. But those five years between 2010 and 2015 are kind of a blur at times. Seeing the lights switched on at the campsite last night really took me back to the good old days."

Just then, Will and Gard heard Hayden take fire at the cans once more. The two could see the lifeless eyes of Hayden as he fired the gun with no emotions. Hayden hadn't expressed anything since he'd been back at the swamp. No grin, no laugh, no whimsical look when he saw the lights of the campsite back on again. Gard asked Will if Hayden had reached out to anyone about what had happened to him during his five years.

"He hasn't said anything to anyone. After I volunteered to help James fight for the order of the balance, he was the only one to stand up to join us. Whatever happened to him, he's bent on revenge."

"We need to get this guy some fighting action, maybe then he'll enjoy himself," Gard said just before the walkie-talkie went off with Timber's voice calling in the three back to camp. The three gathered up their stuff and hustled back to camp.

James was standing not too far away from the campsite waiting for his friend to arrive. James's friend teleported in front of James as instructed. This angel was Boston, the spirit who worked in the armory up at the gates of Heaven. Boston was carrying a large bag in each hand and another large bag strapped to his back. The two smiled at each other and said hello. Boston was telling James how impressed he was about how the Hogs already took out two spirits. James was excited for the group to meet him, so he led him back to camp.

"There's been a lot of talk upstairs, you know," Boston said.

"Isn't there always?" James carelessly replied.

"The Saints were shocked that an archangel came to you guys. The Saints never received help like that from them before."

"Well, I wish he would have stuck around. We could have used him."

"There's a betting pool taking place on whether or not you guys are going to be able to kill Memphis, or he's going to kill you."

"What are our odds?"

"Not good. But someone new is giving us an advantage."

"What do you mean?"

"Let's discuss it with the group. I'm excited to meet them," Boston said as they entered the camp area.

By this time, Will, Hayden, and Gard had returned. The three first asked where Eric was. Timber informed them that Eric grabbed his stuff and took off. This made the three highly concerned. Gard was upset that Eric didn't even stick around long enough to say goodbye. Will wanted to know if it was even safe for Eric to go back to his home, given the fact that in the past two days, different members of the group were attacked by their spirit. He was afraid that Eric may be next.

James said that right now, Eric was making a drive back to his office, saying that it's a several-hour drive, so they had time to catch up with him there through the power of teleporting. In the meantime, he introduced the group to Boston. Boston said that he was a weapons expert up at the gates of Heaven. He said that the Saints had sent him to equip the group with some of their best artillery.

"If the Saints are helping us now, can they find out where Eric's evil spirit is?" Gard asked.

"The horseman Famine was assigned to watch Eric. And all of the horsemen have the power to sensor themselves from Heaven's eye," James stated.

"Tell us about the weapons!" shouted Hayden, wanting to get to the thing he was more interested in.

Boston had five angel rifles along with tons of ammunition. Hayden was happy about this; for now he could do some target practice with the guns without fear of running low on bullets. Boston also had some extra parts to help build bombs and other helpful devices that could affect all types of spirits. Boston then showed off a sword sheath. This was a personal request from James, saying to keep it top secret. Boston wanted to see the sword.

James didn't straight up tell Boston about the sword, but it was obvious that they had one. Why else would they ask for a sheath? James then handed the sword over to Boston. Boston was fascinated by the weapon and asked if it was the tool that helped the Hogs kill the devil. The Hogs told Boston that the sword was pulled out of the barrier from inside the Garden of Eden by one of Logan's friends. They informed him that at first touch of the sword, it would give them this blast of positive energy, making them feel like there was no fight they could lose.

"Well, it is possible to lose a fight when holding that blade," Timber added as he remembered Cain dying with the sword in his hand when he went up against the devil.

Boston could feel that quick blast of high spirits when he first took hold of the handle. Boston had an educated guess on the origin of this weapon. "I think this sword was made right out of God's hand."

This statement made everyone pause in disbelief.

"When God made the Ten Commandments, he made them right out of his hand and gave them to Moses. When Moses touched the two slabs of carved stone, he felt this excited feeling, just like the ones you all described while touching this sword."

The Hogs never really put that much thought on the sword now that they thought about it. They always just saw it as a helpful tool that got the job done.

"It glowed when it was close to the devil," Juice brought up.

The Hogs forgot about that detail. The sword presented a gold glowing light whenever it was close to the devil.

Boston also had a theory on that. "If this was made out of God's hand, then it's an extension of himself. Prayers talk about how God is your protection while you walk through the darkness. The sword embodies that. The sword will shine the light on the evil, and because it's a weapon, you can defend yourself with it."

This explained why the sword was as special as it was. It was made from God's hand. That weapon could overpower anything that God or anyone has created. Boston said that with this weapon in the hands of the Hogs, he now regretted making his bets in the betting pool he made up at the gates of Heaven.

"Boston, you said we were getting help outside the Saints?"

"Yesterday the Saints received information on Memphis and the things he's been up to."

"Who sent this?" wondered James.

"Do the Saints have a spy in Memphis's army?" questioned Will.

"The Saints have no idea who delivered this information, but it's clear that someone on Memphis side is a trader. Whoever this spirit is gave us all the information on Memphis's project titled Project Cider."

"Project Cider?" asked Gard.

Boston informed the group that Project Cider was started when the evil spirit known as Siren discovered a split personally resting in Juice's brain. All eyes were on Juice with wonder.

"The project was to pull that personality out of Juice, making the first human-spirit hybrid. And Memphis received confirmation that the project was a complete success. Cider walks."

"Wait, what?" Juice uttered, finding this hard to believe.

"Are you telling me that there are two Juices out there?" Hayden nervously asked.

"Oh, I get it. Apple juice and apple cider," Miles said, feeling clever.

"Well, I'm glad Memphis was thinking of me as more of an apple juice guy instead of an orange juice guy. I hate orange juice," Juice replied as he started to raise his voice.

"The project was to have the Siren implant an empty spiritual egg inside your brain on top of the infection. It built up energy from your dry Loomation over time, such as a plant feeding from the sunrays. But the Siren wasn't powerful enough to give it its own body. The infection had to be removed from your head by someone pretty powerful in order to give it a body," Boston explained.

"Like an archangel?" Juice said, squinting his whole face as he just realized that he may have made a mistake.

"Juice, what have you done?" Timber asked.

"This does explain why Gabe felt so out of breath after he removed the infection. The egg must have taken enough energy from him in order to give itself a body. Wait, I was there when it happened, and I didn't see any copy of me."

"Did you check?" Gard said.

Juice opened his mouth, about to say that of course he checked. But he didn't say anything because after giving it a second thought, he said, "I may have left right away and didn't bother to check. But to be fair, who would look for something like that!" Juice's voice rose up, and he started to pace back and forth.

"Why would Memphis need a second Juice out there anyway?" questioned Will.

"He wants to know how you killed the devil," James replied. "The reason why each of you had an evil spirit attached to you over the last five years is because Memphis was never given the information on how you guys killed the devil. And being in the dark of that scares him. He was hoping that during the five years, one of you would have mentioned the actions taken to kill the devil to someone. But since none of you have said a word of that day, he's still scared of you guys. If there is evil Juice out there, then maybe Memphis will get the details from him."

"He could have tortured us for the details or something," Will replied.

"He was never in a hurry to find out. He figured the angels don't know either, so no need to know now. Plus, the spirits don't like it when the humans know that they're the ones responsible for all their bad days. Most of the time people blame God when things don't go their way or when things take a turn for the worse. So the spirits won't make themselves known if they can help it."

"Since most of us are now fighters for the balance, he's going to want to know about that sword now more than ever!" Gard shouted as he stood up from his chair.

"Since we all now know about the spirits, they won't hold back. They'll attack us on sight and make us talk," Hayden added.

"We got to find Eric! It's not safe for him to be out there now!" Gard yelled.

"We also need to find Cider!" Juice shouted. "He may still be in New Mexico. I had the infection removed when I was in the white sands out there. He may still be there."

"Juice is right, we've got to find Cider before Memphis does," Will mentioned.

"Can't the Saints find him?" questioned Timber.

"The Saints have tried, but they can't. Cider has a quarter of Juice's soul in him. The majority of the soul lies with Juice. Every time the Saints try to located Cider, they track the soul and always end up finding Juice," Boston explained.

"Can Memphis or any of his followers track us?" Timber asked in a panic.

"Tracking down a soul takes time. The devil being as powerful as he was took him four weeks to track them down," James added.

"Yeah, but Cider has all of Juice's memories up until he was separated," Boston sadly added.

"Which means he knows where the swamp is," Miles uttered.

Tons of panic was catching on from all this news. The Hogs had trouble thinking clearly. They knew that they had to find Cider before Memphis did, and the whole second Juice being out there was already crazy to think of. Gard wanted to find Eric before his spirit got to him first.

James said that since they knew exactly where Eric was heading, he would send out a small search party for him. He had Hayden, Gard, and Miles to head to Eric's office building to bring him back to the swamp.

The rest of the group—Will, Juice, Timber, James, and Boston—would head to where Cider was born and check the towns around that area, praying that the hybrid didn't wander off too far.

Breaking the Habit

Hayden, Gard, and Miles appeared on the sidewalk across the street of the skyscraper Eric's office was in. Their sudden arrival from the teleporting trip was only seen by a homeless man sitting on a nearby bench. The homeless man flinched when the three entered his view from literally out of nowhere. Gard looked over and saw that they were spotted by the homeless man, and then insisted on him and his friends to get walking.

"You couldn't have brought us to a more isolated place, Miles?" questioned Gard.

"Sorry, but you know I can only teleport to places that I've seen before. The photo James showed me of Eric's work building didn't come with a private teleporting entrance location," Miles replied.

"We were only seen by a homeless person. It's not like we popped up in the middle of the street during rush hour," Hayden added.

"If we head to the parking garage, we can meet up with Eric when he gets there," Gard told his friends as he led them to the location.

"Yeah, about that," Hayden uttered.

Gard put the march to a halt to ask what was on Hayden's mind.

"The evil spirit who haunted Juice was his landlady. So it's possible that Eric's evil spirit is someone who can get close to him."

"You think the horseman Famine is someone who works with Eric?" asked Gard.

"It's possible," Hayden said.

Both Gard and Miles had a chilling thought that the horseman could be in that office building right now. This made Gard think that the mission should be bringing Eric back to the swamp as soon as they ran into him. But Hayden had another idea in mind. Hayden revealed that he smuggled an angel rifle and the sword contained in the new sheath as Miles was teleporting them. Hayden showed off some extra ammo for the gun, saying he stole it from Boston's bag before leaving.

"Something tells me that's not for protection," Gard said.

"We can kill the horseman," Hayden replied with confidence.

"Shouldn't we wait until the whole group is involved before we start making attacks?" asked Miles.

"The three of us can take out one steed! Juice and Kate killed the Siren, and you killed the Grim Reaper," Hayden replied, now starting to take on an aggressive tone.

"Juice and I were both almost killed during those fights. And according to James, a horseman is on a different strength level. The rifle may not be strong enough to kill him," Gard mentioned.

"That's what the sword is for. It killed the devil, which means it can kill anything!" Hayden added as he started to come off as desperate.

"What about Eric? We came here to get him out of danger," Gard reminded them.

"Eric may lead us straight to Famine."

"So you want to use him as bait then?"

"Don't act like you've never used a friend as bait before," Hayden said in rage.

Gard took a moment to settle himself down from bickering with Hayden. Just yesterday, Gard would most likely have lost his temper and start to yell. But Gard could tell that Hayden just wanted a fight. Gard knew that Hayden had a point; if the end goal was to attack Memphis, then they should start getting some battle experiences.

Gard stressfully pushed back his hair with his hand, and he then looked over to Miles and asked, "What about you, Miles? You ready for a battle?"

"Guys, a simple teleport here and there I can handle. But I haven't done anything beyond that in five years." Miles took a look at his hands. He started to wonder how he would behave when he saw the light being released from his body once again. Miles feared of having another full mental breakdown like he once had before.

"Hey, you'll be our escape plan, okay?" Gard said to his friend to ease his fear.

Miles agreed to that and decided to go along with the plan. Hayden handed over the sheathed sword over to Gard while he armed himself with the angel rifle. The plan was to wait until Eric showed up at the parking garage. After that, they'd take the stairway up to his office floor, hoping that Famine was somewhere inside.

⁕

As Eric was driving to the work building, he cranked up the air conditioner in his car. His body was feeling flushed in a way. He was wiping off tons of sweat from his body constantly, and his road rage was easily being triggered. Leaving the swamp and the responsibility of restoring order to the balance was bearing on his mind. He saw the balance as no longer his problem. Before, he felt guilty for not giving Gard that loan and always felt responsible for his death. His conscience felt clear after saving his life twice since then. Now all he wanted was his pills he left in his office.

As Eric arrived to the roads that bordered the skyscrapers, he looked up and saw heavy dark clouds covering up the sun. Then the rain started to fall. Eric spotted a street parking spot close to his building, so he took it. He was still scheduled to be on vacation, so this was just a get-in-and-get-out visit. Eric did a quick check in his car for an umbrella. He saw none, so he just exited the car with no attempt to shield himself from the heavy raindrops. He figured that the rain would disguise his heavy sweat.

Eric reached the front doors and pulled them open. Eric didn't know this, but he was being watched by Hayden, Gard, and Miles from the building across the street. Now that they saw that Eric was in the building, they dashed to the parking garage. Gard had been to Eric's office before and knew that there was a stairway from the parking garage to inside the building.

Eric gave a nod to the security guard by the front door. The guard welcomed him back by name and asked if he decided to go casual today. Eric didn't realize it, but he wasn't wearing his usual businesses work suit; he was wearing Levi's and an untucked shirt. Eric reported to the guard that he was there to retrieve something, and he'd be on his way. Eric walked to the elevator doors, pushed the button, and boarded the elevator.

As the lift was bringing him to the top floor of the building, Eric started to think of his cover story. He left so suddenly, saying he had a family emergency and would need a few days off. Eric thought about using the sick mother excuse, a possible deathbed situation. He figured if anyone asked him to elaborate, he would just say it was too painful to think about.

When the doors opened, he saw a lifeless, dark work floor with nothing but empty cubicles. Eric checked the elevator doors and saw that he was indeed on the right floor. Eric couldn't understand what was going on. It was early work hours, so this place should have been packed with coffee-filled employees scattering about. The place looked like it was closed down, and everyone was laid off. The natural light from the windows was the only light source, and since it was cloudy with a heavy rainstorm, the whole room looked dark gray. The only sound was the rain slamming against the windows, which was a little disturbing. In fact, the whole floor was slightly chilly.

Eric saw his office across the floor, and before he could take one step in that direction, he heard someone yell out his name from the right side of the room. Eric knew that voice. It was his boss. Eric looked over and saw his boss walking over to him.

"Mr. Clay," Eric said in shock and also in relief.

"What are you doing here? I thought you were out for a few more days."

"Yes, that schedule is true, but I just had to grab some things from my office first."

"Look at that, a few days from the office, and you find yourself wanting to bring work home with you. Always putting work first is how you managed to climb as high as you have in such little time!" Mr. Clay said just before leading Eric to a detour route to his office. "We were going to have all the remodeling finished by the time you got back."

"We're remodeling?" a confused Eric replied as he followed his boss.

"Yeah, a construction crew left a lot of their equipment lying around the middle of the floor. Normally having one of my subordinates trip over one of their extension cords could lead to a lawsuit, but since I like you, I'm leading you away from all of that."

Eric couldn't recall any mentioning of a remodeling job planned for the office. He thought a memo would have at least been e-mailed to him. Mr. Clay said that all the workers were working from home online right now. Mr. Clay led Eric all around the cubicles, which was a longer way to get to his office. Eric could have been to his office within seconds if he would have just cut through the middle of the floor like he did every day when he got there. But going all the way around the room just stalled the process and made his desire to get the pills more annoying.

When they reached the office door, Mr. Clay let Eric open his door himself. Eric opened the door and was relieved that the light switch was still working in his office. Eric eyed his file cabinet that contained the box of pills he hid. Eric thought that his boss would just walk away, but the man walked in and sat in one of the guest chairs. Eric felt the need to grab something from his office; otherwise, his boss would get suspicious.

Eric went to his desk, a solid wooden rectangle with a wooden center leg holding it up. Eric wished that the desk now had drawers so that he could retrieve something in it. Eric went to the file cabinet behind the desk. He opened it up and started to grab some files. Resting in the cabinet drawer was the box of stashed pills. After Eric had a handful of files, he reached for the box. Eric, with his box under a stack of files, said he now had what he needed, so he was ready to go.

"Hold on now," Mr. Clay said as he walked over to the liquor cabinet. "How about a drink?"

"It's pretty early for a drink, isn't it, sir?"

"Come on now, you're on vacation, which means drinking time is whenever you're awake, am I right!" Mr. Clay handed a glass over to Eric.

Eric had to place the box and files on the desk in order to take the glass.

"You really look like a guy who could use a drink."

"Cheers," Eric said as he gulped down the liquid.

"Take it easy now," Mr. Clay said as he refilled the empty glass. "Sit down, relax, tell me about your time off."

Eric sat in his office chair behind his desk and now took his time sipping from his glass. "Just had to meet up with a lot of people from my past. It was pretty overwhelming." Eric was stunned by what he said. That was too close to the truth and not the planned lie he was going to deliver when asked about his time off. Eric being so close to the drugs was making his brain lose focus.

"Yeah, I know reunions can be rough," Mr. Clay said as he sat back in the guest chair and placed his feet up on to the desk. His feet landing on the desk caused the box to jump and almost fall off the edge. It took everything Eric had to keep himself from reaching out and grabbing the box after he saw it almost fall over. His sweat was now dripping so much, it looked as if he was standing next to a fire. Eric didn't like the way his boss was having his feet up on his desk. His feet were so close to nudging the box over. But it was the boss, which means he could do whatever he wanted.

"So what did you and your friends talk about?" asked the boss.

Eric thought that if he would indulge him with the conversion, maybe he would leave him alone after he ran out of questions for this small talk. Eric talked about how he had to discuss the actions he and his friends did a long time ago. He said that he had to testify in court even. Eric wasn't even paying attention to what he was saying anymore; he just wanted what was in that box so much.

"What was it that you guys did?"

"We were accused of killing someone."

"Killing him with what?"

Eric was about to reply, but he found himself frozen in confusing thoughts. Eric didn't give away if he and his friends killed a man or a woman. Eric felt that any other person he would share this information with would be more shocked than asking leading questions. Eric then remembered that the information on how the devil was killed was always kept secret. Eric couldn't believe it. He almost gave away the Hogs' biggest weapon against the evil spirits. Eric made hard eye contact with his boss and started to wonder if he was human.

"Alright, enough of this charade!" Mr. Clay said just before he kicked the box of pills off the desk. The box broke open, and the pills scattered all over the floor. Eric desperately scrambled around his desk to gather up the pills. Eric dropped to his knees to gather up the drugs.

"Tell me what you and the other Hogs used to kill the devil!" Eric's boss roared.

Eric now knew that he was in the same room as the evil spirit Famine, and he had enough pills on the floor in front of him to ease his stress. Eric didn't know if it was the situation he was in, or if Famine was using his powers to raise Eric's addiction to take the drugs.

"You can feel that temptation, can't you. With the amount of addiction I'm pouring into your mind right now, you'll swallow every pill on that dirty floor and be begging for more! That is if you don't die from overdose first. Now if you want this addiction to stop, tell me what I want to know!"

Eric pulled himself away from looking at the pills and used all his will power to force himself to his feet to look at Famine dead in the eye. "I won't bend to your power! You can force the pills down my throat yourself, but I'll never give up the advantage my friends have over your kind!"

Outside the office, Hayden, Gard, and Miles made it to the floor from the stairs. Gard pointed over to where Eric's office was. The office door was closed, so they couldn't see Eric and his boss talking. Gard wanted to get closer to Eric's office to see if he could hear what was going on inside. Gard started to walk down the aisle in the center of the floor, between the cubicles. After he marched forward into the aisle, he was spotted by something hiding within one of the cubicles.

A disturbing, chilling growl suddenly triggered Gard's fear, so he quickly faced the sound and saw a large monster squatting down in order to hide within the cubicle from the people outside the center aisle. The monster was a hatched egg spirit. It was a tall gray beast with wide mighty shoulders with a hunched over–shaped body. The growing sound alerted the rest of the six other hatched egg monsters hiding within the other cubicles. The three Hogs were surrounded by theses angry, threatening-looking spirits.

Hayden brought the gun up to the ready-to-fire position while telling Miles to find a place to hide. Gard had three of the egg monsters on his left and right to walk past in order to reach the door. With all these spirits in the building, it was clear that this was a trap, and it was now time for action. Gard shouted out to Hayden that he was making a dash toward Eric's office and to lay down cover fire for him. Gard went into a dead sprint to the door, easily getting past the first creature. Thanks to Hayden firing off his gun a few times, the second creature trying to stop Gard was struck in the head by three green baseball-shaped orbs. Hayden then took fire at the final monster between Gard and the door and managed to push away the monster's tackle attempt on Gard.

Gard shoved open the door with his shoulders. Eric was hit by the impact of the door being forced open wide, and he landed on his desk. Eric pointed to his boss, shouting at Gard that he was the horseman. Famine, with all his might, pushed the desk that Eric was on top of out the window. While that action was taking place, Gard lifted the sword and removed the sheath close to the spirit's face.

Once the blade was exposed, the glowing feature that it does whenever it is close to an evil spirit was finally released. Containing that glow for so long within the sheath caused a buildup of energy, and when that energy was released, it attacked the spirit as if it was a powerful defense spell. The blast of the blade attacked the spirit just as Famine shoved the desk to the window. Simultaneously, Eric and the desk he was on crashed outside the window while Famine was thrust out the office wall, knocking him back on the floor with all the cubicles.

Gard moved as fast as he could to grab Eric as he was falling out of the forty-second-floor story window. Eric grabbed hold of the desk table on one side while Gard managed to grab hold of the other side. The center leg of the desk snapped off as the desk swung to the side of the building. Gard's body was lying on the floor, his armpit on the edge of the shattered window and his right hand clinging to the desk. The shattered glass from the bottom edge of the window was tearing up Gard's armpit. The finger holes dug into the table were starting to drag down, causing his fingers to get scratched up and fill with splinters. Eric, on the other side of the table, was having the same problem with his fingers. Eric was sliding down and had to use his other hand to drive into the table to help support his body from falling. With the heavy rain falling all around, it was making the attempts to hang on even more difficult.

"In case one of us slips, I need you to know that I'm not mad at you for not giving me that loan!" Gard shouted. Gard was in no condition to pull the desk table back into the room. He was afraid that one false move could lead to him losing grip of the table, and Eric would fall with it.

"I could have done more than just say no to you! You were clearly in some troubled times, and all I did was throw you out of my life!" Eric said as he pierced some new finger holes higher up on the table to climb his way up. "Then I found out that you died in a plane crash afterward." Eric started to pull himself up the table. "I felt that your death was my fault!" Eric then dug his fingers higher up on the table and felt the whole thing start to split in two with Eric being on the falling side.

Eric and Gard made eye contact, and just before the table split in two, Eric pushed himself up off the table, and while in air, Gard let go of the table and used his free hand to grab Eric's hand. Gard dragged Eric's body over him and back to the floor next to him.

"That's why I went back to the Hogs. I found my chance to undo a mistake."

"You didn't make a mistake, Eric," Gard said as he got to his feet and offered a hand out to Eric. "It was my fault for the situation I was in. Even if you did give me the loan, I still would have ended up where I did. I'm just happy that I was here to save you."

Eric took the hand and got to his feet. "We're not saved yet. We still got the horsemen to take care of. And I think I got a plan on doing that."

Back by the cubicles, Hayden was firing off his angel gun all around him, keeping the hatched eggs at a safe distance. Hayden spotted the last egg monster heading over to Miles. Miles was squatting by the wall with his head covering his face, so Hayden rushed over to protect him. Hayden fired off his gun, but it was empty. Hayden then removed his hunting knife with the Garden diamond chips embedded at the tip of the blade.

"I'm just the escape plan, I'm just the escape plan, I'm just the escape plan!" Miles's fear and the overwhelming feeling of this battle caused Miles to lose his thought process. Miles's mental problems were acting up again, and he was having a hard time keeping himself calm. Miles looked up and saw one of the egg monsters on the verge of making an attack at him. But Hayden came just in time, shoving his hunting knife deep into the back of the monster. Hayden swung a leg over to trip the beast, and while it was on the ground, Hayden stabbed the beast until it was dead.

Over by the center of the floor was Famine, lost in his thoughts. He sensed a whiff of the power that took out the devil. He didn't get a good look at the weapon, just the sheath. Famine thought if he could steal the weapon, then he could be the new leader of the evil spirits. Famine got to his feet and saw Hayden and Miles.

Hayden quickly reloaded his gun and started to shoot his gun at the spirit. The spirit caught a slight whiplash from every shot he took. Every time his body flinched, it started to transform, and before Hayden knew it, he was charging at a large raging, mighty horse.

"Okay, so he's a horse now," Hayden uttered to himself as he continued his charge. Once Hayden's gun was empty, he swung his leg up and around the horse's back. Hayden reached around the horse's neck and started to pull back on the rifle in an attempt to choke the spirit. Famine was jumping like a wild bull. Hayden did his best to stay on top of the horse, but in time, He was flung right off and smashed against the wall, knocking him unconscious.

The steed then eyed Miles and took charge at him like a running bull. Miles fired off the gravity spell onto the spirit. The blast coming out of Miles's hand was draining his entire strength from his body and caused him to land on the ground, almost passing out. The effects of being hit by the gravity spell caused the horse to go down, but wasn't enough to pin him down.

"Hey, donkey!" shouted Gard.

Famine stopped his charge at Miles to look over at Gard. Famine spotted the sheath in Gard's hand and so started to take charge at Gard. Gard then followed the spirit's lead and ran up to the beast. Famine was going to use his mighty hooves to stomp Gard to death. Gard was lucky that Famine was moving slower than his usual pace due to being hit by Miles's spell; otherwise, this plan wouldn't have worked. Right before the two collided into each other, Gard slid under the beast's belly between his hooves. Once Gard was out of Famine's point of view, he saw that Eric was hiding behind him, holding a gold glowing sword. Eric swung the sword straight at Famine.

The sheath was in Gard's hand to get the spirit's attention, but Eric had the sword all along. Famine thought that Eric had fallen out of the window, so he didn't expect him to be standing behind Gard. The sword was swung at the horse's neck, killing him with one strong swing. The horse tipped over and started to slowly turn back to Mr. Clay's body.

Gard walked back up to Eric to hand him the sheath. Eric used Mr. Clay's suit to clean the blood off the sword before returning it into the sheath.

"Not a bad plan," Gard said.

"I could have sworn that the sword glowing was going to reveal me, but we were lucky Famine didn't see it."

"I think whatever Miles hit him with was what made the plan work. The horse would have killed us if it was at full speed," Gard added.

Eric ran over to check on Miles while Gard went over to check on Hayden. Gard eased Hayden awake before helping him up. Hayden asked if they won the fight. Gard smiled and said yes. Hayden, with a blank look on his face, placed his knife back into his sheath. Miles, on the other hand, was awake but barely. He was whispering to himself, telling himself what's real over and over.

Eric looked over at his friends with concern.

"He was like this when Juice and I picked him up, but not this bad," Hayden stated.

"We'll take my car back to the swamp. He's in no condition to teleport," Eric replied.

"So you're with us now?" wondered Gard.

Eric said that he was with his friends until the end. Last thing he needed was to find out that all his friends died trying to fix the balance while he stayed safe in his nice office. Eric helped Miles up and assisted him on walking to the elevator. As they walked over to the lift, Gard looked around the room. He saw that Hayden had single-handedly killed all the egg spirits. Hayden was a one-man army; he was a little frightening with his vicious actions. Hayden acting wild and being a strong fighter wasn't anything new to Gard. But Hayden, not having any emotions in his life, showed that he was still in need of help.

Eric was very concerned about Miles. Miles was the first to show a sign of friendship to him at the swamp, and now Miles's mind seemed lost worse than ever since he had to use the power he was too afraid to use. Miles played a big part on killing the spirit, but he couldn't celebrate with the others.

The four returned to Eric's car. They didn't want to interrupt the others on their search for Cider, so they just drove back to the swamp. They picked up some fast food on the way. Eric asked Gard to take over and drive. Eric may have been free from Famine's power of the heavy addiction to the drugs, but the side effects from the withdrawal was making it too hard to keep driving.

When they returned to the swamp, they reunited with the rest of the group. They put Miles to bed, hoping that a good night's sleep would do him good. Gard told Eric that he should go to bed too. Eric was heading to his camper, but then he stopped and faced everyone. He opened up about his past five years. He said he was feeling in such a sick mood because he had been on drugs for a while now.

He said that it all started when he started working at his job. After a few weeks of being one of the people in the cubicles, he was invited to Friday night drinks after hours. He hated it, found all the coworkers as annoying cocky suits. Still, he felt that if he wanted to climb up the career ladder, he thought he should get to know the other workers better.

Then one night, the coworkers were robbed at gunpoint after a late night at the bars. One of the workers tried to be a hero and fight back. The guy was very overweight and was very easily overpowered by the robber's might. Eric said that he took a bullet for his coworker. Eric didn't really see that as an act of bravery due to the bullet barely hurting him. But Eric played along and pretended not to have a dry Loomation that made him very strong.

Eric was patched up at the hospital and was given some pills for the pain. The pills would become his obsession in time. For Eric to play along with having a regular human body, he took the pills from time to time. He just wanted to use up all the refills so no one would get suspicious. Eric was taking the pills for pain when he wasn't suffering from any pain. Eric did find that the pills did, however, relax him.

Eric found out that the coworker who he took the bullet for was part of a higher board member's family. After that, Eric's career received so many extra favors, and before Eric knew it, he had a large job title, a fancy new office, and a ton of work that he was unprepared for. It all came so fast, and it led to tons of more stress. Eric took the pills for stress and got hooked. He was buying them from dealers inside his own office building. Eric was ashamed of his addiction and found it hard to open up to his friends about it. Now Eric was having a heavy reaction from the withdrawal and told the Hogs that he was going to get through it and was hoping that he could keep off the stuff.

The group assured Eric that they will be there for him during his time of need. After that, Eric went to his tent for much-needed sleep.

James was happy. He saw the Hogs getting along just like they used to. He knew that the group wasn't totally fixed. Gard told James about Hayden's high aggressive actions of the battle. It just looked like Hayden was full of unhealthy rage. That and Miles was worse than ever. James knew that with four Hogs recovering, it should be easy to help the final three.

Troubled Hogs

Sometime in Spring 2016

Not too far from the town she was heading toward, a woman was standing next to her broken-down car on the side of a country road. She waved down two cars. She was desperate for some assistance, but both cars just kept on driving. She thought no one would help her and started to think about walking to the town. Then a third car drove by, and this one stopped to help her.

"Thank you, sir," she gratefully said to the man getting out of his car.

The man was Hayden, and he didn't bother giving any introduction. He simply asked, "What's wrong with the car?"

"It just died on me all of a sudden."

Hayden reached into the woman's car to turn on her hazard lights. Once the lights started blinking, he saw that there wasn't a problem with the battery. "Any smoke coming out from the hood?" Hayden asked as he popped opened the hood of the car.

"No signs of any trouble. It just died."

Hayden took a quick check over the engine and focused on the spark plugs. Everything seemed shipshape. Hayden was more determined to find the problem than talk to the woman. Hayden put the hood back down and walked to the side of her car.

"You know, I waved down two other cars who passed me, and none of them wanted to help." The woman stopped talking when she saw him look under her car. Once she was only looking at his legs, she went on talking. "Being out here in the woods, I lost my cell signal, so I couldn't call for help." She then started to hear Hayden poke something from under the car. She had no idea what he was doing, so she just kept chatting. "I thought my only option was to walk to town and find a mechanic."

By this time, Hayden climbed back up from under the car; he looked at her and said, "I'm a mechanic." Hayden walked over to the back of his truck and grabbed a gas container. Hayden unscrewed the lid of his container and started to pour it into the side of the car. Shortly after he started to pour, he asked her to try to start the car. She got into her driver's seat and turned the key. The car started up right away.

"Are you kidding me? I was out of gas!" she said in shock. The girl felt so dumbfounded by this news. She felt that she should have been smart enough to know if she was running low on gas.

Hayden looked over the dashboard of the car and saw that her fuel gauge had her sitting at half tank. "Your gas gauge is broken." Hayden then went back to pouring the rest of the gas into her car. "This will get you to town. I recommend you find a gas station when you get there."

"And what about my gas gauge?"

"There's a car repair shop that can fix it for you," Hayden said as he capped his gas container and headed back to his truck.

"Well, thank you! I didn't think that there were any more Good Samaritans out there."

"Well, the thing about meeting a Good Samaritan is that you'll have to be visited by two jerks first."

"Well, I would really like to repay you."

"No payment needed."

"Okay then, how about this. I'm the new manager at the bar in town, the Bends. I start my first shift tonight, and tomorrow I start doing the boring paperwork. If you stop by tonight, first drink's on me."

"I might be there," Hayden said with a nod. Once Hayden turned away from the woman, he heard a faint sound from deep in the woods. It was a woman screaming in pain. Hayden recognized that sound; he knew that scream all too well. Hayden looked around and started to remember being here before. He remembered helping this woman on the side of the road. He remembered going to that bar and spending the night talking to her.

He then heard the sound of a woman screaming again. This time the sound was much closer. Hayden turned to face the woman who he just helped and saw her burning in flames. She was burning like a hot torch while she was screaming in pain.

Hayden then woke up from his nightmare.

Wednesday, October 7, 2020

Hayden had a tight grip on his hunting knife that he had slept with every night since he arrived at the swamp. Hayden was breathing hard and was trying to calm himself down. After Hayden managed to get a hold of his breathing, he forced himself out of bed and got dressed. Hayden exited his pop-up camper with his backpack in hand. He marched over to the picnic table to fill his bag up with some food and water. He always ate his breakfast during his morning hike in the swamp.

As he got closer to the table, he saw a number of people under the canopy that rested above the table. He saw Eric and James sitting next to each other talking. Boston was under the canopy also, but he wasn't sitting. He was looking through one of his bags full of weapons that rested on the table. Hayden figured that he was checking his inventory to make sure Hayden didn't take more than what he said he did. Hayden did take some ammunition yesterday, but he already confessed to that.

Once Hayden reached the table, he saw that Timber was also packing up some water bottles. Timber explained that he was teleporting out with James and Boston to continue the search for Cider. Timber asked Hayden if he wanted to join them. Hayden passed; he didn't want to waste time searching for some half-human, half-spirit hybrid. He wanted to go on battle missions or search for his own evil spirit. James already told him that there were no leads on who or where his spirit could be.

The spirit normally worked from inside the spiritual realm, which meant that it mostly attacked Hayden's mind.

Eric and James's conversation came to an end, and Eric headed back to his tent. James rose to his feet to ask Boston a question. He leaned in close and whispered, "Did you bring that special order I requested?"

Boston dug through the bag he was inventorying and pulled out a small glass bottle containing some red liquid. Boston whispered to James while handing it over, "If the Saints find out that I didn't dispose every ounce of this serum, they'll retire me."

James patted his friend on the back, claiming that this was going to work. He turned around. "Hey, Hayden," James called out.

Hayden eased his way over to James while James did the same. James told Hayden that he wanted him to have the bottle.

"What is it?" Hayden asked, not being very interested in the gift.

"There was a time when the Saints were building a weapon that could harness the power of fire. They ordered Boston and a few others to develop this weapon. They made a serum that could cause the person who drinks it to grow fire from their skin."

"Not interested!" Hayden said as he backed away.

"Hayden, you're the only person who this serum would work on!"

This made Hayden stop dead in his tracks.

"The serum works, but the fire would burn the person's skin off. You're the only one with a fireproof body!"

"You read my file! You know what fire reminds me of!" Hayden said, keeping his back on James.

"I know that the images in your mind haunt you, and I admit that they're not going to ease away by simply talking to the others about it. I think you need exposure therapy."

"I need to kill my spirit, that's all!" Hayden shouted as he turned to James.

"Your spirit knows exactly how to bring you to your knees. She can show you images of fire, and you'll be begging her to kill you!" James said as he moved in close to Hayden. "Why don't you hit her with something she won't expect? Why don't you use your fear as a weapon?" James then shoved the serum at Hayden's arm's reach. "When you received your

Loomation, it was able to read the tolerance of the fire's heat that you've built up over your life. When it dried up, it made your body fireproof." James then changed his voice to a softer tone. "Hayden, your motto was once 'Everything burns.' Then after you got your power, you changed it to 'Everything burns—"

"But me," Hayden said, quietly finishing the quote.

James once again begged Hayden to take the bottle, and this time Hayden accepted.

<hr>

Later that day, James took Timber and Boston out to search for Cider while some of the Hogs stayed in the swamp. They passed time by hitting golf balls. The clubs were left inside the truck that sat at the swamp.

Gard knocked the golf ball hard off the tee, launching it out far away.

"*Fore!*" shouted Juice to no one.

"You know with our dry Loomation inside us, we could go pro in the golfing business," Gard stated.

"You may have a big advantage with your long drives, but your putting is garbage," Juice said just before he gave his golf ball a whack. "Oh, I sliced it!"

"That's a bad thing, Juice," Will said as he slipped on a hooded sweatshirt due to the misty weather they were having.

"You feeling the first shiver of fall?" Juice asked Will.

Both Will and Gard gave Juice an odd look.

"What? My father says it every year," Juice said as he set up another golf ball on a tee. "Man, I love the fall. It gets cold enough to wear pants and hoodies that keep you warm. That and those long sleeves keep the bugs from walking all over your exposed skin."

"Nighttime comes sooner, which gives more stargazing time," Will mentioned as he took a seat in one of the chairs.

"It's the best time to have a fire when it actually keeps you warm instead of making you sweat more," Gard added.

"Yeah, too bad Hayden won't let us have one," Juice uttered as he hit his golf ball.

Gard told the two how Hayden acted during their fight with Famine and the hatched egg spirits last night. Gard describe Hayden's action as a soulless killing robot. Will was upset that they took on Famine and didn't involve the rest of the group. Gard said that it was all Hayden's idea, but Gard couldn't blame it all on him. Gard did go along with it. He stood by what they did; otherwise, Eric could have died.

Eric walked up to the three with a blanket on his shoulders. His friends asked him if he was alright. He said that he was getting theses cold chills here and there. He sat down in one of the chairs and claimed that it was a side effect from the withdrawal. Juice thought that after killing Famine, Eric would go back to normal.

"I talked to James about that this morning," Eric said before he took a swig of water. "Famine just made me crave the pills on a very high level. He had nothing to do with how the pills made me feel or how I feel after I stop taking them."

"Do you still have the craving for them?" wondered Will.

"Not as much as I used to. James told me that now that the horseman is dead, everyone in his territory is free from those heavy cravings. But people have done it for so long, it's now instinct for them. They are so used to doing it that even without the cravings, they don't know how to stop. The habit won't break for them until some good spirits come to plant some better ideas in their minds. Many good spirits are responsible for putting the ones who are alone into rehab. The ones who are not alone have friends and family looking out for them. I'm one of the lucky ones. I have all of you guys, but many people right now aren't as lucky."

"Well, if you feel the desire to take more pills, just tell me, and I'll give you a good smack!" Gard said as he swung hard at the golf ball. Gard completely missed the ball and was the first to make fun of himself. "Woo, I got a hold of that one!"

This caused the group to have a good laugh. Eric stood up from his chair to reach for Gard's golf club, which he handed over. Eric took a mighty swing at the ball, and everyone was impressed by the drive and accuracy. Eric explained that he had a private golf coach who taught him how to play due to him having to play with his bosses and rich clients. Eric then sat back in his chair to wrap himself up in his blanket again.

"The positive spirits and the rest of the angels won't come down until Memphis is dead," Juice sadly stated. The Hogs remembered their overall goal of what they were doing, and that was to kill Memphis. The Hogs were skeptical about being able to accomplish this task. Gard believed that the group was now ready to take on Memphis. Eric mentioned that they still haven't killed Hayden's, Timber's, and Miles's spirits, reminding Gard that the plan was to first take out their evil spirits before taking on Memphis.

"I know Hayden was a strong soldier last night, but I'm worried about his state of mind," Will admitted. "Gard, you agreed to take on Famine because you were worried about Eric. But I think Hayden was itching for a fight, and with that motivation, he brought Miles into a battle that he wasn't ready for."

The four looked over to Miles, who was sitting by himself up on top of a hill just outside the campsite. His mind was suffering after the battle with the horseman last night. This morning he seemed better, but he was keeping his distance and not saying much. Eric and Gard gave Miles credit to him, saying that if it wasn't for him, they would all have been killed by Famine. Will mentioned that if they wanted to take on Memphis, they'd need Miles at full health, and they couldn't afford him to break down every time he used a powerful attack.

"When I was at the gates of Heaven, the craving feeling for the pills was completely gone. Things got very stressful up there, and I didn't even think about reaching for my bottle," Eric stated.

"He did start acting fine when we got up there," Juice uttered.

"Maybe being that close to Heaven heals the mind, such as the Garden of Eden heals the body," Will said, thinking out loud.

"Maybe the sickness that his spirit put on him was slowly returning after he returned to earth," Gard theorized. "After he used that much active Loomation while in battle, his mind just went straight back to the illness he was carrying before he went up to the gates."

"When Hayden and I picked him up at the hospital, he at first didn't even know if we were real. I feel bad for him. He's the only one with that power, and if he ever told anyone outside the group what he can do, they would tell him that it's not real, that it's all in his head, and that he needs mental help. It's not healthy for him to hide what he can do. The results made him unable to identify what's real and what's not. And when you add the effects of the horseman Pestilence, you get one troubled person," Juice said as he returned his club into the golf bag.

"I think a blast from a cube could help him," Eric replied as he stood up from his chair. "I think a fresh blast of Loomation could clear his mind again."

The Hogs thought it was worth a try, so they all gathered up to the fire ring. As Eric was solving the cube, Hayden returned from his hike. Once the cube was all set up, Eric handed it over to Will. Will recommended Eric to take a blast from the cube as well. He thought a blast would speed up his withdrawal sickness. Eric said that he didn't want any shortcuts from this dreaded feeling. He said getting though this the natural way will make him stronger in the long run.

Will took the cube and asked Miles if he was ready. After Miles gave consent, Will crunched down on the cube. Everyone saw the cube glow a bright white light. Will released the pressure he had on the cube, and the blast of Loomation was released, striking down Will and Miles. Gard was standing behind Miles, ready to catch him and to ease him to the ground.

Miles opened his eyes and felt fine. His mind felt clearer now, and he was able to keep himself from uttering nonsense. Miles reported that the cube felt like a temporary fix, that in time he'd lose his mind again. The process of that will speed up if he did defense spells again. Hayden raised his voice, saying that they needed to take out Pestilence, claiming that as long as he's alive, Miles will never be able to escape his health problems.

"I think he's at the hospital I was at when you guys picked me up," Miles reported.

"I know where that is. I can get us there within the hour if someone would lend me a car," Hayden stated.

"Now let's calm down for a moment. Maybe we should wait for James and the others to get back before we go anywhere," Will replied.

"I say we at least hit the road. Once we reach cell phone range, we can give James a call and tell him what we're up to, and he can teleport to the hospital. Us driving there instead of just teleporting gives us more time to think of a plan," Gard suggested.

"Miles, this is your evil spirit who we're going after. What do you think we should do?" Juice asked his friend.

Miles didn't want to return to his scared and uncertain ways. He knew that Pestilence was at that hospital; he could feel it. He knew that until that spirit was dead, he'd never fully be able to help his friends. Miles said that they should go and face the horseman so that he could have his mind free from his sickness once and for all.

Will, Juice, Hayden, Gard, and Miles all packed up in Will's car and drove out of the swamp. Eric was currently in no condition to fight, so he stayed behind in case James and the others returned before they could receive a call from the group. He wished his brave friends good luck and to come back safe. The car made it to the road that bordered around the swamp, and they headed to the mental hospital.

Deadly Disease

A mysterious woman marched up the steps leading up to St. Anthony Hospital's front doors. She seemed to be in a hurry as she entered the building. She saw that there wasn't a human in sight, but she wasn't there to see a human. When she approached the front door of Dr. Angelo's office, she didn't bother knocking, just turned the knob and entered.

Dr. Angelo was surprised to see her. "What are you doing here, Cindy? You know that this is my territory."

"During the search for Cider, I discovered that a gas station camera had spotted Juice and four other Hogs not too far from here," Cindy reported.

"They're heading here," The doctor stated as he leaned back in his chair. "After the attack on my brother Famine, they must theorize that I too stayed in a position close to the Hog I was assigned to." The doctor eased his swivel chair over to the window. The calm doctor's tension started to rise as he glanced out the window. "After the birth of Cider was announced, Memphis lifted the ban on killing the Hogs. And since then, I've been conjuring up something that will kill them painfully slow!" the man said, pounding his fist into his palm.

"I came because I want to take care of Hayden personally. I don't trust anyone besides me to kill him."

The doctor turned his chair back toward the woman. He was insulted by the fact that she didn't think that he could handle the kill himself. The woman was Hayden's evil spirit, and she knew that Hayden was present when Famine was killed, so she wasn't sure if one horseman was capable of doing the job. Now that they managed to kill a horseman, the weaker spirits were now starting to fear the Hogs.

"They've already killed Susan and the Grim Reaper. They are obviously targeting their spirits, which puts me on their hit list."

"This explains why they're coming for me," Dr. Angelo stated.

"That's why I want Hayden dead. As long he's alive, they'll have a reason to go after me."

"Well, they're in my territory, and that allows only me to do anything to them. What would you be willing to trade for the right to kill Hayden?"

"I'll be willing to pardon off half my territory to you," she said with no hesitation.

"Deal," he said as he offered his hand.

She shook the spirit's hand and was slightly shocked that the deal was made so easily. After the deal was made, they started to work up a plan on killing the Hogs. They had an advantage; the Hogs were coming right to them.

⥈⋙∙∙∙⋘⥈

Sunset was underway when the Hogs arrived at the hospital. They talked to James over the phone while on their way. James had confidence in the five Hogs to take on the horseman by themselves if they wished. Everyone knew how important it was for them to find Cider before their enemies, so they told James and the others to carry on their search.

In the parking lot, the five armed themselves with their special arsenal. Will, Hayden, and Gard all carried angel rifles. Miles wasn't given any weapons; he had his active Loomation powers to defend him. But he was hoping to avoid having to use it. Juice was given the sword encased in the sheath. Juice was informed that when the glowing feature was brought out, it would release a powerful blast when exposed. The blast was strong enough to knock a horseman through a wall. This made the plan of taking out the spirit quite easy. Plus the sword glowing in the presence of a dark spirit would expose their target.

The five exited the car and made their way to the front entrance. The windows along the side of the building all had dark shades covering the glass. The place was old, with faded red brick and gothic-shaped windows outlining the walls. Walking up the steps, some of the Hogs started to feel a touch of fear creeping underneath their shield of bravery. The fear of hospital security putting a stop to them before making an attack on Pestilence was a possibility. The Hogs knew that they could overpower simple security, but the idea of hurting innocent people was unsettling. The front door was open, and the Hogs started to walk in.

Hayden, who was on the bottom of the steps, was about to move up to the door when he heard something from the woods. This sound was of a woman screaming, the same scream that haunted his dreams. It was only heard by Hayden. Hayden turned his head away from the front door and toward the source to the sound. Will called out Hayden's name, confused as to why Hayden seemed motionless.

"Hayden, come on," Will insisted with a concerned plea. But before Hayden could move his head back to Will, an invisible force slammed the door in Will's face. Hayden, being the only Hog outside of the building, charged up to the door and used all his might in an attempt to pull open the door.

Inside, Will, Juice, and Gard all tried to push open the door, but it was no use. The door wasn't budging. Pestilence had put a spiritual lockdown on the building, and the Hogs inside were trapped.

The Hogs inside were yelling out to Hayden, wondering if their voices could carry over to the outside. But Hayden heard nothing but silence from inside the building. The Hogs inside couldn't hear Hayden's hollers from the inside either. The Hogs inside put their tug-of-war with the door to a pause when they heard a gust of wind from behind them. They all turned their heads and saw a green cloud drifting their way fast. The green smoke permeated all the rooms of the building and covered up all the windows and doors with a thick coat of smoke. The green fog engulfed the four Hogs at the door.

Outside, Hayden backed away from the door, removed his gun from his side, and pointed it at the door. Hayden fired at the door a few times. The bullets dug holes into the door, but they disintegrated when they touched the thick green smoke that covered the inside of the building. Hayden maneuvered himself away from the door, positioned himself in front of a window, and took four shots at the window, resulting in the same outcome. Hayden started to eye the roof to see if there was a chimney or something to find a way in. But he heard the screams coming from the woods once again. Hayden took his attention away from the building and focused on the woods. He was tired of hearing the screams, and he knew that if he faced his fear right now, he would encounter his dark spirit. Hayden was ready for a fight, and with a heavy grip on his angel rifle, he charged into the woods.

Inside, the three of the four Hogs were on the floor emitting nasty coughs. Will, Juice, and Gard had fallen awfully sick after being exposed to the green fog. The green fog was lingering in every room, giving off a smoky atmosphere. The symptoms of the sick Hogs were pounding headaches, stomach pains, and nausea.

Will looked at his forearm and saw it was starting to bleed from cuts that were spontaneously appearing. Both Juice and Gard had also started to bleed from fresh cuts that were appearing all over their bodies. The infection from the green smoke had caused the Hogs' dry Loomation to tear up their body from the inside.

Due to Miles having an active Loomation, he was immune from the sickness. But as he looked at his mighty friends writhing in pain, he grew very overwhelmed and frightful. Miles tried to perform the healing spell on his friends, but it failed to cure them of this deadly disease. Juice felt that this fog action must mean that Pestilence was indeed in the building.

"I think that was obvious, Juice!" Gard shouted as he tried to get to his feet. Gard felt his legs lose all strength halfway up, and then he helplessly plopped back to the floor.

"Well, it's a good thing we're in a hospital because this horseman is going to need one," Juice struggled to say as he tried to fly his body off the ground. He too ended up like Gard, flopping back to the floor almost immediately after trying to get up.

"You guys are in no condition to fight. We should just retreat," Miles suggested.

"Miles is right. We should teleport out of here, regroup, and take on Pestilence another day," Will agreed.

But Miles was unable to teleport out of the building. They figured that there was an anti-teleporting symbol up in the building somewhere. Will grabbed his phone in attempt to call Hayden, but there was no signal. The Hogs were trapped in a building, and there was no help coming for them.

Miles assisted the three sick Hogs over to the main waiting room where he placed them on the couches.

"Where's Pestilence?" asked Gard.

"I bet releasing this fog had worn him out, so he probably released his attack in a place where he would have felt safe to recuperate afterward," Miles theorized.

"If that's true, then we have a few minutes to plan our attack," Gard stated.

"Yeah, but we can't even stand right now! How are we supposed to take on a horseman?" questioned Juice.

At this point, Will revealed that he had the cube in his possession. The Hogs believed that a blast from the cube could wipe Pestilence's disease from their bodies. But due to the smoke still clouding the air of the building, they would just get infected with it again. They figured that once they get a hit with the blast from the cube, they may be able to fight off the infection for maybe a minute before they got sick again. With that thought in mind, they started to come up with a plan.

Outside in the woods, Hayden was following the sound of the screams. Hayden couldn't figure out if the screams were real or all just in his head. Hayden had heard the sounds of the screams in his nightmares most nights. Hearing them while awake made him feel like it wasn't all in his head, so he kept marching. Hayden sensed that his evil spirit was calling out to him, leading him to his death. Hayden stopped his walk and looked back; he was now so far away from the road, he no longer saw it. Realizing that he was now isolated in the woods, he felt a disturbing familiarity.

As Hayden stood alone, he remembered the time he moved out to his house in the woods almost five years ago. At first, he found comfort living in nature away from the city. The enjoyment of being isolated didn't come until what happened to Amy. When Hayden though of Amy, he gave off an uncontrollable shake and had to press his hand up against a tree for balance. Hayden told himself to never think about Amy if he could help it.

Hayden told himself that he wasn't a good friend. He told Amy that he would protect her, and his failure was a never-ending torture for him. When Juice came for him, he was told that there was evil out there responsible for all the awful things that has happened to him. Ever since then, Hayden was driven by the chance of gaining revenge for Amy. Hayden once again heard the screaming in the woods. His fight with his evil spirit was close by, and he was willing to do whatever it took to win this fight. Hayden pulled out the small bottle he received from James and swallowed the liquid inside.

Back inside the hospital, Miles was searching for that anti-teleporting symbol while the other Hogs were in the waiting room. Miles had the layout of the building memorized in his head, so he knew his way around. The whole building seemed to carry this green mist, making it hard to see. He came to his old room and saw that it was just as he left it. Miles looked at the sheet resting on his bed and remembered that he once fashioned it into a noose.

"Ready to come back home?" asked a voice from down the hall.

Miles turned to face the man speaking and saw Dr. Angelo. But by now, Miles knew who he really was. "Pestilence," Miles said, being unafraid.

"How are your friends downstairs doing?" asked the horseman.

"What did you do to them?"

"It's a powerful disease that affects humans who carry dry Loomation. I made it special for this occasion. After what you did to my kind, you all deserve the slowest, most painful execution I can deliver."

Miles's hand started to quiver as he was eager to fire off a defense spell, but he was too afraid to fight. "Why let me walk free unharmed then?"

"You're no threat! Your power is much too weak against me. And besides, one attack out of you, and your mind would once again lose all control!"

"I have you to thank for that! All the sessions with you talking about my gifts gave you the opportunity to make me doubt myself. You drove the idea that I had no power in me, that it was all in my head. When I saw the power released from my body or felt it inside me, I would think that it wasn't real, but when I felt and saw the proof, it made me think reality wasn't real."

"Never during any of our sessions did you mention how you and the others killed the devil! I thought that was going to be a secret you would take to your grave."

"The more things you told me that wasn't real made me block out the fight with the devil even more than I normally did!"

"Well, I'm sure your buddies brought the weapon with them. They should be too sick by now to even walk, so I'll just go get it and use it on them, and then I'm going to use it on you!"

Pestilence turned and headed toward the main hall, but Miles waved his hand to fire off a few defense spells. A few blasts of violet light came from Miles's hands, striking the spirit's back. The blast might as well have been a splash of water from a calm fountain. Miles was so out of practice with his defense spells that he couldn't pull out the stronger attacks.

Miles dropped to his knees in exhaustion. Miles seeing the light coming out of his hand caused his mind go a little unstable. Miles felt that he had already started to slip back to his uncertain thoughts.

Pestilence, no longer bothered with Miles, figured that he was done with the fight. Now that the only Hog unaffected by the disease was out of the fight, Pestilence felt comfortable approaching the Hogs in the waiting room.

Outside, Hayden felt an annoying heartburn and figured that the serum was starting to kick in. Hayden kept going and reminded himself that he was doing this for Amy. Hayden and Amy never were even a couple; she was just a friend who needed his help from time to time. Amy was recently divorced, claiming that her husband was an abuser. She moved away from him to start fresh, and before she even made it to the new town, her car broke down.

When she discovered that her lights weren't working in her house, she asked Hayden if he could fix it. Hayden had experience with wiring and helped her out for more free drinks at the bar. She was new in town, far away from any living relative, and really needed a friend like Hayden. He helped her reach the town by giving her some extra gas. He helped with her house lights, and he managed to protect her when her ex-husband came to her demanding money. Hayden and his advanced strength was able to shove off the heavily built guy like he was nothing. Hayden could have broken the guy's bones and deliver two black eyes, but instead he just shoved him like he was a rag doll. After that, Hayden was given free beers for life from Amy.

When Hayden no longer heard the screams in his head, he came to a complete stop and looked around. Then harsh, torturing memories were being visualized in his mind. The memories of Hayden walking to Amy's house carrying flowers came to his thoughts. The memories were causing not only mental pain but physical pain as well. Hayden dropped to his knees and felt that his will to push out the bad memories were causing this physical pain. Hayden was screaming with his hands on his head, but the only one around to hear his screams was the evil spirit of Phobia, who was attacking Hayden from the spiritual realm.

The memories the spirit was firing into Hayden's mind made him remember the first time he heard Amy's screams. Hayden remembered that night; he dropped the flowers he was carrying and ran to the house. When he had the house in sight, he saw it glowing in flames. The house was burning everywhere, and the screams were coming from the second floor. These memories made Hayden believe that a man could die from reliving the haunted past. Hayden felt his body's energy quickly draining and his heartbeat going out of control from the amount of pain that was coming from revisiting his memories.

The spirit was trying to kill Hayden, and every time Hayden tried to block the past, she piled it on even harder. Hayden started to remember barging into the front door unafraid of the flames. Inside the house, the screams were so loud, Hayden knew he had to act fast to save her. Hayden hustled up the steps, and when he reached the halfway mark, the stairs collapsed under his feet. The fire and burned rubble buried him. If it wasn't for his dry Loomation making him strong and fireproof, he would have surely died. Nevertheless, the air was thin, and Hayden was on the verge of suffocating. He couldn't believe that Amy was still able to scream after all this time. Hayden got to his feet and took a mighty jump up to the second floor. He caught the upstairs with his forearms and managed to pull himself up. He then had to run because the floor was starting to give way. Hayden jumped into Amy's room and saw her burning in the fire like a hot coal.

Hayden grabbed her and jumped out of the window, landing in the yard with her in his arms. Hayden ran away from the house to be clear of any falling rubble. He then placed her on the ground and used his hands to douse the flames. When he saw her with the flames out, he couldn't bear the sight of her. She was covered in third-degree burns and was no longer breathing. She was dead before Hayden even got to her.

Hayden remembering all this made him fall to the ground, face to the dirt and eyes closed. In that state of mind, he heard the spirit talk to him.

"I made sure that every time you would see or think about fire, you would see her burning. I made sure that the screams would come to you whenever you would try to help others. I was assigned to turn you into a slithering coward. But you still wished to fight with your friends despite everything I did to you."

Hayden was in such misery as his whole body was in pain by trying to block out the depressed memories. His mind was nothing but haunting images. He just wanted the spirit to end his life right there, but she kept on taunting him.

"At least I kept you afraid of fire. You know the investigation called it an electrical wiring accident, which always made you think the fire was caused by you. But the truth is that I started that fire. I then disguised myself as the fire investigator to trick you into thinking that it was always your fault."

Once Hayden heard that last piece of information, his memories became altered. He knew that the wiring in that house was fine, which made him believe that the fire was caused by an evil spirit. He just forgot about that when the spirit was hitting him with his blocked memories. Hayden's passion for revenge came to him. Now knowing that the fire wasn't his fault caused him to lose that fear of seeing the element again.

Hayden tossed his arm out from under his chest in a strong motion. Fire was tossed out of his arm like a defense spell, and it seemed to hit something. The flames being hurled out of Hayden's body could hit someone while they were in the spiritual realm. The spirit of Phobia suddenly felt the burning flames, and that caused her to appear in physical form, burning and shrieking in pain.

The sound of the spirit's shrieks was a joyful sound for Hayden. It was nice to hear the evil that caused Amy's death holler in pain.

Hayden got to his feet and approached the burning spirit. He then used both hands to release out enough fire to burn the spirit to ash. Once the spirit was no more, the fire vanished away, and Hayden dropped to his knees to catch his breath. He did what he set out to do; he now felt stronger and knew that the nightmares would now stop.

Hayden eyed the way from where he came; he rose to his feet and dashed toward the hospital to help his friends.

In the waiting room, Pestilence saw the three Hogs resting on the floor, too weak to defend themselves. As the spirit walked in close, Gard, with all his remaining might, twisted himself from belly to back and lifted the sword up as high as he could. Gard then removed the blade from its sheath, exposing the glowing feature it emits when exposed to evil spirits. Just like last time, the glowing feature being released after being concealed came out as a powerful blast that jolted the horseman back away from the Hogs.

"*Will, now!*" Gard instructed.

Will was resting with the cube under his hand placed in the crunched-down position this whole time. When Pestilence was knocked off balance, it was time to go in for the kill, and to do that, they would need a rush of energy to be blasted into them. Once Will eased off the cube, the three were hit with a fresh burst of Loomation, wiping out the disease inside them.

"*Juice, go!*" Will yelled after the blast cleared.

Juice floated his body up into the air and bolted his way to the sword still in Gard's hand. Once he had the sword in hand, he rocketed himself straight to the spirit with the tip of the sword leading the way. As Juice was charging, the effects of the green fog had already sunk in, causing Juice to fall ill once again. Juice managed to impale a bit of the blade into Pestilence's chest, but before he could deliver the fatal blow, he collapsed to the ground, losing his grip on the handle.

Pestilence was leaning up against a wall while he tried to ease the sword out of his chest.

Miles stumbled his way into the room and saw his friends on the ground in a life-threatening condition. Miles looked over and saw Pestilence struggling to ease the sword out of his wound. Miles had to act fast for there won't be another chance to fight if he stalled. Miles saw the glowing sword and remembered how Logan managed to use that glow as a weapon. He rushed straight toward the glowing weapon and blasted out a defense spell from his chest. The attacked infused with the glowing of the sword made it twice as powerful. The renewed force of the attack thrust the blade deeper into the horseman's body, ending his life.

Once the spirit was dead, the lingering smoke cleared up, and the sick Hogs now felt fine. Due to the recoil of firing a defense spell from his chest, Miles was knocked to the ground. Juice helped his friend back to his feet while Gard removed the sword that was stuck into the wall with the horseman between the wall and the handle.

"How are you guys feeling?" Miles asked.

They replied that they all felt fine and were wondering how Miles was feeling. Miles felt a little out of strength due to his defense attack, but his mind felt at ease and clear. Miles would no longer suffer from his grip on reality and would be able to use his active Loomation again with no mental consequences.

Just then, the front door was forced open with a fiery blast. Hayden came running in with fire burning in his palms. "Where's the danger? I got high fever and need to burn something!" Hayden shouted as loud as he could with wild eyes.

This entrance at first put the Hogs on guard, but when they saw that it was just Hayden, they released an impulsive laugh.

"Hayden, the battle's over. You're a little late," Juice replied.

"I see you've been busy," Will mentioned.

Hayden looked down at his hands, feeling embarrassed for charging in for no reason. He doused out the flames. Gard pointed out that

Hayden must have gotten over his fear of fire. Hayden informed his friends that he killed his evil spirit.

The five Hogs had a big victory today; they managed to eliminate two dark spirits who were breaking the order of the balance. Hayden got over his fear of fire, and it seemed to have warmed his heart.

That night, the Hogs sat around a warm fire. Hayden was almost skipping as he circled the fire ring, feeding the flames with sticks and logs. With the campsite having its lights up, the tents set up, and now the fire burning bright, it looked just like the good old days.

The Hogs were drinking their beverages while Hayden told them about his past five years. He told them about Amy, that she was a good person and a good friend. Hayden knew she just had a divorce, so he didn't want to ask her out right away. He just enjoyed the company of a friend, something he was lacking at the time. On the day he was going to ask her out was the day she died.

Hayden's friends all expressed their condolences upon hearing about Amy. Hayden explained that it was his evil spirit who was responsible for her death in an attempt to have him tremble at the sight of fire. Hayden gave in to the fear and avoided fire. Every time he saw a flicker of a flame, he would be reminded of seeing Amy's burns. But now that the evil spirit was dead, he could move past that fear. He covered his memories of Amy with joyful ones. He saw her in his friends: the warmheartedness, the joyfulness, the occasional air-headiness was all within her as well. When he saw the fire now, he remembered those dark nights camping out in the woods when he was just a kid. His family always put him in charge of the fire. At the time, he was afraid of the dark, so he made sure that the fire was always burning brightly.

Hayden looked down at his hands, feeling slightly upset that the serum that gave him the power to make fire from his body had waned off. But he was happy to be able to make fire the old-fashioned way again.

Peace with Death

Thursday, October 8, 2020

That afternoon in the swamp, a few of the Hogs were with Boston on the northern hill that overshadowed the campsite. Hayden was chucking firewood logs into the air for his friends for target practice. Hayden found this as an amusing way to chop up firewood. After Hayden tossed one high across the sky, Miles was able to blast it into two pieces by hitting it with one of his defense spells.

"Hey, that one was blue!" shouted Hayden in celebration. The strength level of the defense spell was reflected by the color of light it presented. The rainbow was the chart of the power levels. Purple was the weakest, and red was the strongest. Miles knew that purple would only drive away small animal critters and would have no effect on any of the spirits. Miles's highest level of attack he had ever achieved was green. He was informed by Boston that green would do some damage to a lot of spirits.

"Last time I had to train from the ground up, it took me a few days to reach the blue stage," Miles stated.

"Just because you haven't trained in such a long time doesn't mean you have lost your progress. The muscles are still there, you just need to flex them a bit," Boston informed.

Miles was happy to hear that he didn't have to start from scratch, which gave him high hopes of reaching green soon. But due to him not having that advance strength, he had to take scheduled brakes while training so that firing off the blast from his hands didn't tire him out too much. Miles made his way back down the hill to grab some food.

Hayden approached the hill from the other side. While standing on top of the hill, he chucked the fire logs as close to the campsite as he could, noting that he'll pick up the pieces later. As he and Boston were standing on top of the hill overlooking the campsite, Boston gained a newfound sense on just how amazing this place really was. From up there, he could see the small campsite surrounded by acres of decaying swamp land.

"How did you guys manage to find a place like this?" asked Boston in a sense of wonder.

"Pure luck," Hayden replied. "The place was bigger when we found it. But after I took some of the diamond pebbles out from under the ground, the blessed land shrank a bit."

"Diamond pebbles?" Boston uttered as he issued a confused look toward Hayden. Hayden thought that Boston read the Hang Out Group members' files, which was why he was slightly vague in his details. Boston said that any details that could have been an indication on how the Hogs managed to kill the devil were redacted. So Boston had no idea what diamond pebbles Hayden was referring to. Boston asked if he could see them.

Hayden took Boston to the cabin that sat in the center of the campsite. The cabin was titled Diamond in the Rough. Hayden lifted a small throw rug from the floorboards, revealing a hatch door. He pulled on the handle, lifted the door, and exposed the dirt. Hayden informed Boston that the remaining chipped-off diamond pieces were tucked under the dirt that they were looking at.

Hayden informed Boston that the chips were fragments from the diamond that powers the great Garden of Eden. The pieces, once exposed to dirt, would bless the land around it. That's how the campsite was so blessed and rich. Hayden said that he took what he could from the dirt to help him build his bullets that he used in the battle against the devil.

Boston was fascinated by how much power the pieces had. They only seemed to bless the land and any heavy weight sitting upon it. This would explain why the cabin and the truck were still in perfect shape. Boston was impressed by the way Hayden was able to arm the pieces, and this caused him to wonder what he could build with them. Unfortunately, Boston was under law by the archangels that no angel, spirit, or saint could build something too powerful. But Hayden was human; no rules were bonded to him. If Hayden could build something with Boston's assistance, that could be a loophole.

Around the fire ring, James had a breakthrough on the Cider mission. A photo of someone who had the identical face as Juice was spotted on a bus station security camera. James showed a photo of the man. Confirming that the hybrid was real gave the Hogs a chilling feeling.

Juice was worried about what kind of trouble this guy could have gotten himself into. The hybrid having his face could make Juice a wanted criminal. James assured Juice that if there was a crime bluntly done by Cider, it would have been easier to find him. Cider was keeping a low profile in order to stay safe and hidden. James reported that whenever they leave the swamp, they were constantly monitoring any of Juice's online accounts. Logging into any banking accounts, shopping accounts, or social media accounts would alert them on his location. Gard opening his social media account was how the Grim Reaper found him.

James said that Cider was spotted on that bus station camera late last night. The location was just an hour away from where Juice was living. It was also an hour away from Juice's hometown, Maze. The Hogs believe that Cider could be heading toward a place that he would feel like he would belong. Since he had all of Juice's memories, he was, in a way, Juice, just with a different personality. They didn't know if he was heading to his childhood home or his current residence.

"When we find him, what are we going to do next?" questioned Juice.

"Us getting to Cider first assures our safety. Our hideout here in the swamp and our secret weapon would all stay between us," James replied in a heavy tone.

"We know what Memphis will do if he finds him, but what are we going to do if we find him first?" asked Juice.

This question was one that the rest of the group didn't think to ask until now.

"Are we going to hold him someplace against his will? Are we going to hope for the best, and he teams up with us? Or are we going to kill him?"

The people at the campsite were speechless. They had been so focused on getting Cider that they had no idea what to do with him after they found him. Until now, the Hogs had always known what to do when new things happened to them; run, hide, or fight were the usual responses. James said that the Saints would know what to do with Cider when they found him. The threat of him being found by Memphis was still at hand, so they were anxious to start searching.

The plan was to build two search parties; one will go to the town of Juice's apartment to see if he returned there while the rest would head to Maze. Right away, Hayden said he wanted to hang back at the swamp to help build a new weapon with Boston. Juice wanted to excuse himself from the search as well. He said that his presence may be a little misleading; he was afraid when asking people if they had seen Cider, they may get him confused with himself. Miles wished to stay in the swamp as well; he wanted to keep working on his defense spells.

When the search party came down to just Will, Timber, Eric, and James, James thought it would be best to search in Juice's current residence only. Knowing that Timber lived in Maze meant that the horseman Death must be there too, similar to how Famine and Pestilence were living close to Eric and Miles.

James was nervous about going after Death. During all the battles within the war of the broken balance, Death never stepped in to assist Memphis with any of the fighting. Death was a nuclear bomb that Memphis had. Fortunately, Death always passed on the battles when asked by Memphis. Death could kill just by looking at you. So James felt safe staying away from this horseman. James did a character study on Timber since they entered the swamp and sensed that there was no lingering haunting thoughts on Timber's mind like the others had. Timber never talked about any problems. In fact, he was very cooperative with everything. He volunteered to help restore the order of the balance the very first night and had been a good extra pair of eyes for the search for Cider this whole time.

"Timber, this is your evil spirit. If you think we should go after him, you make the call," James said, looking at Timber.

Timber gave a quick moment to think about it and said, "I don't think we should go after Death. I think we should keep our eyes open for Cider."

Will didn't sense any fear in Timber's voice. He believed that the search for Cider should be top priority and not just trying to find a way out of the fear of facing his spirit. Will figured that if Timber was feeling fine, his evil spirit can wait another day. Will volunteered Timber and him to search the city of Maze for Cider. James warned them to only be looking for Cider. If they sense that they have found Death, they should turn and run the other way immediately.

Eric, Gard, and James were all teleporting to Juice's apartment while Miles was going to do a quick teleporting trip to Maze to carry Will and Timber. Before Miles returned to the swamp, he told them that he'll be back in four hours to check on them.

After Miles left, Will and Timber started walking around the town. As they walked, Will started to reach out to see if he could get Timber to share about his past five years. The usual theme was that a Hogs wouldn't open up until after they defeated their evil spirit. Will saw this as a test; if Timber would be easy about opening up, then maybe he truly was fine.

"So Eric's spirit was his boss, and Miles's spirit was his doctor. You got any guesses on who your spirit could be?" wondered Will.

"I haven't had a boss since 2015," Timber uttered. "I was searching all over for a job before that. Then I got an offer from Maze's funeral home. I would be made partner and the one chosen to take over when the current owner retires." Timber then looked up and saw that the sidewalk they were walking on was leading up to his funeral home. Timber redirected the walk to avoid that place. "I was interested in moving away from here like the rest of the Group did or was in the process of doing. But an opportunity like this was rare and would have been a bad career choice not to take."

"Yeah, I remember hearing about that; it was a great job offer." Will replied.

"Not too long after I took the job, my boss died, and I became full manager and owner of the business."

The two came to a bench and took a seat. Timber was a little relieved to be talking about this for once. Timber went on to say that the body count kept rising after that. Maze and all the small towns that circled it had tons of young people dying from fatal accidents. Timber couldn't believe it, but within the five years of working, he hadn't picked up one senior citizen who died from natural causes. In fact, he didn't pick up any senior citizens. Hard to believe that during this whole tipped-balance era, the retirement homes received the least amount of deaths.

"The numbers were scattered. I would have a lot of funerals one week, and then three weeks would pass with nothing," Timber said, keeping his head low. "I felt that no one lived long anymore. You die young, or you don't die at all. It was weird, the thought of never dying frightened me the most." Timber gave a slight turn of his head toward his friend.

Will was leaning on every word as Timber continued to talk.

"I found myself standing on a bridge from time to time, the same bridge that goes over the river when you're coming back to town from the south side," Timber said as he brought his shoulders up and pointed south. "I thought that if I don't jump now, I'll never die. I just kept seeing the young die and the old keep on living. The fact that I have this power inside me, my aging slows down. With my aging moving as slowly as it does, it would take years to die of old age. I just didn't want to be alone for that long, you know."

"I know what you mean. Life for us is long, and that does sometimes scare me. Family and friends will all die while we will still look half our age. The fear of outliving everyone around you can be overwhelming. But you're not alone. You got the whole Hang Out Group."

"I think that's why I've been feeling better since I returned to the swamp. I was reminded that I am not alone."

The two passed charming smiles to one another before lifting themselves up off the bench. The two wanted to cross the street, so they looked both ways. They saw only one vehicle, a black van. The van driver waved at them to walk over and that he'll wait. Will and Timber walked across the street, and as soon as they made it to the other side, the van pulled up next to them. In a matter of seconds, two men exited the van and slapped a rag drenched in chloroform over their mouths. Will and Timber tried to fight back, but it was too late for them. Their eyes closed shut before they could fully wave their fists.

About an hour later, Timber woke up chained to a chair. Timber tried his best to flex out of the chains, but due to him overcoming the effects of the chloroform, he failed to break the shackles.

"If he tries that again, give him another sedative!" said a voice from behind Timber. The voice was of a man, and he walked around Timber so that they could make eye contact. The man bent down to get at eye level with Timber. "You don't remember me, do you?" the man asked.

Timber was thinking that this man was his evil spirit, the horseman Death. But what the man said next proved him wrong.

"Last time we met, you were tied to a chair back at the Renshaw Mansion!" the man yelled. "I was just another poor member of a broken team back then. After you and your friends burned down the mansion, I bailed on the group. This turned out it was a smart move because the rest of the group was either arrested or killed. But luckily for me, the group gained new life. Some old members who quit the group years ago got together and started it up again."

Timber couldn't believe that he was facing a past threat after all these years. The Havocs were an extinct threat for the Hogs. They hadn't been a problem since 2010. Timber did now remember Juice mentioning that the group was back, but Timber didn't expect to run into them. His mind was too wrapped up with the spirit threat.

"What do you want from me?" asked Timber.

"I thought that was obvious. The cube."

This information made Timber let out a soft chuckle. He claimed that he hadn't seen the cube in years. He lied, telling them that he couldn't even remember when he saw it last.

The man put his head down, wishing that Timber would have said something more helpful for them. The man brought his phone to his head and said, "Give him a shock."

Timber then heard the screams of his friend from the other end of that phone call. From the sounds coming from the phone on speaker mode, Timber could hear electric shocks followed by Will shrieking in pain. Timber demanded the man to put the torture to a stop, saying it's pointless because neither of them knew where the cube was.

"I don't believe you! You expect me to think that you let something as powerful as the cube get lost as if it was a common remote! *Hit him again!*" the man shouted into the phone. More screams from the phone were heard by Timber. The man once again asked Timber where the cube was, and Timber stuck to the story that they lost it. This made the man angry for he still did not believe him. The man said over the phone that he was going to count to five, and if Timber failed to reveal the whereabouts of the cube, Will was going to be killed.

When the man said one, Timber shouted that he didn't know where the cube was. The man said two, and Timber attempted to bribe the man, saying that he'll do anything. The man said three. Timber shouted that he'll take Will's place and that he would rather die. The man said four.

"Please, you don't understand! The world has gone to a dark place over the past five years! My friend who you're threating to kill and I are trying to fix it! We're trying to bring hope back to the world! Things can be better again for everyone! We can't do this without him! His will was the strongest of us all. So please just let him go, and I'll tell you where you can find the cube!"

This was what the man wanted to hear. He didn't care about any of the other things said; to him, that was all just nonsense. The man said over the phone to hold back the kill order. But there was no response. The man feared that there was no reply. The thought that Will had overpowered his torturers had crossed his mind. The man ordered his men in the room to go and check on the other room where they were keeping Will. Two men who Timber didn't even see walked past him and headed toward the door.

Just before the two reached the door, it was kicked open, and a stranger barged in, a person who neither Timber nor anyone else in the room had ever seen before. The two men close to the door started to charge at the stranger, but all of a sudden, they dropped to the floor lifeless. The stranger looked at Timber and then turned his head to look at his kidnapper. The kidnapper pulled out a gun and fired it at the stranger, but nothing happened. The bullet just pierced his shirt while the body didn't even flinch. The stranger tilted his head, and the abductor fell to the floor, just as the other accomplices. The three men were all dead, leaving Timber and the stranger alone.

Timber knew who this person was. It was the horseman Death.

"It's time we talked," Death said to Timber.

Timber, now with all his might, tried to break the chains that kept him bound to the chair. He had to get to his phone to call for backup. This was a search-and-find mission, so he didn't have a sword or ever an angel weapon. As Timber struggled, Death picked up a chair and placed it in front of Timber.

"Don't get up on my account. I'm not here for a fight," Death said as he sat in the chair across from Timber.

"Did you kill these people?" Timber asked.

Death twisted his head around to look at the corpses on the ground. "Yes. But I did them a favor. These men were married to their criminal activity. They were never going to change, just get worst. Cutting their life short discontinues their souls from growing more foul, and it improves their odds of ending up in Heaven better than if they would have lived a full life."

"Will…is he alright?"

"Will is fine. I killed the men who were hurting him before teleporting here. He'll find you soon, giving us enough time to talk."

"What do you want to talk about? Aren't you my evil spirit? Shouldn't you be trying to kill me?"

"I was the spirit assigned to you, and in exchange, I was granted a large amount of territory. But I never placed a curse on your way of thinking like the others did to your friends."

"But I've been depressed."

"Yeah, you had been living in a world with no good on the balance. That'll make the happiest person grow gloomy at most times."

"So you're saying it's just been me this whole time? No evil something to blame for my depression?"

"Believe it or not, not all bad things and all bad moods are caused by evil spirits. Sometimes crap happens, and people get upset," the spirit said as he gave a tug on the chains wrapped around Timber. With a small tug, the chains loosened its grip, and Timber was able to break free. "I'm not even an evil spirit. I'm a neutral spirit."

"The horseman Death isn't an evil spirit?" Timber asked, confused.

"When humanity started, God asked me to find a way to get the souls to Heaven after they were done with their human bodies. I said the only way for them to fully escape their human bodies was by death. Death is a bridge to the afterlife, to God's home for most people. The living can't see the bridge, so they have the illusion that their loved ones are gone forever. And because of that, I get a bad name for being evil. True, I do take people's lives early. Sometimes it's for their own good, but there are times when death can send a message. Death can be an alert for dangerous locations, food, water, or people. It could be a reminder for how short life is and how fast it can go by. But going to the next life isn't a bad thing for the ones who have passed away. The pain comes to the ones who are still here now having to live in a world without that person."

"If you're not evil, then why are you working for Memphis?"

"I said I was neutral spirit, not a good spirit. Memphis was built as a neutral spirit as well. He saw himself more as an evil spirit. Having to be the enforcer and executor for whoever broke the balance made him feel like he was the bad guy. He wanted the evil spirits to be free to do as much as they wanted, and I was on board with his message. In order for me to get my territory, I had to take a job on watching one of the Hogs. I had to see if you ever mentioned the details on how you and the others killed the devil. But I never planted any lingering haunting images in your head. Your depression was on your own, and you improved by hanging out with your friends. I can see that the person in front of me isn't the same person you were just over a week ago."

This was all hard for Timber to take in. A lot of what Death was saying made sense to him; it was just odd hearing it.

Death went on to say that he enjoyed how the balance was going when Memphis was in power. But now he's tired of it and wished for things to go back to normal. When the Hogs started to fight for the order of the balance, it was a wake-up call for him. Death saw that things got so bad that humans were now trying to fix the balance. This made him remember that earth was made for the humans. The balance was put in place for them to make choices. If the only choice people were granted were negative ones, they didn't stand a chance making it to Heaven. Death's job was to help people get there, and he being a part of the broken balance made him unable to do his job. This was why he was putting his damaging production on disrupting the balance to a halt.

"You're going to give up your territory?" questioned Timber.

"Not only that, but I'm going to fake my own death. Make the other spirits believe that I was killed by the Hogs."

Death explained that most of the spirits grew concerned of a threat from the Hogs after Famine was killed. After Pestilence was killed, many of the spirits were threatening to leave earth. After Death faked his demise, he knew that the remaining spirits would fully fear the Hogs and refuse to perform their negative actions until the Hogs were dead.

"So would you be helping us then?" wondered Timber.

"I helped enough. I was the one who let the Saints know about the birth of Cider and that Memphis was looking for him. And you guys did a bad job on finding him, by the way. Memphis's followers already found him this morning."

"Wait, Cider was found?" Timber replied with a shock.

Death said that Memphis will get Cider to spill every secret the Hogs have. Death was able to give a play-by-play on what was going to happen next. He said that after Memphis gets all the details he needs from Cider, he'll make a plan of an attack on the Hogs. Memphis will be in a rush to come in for the kill after all the spirits retreat from earth. The Hogs will be the reason for the evil spirit's abandoning the thing they love to do, which is going to make Memphis want to eliminate the threat right away.

Death could hear Will walking toward the room, so he gave his last words to Timber before teleporting away. "Good luck."

After Death vanished, Will arrived. Timber got to his feet and hustled over to him. Timber said that they should get out of there—too many dead bodies lying around. Will asked what happened to cause that. Timber explained that Death came to him and saved them both. After the quick highlights of Timber's visit with the horseman, the two contacted James for a teleporting pickup.

Back at the swamp, the news of Cider being found by Memphis was discussed. Death's warning that Memphis was coming in for the kill hung over the Hogs' heads. They wouldn't have the element of surprise with the sword, but Hayden and Boston believed that they had a new weapon to use on the spirit. All that day, the two were building a bomb. Boston told him a few instructions on how to build one with the angel weapons, and Hayden really ran with it. Due to the minimum amount of resources they had, the explosion wouldn't be enough to kill Memphis.

But Hayden knew a special ingredient to add to the bomb, one that would heavily increase the power of the blast. It was the remaining diamond pieces buried under the cabin. The additional power that the pebbles give to the elements that are in the bomb will generate an explosion powerful enough to kill Memphis.

The Hogs were a little leery on giving up their home for they knew that once the diamond pebbles were all removed from the ground, the campsite would lose its blessed features, and the land would grow damp and dead.

"Guys…look," Timber said in a whimsical tone.

Everyone looked over to the glowing hologram of the balance displayed within the campsite. Due to it now being nighttime, the glowing feature was clearly visible. After all this time, the Hogs didn't pay close attention to it as much anymore. Timber wanted to see if what Death said was true, and by looking at the balance, it seemed that he wasn't lying. The evil side of the balance had vanished, meaning that the remaining evil spirits had retreated from earth. With no evil spirits on earth right now, all territories were abandoned, freeing everyone from the negative thoughts.

"Does this mean that good is coming back to the world?" asked Juice.

"The evil spirits may be gone, but the good spirits are still not back," James sadly replied.

"They're waiting for us to kill Memphis, aren't they?" Gard asked.

James replied with a meaningful nod. The Hogs knew that humans would still feel as bad as they once did, even with the evil spirits now gone. In order to change that, they must bring back hope to the world. The Hogs were lucky; they had each other to restore their old kind ways.

But people have been in the dark for so long, the ones who are alone won't notice the light without a positive spirit guiding them. The Hogs said that Memphis was next. They will use the pebbles from the ground to create a bomb strong enough to end this dark time.

That night, the Hogs stared at the glowing balance as if they were stargazing and viewing their achievement with a sense of awe.

One to Go

Friday, October 9, 2020

A man woke up on a cold rocklike surface. At least he thought he woke up. His sight was so dark, he wasn't even sure if his eyelids were open. With his hands at his side, he started to pat the ground around him. As he slowly stretched out his arms, his right hand came up to a rock wall of some sort while his left hand came to an edge. To the man's left was a ledge, and he couldn't see how far the drop was. The man brought his hands to his chest and reached them over his face above his head. His hand touched another rock wall just like the wall to his right side. The man reached out his right leg, and his foot quickly felt another rock wall.

The man theorized that he was lying in a hole within a rock wall. The size was about the size of a twin-size bed, and since the man hadn't stood up yet, he didn't know the height. He slowly got to his feet, making sure he didn't lose his balance and fall over to the right side, which for all he knew, was a bottomless pit. He was able to fully stand up, but when he stuck his hand up, he found the height of this hole was just a little higher than his head. Taking a chance in the dark, the confused man shouted, "Hello?"

A couple of bright flash flood lights were switched on moments after the man spoke. One was pointing right at him; he had to raise his left hand to shield his eyes until they adjusted to the light. With some lights shining bright, the man saw that he was in a very large cave. He was indeed within a hole in the cave wall with a very deep chasm between him and the ledge. The distance between him and the ledge wasn't too far, but in order to make the jump, he would have to take a running start. Due to his tight confinement, he had no room for a running start and seemed to be trapped in this hole that seemed to be perfectly fitted for him.

The man wasn't afraid of the deadly drop that was just in front of his position. But he was concerned about whoever it was who turned on the lights. The man felt safer in his little hole away from the grounds across the chasm. As his eyes adjusted to the light, he was able to get a clear look at the person who turned on the lights. "You're Memphis, aren't you?" Standing on the other side on the pit was the mighty spirit Memphis, grinning with delight.

"And you are Cider," Memphis stated, giving the man his name.

"Cider, is that what they are calling me?" This man was the person who both the Hogs and the evil spirits were searching for ever since the Siren announced his birth. Memphis was able to find the wanted hybrid first, and now he was going to learn everything he didn't know about the Hogs.

"I saw that the Hang Out Group member Tyler went by the nickname Juice. I felt that his counterpart should be something similar," Memphis replied. Memphis didn't deliver any threatening tone when he talked to Cider; he spoke to him with respect and kindness.

Cider saw the connection with apple juice and apple cider and thought the name was fitting for him. Cider looked down and saw more floodlights attached to the side of the cliff across from him, under the ground Memphis was standing on. The lights were shining all the way to the bottom where many car-sized eggs were resting. The whole bottom of the chasm was covered with these eggs.

"Just a little less than five hundred spirit eggs down there," Memphis informed Cider as he saw him staring down at them. "I made them all last week, and by nine thirty or so tonight, they'll be fully ready to hatch!"

Memphis walked up to the ledge to take a peek down. "I had to hatch six earlier this week to deliver to Famine. Since they were hatched early, they weren't at full strength, which was probably the reason why the Hogs were able to defeat them so easily."

Cider saw a small army down that pit just waiting to hatch, all under the command of Memphis.

"I was once at that stage," Memphis said. "Making a powerful spirit such as myself takes a lot of active Loomation. But making a simple soldier takes the bare minimum. Just get some water and heat it until it starts steaming. Then use your active Loomation to turn that steam into a solid container, one that breathes life into a new spirit."

Memphis explained that this was how you built a spiritual egg. Memphis said that if the Saints would have given him the access to tap into more of his active Loomation powers beyond the bare minimum, then he could be making horseman-powered spirits. But that didn't bother Memphis; he was still able to build hatch eggs spirits that gave him the power to build his own army.

The reason why Memphis was breaking down the spirit-making process was because he did something similar to create Cider. He gave the details of his birth, saying that when the Siren was affecting Juice's mind, she found an infection in a type of hibernation stage. She made a few attempts to wake that infection up and did succeed once when Juice was at his highest level of rage. Still, it wasn't strong enough to keep Juice from reclaiming the wheel once again. Memphis told Cider that Juice's evil spirit placed an egg inside Juice's mind. It was living off the Loomation inside Juice's body. And when it was removed, it was able to take power from the archangel to form its own body.

Memphis told Cider this, hoping that he would in return pledge a type of loyalty toward his creator. So when Memphis asked Cider how the Hogs managed to kill the devil, he was hoping he would comply.

Cider wasn't sure if he should take sides in this war of the balance mess. He was told that he was a hybrid of being a human and spirit, so he felt that he shouldn't take a side.

Memphis took a look down the pit to look at the unhatched eggs. "I started in that stage when I was made. I was made by the Saints to be a fighter for the order of the balance. They wanted me to be controlled by them and to be feared by all spirits. But that wasn't what I wanted. I wanted to be loved. I knew that I would never get that from the Saints. They simply saw me as a tool, a tool that would just sit in a drawer until they needed me. And since all spirits were meant to fear me, I knew I would have been hated by them.

"So I exercised my free will and sorted out a different option against the one that was made for me. The spirits made me a killer and a person to be feared, so I saw myself more as an evil spirit, and so I wanted their love. I set them free with the news of the devil being gone and that the Saints and angels weren't strong enough to stop them." Memphis then looked at Cider with his pitch for him to join him.

"It wasn't hard for me to choose my side. I was made evil, and so I chose to betray my creators. Cider, you were made to be opposite of Juice, and Juice is a fighter for the order of the balance. There is no place for you out in the human world. They already have a Tyler Bluth wandering the earth. They don't need another. So embrace your spiritual side and join us, the ones who fight to get what they want! If you help me with the information I need, I'll grant you territory just like I did with my other followers."

"What am I going to do with territory? I can't affect people's minds like the other spirits."

"Oh no, Cider, you're not looking at the bigger picture. The army I have down there is the first step into the next part of my plan."

Cider gave an intriguing look at Memphis.

"Phase one was to get the evil spirits doing as much damage to the world as they wanted. They have been so used to doing their thing in the spiritual realm or disguising themselves as a doctor or a coworker. I knew the angels would attack, and I knew they would one day surrender. The plan after they surrender was to step into phase two, but the Hogs started making their attacks, so phase two has been put on hold."

"What is phase two?" question Cider.

"We step into the spotlight. We no longer release our negative energy in secret and start making hell on earth a reality. My army down there will start attacking towns like wild monsters."

"The angels may have given up on fighting you, but humans will fight back. The military can take out your army not too long after your riots."

"That's the beauty of the power of teleporting. I know how to shut it down, and I know how to turn it back on. If the human militaries try to stop me, we can always retreat. George Washington has more retreats than victories, and he won a country. Think about it, Cider. The world could be ours! It'll take years, yes, but with your aging, you can be able to see the takeover." Memphis spoke very highly of himself. "The only humans who pose a threat is the Hang Out Group. And when they are dead, the evil spirits will come back to me and start doing what they love again. And they will once again love me."

Cider thought that Memphis was right. There was no way the Hogs were going to defeat that army that rested at the bottom of the cave. And a world being taken over by evil spirits made the offer to join with the leader more temping. So Cider said that he'll tell Memphis everything he needed to know before going up against the Hogs.

Memphis grinned and told Cider that he'll drag the ladder over so he can walk out of that hole. But Cider said there was no need because he could fly across the pit. Memphis placed Cider in that hole in the wall so that he wouldn't escape in hopes that he wasn't able to fly. Now knowing that Cider could have escaped at any time made Memphis trust him even more.

⎯⎯◆◆◆⎯⎯

That morning, the Hogs removed the final diamond pebbles from under the cabin. Once they were removed, the blessed area started to be retaken by the rotten dead land that surrounded it. It was very sad to see the place that housed the Hogs for so long fade away, but they knew that they were making a sacrifice. Hayden and Boston added the pieces into their bomb to charge up the explosive chemicals inside it. With this extra feature, the bomb's blast will be much mightier.

Boston said that the bomb will release a huge fiery explosion with a powerful force wave. The damage will be equal to any human-made bomb; it'll burn the ground, cause a crater, and be really loud when it goes off. Eric asked about the type of side effects from the bomb, such as a lingering radiation poisoning. Boston said that the chemicals were made from Heaven's arsenal building within the lab department. He claimed that the radiation from the bomb was harmless, and it may, in fact, replant the ground into something new.

Once the bomb was fully built and ready for detonation, Hayden hid it within one of the tents in the campsite. Once the group knew that Cider was captured by the enemy, they predicted that Memphis will be coming in for an attack at some point. Memphis will think that he'll be coming in for a sneak attack, but on the contrary, he will be the one falling into a trap. The Hogs weren't going to be at the campsite when Memphis showed up; they'll be at a safe distance keeping constant surveillance over the area. When they see the spirit teleport into their trap, they'll remote-detonate the bomb, and that blast will strike Memphis so fast, he wouldn't even have time to think about teleporting away.

Since the campsite was about to be destroyed, the group was taking mementos from their home away from home. Will took the license plates from his old truck that had been parked there for many years. Hayden took a few bricks that were a part of the fire ring. Since they had to create the illusion that they were still living there when Memphis showed up, they couldn't take much.

Gard was removing the sign that hung over the door of the cabin that read *The Diamond in the Rough*, saying that they'll need to find a new place to hang it. Juice exited the cabin carrying the framed newspaper article of Logan and his friends selling the large diamond. Juice placed it down next to the door so his hand would be free to pick up the other framed photo he wanted to save. The framed photo of the Hang Out Group standing within the Garden of Eden was still hanging on the outside wall of the cabin. Juice was about to lift it off the wall, but he suddenly noticed something.

"This photo is crooked," Juice said, dumbfounded. He turned his head to see his friends. "Was it always like this?"

The rest of the Hogs just shrugged their shoulders and gave off careless expressions. Juice turned back to the photo to lift it off its nail. All the keepsakes were gathered up and handed over to James. James said that the safe house where all the Hogs met up before their trial was a place where he could put all the items. James then teleported away with the souvenirs, saying he'd be back in a minute.

The Hogs then looked around the campsite and could see that the land was getting worse and worse by the second. The place still had all tents up, the string of lights were still hanging over the area, and there was still a fire going in the pit. But it just wasn't the same for the friends. The thought of the land dying around them felt like an omen of things to come for their final mission.

"This land has been good to us over the years," Will said as he sat in one of the chairs.

"Remember our first night here?" Eric chimed in while sitting in the chair next to Will.

"I remember getting terrible directions from Timber, and the three of us were wasting gas driving around this place trying to find you," Gard mentioned as he gestured over to Eric and Miles. A small laugh came from that comment while Timber defended himself, saying that Gard missed his turn.

"This is where I first flew," Juice said in a nostalgic way.

"First place where you crashed too," Miles added.

"This place still has one more job to do," Hayden stated. Hayden was referring to their campsite now being a trap for Memphis. Hayden was happy to know that their special hangout place was going out with a bang.

Boston came walking over to the fire ring. He was briefly gone, hiking away from the campsite to find the best place to set up a stakeout. Boston said that he found the perfect place to hide, saying that this location will be out of the bomb's blast range while being the perfect place to keep a good vantage point for when Memphis arrives.

"You really think that this is going to fix the balance?" wondered Eric.

Boston explained that the remaining angels were enough to continue the fight for the order of the balance. Since they still feared Memphis, they wouldn't fight until he was dead.

Will pointed out that there were more evil spirits than Memphis. Boston said that Memphis was a one-man army who was responsible for the death of many of the angels. But it wasn't just him who was a strong obstacle; the horsemen were also heavily responsible for the negative spirits' victory. Now that they were no longer a problem, the angels would have a better chance at regaining the order. Boston said that the balance may not be perfect, but it won't get this far out of hand ever again.

"So when we take out Memphis, we can go home?" Timber asked.

That very much seemed to be the case. Once the angels came back, the order of the balance would no longer be the Hogs' concern.

"Well, now that we have our lookout spot, shouldn't we go there now?" wondered Juice.

"I can stay there by myself. I got the detonator, and my eyes don't blink," informed Boston.

"We're not leaving you out there all by yourself. We're in this until the end," Will responded.

Boston said that it's more likely that Memphis will show up at night, and it was going to be a while until then. The Hogs discussed it and felt their hunger starting to take over their concentration. They didn't eat all day due to the nasty order of the swamp destroying their appetite. So they figured that they'd go into town for dinner.

Shortly after thinking of this idea, James returned to the campsite. Boston said that he and James had a spiritual telepathy, one that can be reached anywhere. So James would go with the Hogs into town so that they could stay in touch with Boston as they were out to dinner. The Hogs wanted to go back to their favorite pizza place in their hometown, so James teleported them all there.

The Bigger They Are

The Hogs were sitting in their favorite pizza joint in their hometown of Maze. They were, in a way, having a victory dinner celebrating how far they came since they were first gathered up for their court date. The Hogs felt that they had been on a special retreat over the course of fixing the balance. Getting away from their usual routine of their daily lives made them see the depressed people who they had become. Spending time with their best friends while being away made it very easy for them to open up about their past. The fact that the Hogs were Loomation carriers severely limited the people who could relate to their dilemmas when expressing their fears of how the power affected their lives. The Hogs were happier while being together, and now seeing how bad things could get when they were apart really showed how important their friendship was.

As the Hogs were waiting for the pizzas to arrive, Gard caught a glimpse of himself in the metal napkin dispenser. Gard picked up the dispenser and held it up to him like a mirror. "Guys, this wig looks awful on me!" Gard shouted. Gard was wearing a long wavy wig along with a baseball cap on his head. Since the group returned to their hometown, they were afraid of someone recognizing Gard and growing confused due to him being legally dead. To avoid that uncomfortable conversation, the Hogs threw a wig and hat on him.

"It looks nothing like you," Juice uttered to Gard.

"That's what it's supposed to do, Juice!" Eric replied.

Just then the waitress carried over two large pizzas and set them on their long table. Juice hurried to pick up a slice and asked if anyone was going to join him in a game he liked to call Burnt Mouth. Hayden snatched a slice saying he would love to, but Juice claimed that Hayden was permanently disqualified due to his high tolerance to hot temperatures.

"What's Burnt Mouth?" questioned James.

"Burnt Mouth isn't a game, it's just quickly taking a bite out of pizza that just got out of the oven before cooling off," Will explained.

"What's the point of doing that?" James said with a confused tone.

"You burn your mouth, and it's funny," Juice added excitedly before taking his bite. Juice's reaction to the hot food caused him to flinch and emit a small squeal. Gard then took part in the activity, followed by Will and Miles.

"It's stupid! I've never done it," Eric stated.

"It just burns your mouth for a while, and until it heals up, the pizza tastes like nothing," Timber reported.

The Hogs did admit that it was a silly thing to do and that they hadn't done it since high school. But in the light of revisiting old hangout places, they found doing the game again fun.

The waitress came to the table once again, dropping off a pitcher of water for the group. Before leaving the table, she turned to Eric and recognized him. "You're Eric Derole, aren't you?" she asked.

"Yeah," Eric kindly replied.

"I remember you from high school! You were a senior when I was a freshman. We were on the quiz bowl team together!" She said joyfully. Eric was sorry, but he didn't remember her. She explained that she was barely on the team and that it's easier for the freshmen to remember the team captain than for a senior to remember the little freshmen. She looked over and recognized Will from him being in charge of the student council. The last person who she knew was Juice, just because she remembered him running down the halls every Friday during third period.

"My recycle class and I were trying to see how fast we could gather up all the paper and cardboard within the school," Juice stated.

"I remembered you once screaming that John was *it*," she said with a grin.

"We may have also been playing tag through the halls," Juice uttered.

"I knew it!" she said with a joyful laugh. "It's so cool to see you guys again. I vaguely remember you guys calling yourselves…what was it, the Hang Out Club?"

"Group!" Juice said with pride. "If we called ourselves the Hang Out Club, our initials would be HOC. Then we wouldn't be the Hogs."

"Well, technically, *hangout* is not spelled with a space. So our initials should be just HG," Eric explained.

"We purposely spell *hangout* with a space so that we can call ourselves the Hogs!" Juice replied.

This made the waitress laugh again; she then calmed down and told them to enjoy their meal. Then she bowed her head and told them she was sorry for the loss of their classmate a couple years back. The Hogs said thanks, and she walked away. The Hogs were happy that the girl didn't recognize Gard under his wig, so the disguise worked.

Once she was far away from the table, Gard asked, "Did any of you attend my funeral?"

An awkward hush fell over the table, and no one made eye contact with Gard. The truth was that none of them went to the funeral. Will said that he wanted to go, but that didn't matter since he had no excuse missing it. Hayden found that to be an odd question, thinking that's not a question you hear every day. Juice took another bite out of his pizza, and when it burned his mouth, he emitted a small holler due to the pizza still being hot. This caused the awkward silence to turn into a laugh, and the Hogs carried on with their dinner. Gard even mentioned that he didn't care if anyone showed up, saying that he probably wouldn't have gone to any of theirs if they would have died.

James didn't eat, saying that his active Loomation he received from Heaven keeps his energy up as a replacement for food. James said that he was going to go out for some air. Since he couldn't participate in the burnt mouth game nor on the food and drinks, he would go and find another way to spend his downtime. The Hogs told him that they would meet up with him by the school when they were done eating.

Once James left the building, the Hogs were upset that James couldn't have stayed with them. They grew to enjoy James and started to see him as a friend. They all owed him a lot, and it was going to be sad to see him carry on his angel duties while they returned to their lives after all this was over.

James strolled on the sidewalk that was next to the main street. He was looking at the traffic lights and the local stores. The town seemed empty due to most of the locals attending the big high school football game being played out of town. James felt the comfort of a small town, and to his delight, he felt the pleasure of fighting for the planet against evil forces. He saw the beauty of the world, and with his time spent with the Hogs, he saw the beauty in people.

Then James spotted a church down the street. James made his way into the church and found it empty. There were a few lights on, so James could see the fascinating architectural work of the church. James sat down at the front of the church and looked up, thinking about his future. He knew that once he and the Hogs take out Memphis, the rest of the angels would come back. James knew that the Saints would make him a commander after that. James knew that the balance could still be threated without Memphis being around.

"You should have stayed at home, James," a sinister voice said to James from a short distance behind him.

James knew that voice, and his skin started to crawl when he turned to face the man who spoke. With a chilling fright, James was looking at Memphis. Memphis was big, tall, and muscular. His skin looked to be made of steel, and his eyes were dark blue just like the deep ocean. He was carrying weapons on his body. A hand angel gun was strapped to a belt around his waist along with a knife. On his back was a sword.

James stepped out of the pew he was sitting in to enter the center aisle to be in Memphis's sight. James sent a telepathic message to Boston warning him of his visit with Memphis within the church. James told Boston to inform the Hogs first and that they were at the pizza place not too far from the church.

When Boston received this message, he quickly grabbed his bag full of weapons and teleported to the town of Maze to find the Hogs.

"You and the humans have done far more damage than the Saints ever accomplished. You should be proud of that," Memphis said as he slowly made his way up toward James.

"You here to discuss terms of surrender?" asked James, keeping his ground.

"I'm just getting started. I see what you and the Hogs have done as a minor setback."

"We killed some of your most powerful followers. You can't survive by yourself. Your kind is going to lose."

"You still haven't killed me," Memphis said as he removed his knife from his belt. "Once you and the rest of the Hogs are dead, the good side of the balance will lose what little hope they have. The evil side will be forever free to roam the planet and cause havoc to all who live on it."

James spotted the knife Memphis had in his hand. He knew that this was one of the knives that could remove an angel's power. James was doing his best to keep his cool; he didn't want to show the spirit his fear. With a quick draw, James pulled out an AG handgun, which was strapped to his belt under his jacket. He aimed and fired it three times. This attack inflicted no pain to Memphis, causing only minor flinching.

Memphis now took a heavy charge toward James. James didn't know what to do. He knew that he didn't stand a chance alone against this powerful foe. He already tried to teleport away, but Memphis must have already put up an anti-teleporting symbol, a trademark Memphis uses to trap his prey. Still, if he could manage to stall him until the Hogs arrived…

James took a charge toward Memphis. The two collided at the center of the aisle, and the fight began.

Boston teleported outside of the pizza place and sprinted inside. He saw the Hogs all sitting at a long table and shouted out that Memphis was at the church. The Hogs jumped out of their chairs and hustled to the door. Eric popped out his wallet and threw all of his money at the table to pay for the meal. Boston was holding the door open for everyone as they rushed outside.

"Do you have the sword?" asked Gard to Boston.

"That and more," he replied.

"Where's James?" wondered Will.

"He's at the church with Memphis," Boston explained.

"We better hurry then!" Timber shouted.

Will was leading the people to the church, and since Miles was the last one out of the building, he and Boston formed the caboose of the line. Lucky for the group, the roads were clear at the time, so they could easily cross the street and even run down it. Everyone was eyeing the tall structure of the church's bell tower in the distance, so they never noticed a flying man landing behind the group.

"Sorry, guys, but no active Loomationers allowed!" This flying man was Cider, and he was holding a huge gun in his arms. This weapon was short, but it had a barrel the size of his chest. It took both of his hands to hold and to aim it. Cider fired it, and a stream of energy was blasted out of the barrel.

Boston, in a hurry, positioned himself in front of Miles to shield him from the blast. Boston took the full hit, but the impact pushed him back onto Miles hard. Boston being slammed into Miles caused him to be knocked unconscious.

The shock of seeing Cider for the first time made the Hogs gasp in disbelief. His likeness to Juice was a perfect mirror image. The Hogs, in a fit of rage, took a step toward their attacker.

Cider aimed the gun at the rest of the Hogs, telling them to freeze. "My job was to take out the one who can perform the heal spell. Memphis wants no heal spell performed inside the church. Now you can ether attack me or go save your friend!"

The Hogs looked over and saw that the church was close and knew that Memphis had already started his fight against James. If they didn't come to his aid now, James would surely die. Cider's threat seemed to cause a standstill, which made the Hogs suspect the church being a trap. The Hogs didn't fear Memphis, so they chose to ignore Cider and made their way to help James.

Hayden went to check on Boston. He seemed to be paralyzed from the stun of the blast. Boston said he'd need a few minutes to recover. Until then, he'd stay outside and tend to Miles until he woke up. Boston handed the bag of weapons over to Hayden, telling him to kill that spirit once and for all. Hayden picked up the bag and hurried to catch up with the others.

Juice was the last one to head to the church. Juice wanted to take a moment to look at his alter ego. The two stared at each other for a few seconds. Juice hadn't forgotten what Cider did to his friends back when he was in control of his body and longed for his revenge. But Juice knew that the fight with Memphis was more important right now, so he turned away and followed the others.

Inside the church, James's knuckles were bloody and swollen, and after he fired all his bullets on Memphis, his attacker was still coming at him with full strength. James's exhaustion got the better of him, and Memphis was able to grab him by the neck. Memphis lifted the wounded angel off his feet while allowing him take tiny breaths. Memphis then shoved his dagger into James's stomach. Sliver sparks were flickering out of James's wound, similar to the past angels who were stabbed by this type of weapon. James could feel the sharp blade pierce his torso, but what hurt more was the feeling of his active Loomation being drained from his body. James squirmed around in an attempt to break free, but it was no use. He could feel his strength and power fade away.

At that moment, the Hogs barged though the back door of the church behind Memphis. Memphis turned his head around to eye the Hogs. Memphis grinned and chucked James across the altar, causing him to crash through the wall and land in the dressing room. The Hogs felt that they were too late, thinking that Memphis had already killed James.

Enraged, most of the Hogs charged at the spirit. Memphis took a large stomp at the floor, causing it to fissure all the way up to them. The Hogs all tripped on the swerving floor that was popping up at their feet. Hayden, who was smart enough to stay behind, took out one of the AG rifles and started to take fire at Memphis from across the hall. The Hogs on the floor rushed over to the bag full of weapons to arm themselves.

Juice took the sword and removed it from its sheath. He said that he was going in for the stab. Juice, with sword in hand, flew across the damaged floor, charging with the tip of the blade head-on. The sword started to glow once it drew closer to the evil spirit. Memphis then removed his weapon that he had strapped to his back. Memphis brought his own sword to the battle and was ready to challenge the Hogs' sword.

Juice's jab attack was warded off by Memphis's blade. Juice circled around Memphis to attack from behind. Memphis was able to block all of Juice's attacks with ease.

"How is this possible? That's the sword that can cut through anything!" shouted Timber. "It should be slicing through Memphis's blade with ease!"

The Hogs took a closer look at Memphis's weapon and saw that the blade was pushing back the glowing sword wielded by Juice. It had the effects of a reverse magnet pushing back the weapon that came into its space. With this power, Memphis was able to repel the unbeatable sword of God.

Juice was using his power of flight to avoid attacking the same location twice in a row. After he was blocked from one side of Memphis, he would fly across his shoulder or around his waist to attack from another angle. Memphis was a master with his sword, and he was able to push back Juice regardless of whatever angle he approached in his attack. Juice was using all his might with every move he delivered, and it was causing him to sweat and grow winded. Memphis was way too strong to tire from simply defending Juice's attacks.

"Juice can't get a hit on him! We need to come up with a plan!" Eric yelled.

"I'm all over it!" Gard shouted as he took one of the AG handguns from the bag and charged into the center of the aisle. Gard had to take carful strides while crossing the cracked floor while in a sprint, eyeing each stable part of the floor before taking his next step. When he got up to Memphis, he dove down in front of him, ducking under Juice's flight path. Once on the floor, he started to use his gun to fire at Memphis's hand. Gard was hoping the rapid gunfire would weaken his grip on the weapon. With Gard on the ground in stomping distance of Memphis, he had to start rolling around to avoid being smashed by Memphis's huge feet.

Memphis had Juice flying around his upper body, taking stabs at him with the one sword that could kill him, while he had Gard rolling around the floor taking fire at his hands. In his mind, he was swatting a fly while trying to stomp a bug.

"Timber, head upstairs to the balcony!" Hayden ordered as he handed one of the AG rifles to him.

Timber bolted up the steps to the balcony.

"Eric, go to the right side of the pews and take cover!" Hayden said as he handed him a rifle. "Wait for my signal before firing."

"I'm going to go check on James! He could still be alive!" Will shouted.

Hayden instructed him to go across the church from the left side and be quick about it. Will took off on the left side while Eric took off on the right side where the floor was still intact.

Memphis's hand started to heat up from Gard's constant attack. Memphis couldn't handle this annoyance for much longer. Sooner or later, he was going to lose his grip on his weapon or bring too much focus on trying to squash Gard, leaving his protection from Juice unattended and possibly getting himself stabbed. Memphis made a risky move and shoved his fist at Juice. A punch came at Juice fast, but Juice managed to drive a large cut into Memphis's forearm before he was hit in the chest. Juice was knocked back and was slammed into the wall. Juice crashed to the floor hard, losing his breath, but the sword was still in his hand.

Memphis raised his sword up and brought it crashing down on the floor toward Gard. Gard rolled into the pews and started to slide his way down the rows to flee from the attack. Before Memphis could start swinging his weapon again, he was hit by AG bullets from three different points. Point one was fired by Timber from the balcony, the next was fired from the right side of the church by Eric, and the spraying came from Hayden straight down the aisle. The spirit started to use his sword to block and redirect the shots at him. A lot of the ricocheted bullets came at Timber from the balcony, causing him to duck for cover.

When Hayden and Eric saw that their attacks were being easily repelled, they put their trigger fingers to a halt. Memphis then grabbed a handgun from behind his belt and aimed it at Hayden. Hayden quickly jumped behind one of the pews to his left to get some cover from the coming blast of Memphis's gun. Green spear-shaped bullets were blasting through the splintering wooden seats of the church, whizzing above Hayden's body. While on the ground, Hayden saw Gard roll over to him from under the pews.

"We need more firepower," Gard stated.

"There are some AG grenades in Boston's bag, but with his sword, he'll just swat them away," Hayden replied.

"What if we hide the grenades in something he wouldn't expect?" Gard theorized.

"I'm open to ideas!" Hayden said as he popped his head up to fire off a few rounds at Memphis. Hayden then lowered his head back under the wooden pews.

"Remember that first summer after we graduated, when we helped the church with their renovation?" Gard asked Hayden.

"Yeah," Hayden replied.

"Remember impressing the priest by moving that heavy thing without the need of a construction crew?" Gard cleverly implied.

Hayden looked up at the celling, knowing exactly what Gard was talking about. Hayden gave an acknowledging nod and instructed Gard to keep Memphis in the center aisle. Hayden then rushed out of his hiding spot and dashed toward the duffel bag of weapons. Once he had the bag in hand, he headed upstairs to the balcony to meet up with Timber. Once the two were together, Hayden handed over his diamond-tipped knife to Timber and gave him the same instructions he gave Gard: make sure Memphis stayed in the center of the middle aisle.

When Hayden made his way to the stairs, Memphis was about to take fire at him. But he was shot by Eric from his left. Eric was shielding himself behind a large support beam while shooting off his gun. Memphis ignored both Hayden and Eric because he saw that the Hogs' sword was close by. Juice was to Memphis's left, and his butt was on the floor with his back leaning up against the wall, his right hand barely gripping the sword.

Memphis took one step in the direction of Juice, and Juice moved his body back into a fighting pose with the sword now tightly gripped with both hands. "I got a cut on you once, Memphis. You think you can handle round two?"

Memphis grinned, knowing that Juice just managed to get a lucky slash on him when he was fresh for the fight. Now that Juice was recovering from a heavy punch to the gut while also being exhausted from round one, Memphis saw the chances of receiving another slash from Juice at this stage would be highly unlikely.

Juice stumbled to his feet while keeping his fighting pose. Memphis was taking charge at Juice. Juice was too weak to move but still desperately stood his ground. Memphis knew that all he had to do was to snatch the weapon out of Juice's hands, and all hope for the Hogs winning this fight would be gone.

Memphis was quickly bearing down on Juice. Heavy eye contact was all that they could focus on. Right when Memphis was one step away from Juice, Eric hopped between the two and started to fire his gun rapidly in Memphis's face.

The unexpected blast to his face caused him to lose his balance, and he started to tumble backward. Memphis was backing his way to the center of the church while being attacked by Eric. Gard ran down the left aisle, and once at the front of the church, he started firing his gun at Memphis's head from behind. Memphis, in slight agony, did something that made the skin of the Hogs shiver. He started laughing. Memphis, now in the center of the church, turned his body to have his back at the altar so that bullets being fired were now striking the left and right side of his head as he continued to laugh.

Juice got himself hovering, and he launched himself behind one of Eric's bullets with the sword charging his way once again. Memphis spotted Juice coming his way in the corner of his eye. Memphis once again gripped his sword, ready to defend himself. Memphis stopped his laughing and used his blade to block the sword from striking his head. In a quick motion, after blocking the sword, Memphis used one of his hands to grab Juice's shoulder. Memphis swung Juice into the ground in front of him hard, causing Juice to lose grip of the sword.

"Get Memphis's weapon!" Eric shouted as he pressed his hands on the handle of the weapon in Memphis's hand. Eric was driving his fingers into Memphis's grip in an attempt to pry it out of his hand. Memphis easily chucked Eric behind him. The Hog was tossed back to the dressing room behind the church wall where James ended up. As Memphis was turning his body back toward the front of the church, his laugher grew even more joyful. Memphis never expected a fight with humans to last this long. He completely destroyed and clobbered the angels with ease. Angels were Heaven's most powerful soldiers, and these humans who barely carried

Loomation inside them were more of a threat to him. Angels were made to protect the humans—what a joke he thought that was.

But the laughing came to a stop when Gard managed to shove the barrel of his gun into Memphis's mouth and pulled the trigger. Smoke was exiting from his mouth and nose; the attack didn't damage anything inside his body, but it delivered a powerful burned mouth. Memphis's eyes tightened up with rage. He bit down on the barrel, smashing it, and then delivered a mighty kick to Gard. Gard flung back, crashing into a line of pews; he plowed past five pews before his body came to a stop. As Memphis brought a hand to his mouth to comfort his burned tongue, Juice used his flying powers to perform a back flip, driving both his feet up Memphis's chin. This action caused Juice to break both of his feet along with possibly shattering both his shins, but it was worth it because Memphis fell on his back—the first time the beast was ever knocked down.

Timber, on the ground floor in the back of the church, saw his opportunity to end this fight once and for all. Timber saw the God sword lying not too far from Memphis, and he saw Memphis slowly getting to his feet. Timber was running as if the whole fate of the world depended on it because Memphis was now reaching for the glowing gold sword. Timber looked around and saw both Juice and Gard in too much pain to continue the fight at the moment, so they couldn't attempt to reach the weapon first. Timber wasn't fast enough, and Memphis was already too close to the glowing blade. Timber stopped in his tracks, aimed his gun, and pulled the trigger.

The bullet blasted out of Timber's barrel and hit the golden sword, knocking it away from Memphis's reach. Memphis paused in frustration after seeing the sword being knocked away from him. During that pause, Timber made his way up to the spirit and used Hayden's knife to impale the knife into Memphis's forearm. Memphis didn't give out any sound of pain; his skin was so thick that the stab barely released any blood. The blood felt the same as human blood, but it was clear instead of red. Timber had to use more strength to remove the knife from the spirit's body, but that didn't stop him from quickly making more and faster jabs into the man's arm.

Memphis threw a punch at Timber, but it was slow, and Timber was able to back away, dodging the attack. Timber saw that Memphis was now reacting slower, which meant he was growing sore from this fight. Timber saw more blood slowly pour out of Memphis's forearm where Timber made his stabs. Timber slowly backed up away from Memphis as he was coming toward him. Timber was doing his job by keeping the spirit in the center of the aisle.

Earlier during the battle by the dressing room, Will was desperately looking for James. He could hear the battle from the other side of the wall, and he was praying for his friends to be okay as he was praying for his friend James to still be alive. Will saw where James must have landed when Memphis tossed him. One of the wooden wardrobes was smashed up with James's body. When Will ran up to the broken wardrobe, he found James underneath robes and cloaks. Will saw James's red blood gushing from the large stab wound. Using torn-up cloths, Will did his best to stop the bleeding. James was helplessly shivering in deep pain, barely holding on to life.

"Let me be…go help the others," James said with heavy breaths between his words.

"You're going to be fine, James. You just need to give yourself a heal spell, and you'll be back to normal!" Will said as he was holding pressure on the open wound.

"You don't understand," James said, finding it hard to talk. "He took it away from me…my connection to Heaven. Without that connection, my body is now as simple as humans. I lost my source of Loomation powers. I lost my ability to communicate telepathically to other angels, spirits, and the Saints. I can no longer go home." James was weeping in his depression.

Will was too focused on keeping James's blood from leaving his body to fully let these words impact him. "James, you're still not dead, which means the world isn't done with you yet! Now I'm going to get you out of here!" Will said as he placed his hands underneath James and started lifting him up.

This action caused James to feel more pain, and he started to scream. Will had to place him back down, seeing that any more attempts to move his friend would make things worse. "I could use a little help!" Will shouted to the ceiling of the church.

Just then, Eric crashed through the wall of the dressing room, landing nearby.

"Eric, are you okay?" shouted Will.

"I'm fine," Eric replied. Eric noticed James in his near-death state and asked with a worried tone, "Is he going to make it?"

"He lost his Loomation powers. He can't heal himself," Will regretfully reported.

"If he needs some Loomation, then let's blast him with some!" Eric said as he removed the cube from his pocket.

"Eric, you're a genius!" Will shouted as he grabbed the cube from Eric's hand to bring it up close to James.

"There's no telling that I'll get an active Loomation or a dry one," James uttered.

"If it becomes active in you, you can heal yourself. If it's dry, it'll give you the strength to lift your weakened self up!" Will yelled as he crunched down on the cube, causing it to glow. Eric got in close to the cube to absorb some of the blast also. Will eased on the cube, releasing its boom, and the three were hit with the shock wave.

After the energy wave faded, Will asked James if it worked.

"It didn't become active, but you were right about the dry Loomation giving me the strength to stand on my own," James said as he rose to his feet.

Will and Eric smiled at him, and they too felt a huge amount of fresh energy after receiving the wave of Loomation. The three could still hear the battle behind the wall and knew that it was time to enter the fight.

Up in the attic of the church, Hayden was pulling nails out of floorboards. He was weakening the floor so it would easily break when something heavy landed on it. After that, he climbed back up to the bell tower where he spent most of his time after leaving the battle. Hayden eyed the chain that was holding the church bell into place. Hayden aimed his gun at the chain and had to hope that Memphis was right where he should be, and the Hogs would be clear when it came crashing down.

Hayden closed his eyes, praying that this would work, and calmly fired off his gun.

The bullet split the chain holding up the bell, and it dropped fast, slamming into the floorboards of the attic. Hayden, seeing that the bell failed to crash through the floor, was shocked. "Well, that's not good," Hayden softy said to himself.

Back on the ground floor, Timber managed to lead Memphis right where he needed to be in order for the Hogs' trap to work. Over by the altar, Will, Eric, and James saw an injured Juice and Gard close by. Eric said that he'll go check on Juice while telling Will and James that one of them should go check on Gard.

James, now feeling much better after receiving the power from the cube, felt fine running over to check on Gard. Will, on the other hand, spotted the sword lying close by, so he went to retrieve it.

"Juice, can you stand?" Eric said as he helped up his friend.

"No, I'm pretty sure everything beneath my knees are broken. But it's okay. I can fly, I don't need my legs!" Juice said, trying to sound tough.

Over by the pews, James checked on Gard. Gard was doing his best to get to his feet, but James had to help him stand. Gard warned him that there was going to be a time to run out of the church fast. Before Gard could elaborate, the church bell came crashing through the ceiling with Hayden on top in a similar position as someone riding a bull. Hayden even let out a loud "Yeehaw!" as he was falling down.

Just before the bell landed right on top Memphis, Hayden jumped off and landed near Timber. The impact of the bell landing on top of Memphis caused the top to snap off. The ring and sides of the bell was still intact, surrounding Memphis. Memphis was so strong that his head barely felt any pain from this attack. After the excitement of the crash was over, Memphis started to laugh once again.

"A bell landing on me? That was your big plan?" he taunted the Hogs.

"Well, that was the first part of it," Hayden replied.

Memphis then heard a beeping sound from inside the still-intact bell shell that he was standing inside of. Memphis looked down and saw that the inside of the shell was filled with angel grenades all about to blow. Memphis's eyes widened in terror. One of the explosions went off, causing Memphis to lose grip of his sword, causing it to fly out of his hands.

The shattered pieces of the bell flew toward Juice and Eric, who had to duck for cover. Then the rest of the grenades from inside the bell started to go off one by one. The shrapnel of the bell, the floor, and pews that were caught in the explosions were flying everywhere. The Hogs were in danger of everything being chucked around from these explosions. Will told everyone to head out the way they came in. Will helped James carry Gard out of the church while Eric and Juice made their way out the door. Juice, with his broken legs, had to use his power of flight to glide his way through the rubble. As they rushed to the doors, they kept hearing the devices from the broken bell going off and saw the shrapnel hissing past their paths to the exit.

Hayden and Timber were the first at the door and held it open for the others. Juice and Eric got out, followed by Will, Gard, and James. Outside, they met up with Miles and Boston. Miles woke up from the loud explosions, but he couldn't teleport them out of the area. Boston explained that Memphis still had his anti-teleporting symbol up. So the Hogs had to make a run for it. They had to make it outside of the symbol's range in order to retreat back to the swamp by teleporting.

Memphis was still being attacked by the blast going off all around him; any human would suffer lethal burns from the blast of the grenades going off. Even with Hayden's fire tolerance, he wouldn't stand a chance with those blasts blanketing the whole church. It was too risky to send someone in to stab him with the sword. And after the explosions were over, they knew Memphis would still be strong enough to continue the fight. So they took the opportunity to retreat. The Hogs who could make the run helped the ones who could barely stand. They ran fast, to a point where Boston could no longer feel the force of the anti-teleporting symbol anymore. At that point, he teleported everyone back to the swamp.

Being Human

The shrieking sounds of the first responder sirens were approaching. The church was full of fallen debris. The Hogs were long gone, and Memphis was crawling on the floor of the center aisle. Cider came in from the back door, expecting to see dead Hogs lying all over the building; instead he saw the mighty Memphis helpless and beaten. "I take it we didn't win?" Cider asked as he hovered over Memphis.

"Oh, on the contrary, we accomplished our mission successfully," Memphis said as he struggled to his feet. Even in Memphis's most damaged state, he still carried himself as a victor. "The plan was to take out the angel who convinced the Saints to have the Hogs as fighters for the balance. He may not be dead, but he's no longer an angel, which, to his kind, is pretty much the same thing."

"So we were attacking their morale?" Cider questioned as he brought his dangling legs to the floor.

"I thought with James cut off from his Loomation powers and you taking out the one with the active Loomation, the Hogs wouldn't be able to heal themselves during our battle, assuring my victory."

"Looks like it didn't go your way," Cider said as he reached down to pick up Memphis's sword.

"They were resourceful. They had more weapons than the sword and dagger you mentioned."

"The spirit on their team who protected Miles from my deadly attack was someone who I've never seen before. And I didn't know about the duffel bag of guns and grenades," Cider mentioned as if it wasn't really important.

"I expected some type of extra arsenal from them, but what you didn't warn me about was their teamwork," Memphis said with a slightly frustrated tone.

Cider defended himself, saying that he warned him of all the Hogs' skills. Memphis brought up the fact that he had fought people stronger than the Hogs before, and they all easily fell to his might. Memphis knew that the Hogs must possess something extra besides the standard survival instincts. Cider couldn't believe that Memphis was trying so hard to find an excuse for his defeat.

"The person who chose us to kill the devil was a man named Logan. He said that our powers were based on emotions," Cider informed Memphis for the first time. "He said that the power of friendship and love was the strongest. It's something that the devil didn't have, and that would be our true advantage over him…or something like that."

Memphis couldn't believe that this piece of information was kept from him by Cider. Cider didn't truly believe that emotions were the source of their strength, so he refused to bring it up. Memphis didn't understand how Loomation powers worked inside a human, and with this new detail, he figured that it must be true. Memphis then reached for his handgun that was lying on the floor close by.

"It's okay, we know where they are, and once your army wakes up, the group won't stand a chance against them," Cider said as he thought Memphis was grabbing his things to get ready to leave.

"I think there's a chance to deliver another hit to the Hogs' morale!" Memphis said as he fired the gun at Cider.

Cider flew out of the way of the incoming attack. "What do you think you're doing?" shouted Cider in rage.

"You and Juice share the same soul!" Memphis yelled as he fired the gun at him again.

Cider successfully dodged the assault once more.

"If one of you dies, you both cross over to the other side!"

"Oh, so if I drop dead, then so does Juice? Isn't that a little too simple for you, Memphis? I thought you were better than that!" Cider said, flying all over the damaged church. Cider was still carrying Memphis's sword, and he used it to redirect the coming blast at him. After the blast hit Memphis, the spirit flinched a bit. When he regained his balance, he saw that Cider was gone, and he took the sword with him.

⋙✦⋘

Back at the swamp, the Hogs were now free from their pain, broken bones, and lack of blood due to a heal spell from Miles. Hayden started up a fire as the Hogs sat around the ring to get a chance to relax. Fighting something that strong brought back painful memories of their battle with the devil.

Once the fire was lit, the visual of the flames brought back the frightening images of the night even more. Will used the sword to stab the dirt, making the weapon stick up in the ground. The Hogs all took a glance at the sword, thinking of how the blade had protected them and even saved their lives in past battles. The Hogs no longer saw the sword as an unbeatable force. Due to their failure to kill Memphis during the fight, the weapon now had lost its undefeated record. Knowing that made them feel less safe and unsure if they were the right ones to be the one to kill Memphis.

"You guys did well back there," Boston proudly stated to the group.

The Hogs were embarrassed. They built themselves up with all this false confidence on taking on Memphis, and they failed to kill the spirit. Boston told the group that they lasted longer than any other angel task force that faced him. The Hogs wanted the win; surviving wasn't enough of a victory for them. The Hogs could see the hologram of the balance of good and evil glowing in the dark atmosphere of the campsite. The whole world and all of Heaven was counting on this group to fix the balance, and they weren't certain if they could.

"Cider being Memphis's ally will make him harder to beat," Eric pointed out.

"I'd say that he let us off easy. He could have killed or at least wounded more of us, but instead he let us go," Juice replied.

"He didn't want Miles to deliver us heal spells during our fight with Memphis. He disabled two members of our group so that Memphis could have a better chance to win the battle. If he was really on our side, he would have let us go untouched," Hayden explained.

The debate of what was going through Cider's head didn't last long. Juice admitted to himself that he wished to see some light within his evil clone.

"James, how are you feeling?" Will asked his friend. After the Hogs returned to the swamp, they were a little unfocused with clouded minds. The aftershock of a big life-threating battle would do that to a human. Now that James had lost his connection with his Heavenly powers, he was now one of the humans.

James was standing opposite the Hogs with the fire ring between them. James didn't look at his friends; he had his back to them and was looking up at the stars with a tear in his eye. James may have escaped death, but he knew that his life was now over.

Will stood up from his chair and once again asked him how he was feeling.

"I was made to serve, to be a soldier of Heaven. I was made with a strong loyalty and a huge desire to fulfill my missions given to me." James slowly turned his head away from the sky and slowly turned his body to the Hogs. "Now my purpose is gone. I can never serve Heaven's orders again. I can't communicate with the Saints, angels, or spirits."

The Hogs felt a touch of sadness hearing their friend had lost things that were so dear to him.

"Memphis didn't want me dead. At least, I don't think he did. He knew there was another way to end my life."

For the ones who didn't know, James explained that Memphis built a knife that could cut off the link an angel has to Heaven. That link was their source of power, their Loomation—it's what made them angels. Without that, their body matched a human body. James told his friends that Memphis had done this to angels in past battles. James said that some of them died from the attack, while the others who lived out the rest of their time as a human eventually committed suicide.

"Why would they do that?" wondered Will.

"Because they felt that they no longer have purpose in their life. Angels are made to serve Heaven until death. If they come into a position where they can no longer do that, they end their lives. They don't know how to live a human life. They weren't meant for that."

Gard stood up out of his chair and yelled, "You still have a purpose, James!"

"James, we're humans, and we have been serving Heaven for the past week now! You can still serve!" Hayden said as he rose up from his chair.

"We still got the balance to fix, and we're not fixing it without you!" Timber added, also getting out of his chair.

"And you're not some average human. The blast from the cube you received gave you a dry Loomation. And even without that, you're still a strong member of this group!" Eric added as he, Juice, and Miles stood up.

James was touched by everything the Hogs said. But he was still unsure if he could handle being human. The Hogs did warn James of the negative aspect of being human. They brought up the fact that life is hard and not fair. They told him that there were going to be some bad days. They also told him that there will be some great days as well. There will be moments that would let you forget your troubles and express the joy of living. Moments like that come when you're hanging out with your friends. They told James that he had friends.

"Your friends will help you when you need it and even when you don't." Will walked next to James. Will then took a good look at all his friends and said, "Your friends will keep you company when you suffer a bad breakup. Be there for you when you lose a loved one. Strongly advise you to get out of a dangerous habit. Help pull you out a jam. They'll keep you sane and from getting lonely."

The Hogs hearing this made them realize just how much they missed each other over the last five years. So many bad moments of their lives could have been eased if they would have just been there for each other. They blamed it on how life works. You grow older, you move away, you lose touch—that's how life goes. They thought they were stronger than that, that they would stick together during the hardest of times. When they all realized that James was the one who brought them all together again, they made a deep confession.

"James, I was ready to end my life before you knocked on my door," Juice stated while lowering his head. "I had the sharp glass in my hand and an exposed wrist ready to release blood. But then you knocked at my door and gave me a purpose to keep going." Juice raised his head back up. "James, if you ever think about ending your life the way I did, find me and let me help you."

"I wanted to put a bullet in my head before Juice found me," Hayden admitted.

Everyone was now looking at Hayden.

Hayden corrected his words by saying that he wanted to see if there was a bullet still left in his gun by shooting it at his head, but same results. In this line of confession, Timber, Eric, and Miles all stated that they were on the path of ending their own lives until they were called by James to come together. Gard said that he never had a moment when he was ready to end his own life, but he did have thoughts on how his pain and suffering would go away if one day he just died. Almost all of the Hogs had James to thank for their lives, so they felt that they owed him theirs. They knew James was entering a new way of life, and they wanted to be there to help him every step of the way. They owned him that much and were more than happy to do it.

James knew that a new life of being human would be a tough adjustment. He knew that he would have to find a place within the world that fit him. He would find goals and use every day he had to achieve them. Fixing the balance was the goal he could still work toward.

James then looked over to the balance hologram at the campsite and reflected on his reasons for wanting it to be fixed. He wanted the humans to live with a fair amount of good and bad situations that would affect their free will. Now he was one of them humans that he so valiantly fought for, he had a better understanding on how important the balance was for everyone.

James then looked over to the Hogs. He knew that having them as friends meant that he wouldn't face the bad time alone.

All seemed well at the campsite. They thought the fight was over, and they could gain a good night's rest and plan on taking on Memphis in the morning. Up until now, that was how their days were going. But this wouldn't be like the other nights when they had a heart-to-heart talk and take on evil in the morning. The calm night of chatting around a warm fire was disrupted by a shadowy figure in the starry sky.

"Heads up!" Boston shouted.

Everyone brought their eyes up to the sky and saw a person flying in their direction.

"Cider!" Juice said with an uneasy tone.

The group grew worried that Memphis was close by, so Hayden hurried himself up the hill north of the campsite. Boston said that he'll circle around the campsite to check for any other intruders. Gard pointed a gun at Cider, just in case their visitor was going to try something menacing. The rest of the group just stared at the flying man as he slowly descended to shouting distance. Once he reached the light coming from the campfire, he hovered over it, remaining still within the air. He didn't feel safe on the ground while visiting these people.

"You're probably wondering why I'm here," Cider said.

"Are you here to hurt us again?" Juice asked.

"Let's move on from that," Cider replied.

"Move on from that? It wasn't even an hour ago since you shot at one of our guys and led us to get our butts kicked by Memphis!" Eric shouted.

"I regret my actions, okay? We all good?" Cider painfully uttered in hopes to show that he came in peace.

"You're working for Memphis! Give us one good reason why we shouldn't kill you right here and now!" Gard yelled.

"Because if I die, then so does Juice!"

This caused the group to grow silent. They were shocked by this news and became worried for Juice.

"Our souls are one of two halves. Since we were split, if one part of the soul crosses over, than so does the other."

The Hogs all turned to James, wondering if he could give some kind of confirmation on this. James did believe that the hypothesis did have a strong outcome. Will spoke out to Cider, asking him if he knew this. And if so, why would he put his own life at risk by letting the Hogs fight Memphis? Cider lied to the Hogs, saying that if he didn't cooperate with Memphis's request, then the spirit would kill him on the spot. Cider then added to his lie, saying that he was rooting for the Hogs to kill

Memphis the whole time. He claimed that he set the gun that he used on Boston to stun so that it wouldn't kill him. Cider said he needed to find his chance to get away from Memphis, and after his battle with the Hogs, he found his chance to be free of him.

The Hogs didn't know if they believed the hybrid's story, but Cider didn't care. He came to the Hogs to give them a warning to assure himself to see tomorrow.

"Memphis is coming here tonight."

This statement sent a horrendous chill down the Hogs' spine. They delivered a heavy beating on Memphis; it was amazing that he was alive, let alone ready to come in for another fight on the same night. When James asked when would the spirit's next attack be, Cider replied that James's question was a dumb one.

"You should be grabbing what you can and getting out of here pronto! Memphis's attack at the church was just to get to the angel. He wanted to take care of the one responsible for turning the Hogs into fighters for the order of the balance personally. After that, he wanted to face the rest of the group to see if he could defeat them or to attack again with reinforcements. After what you guys did, he's bringing the entire army."

"How many we talking about?" questioned Hayden.

"He said close to five hundred. Five hundred Egg spirits all set to hatch at nine tonight."

It was already a half hour away from nine, making the Hogs feel like they were on some sort of a countdown. Cider informed the Hogs that he delivered the location on where the swamp was to Memphis. Cider said that since he didn't have any photos of the campsite, he showed the spirit a photo of the road north of this location by using a map of the roads he found on the internet. Cider said that Memphis, along with his army, will approach from the north due to them only being able to teleport to a location they have seen before. Cider warned the group that Memphis will set up an anti-teleporting symbol after showing up to keep the Hogs from retreating. "After that, you guy are finished. You're not strong enough to take on his army!"

James asked Cider if he knew where Memphis put this symbol during battle. Cider did know that answer, saying that Memphis placed it on the back of his belt buckle. Having the symbol on his body was a way to control who and when people can teleport. Cider once again begged the Hogs to leave while they still could. Cider didn't want Juice to die that night. He said that he's new to living and doesn't want his life to end before the next sunrise.

The Hogs passed uncertain glances among one another. They didn't know if Cider was telling the truth or if he was still working for their enemy.

Cider brought something to the Hogs to show that he wasn't working for Memphis. He removed a sword that he had tied to his back and chucked it down to the dirt, making it stand upright. The Hogs recognized this weapon as the one Memphis used to defend himself from the Hogs' sword.

"Just because you brought us our enemy's weapon doesn't mean you're on our side," Gard said, not impressed. "For all we know, Memphis has another one just like it."

"Oh no, he does not," Boston stated with a shocking tone. "This here is the Blackout Sword, a weapon made to deflect Loomation-powered attacks." Boston, now having everyone's attention, told the group that he helped work on this weapon years ago. "The weapon was given the usual assets Heaven has to offer: never grows dull, made to be perfectly balanced, and able to tear through the skin of angels and spirits." Boston walked up to the blade, gripped it by the handle, and pulled it out of the ground. "The special effect of blocking Loomation was a tricky one to apply. We attempted this feature on six different weapons. First, we locked them into a chamber for a quarter of a decade. A chamber of absolute darkness, a place that has never seen the light of Loomation before. After that, we pinned all of the six tools around a dying star, where all light in the area was pulled into a black hole. During this time, five of the six were pulled into the hole, being destroyed. The sword was the only one that was able to be retrieved. In the end, we made a weapon that could repel all Loomation."

Boston went on to say that the weapon was used in battle against Memphis during the war. The angel carrying the sword was killed, and the sword was stolen by Memphis.

"Cider must have told Memphis that the sword the Hogs used on the devil started to glow a golden light when near the threat," James said as he looked up to Cider for confirmation, which he gave by a reluctant nod. "Memphis must have thought that the sword would glow in his presence, and that glow is just Loomation."

"So if he had a weapon that could deflect Loomation, then he could find a way to block our unstoppable blade!" Eric shouted in frustration.

Once the Hogs learned that they been carrying God's sword in battle, they felt that they had the most powerful blade in all creation on their side. Seeing their enemy find a way to block the most powerful weapon made them lose that feeling, as if the odds were once again even.

"There's no way that Memphis would willingly give up his only chance at defending himself," Hayden stated.

"Now that we have both swords, the odds are once again in our favor," Eric pointed out.

Seeing that Cider stole Memphis's most important weapon and then delivered it to the Hogs made them believe that he was telling the truth. If Memphis was going to defeat them, he would have to bring an army.

The flying messenger felt that he did his best to convince the group of the imminent attack. There was nothing more he could do, so he turned away and flew off in the sky. The Hogs were left to make a choice, and they didn't have much time to make it.

It Takes an Army

Hayden headed to his camper to pick up a pair of binoculars. Once in hand, he headed up the hill on the north side of the campsite. The other Hogs met up with him on top of the hill to look out in the distance. The night sky was full of visible stars brightening up the land, making it easy to spot an army of hatched egg spirits coming their way. The long field between them and the road was empty, not a spirit in sight.

"How much time do we got?" questioned Timber.

"Twenty-three minutes until nine," Will quickly responded.

The idea of a major attack coming to the Hogs in such a short amount of time had them feeling on edge.

"The bomb trap could still work," Miles said with a force of belief in his words.

"Back when we thought it was just Memphis coming for us, it would have," Boston replied.

"He's right! With an army now coming, one of Memphis's chess pawns would check the campsite first and report back to Memphis when they find the bomb hidden in one of the tents before Memphis enters the blast zone," James regretted to inform.

"We know he'll teleport by the road, so we replant the bomb there," Eric suggested.

"Still might not work." James sadly shook his head before elaborating. "Say we hide the bomb on the left side of the road, then Memphis arrives on the right side of the road. With his army between him and the bomb, he could survive the blast."

"I thought this bomb was supposed to be strong enough to kill this spirit!" Timber yelled.

"We're not sure if it'll work or not. We know it has a better chance of killing him if we can get it as close to him as we can," Hayden chimed in.

"What about an air drop?" Juice spoke up, grabbing everyone's attention.

All eyes were on Juice for what he was suggesting was something a little too dangerous to think about. Juice said that he could fly right over the army and drop the bomb on top of Memphis.

"He'll kill you by shooting you with his AG handgun before you get close to him," Will stated.

"Make sure he doesn't look up. And that Blackout Sword can deflect the ammunition. I saw it done by Memphis back at the church," Juice said with confidence. "Once I get to a drop point, I'll let go and sky-rocket myself up so that Hayden can push that detonation switch that he's so eager to push."

The Hogs thought about the plan, seeing it as their best chance at winning this battle. James then brought up the fact that Memphis had the power to teleport. The group learned that Memphis sets up an anti-teleporting symbol on the back of his belt buckle in order to keep his prey from getting away. He still had the power to take down that symbol if he felt that his life was in danger.

"Let's be the one who traps Memphis this time. Once he enters our territory, we'll set up our own anti-teleporting symbol so he can't retreat from our attack!" shouted Gard.

This got the group in high hopes. Having the idea of trapping their enemy in a deadly setup sounded like a good plan.

"We know where they are coming from!" Hayden shouted as he pointed toward north. "That way!"

"We know when they're coming!" yelled Gard as he lifted his arm up along with Hayden's.

"Which is pretty soon, just for the record," Eric added.

"Tonight, the order of the balance will take out its biggest threat!" Boston said with pride in his voice as he raised his fist into the air.

There wasn't much time, so the Hogs acted fast. They started to build dirt piles on top of the hill so that they could be well hidden as they were in the crouch-down shooting position. They armed themselves with AG rifles and handguns. Some members even carried grenades. Hayden even duct-taped his hunting knife to the end of his rifle to make a bayonet.

Juice had the bomb on the ground right in front of him. He felt a little unsettled about the idea of picking it up. Will saw his friend in a frozen state and gave him an encouraging pat on the back, reminding him that he can handle this task. James also delivered an encouraging nod to his frightened friend. Boston then walked over carrying a belt to wrap the bomb around Juice so that he doesn't lose it in flight. Boston wasn't as gentle with the handling of the bomb as Juice would have liked. There was a moment when Boston almost dropped it while attaching it to Juice.

"Is this a seat belt from one of the cars?" Juice shockingly asked.

Boston said that he took the seat belt from Juice's car. Juice was now mad on two terms: the powerful bomb being strapped to him by a simple seat belt was the first one, and the other thing he was mad about was that Boston stole it from his car.

"Oh, these things keep you safe in dangerous situations every day," Boston said in a reassuring voice.

Some of the other Hogs started to thank Juice for his bravery in this mission. Juice thanked his friends, just before asking any of them if they wanted to switch roles. He was happy to trade his flying powers with anyone at the time. Juice was using poor comedy to cover his fear, but in all honesty, he felt capable of completing this task. Once the bomb was secured to Juice by the seat belt, Boston informed him that all he had to do was push the red button on the clicker in order to release the weapon.

"Release the bomb while up in the air. After that, take off to the high skies, and once you're clear, I'll detonate it," Hayden instructed Juice.

"Take cover over by the woods on the east side of the swamp. Keep your walkie-talkie close to you and wait for our order before approaching the army," Will added.

The final object handed to Juice before taking off was the Blackout Sword. This was handed to him by James.

Juice swung the long oblong-tubed shape shell behind his back, finding the maneuvering of it surprisingly smooth. Juice then took off to the east trees with his friends wishing him good luck. Once Juice was hiding up in the trees, the rest of the group all made sure their weapons were loaded and that they were carrying plenty of ammo. Now that everyone was ready for the attack, all they had to do was wait.

The road north of the swamp was one boring straight road that went from the east to the west. There was nothing to the north side of the road except empty fields. To the south of the road was the muddy swampland with the Hogs' campsite less than a mile inland.

The time was four after nine, and in the blink of an eye, the road became engulfed with Memphis's hatch egg spirit army with Memphis in the center of the pack. The arrival of so many spirits teleporting to that location all at once dramatically shifted the air.

All the way back to the top of the hill, the Hogs could feel and even hear the eerie gust of wind racing overhead. They literally felt the chill of war coming their way. The Hogs were smart enough to understand that this was their portent of the battle to come.

Hayden put his eyes to his binoculars once again and checked for the approaching army. Hayden maintained his posture completely still until he saw the spirits coming. "They're marching in," Hayden said over the walkie-talkie.

The Hogs on the hill tightened their guns and raised them up to their eyes, ready to fire. Keeping their eyes out in the field, waiting for the monsters to enter their shooting range was all they could do. In time, the spirits came in sight of the Hogs on the hill without Hayden's binoculars.

"This is it!" James yelled out.

"Anyone have eyes on Memphis?" Will asked.

"He's right in the middle of the pack! I see him!" Hayden said, focusing his binoculars on the steel color–skinned monster. It was almost hard to spot him out in the crowd of white hatched egg spirits, but

Hayden was determine to receive visible confirmation that Memphis was in the pack. Hayden couldn't believe how well the spirit looked. Not too long ago, the spirit was blasted by tons of explosions, and that was after taking a severe beating from the Hogs. The Hogs were slightly flattered by this attack. Memphis had never brought an entire army to take out his enemies before.

"They're getting closer. Begin firing?" asked Timber, eager to start the battle.

"Hold on, something is happening within the pack," Hayden said with wonder.

All of a sudden, many hatched egg spirits started to stretch out their body, and from their backs, wings started to spread out from their torsos. Many of these spirits had wings, and they stated to take flight into the air. The Hogs tried to get a count on how many launched into the air, but there were too many to count, and they just kept coming. There were about fifty in the air, and they were rapidly flying toward them.

"What are we going to do now?" Eric yelled.

"We need to stick to the plan," James replied with confidence.

"The skies are no longer safe!" Will pointed out.

"By now, Memphis would have set up his anti-teleporting symbol, which means we can't retreat. It's fight or die time!" Gard yelled out loud.

At that moment, Boston stated to brand their own anti-teleporting symbol into the dirt near their position as planned.

"Once Juice starts moving, the flying eggs are going to be after him, so we do our best to cover him!" James instructed as he aimed his rifle at the flying spirits. Hayden lifted the walkie-talkie up to his mouth again to inform Juice that they would be shooting the winged egg monsters away, so he had to be on high alert while flying. Once Juice copied that detail, he was then instructed to make his charge toward Memphis.

Juice flew out of the trees and quickly moved to the center of the army where Memphis was. He was spotted pretty quickly by the flying creatures, and they abruptly turned to him and rushed in for an attack. The flying monsters weren't handling their power of flight too well, so they found it difficult to move in a straight path. Juice didn't need wings to fly. He was very agile in the sky. He was able to do barrel rolls, rising and dropping his altitude to skillfully avoid his attackers. The winged creatures struggled with their maneuverability skills, but since there were so many, they still provided a challenging hurdle for Juice to get around.

On top of the hill, the Hogs were using their AG rifles to take fire at the flying spirits. They first targeted the ones getting too close to Juice and then shot at the ones who were between Memphis and Juice. Juice didn't like all his quick moves, in fear that the bomb could go off with any sudden jolt. When he got a good look at Memphis, the spirit saw that Juice was carrying a bomb. Memphis then sent the front half of his army at the Hogs on top of the hill. He figured that he could take out the ones providing Juice cover fire.

"We got another thing to worry about!" Timber shouted as he saw the front of the army now sprinting toward them. Luckily, there was still plenty of field between them and the front of the pack, but that didn't mean it was safe to ignore them. Timber, Eric, and Miles all took fire at the eggs charging their way, just long enough until Juice released the bomb.

Juice knew that he had to ditch the bomb soon and make a quick exit. The flying eggs were getting too close to him. Juice told Hayden that he better have his finger on the button because he was ready to release the bomb. Hayden gave Juice the order to release the mortar. Juice pushed the red button on his belt and took hold of the device. He saw his open space between him and Memphis and chucked the shell at the spirit hard. Immediately after that, Juice pulled up into the air as Hayden waited for his friend to get in the clear.

Memphis reached for his belt buckle to remove the anti-teleporting symbol. Once he removed the symbol, he was shocked that he couldn't teleport away. It took him a hot second to realize what happened. The Hogs must have set up their own symbol. Memphis was trapped by his own devices, the exact ploy he had used on so many of his prey. Memphis had to act quickly, so he ordered the rear of the army to dogpile on him right away.

All at once, the closest hatched eggs near Memphis covered him with their own bodies, causing a huge pile of spirits doing their best to shield their leader from the blast.

After Juice reached the needed altitude, Hayden activated the bomb, and the Hogs on the hill ducked for cover from the blazing light.

The blast was silver colored and very loud. A noise from the blast echoed through the swamp and all the way up to the hill where the Hogs were seeking shelter. The rear of the army was blown to bits by the explosion, but most of the front of the pack seemed unaffected. The remaining army all stared at their leader. The flying monsters also stopped in midflight to take a look down.

After a moment to let the blast die out, the Hogs took a peek above the dirt wall to check on Memphis.

Thanks to Memphis's servants shielding him from the energy, the spirit was still alive, but just barely. He was too weak to get to his feet, and his whole body was on fire. He started to slink south, away from the Hog's anti-teleporting symbol. As he crawled, he had to pound his body into the hot dirt to douse the flames. The pounding of his body to the ground was more painful than the flames, but the flames were slowing killing him.

The Hogs couldn't believe that the spirit survived that blast. For a moment, they thought of him as being unkillable. James took a look at the God sword and knew that it was now or never. James lifted the sword high about his head and said that he will end this fight once and for all.

"James, we still have half an army to make our way through. We're way outnumbered! We'll never make it!" Eric pointed out.

At this time, Will sprinted over to the campsite to get to the old truck that had been parked on the grounds for a long time.

"Guys, we'll never see Memphis this weak again! This is our only chance to kill him!" Gard stated as he agreed with James's plan.

"Some of us may die, but I'm willing to make that sacrifice if it means we kill this spirit and help bring back the good to the balance again!" shouted Hayden.

"For the balance!" shouted Timber.

"For hope!" Miles cheered.

"For humanity!" yelled James.

At that moment, the sound of the truck turning over caught the Hogs' attention. Will drove the truck up to the top of the hill and told everyone that together, they could get past the wall of soldiers.

As they loaded up on the back of the truck, James told Boston to stay behind, stating that someone needed to protect the symbol. If Memphis's men can't stop the Hogs, then he'll send what's left of his army to destroy the symbol so that he can teleport to safety. Boston agreed to this job and told them that they can count on him. Once everyone was loaded in the back of the truck, Will hit the gas hard, charging straight into the army.

Juice was still being attacked by the winged spirits. He had nothing but the Blackout sword to defend himself with. He knew that if he could get the flying ones attacking him, his friends in the truck would have fewer enemies to worry about. As Miles saw Juice imperiled by the flying forces all attacking him at once, he took the walkie-talkie from Hayden to speak to Juice.

"Juice, when you see me up there, you catch me, okay?" Miles instructed.

Juice had no idea what Miles was talking about, and he was too busy turning and rolling around the air to ask any questions.

Miles looked over to Hayden and asked him to toss him up as high as he could into the air. Hayden didn't hesitate and did as he was asked. Hayden grabbed Miles by the armpits and thrust him upward as high up as he could. As Miles went up, he used his defense spells to blast at some of the winged monsters.

Juice saw the lights of the spells and spotted his friend rising to his level. Juice acted fast and caught him before he fell to the ground. Miles climbed on Juice's back as if he was getting a piggyback ride. Using the seat belt as a handle, he started acting as a gun for Juice. With Juice's flying ability and Miles's defense spells, the two were shooting down the winged eggs, keeping them away from them and the truck.

The truck was moving fast, heading toward the wall of hatched eggs. Once they pierced past that front guard, the path to Memphis would still be a challenge. The bomb drove a massive pit between them and Memphis. They had to either drive around or drive through it. The pit was very wide and very long, with scattered fires burning within it. The pit was deceptively deep, but with their dry Loomation, they would have the strength to pull themselves out.

As the truck drove on, the Hogs in the pickup started to use their guns to blast the spirits blocking their way and the ones charging at them. The truck had to drive over the shot-down monsters, but it found a gap in the army to breach into. Once inside the pack of the army, the creatures started to close in on the truck. Even with all the blazing bullets on the back of the vehicle, they failed to protect themselves from the oncoming army. The truck was tipped and landed upside down, causing everyone to jump off to safety.

Will had to crawl out of the driver-side window. The Hogs around him were firing off their guns like crazy to push back the eggs coming in for an attack. Will looked on the other side of the truck and saw a dozen or so coming in from that direction. Will, with all his might, pushed the truck like a superhero at the oncoming attackers. Following that action, Will fired at the truck around the gas tank, causing it to blow up in flames. The blast destroyed most of the immediate threat, but some still stood. Hayden charged toward the flames to forward his attack. Timber, not liking his friend going off by himself, ran after him.

Hayden ran right through the flames and caught the monsters off guard. He wanted to save his ammo, so he brandished his rifle like a bat to drive his bayonet into the heads and hearts of the monsters. Hayden didn't stop there; he continued on running into more of the monsters, making his way toward Memphis from the east side of the pit. Since Timber had to go around the flames, he had to run in order to catch up with him.

Over by the rest of the grounded Hogs, Eric stated that the eggs can kill them all at once easier if they remained in one place together. Gard shouted out that he'll lure the army away from James, since he's the one carrying the weapon that can kill Memphis. As Gard ran to the west side, Eric ran along with him. Will hated the way that they were splitting up, but James pointed out that there was a clear path toward Memphis, and they should take it while most of the army was going after Eric and Gard.

Eric and Gard found themselves close to the massive pit. Before they knew it, they were heavily surrounded. "Well, our plan to keep them off James and Will worked too well!" Gard shouted as he chucked his final AG grenade into the pit. After Gard made his toss, Eric pushed six eggs into the pit, right where the grenade landed, causing them to die in the explosion. Eric looked over to Gard, feeling like this was going to be it for them. They were running low on ammunition, and there was no way to make a run for it. Gard had similar thoughts, but he still continued to fight as he reloaded his weapon.

Eric and Gard were standing close when they saw a large pack of eggs coming toward them. Eric pulled the pin of his last AG grenade and dropped it in front of them. The two turned and jumped down the pit, sliding alongside the hot dirt. As their butts landed on the bottom, they heard the grenade go off, followed by the screams of the killed eggs. They took a moment to catch their breaths, and once they did, a herd of egg soldiers came leaping down at them from the top of the pit. The two lifted their rifles and fired everything they had at the coming threat, but it wasn't enough. The eggs reached the two friends, and just before being ripped to shreds, the two brave Hogs vanished. There was a heavy gust of wind present just before and just after the two disappeared.

Hayden was going around the pit on the east side of the field. He was keeping an eye on his friends Will and James, who were in the center of the pit making their way across it. Hayden then looked past the pit and saw Memphis still crawling away. He then stopped to take a peek up to the skies to check on his friends in the air. Hayden saw that Juice's speed was slowing down, and Miles's range of his defense spells were losing their momentum, meaning that he was exhausted. Hayden raised his gun up to take out some of the winged angels to assist Juice and Miles.

Hayden was too busy checking on his friends that he didn't bother to check if he was safe. Once Hayden put his run to a halt and took a moment to aim his gun, he was attacked by eggs who were chasing him. Hayden's neck was nabbed by a monster and was being squeezed tight. Hayden's sight was about to go fully black, but Timber fired his gun at the threatening egg, killing him on the spot. Hayden dropped to a knee, desperately trying to catch his breath. As he looked up, he saw that Timber was being swarmed by many eggs. Timber tried to fight back, but the monsters tipped him over, causing him and his attackers to fall into the pit.

Timber's body tumbled against the slanted dirt on the way down, twisting, rolling, and smashing his helpless body against the hot dirt and rocks. The spirits shoving their feet, elbows, and heads into him at the bottom made his bones break. Hayden, while in a knee-down position, raised his gun up and fired at all the spirits on top of Timber before they could do any more harm to him. After Hayden killed off the last spirit, he couldn't see Timber down there. Hayden could have sworn that he saw Timber within the pile down there a moment ago. Hayden could clearly see that his friend was no longer there, which he found odd. Hayden felt that he had to keep moving toward Memphis; otherwise, Timber's sacrifice would have been for nothing.

Up in the air, Juice spotted a group of eggs making their way to the Hog's anti-teleporting symbol. Boston was on guard, but he couldn't take on the entire pack. Juice told Miles that they needed to head over to Boston to assist him on the coming threat. Before Juice could make his turn, he was attacked from below by the winged eggs. Juice's body was swung hard, causing Miles to fall off his back and land into the pit. Luckily for Miles, he was close enough to survive the fall, but he received heavy damage to his body. Miles was able to give himself a heal spell to help himself. Once he felt better, he stood up and looked up to check on Juice.

Juice, on the other hand, wasn't so lucky; Miles looked up and saw Juice get attacked by the remaining flying eggs. They drove him down to the ground and drilled themselves on top of him. All Miles could do was watch his friend being pushed down from afar. He didn't even see where he landed due to the pit covering his view. Miles then checked his area to find someone who could help or see someone who he could help. He looked north and spotted Will and James. Will and James were getting close to the edge of the pit, which would place them right up on Memphis. Miles then saw a herd of eggs charging at his friends from behind. Miles knew that once those eggs get the surprise attack on the two, they wouldn't survive. Even with James wielding the sword, there were still too many beasts going in for the attack.

Miles fired off a defense spell at the eggs and shouted out to them. "Hey, you ugly monsters!" Miles then fired off another defense spell at another egg. "Come and get me!"

Miles's plan on luring the coming threat to Will and James worked. The monsters changed their direction to attack Miles. Miles turned and ran as if his life depended on it. Miles didn't get too far from his run. The monsters caught up to him, and before they could claw their nails into him, he was whooshed away by a mighty wind, disappearing without a trace.

Over by the hill, Boston was firing upon the coming wave of attackers. The eggs were outnumbering him, and all his allies were either gone or too far away. Boston could see that Will and James were now so close to getting to Memphis, so if he failed to protect the symbol now, all their hard work would be for nothing. Boston used up the final bullets he carried in his gun and then started to use his weapons as a club, smashing the eggs to death.

Boston had one AG grenade left, so he pulled its pin, and in the act of chucking it, he was hit by one of the eggs, causing it to slip out of his hand. Boston looked over and saw that his device had landed close to the symbol. Boston knew that if the grenade went off, the blast would destroy the symbol. Boston tried to get to it to knock it away, but he was being pulled back by the eggs. They were all over him, pulling his shoulders and legs away. Boston, with all his strength, jumped on top of the grenade while carrying the eggs attached to his body along with him. The grenade went off, but the explosion was contained under the bodies of the spirits.

Over by the edge of the pit, Will and James reached the top of it and saw Memphis only ten steps away. James, brandishing the sword, charged in quick. Memphis forced himself up to prepare for battle. Memphis had to leap out of the way of the stabbing thrust of the sword, which delayed him from retrieving his gun. After James missed his attack, he swung it hard to the right, leaving a hug gash across Memphis's torso. Memphis lost his balance and stumbled over to his left side when Hayden arrived.

Hayden stabbed his bayonet right into Memphis's body and dragged it up, causing a huge cut in his body. Right at the cut lay the barrel of his gun. Hayden fired his last round into the fresh cut, causing Memphis to fall on his back. Hayden used his gun as a spear and thrust it at Memphis's head. Memphis shoved his head to the right, slightly causing the knife to tear up the side of his forehead close to his eye. Memphis looked over and saw James coming in for another attack. Memphis finally got his hand on his gun and fired it at James.

"James, look out!" Will shouted as he pushed James out of the way of the oncoming bullet. Right before the green bullet touched Will, he vanished, leaving nothing but that mysterious heavy gust of wind.

Memphis then turned to Hayden and fired. Hayden was also swept away by the strong gust of wind in the blink of an eye. James in action jumped on top of Memphis and drove the sword into the spirit's heart. Memphis threw his hands up to push back on the guard below the hilt, attempting to keep it from piercing his heart. Memphis looked over and saw his remaining army too far away to save him in time. He could feel his weakened body fail him to keep the blade from driving down into his body any further. He knew he was going to die by the hands of a fallen angel.

"I just wanted them to be free," Memphis said while still trying to push back the sword. "I just wanted them to be happy."

The blade came down by James's push, and Memphis said his final words.

"I just wanted to be loved by them."

And with a final loud grunt from James, the blade drove right through Memphis's heart, killing him once and for all.

James was able to take a much-needed breath of relief. He thought the battle had ended, but when he looked over, he saw the remaining eggs charging at him. James didn't care. He took out Memphis, and all his friends were presumed dead, so he didn't care what these spirits did to him.

But before the army could touch him, he was whisked away by the mysterious wind.

The Job Offer

While in motion of swinging the sword, James suddenly found himself in a dark space. The last thing James remembered was him standing in a dangerous position about to be attacked by a group of spirit eggs. He was moved from that position so quickly that he didn't even know that he was in a different place.

"James, calm down. You're no longer at the swamp!" shrieked Will as he tried to calm down his friend.

James took a few moments to relax his body as he tried to wrap his mind around the idea on how he was in one place then shifted to another without him even knowing. James eyed the place and saw that the Hang Out Group members were all present within this area. Their surroundings were nothing but pure darkness, as if they were looming in a very large shadow. The Hogs were using their flashlights on their cell phones for light, but besides the lights exposing the faces of the members of the group, there was nothing else in the location to see.

The Hogs asked James questions such as what happened to them? Where were they? They feared that they were in hell or something. James had to admit that he had no idea what happened to them and that he had no clue on where they were. Then a large gust of wind came to the Hogs, and they saw a silhouette of something new exposed within the dark.

The object in the dark was a nine-foot-tall dove. The bird spread out its wings as far as they could reach, and from its wings came many large embers of fire. The fire hovered within the air and became suspended, lighting the room up as if torches were now burning. Hayden commented that he liked this bird due to its fire powers. None of the Hogs felt any fear or any kind of threat toward the bird; in fact, they felt an overwhelming feeling of warmth and peace being around it. With the flames in the air, it was now easier to see everyone, but they still seemed to be standing within a shadow. There was nothing around them but empty space in the dark.

"I like this bird," Hayden stated as he looked at the bird now glowing within the flaming lights.

"This makes sense now," James uttered.

"What is it, James?" asked Eric.

"I knew that we couldn't have been teleported away, not with our symbol still intact. The dove is the Holy Spirit, created by God himself. The spirit can move so fast that it seems that everything around it stands still. It is impossible to see when it moves as fast as it does."

"So it saved our lives just before we were about to be killed in battle?" assumed Gard.

"It must have healed us too. Before I was sent here, I had broken bones and was bleeding all over," Timber added.

"Yeah, but I want to know who sent it? This spirit was thought to have been retired and unreachable for centuries," James stated.

"I asked the spirit to retrieve you," bellowed a voice from behind the bird. A woman walked around the bird to present herself to the group.

James recognized this woman as the archangel Laura. The rest of the Hogs had never heard of this archangel before. Laura replied in a rough tone that she likes her privacy and that she never wanted any prophet talking about her. Will asked Laura where they were.

"You're in a private section of purgatory," she replied.

"Purgatory? Are we dead?" Juice asked, coming close to being in a panic mode.

"You're not dead. The bird managed to pick you all up before you were killed. But you are in a spiritual form while being in here."

James was able to shine some light on this information. He described to his friends that Purgatory was a very large sandbox-type place that sat outside Heaven and earth. Any spirit or angel can enter this place and put up some walls and make their own room of some kind. The Saints used to do their work within Purgatory at one point in time. Pretty much every spirit has their own room within Purgatory; it's where they stay when they're not on earth. This dark space of Purgatory was where the Holy Spirit has been resting. This room is only known to Laura.

"Why did you bring us here?" Will asked the archangel.

Laura was the one to inform the group that James managed to kill Memphis before he was carried to this room. The Hogs all looked over to James with proud and celebrating eyes. Laura then mentioned that the Saints had their predictions, and they didn't think that the Hog would succeed. Laura wanted to make sure that the Hogs would survive the battle, so she asked a favor from the dove to remove any member of the group out of the war zone if their life was next to death.

"Well, we gratefully appreciate your help. But we need to go back. There are still spirit eggs at the swamp that need to be eliminated!" James exclaimed.

"Yeah, and we should check on Boston," Hayden added.

"Once Memphis was killed, the angels came down from Heaven to take care of the remaining eggs. The positive spirits also got straight to work once Memphis was dead, and they are already carrying out good actions to the world as we speak," Laura informed. "And as for Boston…" She painfully regretted to tell the Hogs that Boston had died during the battle.

The Hogs were confused; they just learned that the Holy Spirit was assigned to save any Hog member who was next to death. They saw Boston as a member of their group and were outraged that he wasn't saved.

"Boston was giving his life to protect the symbol. If his body would have been removed from the battle, the blast he was covering would have ruined the symbol, which would have led to Memphis's escape. I'm sorry that I told the dove to leave Boston to his demise, but it was the only way to keep Memphis from escaping. He knew what he was doing. He knew the risk, and I didn't want to steal his heroic sacrifice."

The Hogs hated it, but they understood. When Laura explained the situation of Boston in play-by-play detail, the Hogs were touched by Boston's action.

"Why did you save us?" Gard asked the archangel.

"I'm here to talk on the behalf of God. He wants to offer you a job."

The woman explained that she has been talking to God, and God knows that the balance will never fully be under control without a devil in power. God said that there must be a devil to keep the negative spirits in line. With Memphis now gone, it's only a matter of time until another spirit drives for power and tips the balance once again.

James was the first to volunteer to take the job, saying that being a prime manager for the balance would be an honor to have.

"Thanks, James, but this job isn't being offered to you. It's being offered to the people who were responsible for killing God's first creation," Laura said as she gestured to the first seven members of the Hang Out Group.

"No. They weren't meant for a job like that. They are human. The world is theirs to live in. Being a guardian of the balance isn't what they're built for!" James spoke out in a rage.

"All the Saints who are in charge of the good side of the balance were all human once. So asking humans for a job like this isn't anything new. And not to mention, you alone asked these seven men to help fix the balance at the start of all this," she said, looking directly at James. She then faced the group. "When the member who wishes to take the job steps forward, they will have all the powers of the devil and be working from within Purgatory where he'll have more freedom that the original devil did back when he was locked up in the Garden."

"So taking the job means we have to say goodbye to our lives?" Will struggled to ask for he felt that he already knew the answer.

Laura sadly said yes to that question. "This was why the job wasn't offered until God saw you push yourself to the brink of death to fix the balance. He had to see that you were willing to give up your life for something you believed in."

Hearing this did remind the Hogs that they were willing to give up their lives while in battle to fix the balance. Why would taking a job that takes them away from their lives forever be any different? This was all the more reason why James thought that he should be offered the job. James said that he just wanted the Hogs' help on killing Memphis, and now that he's dead, their work for the balance should be done. James said that he has no life waiting for him on earth. He'll miss his old life of serving Heaven, but if he can take this job, he would find meaning and purpose in his life again.

"This job is not offered to you, James. I'm sorry." Laura, when first talking to the Hogs, came off as annoyed to be the one picked to talk to the group. But as she started to recognize everything that this group has gone though and what they were about to do, it made her start to feel sympathy for the members.

She once again addressed the whole group. "Once you decide who will take the job, the one picked will touch the bird, and the spirit will immediately carry him off to God. The rest of you, I'll teleport you back to your homes. The angels on earth will return your stuff from the swamp to your abodes. Since you're in spiritual form, you'll feel greatly exhausted when you return to physical form, so you'll be put in a place where you can sleep it off."

After she took a few steps away from the group, she paused as if she just now remembered an important detail. She turned to James and asked for the sword, saying that the owner wanted it back. James did as he was asked and relinquished the weapon. She then turned to Eric, saying that the cube was also requested. Eric was a little hesitant on giving up the cube. The others felt it too. The cube was what made them who they were, and it had helped save their lives many times during battles. But fully having the cube taken off their hands was a huge relief to the group, and they were happy to see it go.

The Hogs all looked at each other, wondering which one of them would speak out first on who would take the job. The idea of celebrating their victory over Memphis didn't seem worth doing at the time. Going into battle thinking that not all of you will make it out alive is one thing. But having to say goodbye to someone because you know that they won't come back was another.

The Hogs all talked to each other as if it would be the last time talking to that person. The time they sat there felt like hours, but it was really only a few minutes.

They all came to terms that any one of them was willing to take the job. But the job was only offered to one, and no one was returning home until one stepped up. The problem wasn't that no one was stepping up; the problem was getting permission from the others to step up. It seemed that everyone wanted the job but wasn't going to let anyone else take it over them.

They all weighed the options. Who had the most to return home to? Who wanted to return home the most? Who was needed to still be home? It was a blessing to have this choice, but at the same time a curse. The one who took the job had to talk his way into it. They all agreed that once he's gone, the others would act as nothing was wrong. They would never think of him as dead because he wouldn't be. They were told to act as if he just left the hangout early and maybe one day return. They were not to mourn over him or even regret not taking the job over him. The Hogs did get to say their goodbyes. After that, he was gone, and the Hogs were teleported back home.

A Brand-New Day

Saturday, October 10, 2020

James was the first to wake up, finding himself in the same house that he used to bring all the Hogs together for the first time in five years. James reflected on his first time being at this house. He traded the old couple who lived there several pounds of gold in exchange for the building. He gave them extra pounds of gold if they could pack up their personal belongings and leave all the furniture and appliances inside. He must have given them a huge amount due to the couple having no problem with the trade.

James looked at the dining table and found all his belongings from the swamp there. The angels brought back all of Boston's stuff as well. James saw the AG riffles, the handguns, and the Blackout sword lying on the table. Souvenirs from his warrior days of being an angel.

James then looked over and saw his cell phone on the table. He picked it up and added a message to the group text with the Hogs. James hoped that the others received his text, and he was wishing them well as they woke up for this new day.

Later on that morning, a bus pulled over to the sidewalk, and the passengers started to step off.

"Excuse me, sir," the bus driver said as she woke Juice up, who was sleeping in the back seat of the parked bus. "It's time to depart, sir!" She raised her voice to wake the snoozing man. Juice flinched with a heavy shake as he opened his eyes to see himself in a location he didn't recall being in before falling asleep. "Sir, you need to get off this bus now!" the driver demanded.

"Sorry," Juice said as he lifted his hand up to shield the sun out of his eyes as he exited his seat. Juice walked off the bus in a hurry to find out where he was. Once Juice's feet touched the sidewalk, he saw that he was not too far from his apartment building. Juice looked at some of the people in his area, wondering if any other Hogs were people who also got off the bus. Juice failed to see anyone he knew, so he started walking back to his apartment.

Laura told the group that she would return all the Hogs to their homes by morning, so this was Juice's only explanation on how he ended up on that bus. As Juice walked home, he checked his pocket for his phone. He saw that he had an unread group text message from James sent not too long ago. The text said, "Hang out at my place tonight. I'll buy pizza for us. The place is at the house we all met up before your trial." Juice replied, saying that he'll be there.

Juice arrived at his apartment building and spotted his car parked on the side of the street. The angels were nice enough to bring his car back to him from the swamp. Juice's keys were still in his pocket, and he used them to open his car door. He saw his duffel bag full of clothes and snatched it before heading inside the building. As Juice made it to his floor of his room, his neighbor from across the hall ran past him to get to her door. She knocked on the door for her mom to open; she was in too much of a hurry to take her key out and unlock it herself.

"Mom," she spoke with excitement when her mother opened the door. "I got the veterinarian job!" She jumped for joy. This caused the two to embrace in a cheerful hug for the girl could now move on to a new job in a field she wished to start her career in. In addition, the salary raise would allow them to find a better place to live. This put a smile on Juice's face for he knew that the woman was struggling to pay off her college loans for a while now. The woman moved in with her mom since her father passed away, and the two were wishing to move to a larger place for quite some time. Juice saw that the world was now becoming a better place to live by the sight of his happy neighbors.

Juice twisted the knob of his door and found it unlocked. Juice was nervous to enter as he feared that someone was in there. Juice slowly walked into the room and heard the sound of music playing. Juice didn't know if he should be prepared for a fight or not, but his defense pose settled down when he spotted Cider in his kitchen cooking eggs. Cider turned his head away from the pan and was happy to see Juice alive.

"So you didn't die, it seems," Cider said as he turned back to the pan.

"It was a rough night. Almost didn't make it on multiple occasions, but we managed to fix the balance," Juice said as he removed his jacket and placed it on the back of one of the dining chairs. Juice found the music playing to be an odd choice; it was one of his albums from his collection, but one he rarely played. Juice normally played music while he would cook or clean, so seeing Cider do the same thing seemed to be expected.

Cider put the prepared meal onto a plate and delivered it to Juice, who was now sitting at the dining table.

"These are not how I like my eggs," Juice stated before he started eating. Nevertheless, Juice was so hungry that he didn't care. He figured that hunger, along with feeling tired, was another side effect from returning to a physical form.

"I know, but this is how I enjoy them," Cider replied.

As Juice ate, he felt this whole situation was similar to talking to a mirror or how one would talk to oneself. He didn't know what to think. Just last night, this man cooking in his kitchen attacked his friends, and then an hour later, he warned them of a deadly threat. And now he's cooking him breakfast. Juice didn't know if this man was friend or foe.

"I flew here after I left the swamp last night. Knowing that you were going into battle and knowing the fact that if you die then I die kept me up all night. I didn't want to waste my final moments of my life sleeping, so I watched some of your movies, I played some of your songs. I even tried some of your food. And just doing theses mundane things, I already learned a lot about myself."

"Like what?" questioned Juice.

"For starters, our taste in music only overlaps slightly. Most of the things you have I don't care for. Same goes for you movies, and as you mentioned, we like our eggs cooked differently. Oh, and I'm left-handed, so I don't even have your muscle memory built into me," Cider said as he grabbed a plate of food and sat across the table from Juice. "I don't have your same taste buds or your ear for music. It's odd, I learned more about myself by seeing how much I'm not like you."

"You really are someone different, aren't you," Juice said as he took another bite of food.

"Well, when I watched a few of your movies, the ones that you loved from your childhood, they struck a nostalgic chord in me. I can see why you love them," Cider said as he took a sip of water. "Some of the songs that you used to play nonstop back in high school brought back memories from those days."

"So you're remembering our past?" wondered Juice.

"I'm remembering your past. I got only your memories in my mind, and I was afraid that I wouldn't get the chance to make any of my own," Cider replied in a speedy tone before bringing his fork back to his month.

"You know, I didn't fully think about what I was putting on the line when I went into battle last night, and for that, I'm sorry," Juice said, looking at his counterpart in the eyes.

"I spent a lot of time thinking about what I would say to you if I saw you again," Cider said as he put down his fork. "I want a chance to find out who I am. I want to find my favorite movies, find the songs I want to play nonstop, and I want to start making my own memories. But I can't do that being around you. I still have theses force of habits, but they're your habits. I feel like if I'm in your normal surroundings around the people who you're used to, I'll just fall into your normal routine. So I want to get as far away from you and everything you know. That is where I'll find myself."

"I'll worry about you. You have a history of being a criminal, and that scares me. But I don't want to stop you from finding out who you are. Maybe there's a good person inside you after all. But I don't want to put my life on hold for you. If a battle comes and I want to put my life on the line to help my friends or to fight for what I think is right, I don't want to be held back by the thought of what could happen to you."

"I wouldn't have it any other way. You're letting me live my life, I shouldn't stop you from living yours. But only one condition: we forever stay out of each other's business. If my path leads me to stealing and lying, you stay clear. I won't stop you from entering things that could get you killed, and you don't check up on me to make sure I keep my nose clean."

Juice agreed to this and even gave Cider the keys to his car, saying that it was a birthday gift to Cider. It was also a thank-you for if Cider didn't warn the Hogs of Memphis's coming attack, the spirit may have won last night. Juice said that Cider needed his own identity and that he had a friend who could get him a fake ID. Cider grinned, saying he knows he's talking about Kate.

Juice remembered that he promised to call her after the balance was fixed. Juice gave her the main highlights of what happened and informed her to mail Cider what he needed to start a fresh life under a new identity. Cider would stay at the apartment until he received his package in the mail, then he would take off far away.

Juice packed up all his stuff and carried it all in a suitcase. He left Cider there with no desire on ever returning. Juice started walking out of town, heading to James's place for the hangout he was hosting.

⟞⟶⟩⟨⟵⟝

In the town of Maze, a Hog member woke up on a park bench under the shade of a nearby tree. This man let out a big stretch and yawned. The man looked around and saw kids playing nearby. The children's laughter was the thing that woke him up. After a quick rub of his eyes, he stood up and started running for he didn't know where he was. When he reached a recognizable gas station, he knew exactly where he was and knew where to go. Before he continued his run, he heard a man shout for joy. The man was jubilant because he had just won the lottery. "Forty-two bucks!" the man shouted with glee. "You know what? I'm going to take my mom out for dinner! I haven't seen her in such a long time, I know she'll love it!"

The Hog smiled at the man, told him congrats, and went on his way. This Hog came to Timber's apartment building and started knocking. Timber, who woke up in his own bed, rushed to the door and saw a man covered with a hood knocking. The man in the hood revealed his face, and Timber was relieved that it was Gard under the hood. Timber opened the door to let him in.

"I woke up on a bench in the park. I didn't know where to go. I was hoping that the angel teleported you home, so I came here," Gard explained.

Timber confirmed that the angel did teleport him home, and he received a text from James saying to hang out tonight at the house that brought them to the gates of Heaven. Gard was happy that Timber didn't take off there yet; otherwise, he would be stuck in Maze, where he had no car or even a phone. Timber than added that they needed to pick up Juice on the way. Gard was impatient and was ready to get moving, but he wanted to stop to get some fast food on the way.

⋙◦◦◦⋘

Miles knocked on James's front door. James answered the door and let his friend in. Miles explained that he woke up back in his old hospital room. The angel who brought him back home didn't have anywhere else to take him. Miles said that he would have rather ended up on a bench in the park of Maze like Gard instead of being back at the hospital. Miles walked out of the building for the very last time and teleported to the house.

"It was weird seeing it full of people again. Last time I was there, it was empty," Miles stated to James. "I checked, and the reason why it was empty that day was because they were supposed to be fumigating the place, which they ended up cancelling." Miles took a sip of water. "My doctor hasn't been seen in a few days now. No one at the place knows what happened to him."

"What was it like to fully say goodbye to that place?" wondered James.

"Very fulfilling. When I was there, I was lost beyond compare. I stayed because I felt that I had nothing out there for me. I felt that I couldn't be who I am out there. That the light in me wasn't real and that I had to stay in the dark. But this time, I walked out with my head held high, knowing who I am, and that I have friends out there." Miles smiled and looked out the window to see the sunlight beam out from the dark clouds in the sky. "You know, as I was walked out, I saw a lot of visitors. More than I ever had throughout my entire time being there. The patients were thrilled to see family and friends again, and a lot of them were showing strong positive progress. It really put our sacrifice in perspective."

※

Eric woke up, finding himself back at his apartment. He treated himself to a nicely cooked meal and ran on a treadmill to help wake himself up. He looked at his view of his apartment and felt that the sun looked a little brighter this morning. Eric was planning on going to the hangout, but he wanted to take his time unpacking his stuff. Looking at his muddy shoes made him remember the swamp, the place that was his home for the past few days. Knowing that the place was no longer their blessed campsite and that there was no point on ever returning made him want to never clean those shoes again. It was disheartening that this would be the last time he would unpack his bag after camping out from their meaningful place.

Eric took a look around his very nice, expensive apartment, wishing that he could trade it all away for one more night at the swamp with all his friends.

Eric made a quick pit stop by his work building before heading to James's. On the road, he saw many generous people handing out their loose change to the needy. This put a smile on his face as he entered the building. Eric got off the elevator on his work floor and saw the custodian who he normally bought pills from.

The man walked over to Eric to have a chat with him. "What are you doing here? Did you get the memo that all office people are working at home until the remodeling is complete?" the workman asked.

"I know, I'm just here to check on a few things," Eric replied. The truth was that Eric was getting his life back to normal now that the balance was fixed. He wanted to make sure his actions of killing the horseman who was posing as his boss wasn't revealed.

"Well, if you're here to see your boss, you can forget it. The guy offed himself the other day. The police called it a suicide."

This was fortunate news for Eric to hear as he and his friends were the only ones who knew that his boss was a true monster and not human. The fact that he and the others were in the clear of this murder made him feel relieved. The man then informed Eric that with new management coming in, the board hired all part-time workers to full-time as of this morning. The man was happy for now he had a higher paycheck and full benefits. The man was slightly sad to notify Eric that he would no longer be selling drugs; in fact, with the benefits and pay raise, he was going to start rehab himself.

Eric gave the man a tap on the shoulder, congratulating him on new positive changes in his life and the new path he wished to take. He said that he kicked that habit himself. After that, Eric headed back to the elevator, saying that he was heading off to see his friends.

⟫◦◦◦⟪

As Juice was walking on the side of a country road carrying his suitcases and bags, a car drove up next to him.

"Let's go, sir!" shouted Gard in the passenger seat of Timber's car.

Juice was happy that his ride had finally arrived as he was growing bored and tired. Juice chucked his stuff in the back seat and hopped in himself. Timber asked why Juice had so much luggage with him. Juice replied that he moved out of his apartment, stating that the place held too many bad memories for him. Now that Juice was in the car, Gard order Timber to step on it for the sun was going down, and he didn't want them to be the last ones to make it to the house.

Miles and James teleported to Maze to pick up the pizza that James order from there. "You know, I could have just teleported everyone to your house right away," Miles stated.

"No, let the rest show up the natural way. I think the travel would be good for them," James replied. The two entered the pizza place and were met with their waitress from last night.

"Back for more, you guys?" the worker said in a friendly tone.

"Of course!" Miles cheerfully shouted. Once the pizza was placed on the table, Miles had to ask, "Did it just come out of the oven?"

"Yep, right before you entered the door," she informed.

Miles gave James a glance and told him that they got to play burn mouth. James said that now that he's human, he can fully taste food, and he didn't want his first experiences with pizza to cause him to burn his mouth. Miles argued, saying that it would be more fun this way. James was actually eager to try it himself. He said the heck with it and reached into the box for a pizza slice as Miles followed suit. The two took a big bite of the still smoking hot pizza and ridiculously spazzed out due to the hot food. This made the worker laugh joyfully.

Then a man walked into the pizza place who caught the waitress's attention right away. It was her lost boyfriend Billy. She ran up to him and jumped in his arms. Billy had been lost on a hunting trip for weeks now, and she thought she would never see him again. Billy explained that he was trapped in a cave-in during a heavy thunderstorm, and a group of hunters found him this morning. She cried tears of joy from the sight of him, and her heart started to pound hard as she saw him get down on one knee to propose to her. He said that he's lucky to be alive, and he doesn't want to go another day without her being his wife. She happily screamed of course, and both Miles and James clapped for the happy couple.

Another Hog member got out of his car at a mechanic's shop. As he walked up to the front door, he saw a car getting pushed up to the parking area by a group of college kids. Once the car reached the parking spot, the man inside exited the car to thank the boys for their help. The Hog asked what happened and was told the story. The man's car broke down, and a group of college kids out for a run stopped what they were doing to help him get the car to the shop. The Hog saw that there were still negative things happening in the world, but it was clear that there were people out there who were inspired to do some good.

He then walked into the shop and talked to the manager, saying that he's the person who called ahead of time. The manager recalled that phone call and picked up a box from his desk and handed it over to him. "This is all his stuff that he left here," the manager said, handing over the box.

Will looked inside and saw some dirty worn-out gloves, packs of gum, loose change, and a magnet that said I'd Rather Be Fishing. What really got Will feeling sad were the photos in the box. The photo was of Hayden holding a large fish he caught with some of his Hang Out Group friends when they were young kids. Will thanked the manager and headed to his car.

———◦◦◦———

At James's house, the group was all gathered up in the backyard, chowing down on the pizza while cheering for James to start his first campfire. James was having trouble starting the lighter while the Hogs were shouting out that they were getting cold.

"I feel like starting a fire is an initiation of some type around here," Juice stated.

"I got him to play burn mouth when we got the pizza," Miles added, making everyone laugh.

"Is there even any lighter fluid in that thing?" asked Eric.

"Probably not." Gard chuckled.

Just then, a spark was ignited, and the fire started to spread. The group all cheered for James. The glow of the fire made the place light up in a bright warming blaze. James sat down on one of the chairs and started to relax. James was always so worried about getting the balance fixed that he never fully felt relaxed. James was able to lean back in his chair and take a long look up at the stars.

"One thing I still can't figure out," Gard said. "What were those men making us dig for when I was being held captive?"

"I have no idea, but I can tell you one thing. There wasn't any gold out there," replied James.

When Timber asked how James was so certain about that, James informed the group that he used to be a guide for gold prospectors. He used to advise prospectors on favorable digging locations that would lead to the gold. James laughingly recollected that most people chose not to listen to him and chose to dig elsewhere where they found much less than what they could have.

"So you are saying that there is a fortune of gold buried out there, and you're the only one who knows where it is?" questioned Gard. James, not seeing the big deal, simply replied yes. Gard turned his head to Miles and told him that they were going into the gold mining business. Gard figured with James's knowledge, Miles's ability to travel, and his strength, they would be rich in no time.

Eric jumped in, saying, "After we come up with a story on how you survived the plane crash, of course."

"Just say you washed up on an island. There are tons of them out there," said James.

The Hogs went on to discuss a fictional account of Gard's rescue.

Later, the Hogs heard a knock at the house door; they figured that it was Will, so they shouted that they were out back.

Will walked around the house and smiled, seeing his friends all mingling happily with each other. Everyone let out a joyful cheer when they saw him.

"Will, you're up," Timber said as he nodded over to the woodpile. Will let out a deep sad breath. Will squatted over the woodpile, looking for a large log to pick up. Once he had one in his hand, he chucked it in the fire. The Hogs had always planned a type of ceremony of some kind if one of their own ever passed away. They would get together, set a campfire, and while it was burning, each member of the group would toss in a log and nothing more. The fire was their tribute to their fallen member, and each person who pitched in a log meant that they cared and that they will miss the person. As the fire burned, they think or speak what they would say to the fallen member as if the person was still there. As the fire dies out, they would reflect on their goodbyes, hoping that the member would be able to hear it.

"To Boston. He gave his life for the order of the balance," Will said after tossing his log into the fire.

"We would have lost without him," Gard added as he looked at James.

James was taking this loss the hardest for Boston was James's longtime friend while the rest of the group were lucky enough to have known him and were able to fight by his side. The Hogs considered him as a member of the group and always will.

"Should we do something for the member who isn't here?" asked Juice. The Hogs all looked at the empty chair within the circle around the fire ring. The group knew that Hayden wasn't dead, just taking up a job that required him to be away. So they didn't do the fire ceremony for him.

With two members not being present for the night's hangout, the Hogs still had plenty to celebrate. They had fixed the balance of good and evil, which was something the angels and Saints failed to do.

"James, what did you say to the Saints to let us become fighters for the order of the balance? I was always curious about that," asked Will.

James took a moment to personally reflect on that response before speaking up. "I simply asked the Saints to have faith in humans." Now that James was human, he felt new meaning to that. James could see that this answer didn't settle with the Hogs, so he elaborated. "There are believers and nonbelievers out there. The true believers say, 'We don't believe, we know.' But trust me, they never took a stroll down the side of the gates of Heaven before," James said before bowing his head down. "Those people just have strong faith." James lifted his eyes up to look at his friends. "You guys know. And once you know, you lose faith." James went on to say that humans who lost faith due to having undeniable proof lose that wonder in the world.

"In Heaven, there's a phrase: 'If humans believe in God, then what does God believe in?'" James lifted his head up to see the Hogs finding that phrase to be mind-boggling. "The answer is humans. God believes in humans. And for the humans who know that God is real, the only thing left for them to believe in is humans." James went on as if he was speaking from poetry. "Humans can be unpredictable and act against their selfish usual ways in the heat of the moment. Humans have the power to love and to inspire all by themselves. Humans can do the right thing without any spiritual guidance. When they work together, they can perform miracles."

It was nice for the Hogs to hear that the Saints put their faith into them on fixing the balance. They raised their heads up high in pride. The Hogs now had to find faith within their neighbors. Looking around, knowing that they were surrounded by people who would gladly sacrifice their own life to save them, made their faith strong.

Then the question was asked: what should they do next? They all agreed that splitting up again wasn't the right choice. They saw how bad things got the last time they lost touch with each other and didn't want that to happen again. They said that they would have to find a place just for them where they all could grow old together, which for them will take twice as long as the rest of the world. They would have to live without one of their members being around, but his sacrifice would be a reminder that their mission wasn't to get rid of the evil side of the balance; it was to bring the good and hope back to the world. And if it wasn't for the seven high school friends, one ex-angel, and a loyal spirit, they would have failed in that mission.

For some of the Hogs, the nightmares never completely disappeared. But that night, they all received a long, much-needed, peaceful slumber.